Judy Lambini was a mode
how did she end up with a k

"I'm fairly confident I ca
Judith as well," Andrew of
"Farewell, brothers! Rest easy in the knowledge that Laycock Keep shall still be standing upon your return."

With Judy still cradled in his arms, he strode across the hall and began to climb the exceedingly narrow, winding staircase to a floor somewhere above.

"Where...are you taking me?" she asked.

"To bed."

Damn! Judy went rigid in Andrew's arms when she recalled his true intentions. Her mouth dropped open in startled concern as he kicked open a door, banging it against an inside wall, and dropped her roughly onto a bed. When he jumped onto the bed and stretched out beside her, she finally found her voice.

"What the hell do you think you're doing?"

"If you don't know, I shall teach you. I'm told I'm rather good at it."

Oh, geez. She didn't need this. What she needed was a good, long nap—and a seat on H.G. Wells' time machine.

"Listen, I—"

Andrew kissed her, open mouth on open mouth. His lips felt soft and warm, and when his tongue darted between her lips, Judy felt a tremor of sexual excitement. The heat in her belly flared when he began nibbling her lips and his thumb gently stroked the line of her jaw.

Oh, God. Her reaction to him went beyond anything rational. Judy, however, had no intention of giving in to him. Of all the women she knew, she was the least likely to sleep with a man she'd just met. Having never done so in the past, she did not propose to do so now. Most certainly, she did not intend to sleep with a ghostly stranger who'd been dead in his grave at least 700 years!

To my husband, Philip,
and a timeless love.

A Twist in Time

***

Candice Kohl

A TWIST IN TIME

Published by ImaJinn Books, a division of ImaJinn

ISBN: 1-893896-79-X

10 9 8 7 6 5 4 3 2 1

PUBLISHER'S NOTE:
This book is a work of fiction. Names, characters, places and incidents are products of the author's imagination or are used fictitiously. Any resemblance to actual events or locales or persons, living or dead, is entirely coincidental.

Books are available at quantity discounts when used to promote products or services. For information please write to: Marketing Division, ImaJinn Books, P.O. Box 162, Hickory Corners, MI 49060-0162, or call toll free 1-877-625-3592.

Cover design by Patricia Lazarus

ImaJinn Books, a division of ImaJinn
P.O. Box 162, Hickory Corners, MI 49060-0162
Toll Free: 1-877-625-3592
http://www.imajinnbooks.com

One

"His name is Laycock. That's all you know, except that he lives in some town called Wixcomb," Judy commented idly. She and Carla had time to kill. A dozen, black-nosed sheep had ambled onto the road in front of their car, forcing the young women to wait while the animals made for greener pastures through the break in the hedgerow.

"I know he lives in the only hotel in town, which bears his name. And his first initial is V. V. Laycock," Carla elaborated, her hands gripping the wheel as though she continued to steer.

"Hmmm." Judy brushed her bangs off her forehead while peering through the dusty windshield. "Could you imagine if people heading into New York had to wait for sheep to stroll across the highway?"

"There'd be a lot of dead sheep in New Jersey!" Carla laughed. "But we're in England now, and the idea is to kick back and relax a little on this trip, right?"

"Right," Judy agreed, squirming in the passenger seat. She sat with her feet on her tote bag, her knees pressed against the dash, one elbow out the open window, and her hat being flattened by the ceiling above.

Carla honked the car horn, at last scattering several sheep, and cautiously inched the vehicle forward until a few more of the woolly beasts lumbered out of the way. Seizing the opportunity, she accelerated slowly and pressed on through the cluster of animals.

"I liked London," Judy volunteered as they sped along the open road. "I hope we'll have a few more days there before we go home."

"Oh, we will," Carla assured her. "I'm not going to spend a long time doing research on this Laycock person's old family archives. We'll have plenty of time to do the tourist bit in London."

"That means nightclubs, too, not just museums."

"Of course! Honestly, Judy, just because I'm engaged to be married and make my living holed up in my den writing biographies of dead people doesn't mean I'm not up for a good time. Actually, between the two of us, I'll bet I have the better social life. You never have time to date because you're always working, working, working." She glanced at Judy, quickly adding, "Not that I'm not glad you live your life the way you do. You're the best agent I've ever had."

"Well, thanks."

The tires hit a bump in the pavement, and Judy's head thwacked hard against the ceiling of the car. "Ow!" she squawked, yanking off her flowered, burgundy velvet cloche and flipping down the sun visor. She peered into the attached mirror, muttered, "Damn," and flipped the visor up again. "I missed last month's appointment with my hairdresser. What was I thinking? I should never have flown off to England without getting a touch-up first. My roots look awful."

"Put your hat back on," Carla advised casually. "I'm sure we can find a drugstore in Wixcomb. Just buy a bottle of shampoo-in hair color and bleach it yourself."

She put her hat back on, and to help get her mind off her muddy roots, Judy said, "Tell me something more about this Laycock person. How did you ever find somebody with private papers dating back to the reign of King John?"

"The magic of the Internet. I told you. I posted notices with all my sources and resources, and Laycock responded, inviting me to his home to study his medieval parchments, which he says appear to be signed by Lackland himself."

"Lackland?"

"That was sort of King John's nickname."

"Really."

History bored Judy. Carla loved everything old and ancient, including the lives of long-dead souls, while she herself admired cutting edge technology.

"So you're saying you don't know this man from Adam. Carla, did you ever consider that he might be some kind of pervert, luring you to his lair?"

"He's a computer guru, not a pervert. Owns his own company. Develops spam control and antivirus software."

"You know this how?"

"Because he told me."

"He told you." Judy sighed. "I am so glad you invited me along on this trip. You're too trusting. The real world can be a lot more dangerous than you suspect."

"That's why I've got you, to protect me from the dangers of the real world." Carla shot her a fast smile.

But Judy frowned as she attempted to rearrange her bottom in the passenger seat. "Do you think we'll be in Wixcomb soon? I'd like to stretch my legs."

"You'd have more room if you put your tote in the back seat."

"Uh-uh." Solemnly, she shook her head. "My bag is always with me. It's my security blanket in the city, but even more so when I'm traveling. Except for clothes, everything I could ever need is in there."

"It shouldn't be much longer. In fact, there's a sign!"

***

"I thought your Mr. Laycock owned a computer business," Judy commented when they pulled into the small, graveled lot off the street and looked to the building posed atop a hill. Unlike the black beam and white stucco houses they had passed in the business district, Laycock Inn was an imposing stone structure overlooking the town from its southern edge.

"He does," Carla insisted as she climbed out of the car and closed the door with a smart thud. "The inn is probably a family enterprise. But, wow, it's great, isn't it? It looks as though it used to be a manor house."

Judy wasn't sure what a manor house was, exactly, so she said nothing. But as she exited the car and slung her tote bag over her shoulder, she noticed another great edifice on a much higher hill north of town. "Look at that!" She pointed. "Whatever it is, I'll bet it's a lot bigger than Laycock's place."

"I believe that's the remains of an old castle," Carla surmised as she popped open the trunk.

Before hefting her own suitcase out of the "boot," Judy smoothed the lapels on her burgundy velvet jacket and brushed the creases from her black wool pants.

Together, the women headed up the stone path to the inn, though suddenly they found themselves accompanied by a pair of liver and white spaniels. The dogs seemed to know their way around; they bounded through the entrance ahead of Carla and Judy, who paused to survey the huge room they encountered. "I'll bet this was the great hall," Carla mused. "In the old days, the floor would have been covered with rushes."

Judy preferred the area rugs she found now. She strode across them, directly to the reception desk, leading both Carla and the pair of dogs. "Hello," she greeted the clerk, a plump, matronly woman with a cap of gray curls.

"Hello," the woman returned, her glance including Carla. "I see you've met the master's hounds, Duke and Duchess. Don't let them bother you, they're just friendly. Sometimes too friendly." She rested her ample breasts on the high desk as she leaned over it and shooed the animals away. Then, smiling, she said, "Welcome to Laycock Inn, dearies. Are you having a holiday here? Usually we have older couples on day trips from the city or odd ducks, intellectual chaps who come to poke among the ruins or other such things. It's so nice to see pretty young girls like yourselves. Do you have reservations?"

"No," Judy said, shaking her head, "though we would like to stay if there are rooms available. Actually, we're here to meet with Mr. Laycock."

"Mr. Laycock? Oh, you mean the viscount."

"Viscount?" Judy shared a look with Carla as she suddenly realized what the "V" in V. Laycock stood for.

"Yes." The older woman nodded. "The only surviving Laycock is his lordship, the viscount, and he was lost for a while." Suddenly, her eyes widened. "Oh! You're the authoress, are you? The one who's come to look at his old parchments? I never expected you to be so young."

"Actually, Carla Whittaker is the author." Judy gestured to her friend. "I'm Ms. Whittaker's agent, Judy Lambini."

"It's indeed a pleasure to meet you both. I'm Mrs. Haversham. I manage the inn for the viscount."

"It seems to be a popular place," Carla commented. Several people were seated at dining tables arranged near a huge, stone fireplace, and a group wearing jeans and hiking boots were coming down the stairs, chatting noisily as they headed for the door.

"Oh, yes. Laycock Inn is most always full up. It was

a boon to the town when his lordship claimed his inheritance and turned the empty old manor into an inn. Now, when people come to Wixcomb to poke about, they actually stay here and spend their money in the local shops."

"Poke about?" Judy repeated, raising her eyebrows.

"Yes. They poke about in the ruins of Laycock Castle. You must have seen it, up on the far north hill. Of course, today is Samhain—All Hallow's Eve, you'd call it—so we've even more visitors than usual, since the other business brings them round."

"Speaking of business," Judy pressed politely, "I think Mr.—ah, Viscount Laycock—is expecting to see Ms. Whittaker. Could you tell him she's arrived?"

"Oh, yes, of course. Unfortunately, he's on one of those calls where people from other places get on the same line to chat it up, so you'll have to wait until he's finished. Meantime, why don't you have a seat and a spot of tea to refresh yourselves?" She gestured to a grouping of overstuffed furniture that included a sideboard.

Judy spied a warming plate and tea kettle along with cups and a tray of cookies. On cue, her stomach growled, and Carla chuckled, nudging her shoulder. "Come on," she urged. "You're hungry. We haven't had anything to eat since that continental breakfast."

"What about rooms?" Judy asked, glancing at Mrs. Haversham.

"Oh, there's a pair set aside for you, compliments of the viscount."

"But how did he...?" Judy intended to ask how he knew there would be two of them arriving. It had been very last minute when Carla suggested Judy join her on the trip.

But another guest snagged Mrs. Haversham's attention, so they left the desk and headed for the refreshment table.

"I'd kill for a cup of coffee. Real coffee!" Judy confessed after taking a sip of hot tea. "Did you notice if we passed a Starbuck's on our way through town?"

"Not very likely," a gangly fellow of about thirty put in as he, too, helped himself to a cup of complimentary tea. "I'm Ian MacCoombs, by the way," he informed them. "Are you guests here? I don't recall seeing you earlier."

"We only just arrived," Carla explained before introducing herself and Judy.

"You're Americans. I presumed so, though I hadn't thought Wixcomb's reputation had extended so far yet. It's a fascinating area, to be sure. You'll enjoy it. The hills are simply abundant with places of power."

"Places of what?" Judy screwed up her face as she peered at Ian.

"Places of power," he repeated, setting down his teacup and using his big hands for emphasis. "Energy fields. The land around here is well-known for them. Did you know some are masculine and some are feminine? Like yin and yang. The masculine sites fill you up while the feminine ones disperse or dissolve. It's quite remarkable."

"Remarkable," she repeated.

MacCoombs monopolized the conversation, announcing his intent to explain about seven different sorts of places of power. By the time he got around to describing the fourth, the type that served as gateways between worlds, Judy felt her mind as well as her behind going numb. So she abandoned her tea and company and set out for a stroll around the former "great hall." Between two tall, mullion windows, she spotted a glass case atop an ornately carved wooden stand. Wandering closer, Judy discovered a fabulously jeweled dagger lying on a bed of satin.

"Don't touch that, dearie!" Mrs. Haversham warned from her post at the desk. "An alarm will go off if you touch the case. That piece is quite valuable. It's been in Lord Laycock's family for nearly a thousand years."

Judy stuffed her hand in her pocket and marched back to the manager. "Speaking of Lord Laycock, is he going to see us now?"

"Yes, actually. If you'll collect Miss Whittaker, I'll take you to his office out back. Feel free to leave your shoulder bag with your other luggage, dearie," she advised. "No one will make off with it, I promise."

"That's all right. I'm used to carrying it around," Judy

insisted, patting her tote almost affectionately.

Rescuing Carla from Ian's place of power lecture, they followed the hotel manager through the kitchen and out a back door.

"His lordship works in a separate building because of all the power and phone lines he needs for his business," Mrs. Haversham explained as they crossed the brittle, brown remains of a summer garden, heading toward a slate-roofed, stucco cottage. It looked like the sort of place that Lady Chatterly sometimes met her lover. "Here you go," she announced, opening the cottage door and gesturing Carla and Judy inside. Then, without advising her employer of their presence, she left.

Judy blinked, feeling disconcerted. Outdoors, they'd seen a picturesque little cottage surrounded by bracken and climbing vines. Inside, they slammed headlong into twenty-first century technology supported by sleek, satiny black furniture, pearl gray carpet, and track lighting. Hard drives, monitors, printers, shredders and scanners hummed, beeped and buzzed. Keyboards and speakers, their cords dangling disconnected, were strewn helter-skelter, while CDs and floppies dotted nearly every flat surface, much like the leaves in the yard.

"Be with you in a moment," a masculine voice promised, drawing both Judy's and Carla's eyes to a figure hunched over a work station in the center of the room. Laycock promptly spun around in his ergonomic chair, and Judy felt a shock—not of recognition, but rather like deja vu.

"Ms. Whittaker, I presume?" he inquired, coming to his feet and veering straight toward Carla. As he approached, Judy realized she couldn't see the man's eyes through his amber-tinted glasses. Yet the funky glasses seemed to go with the rest of his casual ensemble, consisting of a Cleveland Indians baseball cap, pulled low on his forehead, a Cambridge University sweatshirt, jeans, and Nike athletic shoes. Judy felt a bit alarmed when she found herself thinking that everything he wore fit rather nicely on a body that looked extremely well-muscled for a man who spent most of his time in front of a computer.

Laycock did not suit her image of a viscount. Judy imagined viscounts to be skinny old men wearing tails and striped ascots.

"I'm Carla Whittaker." Carla shook Laycock's hand. "I really appreciate this."

Turning to Judy, he asked, "You are the agent Mrs. Haversham mentioned?"

He's kind of short, but his presence looms large... "Yes," she replied, stupefied by that wayward thought. "I'm with the Edwin Grant Agency, out of New York." Reaching into her pocket, she retrieved a business card. "Judy Lambini. Ms. Judy Lambini."

Laycock took the card but not her hand. Instead, he walked past her, reaching for a pile of spreadsheets stacked in a nearby chair. Picking them up and dumping them on the floor, he indicated Carla should sit.

"I'm sorry," he said to Judy. "I don't seem to have any other chairs available."

She scowled. Perhaps nobility never had to consider the needs and comfort of others, so he didn't realize he was being offensive. More likely, though, guessing his age by the hint of gray in Laycock's dark sideburns, he had been locked away writing computer language for so darned long, he'd lost most of the social skills he'd learned in kindergarten.

"No problem," she insisted graciously. "I've been sitting in a cramped little car all day. It feels good to stand."

"As I was saying," Carla continued, gingerly perching herself in the chair, "I'm really grateful to be here. But I don't want to impose, so if I could, I'd love to see those documents, the ones from the Barons' War, right away."

Laycock nodded. "The drafts of the concessions the barons eventually won from King John," he said. "I brought them out in anticipation of your visit. They're over there." Without turning his head, he gestured to a long, shallow table under a high window.

Glancing where he pointed, Judy saw what seemed to be a few framed pictures on top of it.

"They're encased in glass," he explained, as if he'd read her thoughts. And when Judy looked back at him, she found he'd been studying her profile. That realization gave her a tingle—pleasant or unpleasant, she wasn't quite sure.

Carla shot to her feet and hurried over to the table. "My God! They're so well-preserved!"

"They've been very well cared for. And though I don't mind you reading them, Ms. Whittaker, I must insist you do it here. I wouldn't feel right letting them out of my sight."

"Oh, I understand," Carla assured him breathlessly.

Judy thought her friend sounded like a woman who'd just run into her first love and learned he'd never married. No wonder Carla had gone into writing biographies of dead people. She got off on reading nearly illegible old papers!

The viscount wheeled the solitary spare chair over to Carla, who sat down again without looking, as though Laycock were a waiter seating her at a dining table.

"Could you use some help?" Judy offered.

"Oh, no." Carla waved her hand and shook her head, still not looking up from the papers. "And don't be mad, Judy, but I probably won't be able to meet you for dinner."

"I'm not mad." She wasn't. But she did feel superfluous, and she didn't much like the feeling.

Lord Laycock gestured to the door. "Your room should be ready for you now, Ms. Lambini. Why don't you make yourself comfortable there? I suspect you have work of your own to do. I understand literary agents work seven days a week."

"Who told you that?"

He shrugged. "Just something I heard, I suppose."

It was true enough in Judy's case, but she didn't admit it. "Actually," she said, "I'm here on vacation."

"Then a walk up to the ruins might be in order."

The last thing Judy wanted to do was walk around any old ruins. But she decided to take off while her dignity remained intact. "I'll think about it," she told his lordship. "'Bye, Carla," she added.

Judy headed for the door and reached for the knob, but the viscount, who had kept pace with her, grabbed it at the same moment. Their hands touched, and Judy felt a searing jolt run up her fingers and tickle the length of her arm. She drew her hand away as though she'd been zapped with an electric current.

"Excuse me," he apologized, opening the door and glancing back toward his work station as though he regretted the minutes he'd spent away from it. Judy stepped outside, and he pushed the door closed after her without another word.

"Well, that was rude," she muttered aloud at the door. She didn't know what bothered her more—Carla not needing her, the viscount's shabby manners, or the fact that she felt an immediate attraction to him, despite his shabby manners.

With a sigh, she trudged back across the barren garden, feeling an alien in an unfamiliar world.

Two

"Thank you for bringing all our bags up," Judy said, wishing Ian MacCoombs hadn't insisted.

"It was my pleasure," he returned, crossing the threshold to put both hers and Carla's luggage down inside Judy's room. "Are you sure you won't reconsider joining me for a look at the Samhain bonfires tonight?"

"No. I'm not much into Halloween."

"This has nothing to do with Halloween, but with all sorts of pagan beliefs, those both curious and mystical. One is that the curtain which separates our world from others, past and present, living and dead, lifts to let mortal and other beings pass through." Ian grinned, apparently pleased when Judy shivered exaggeratedly.

"I think not." She grabbed the edge of her door, forcing Ian to back step into the hallway. "Thanks again," she repeated before locking him out.

Alone, she surveyed the room, which seemed to contain all the comforts of home except for a private bathroom or a telephone. Sighing at the inconvenience, she strolled to her bureau and gazed into the mirror. Pulling off her hat and ruffling her hair, Judy again confronted her muddy roots. "Okay, I'll find a drugstore and buy some hair dye." Her stylist could have a hissy fit, charge her a fortune, and repair the damage later.

Quickly, she changed her clothes, replacing her smart, velvet and wool ensemble for black leggings and a powder blue tunic sweater. She also exchanged her pumps for ankle-high, flat-heeled boots. Then, grabbing her tote bag, Judy left the room and skipped down the steps. The dining area had filled up with guests hungry for an early evening meal, but the manager remained at her post.

"Mrs. Haversham, is there a drugstore in town?"

"A what?" The woman looked up from the plate of chicken and potatoes she was attempting to nibble discreetly. "Oh, you mean a chemist. Yes, dearie, there is. But the shop's closed by this hour, and it's closed Sundays as well. You'll have to wait 'til Monday if you need to make a purchase there."

Judy hoped to be gone from Wixcomb by Monday.

"There's a table available if you'd like to have supper now."

She glanced at the dining area and spotted Ian MacCoombs seated alone. "No, thanks." She shook her head. "I'm not hungry."

"You must be," Mrs. Haversham insisted, holding up her plate. "Try a bite. It will whet your appetite."

The chicken did smell good. Judy hesitated only a few seconds before grabbing a drumstick off the plate. She took a dainty taste, swallowed, and admitted, "That is good. Barbecued?"

"You Americans might say that. It's roasted over an open hearth fire with a special combination of herbs. The recipe's been in the viscount's family forever, so he says."

Judy glanced again at Ian, who had his nose in a newspaper. "I may come down for a whole meal before the kitchen's closed," Judy announced. "Thanks for the taste," she added before turning to head back upstairs.

But a door opening onto a library caught her eye, so instead of veering left to the staircase, she veered right into the book-lined room.

The collection couldn't be the viscount's, she decided, after glimpsing several of the titles. The subject matter stored without system on the sagging shelves appeared too eclectic. A book on America's space program stood beside a volume of Burns' poetry. An English language grammar text sat squeezed between a Stephen King novel and a history of the automobile. Surely the Englishman's reading preferences leaned toward the technical. He had most likely inherited all these volumes, collected by his forebears according to their own whims and interests.

Judy ditched her chicken bone in a wastepaper basket and finally headed upstairs, licking her fingers. When she entered her room again, tossing her tote on the bed, she wondered if she shouldn't have borrowed a book from the library. She certainly had nothing much to do here without Carla to keep her company. Her eyes swept the room again—not even a "telly" so that she could catch a round of snooker on the BBC.

I wonder if the viscount is keeping Carla company? Drawn to the window, Judy pulled back the curtains and gazed at the quaint cottage beyond the dormant garden. Dusk had settled, night was fast approaching, but the cottage windows glowed, beckoning little rectangles of warmth and light boldly piercing the gathering gloom.

He's not keeping her company, she decided. Carla was surely poring over the delicate old pages King John once held in his hands, and the viscount—*Does he have a first name?*— was certainly writing binary code, his guest—*guests*—completely forgotten.

"Why is that rude, so-called nobleman on my mind?" Judy asked herself aloud. Then she remembered Laycock's assumption that she had work to do, so she pulled her cell phone from her tote, called the office, and listened to her voice mail. It almost gave her a sense of satisfaction, knowing that bit of "work" would cost a fortune, but that she could expense it.

When she returned her cell phone to her tote, it slid across her laptop case, which she also stored in the bag. Glimpsing her computer, it occurred to her she'd have more e-mail than she did voice mail. It would have been nice to plug in, log on, and download, but her boss would kill her if she used the cell phone for that purpose. Usually, hotels provided an extra jack for guests' computers. But here at Laycock Inn, she didn't even have the convenience of a phone extension in her room. The pay phone on the staircase landing would not allow her to plug in her modem, and she would be damned before she'd intrude into Laycock's lair again, even if he had a hundred phone jacks in his office!

Disgruntled and bored, she pulled a sheaf of proposals from her suitcase. Turning on a pole lamp, she curled up in her overstuffed chair and skimmed the outlines and sample chapters submitted by writers hoping for representation. They all seemed bad until she realized she wasn't even reading, but merely staring at the typed pages. Climbing out of her chair, she grabbed her daily planner from her tote and checked the hour on the digital time piece glued to the leatherette cover. It was nearly ten, London time.

"Enough!" she announced, tossing the stack of unread pages onto her bureau before heading down to the lobby yet again.

Because her stomach had begun voicing its displeasure at being neglected for so long, Judy hoped to find that the kitchen remained open. Obviously, though, it had closed. All the tables in the dining area were set with fresh linens, glasses and silverware. Not a single hotel guest—not even Ian—lingered at one, nursing a coffee or a glass of wine.

It felt spooky, all this vacancy, especially considering how populated the inn had been earlier in the day. Carla remained conspicuously absent, and even Mrs. Haversham had deserted her post. Judy wondered if the town itself had rolled up its streets until the dawning of another day.

"The bonfires!" she said aloud, recalling suddenly what Ian had told her. Everyone had no doubt gone to the bonfires, with the exception of Carla and Viscount Laycock, who could not be torn from their work.

I may as well go, too. It will slay Carla that I saw the Samhain fires, and she totally missed them. It will also make her crazy having to draw every detail out of me so that she can have a clear picture of what she missed. Judy smiled at the thought as she let herself out the front door.

Immediately, she spied the hillside fires. A trio of them burned on the gently rolling northern slopes, which meant she had a bit of a hike before her. Not just the hills themselves, but the trek across town first.

Fortunately, Judy found herself with unexpected companionship, the viscount's dogs, Duke and Duchess.

"You want to escort me?" she inquired, finding them panting at her feet. They seemed willing, because even before she located a flashlight at the bottom of her tote, the hounds were dancing ahead, only pausing to turn back and gaze at her impatiently.

It took Judy a good twenty minutes to make the journey to the nearest of the conflagrations. It surprised her a little that none of the Halloween celebrants appeared to be children. In the States, she believed, little kids would have made up most of the spectators.

But here, they'd been left behind at home. Only adults and teenagers had gathered to sing and dance to the hauntingly eerie music some played on fiddles and flutes.

Ian MacCoombs. Judy saw him among the crowd and quickly circumvented the first bonfire to head toward another farther along. This excursion was getting to be a bit more than she'd ever intended. But if she was going to be on her own tonight, she preferred truly being alone. Or at least, only in the company of a couple of spaniels, with whom she needn't make polite chitchat.

Duke and Duchess must have caught some poor creature's scent, because Judy watched them scurry off, side by side, their noses in the damp grass as they determinedly tracked something that avoided the fires and the revelers.

"Hey, you mutts! Come back!" she pleaded. But they ignored her, and before she knew it, Judy was trailing Duke and Duchess instead of walking straight to the nearest bonfire.

It was then she saw it, the looming, crumbling edifice, black on black, at the top of the highest rise. The meager starlight and crescent moon managed to make some of the ragged stones gleam with a creepy iridescence, and she recognized them as the ruins of Laycock Castle, still impressive in their decay.

She veered toward the rubble, only vaguely aware that all the villagers, the fires, even the hounds, were now well behind her. Judy used her flashlight to search out the way as she climbed the final crest. She didn't wonder why this pile of old rock intrigued her, why it wasn't Carla leading the way while she herself protested. Judy just kept moving forward, upward, unthinking, compelled, driven and drawn.

Duke and Duchess whined. Judy heard their whimpering and understood they had ceased tracking whatever small creature had caught their attention. But they didn't join her, and after a few more whimpers, they fell silent again.

Directly ahead yawned the open maw that had once supported a gate in the now crumbling curtain wall. Judy did not pass through it, into what once had been a courtyard. Instead, she ambled along the outside of the castle's remains, keeping her flashlight beam on the ground. From the corner of her eye, the flickering yellow light of a crackling bonfire gave her a point of reference, until it abruptly blinked out. Judy stopped cold then and spun around as a flash of panic seized her. But though she strained to see the fire, the only light she saw was the wild slashes her flashlight cut through the air as she waved her arm crazily.

Of a sudden, she became aware of her own foolishness, having gone out in the dark to a place no one knew she might go. That she had walked so far, alone at night, for no good reason except an inexplicable whim involving a rock pile, appalled and alarmed her. Struggling to reclaim her calm, she slowly realized that the big bonfire had not gone out. The blaze had simply become hidden from view as the deteriorating wall she'd been following got between her and the flames.

Judy smiled ruefully and shouted, "Duke! Duchess!" as glad for the sound of her own voice as she would have been if the spaniels had come running. They didn't come, though, so she began retracing her steps, intending to find them. But her foot hit a tree root jutting from the ground like a menacing snake. Faltering, she stumbled backward. The flashlight fell from her hand and went out.

Heart racing again, she dropped to her knees and groped the rough, stubby grass with her fingers, searching for her handy plastic flashlight. She couldn't find it, and straining to see pained her eyes, for she was cloaked in palpable darkness. Since she'd lost sight of the bonfire, a cloud had slithered over and shuttered the waxing moon. Now scuttling clouds blanketed most of the stars as well. With the bonfire beyond her view and the flashlight beyond her reach, she may as well have been in the bottom of a deep, dark well.

The wind gusted, swirling leaves and dust that tangled her hair. The wind portended rain—a cold, needling, wintry rain—and though Judy knew she needed to find shelter, she also felt a wild exhilaration that held her in place. In fact, she raised her face to the sky and opened her arms to the wind. And let herself go.

Rationally, Judy knew she remained kneeling in the cold dirt, yet she felt a static charge that warmed her wherever her body made contact with the ground. Then, impossibly, she began to feel lighter than air. She imagined herself a kite that caught the wind and flew.

Madness, it was, but a delightful madness. No toke on a joint in her college days had ever proved this heady! She loved it, so she ignored her sensible, life-preserving instincts, which screeched in a voice like an angry crow's: *Get up! Run! Hide! A storm is coming, a bad storm!* Finally, surrendering to futility, the voice fell silent.

Judy fell, too, across her carryall. Clutching it to her bosom like a pillow, she closed her eyes and drifted. On the wings of the wind that eddied about her, she felt herself carried off, like Dorothy in the tornado on her way to Oz. Giving herself up to the tingling sensation that vibrated through her limbs, it seemed as though she actually exploded, pieces of herself and her soul scattering everywhere, like a sparkling meteor shower.

After that, she had no sense of being. Like the bonfire and the moon and her flashlight, she'd blinked out.

***

Judy woke in a fog. Not only was her mind muddled, but the air glistened with a heavy, swirling mist

It took her a minute to orient herself, and then she began to recall the previous evening in heart-rending fragments. With a start, she sat up, stretched her arms and legs, and began surveying them for damage. Her sweater and the knees of her leggings looked a little dirty, but she saw no bloodstains. Everything, from her fingers to toes, flexed without pain.

Obviously, she hadn't hurt herself. So why had she stayed outdoors all night? A rational person—especially one who'd refused to go to Girl Scout Camp because she would have to sleep in a tent—simply didn't do that sort of thing, not in the rain!

Again, she glanced down and fingered the fabric of her clothes. They felt a bit damp on the surface, but no more than she could blame on the fog and the morning dew. She was far from soaked through, as she should have been had she lain without cover in a pounding rainstorm.

It hadn't rained, then, despite the clouds and the wind she recalled. What the hell *had* happened?

A queer feeling fluttered in her belly, a sensation akin to panic. Something was wrong, very wrong.

"Damn," she muttered beneath her breath. Carla had to be worried sick. By now the poor thing had probably organized a search party.

Judy pushed herself to her feet. As she rose, she grabbed her flashlight and dropped it into her tote. Immediately, she headed in the direction she'd come, slipping on the slick, dewy grass as she hurried to return to Wixcomb and Laycock Inn.

She glanced up. The sun hung low, a small, white circle in a colorless sky glowing like a dim light bulb. As a celestial beacon, it proved a pitiful guide. She would have to trust her internal compass to find her way.

The trek back seemed interminably long—longer than the expedition out. Odd. Usually return trips felt shorter than the original traveling time. At least, Judy consoled herself, the haze seemed to be burning off as the sun continued to rise. There were only little tendrils of ground fog when she reached Wixcomb's main street.

Except it wasn't any kind of street, and the town could not be Wixcomb.

Judy halted, staring with awe and a sinking feeling at the buildings lining the rutted dirt track. None were quaint or sturdy stucco and timber. These weren't shops, either, only dwellings—huts, actually—made of...what did they call it? Daub-and-wattle. They even sported thatched roofs.

"I'm dreaming," she told herself firmly as she watched people coming and going. "I'm still in bed at Laycock Inn. I never went for a walk last night. I never climbed the hill or saw the bonfires. Pretty soon, I'm going to wake up. When I do, I'm going to laugh."

She felt no urge to laugh right now. Despite assuring herself figments of her own imagination couldn't see her if she did not wish them to, she pressed hard against the wall of a cottage at her back. Boy, her imagination had slipped into overdrive! All the town's people appeared to be dressed in costumes. They wore tunics, the men's belted, the women's flowing free. Some wore hoods so deep, Judy couldn't see their profiles when they passed her.

She had the bizarre notion she stood on a movie set, that she'd arrived on location for the filming of *Braveheart*. But *Braveheart* had been made years ago, and this was England, not Ireland, where they had filmed the Scottish tale. Of course, somebody could be making another period movie. Kenneth Branagh did it all the time.

This wasn't a movie set, though. Judy had no explanation for what she saw, but she knew a movie set couldn't be the answer.

"I'm dreaming, I'm dreaming, I'm dreaming," she muttered like a mantra as she flattened herself against the wall. An unexpected, sharp pain interrupted her chant. "Ow!" she cried, drawing her hand forward to examine it.

Something sharp had gouged her palm as she pressed it against the mud wall. It had pierced her skin deeply enough to draw blood. Could you bleed in a dream? she wondered, sucking the tiny wound.

As she fretted, a woman with two small, dirty children clinging to her skirts stopped directly before her. Scowling, the stranger stared at Judy with narrowed eyes. "Who you be?" she demanded.

"I—I—"

Frightened as a hare, she pushed herself off the wall and sprinted up the road, away from town. She'd been seen. No one should have seen her, not in a dream! But that woman had. And she'd bled, too. Judy paused when she had run far enough to grow winded, and examined her injured palm again. God in heaven, you couldn't hurt yourself inside a dream, could you?

She might not be dreaming after all. She might be awake. But she wasn't where she should have been—in her room at the inn or, more rightly, in her New York City apartment. Where in God's name was she? Not Wixcomb.

"I got turned around," Judy decided. She spun about,

gazing again at the strangely dressed people, the odd little huts, and the assorted animals barking, pecking and rooting in the dirt. "I walked beyond the old castle ruins," she recalled, concluding, "I came down the wrong hill in the fog. This isn't Wixcomb, it's—"

The Renaissance Fair. That's what it was, or at least, that's what it was like. That Old English fair in the States, where all the performers dressed in period costume, and they sold roasted pig instead of pizza by the slice, and actors dressed as knights jousted before their medieval "king."

What a fool she'd been! That woman who'd approached her had simply been wondering why a tourist had come visiting the fair so early in the day. They weren't open yet. The ticket booth was neither set up nor manned. Judy hadn't paid her entrance fee, and she obviously didn't belong among the performers.

Well, she'd go right back and ask for directions to Wixcomb. She couldn't have strayed too far.

With new determination, Judy walked the several yards that brought her back to the edge of the village. A man eyed her suspiciously as she approached, but instead of ducking for cover, she stepped directly up to him.

"Excuse me," she said, "but I seem to be lost. Could you tell me the way to Wixcomb?"

He stumbled backward warily. "Wixcomb?" he repeated.

"Yes. I'm from New York, but I'm staying in Wixcomb. Could you tell me how to get back there?"

"Wixcomb," he said again, spreading his arms and gesturing to the left and the right. Then, looking her up and down once more, he dashed off and insinuated himself among several people clustered in a group. He spoke to them in low tones, and they all looked at her with obvious disapproval.

"Damn." What was *that* all about? She'd only asked for directions. Why wouldn't he tell her? Why were the others looking at her so oddly?

Because this place wasn't like the Renaissance Fair—it was like Plymouth Plantation, another American tourist attraction. Judy had gone to the town near Plymouth Rock on a class trip years ago. She recalled the "villagers" lived on site and toiled at the same sort of tasks the original settlers had. Not only did they dress in period costume, they spoke "period" English. Rather annoyingly, they purposely ignored the tourists and any evidence of modern life so that visitors felt as though they'd stepped back in time.

Judy remembered something else: Mrs. Haversham had said people stayed at Laycock Inn when they came to poke about the castle ruins and "the other." Maybe this was *the other!*

Shifting her tote from her right shoulder to her left, she set out again from the theatrical recreation of an old English village. Geez, she found herself thinking testily, didn't they have enough authentically ancient things in Britain that they shouldn't feel compelled to recreate more? First, the *Globe Theatre* in London and now, this village. The Brits were definitely mad. And rude. But if nobody would break character long enough to assist her, she'd help herself. Now that the mist seemed to be dissipated, she'd hike back up the hills and on past the castle ruins. On the far side, she'd make her way down again. At last, she'd be in Wixcomb.

Veering off the dirt road, Judy hadn't yet looked around to get her bearings when she felt more than heard a large horse pounding toward her. Turning slightly toward the rolling hills she'd recently descended, she saw a massively huge beast hurtling toward her as though its rider intended to trample her into the ground.

Instinct should have propelled her to leap out of the way, but Judy froze. In the split second it took for the animal to reach her, she had no time to be afraid, only astounded. She expected soon to find herself either dead or grievously injured.

Somehow, at the last possible moment, the rider steered his horse away from Judy. When beast and man swerved, they came so dangerously close, she caught the scent of horse sweat in her nostrils. Yet she remained on her feet, swaying only a little, and watched, transfixed, as the man reined in his mount and then walked it back in her direction.

Her numb incredulity dissolved, a hot, pulsing rage

replacing it. God Almighty! He was one of them, a thespian, a player, a re-enactor, whatever the villagers called themselves! No doubt he claimed the role of leading man, because he was obviously young and good-looking. Also, he alone wore the clothes of a king, not a peasant. What the heck—did he think he *was* a king?

Judy opened her mouth to berate the idiot actor who'd nearly ridden her down, when he opened his mouth and swore venomously. At least, she thought he cursed her. Judging from his angry glower and the thunderous tone of his voice, he didn't seem to be inquiring about the weather. But she couldn't be sure, because he spoke French.

Judy knew she hadn't wandered *that* far afield. She'd have remembered taking the *Chunnel*. "Speak English!" she demanded, muttering a choice expletive of her own beneath her breath.

"By all the saints, what did you think you were doing?"

Okay. He'd switched to English—at least Judy presumed he had. She caught a few familiar words. But he had an accent as thick as the morning's mist. And it didn't matter what he said to her. She had plenty she wanted to say to him.

"Don't you shout at me, you jerk! You nearly killed me! How dare you race around like that? In another few seconds, you'd be in the village. There are people there, even children. I don't think the rest of your troupe would take kindly to being trampled by you and your damned—" She paused to breathe and glanced again at the animal. It was obviously, very obviously, as male as its rider. "—stallion!" she resumed. "And what if you had paying patrons? If you injured any tourists who'd come to gawk at your quaint medieval village, the lawsuits would put you all out of work! Did you ever think of that?"

She glared at him, forehead furrowed, hands clenched into fists. He stared back at her as though she'd just beamed down from a spaceship. *How dare he*? He was in the wrong, not she—the arrogant, reckless prima donna!

He kicked his stallion's flanks, and the animal

moved even closer to Judy. The beast's nostrils flared and his eyes—at least the one she could see—showed a great deal of white. But Judy held her ground bravely. This was nothing compared to having the half-ton animal charging her at forty miles an hour.

"Who are you?" the man asked. "From whence do you come?"

"America. And Americans don't put up with the kind of crap you just pulled."

He pulled a face. "America?" he repeated, emphasizing the wrong syllables and making the word sound odd, foreign.

"Yes. America. Don't act like you've never heard of it."

"I have not heard of it."

Judy took a deep breath. She had to remember he was immersed in his role. These people were perverse, the whole lot of them. Couldn't step out of character for a second, just like the suspects in one of those murder mystery weekends she'd attended with friends at a Catskills resort.

"Forget about America," Judy said, suspecting it would prove futile to try to make him acknowledge the year as 1998, not 1298. "I suppose Columbus hasn't discovered it yet, that's why you haven't heard of it. How about Wixcomb? Ever heard of Wixcomb? Nice little town somewhere around here. While I'm visiting England, that's where I'm staying."

The young man screwed his well-shaped mouth to the side, letting his skepticism show. For an instant, that mouth seemed familiar to Judy.

But before she could sort it out, she reacted to his sarcastic query, "Are you blind?"

"No," she replied. "But you're rude!"

"'Tis there." He pointed.

Judy looked back down the beaten path to the fake, historical hamlet populated by actors in period garb.

"This isn't funny," she ground out slowly. "I want to know where Wixcomb, the real Wixcomb, is. I got turned around last night, and now I have to get back. Where is it?"

"Are you deaf? 'Tis there, as I said." He narrowed

his gaze contemptuously.

"I'm neither deaf nor blind, and it's not there!" Frustration and impatience made Judy's eyes well with tears. "If that's Wixcomb, it's a re-creation of what Wixcomb might have been a few hundred years ago. I want the real one, the modern one!"

She felt like giggling hysterically. Yesterday, she would never have described Wixcomb as modern. Then, before this cretin actor could drive her to madness by insisting the nearby cluster of thatch-roofed cottages was the town she sought, Judy added, "I'm staying at Laycock Inn. I have to get back to Laycock Inn. I have a friend waiting for me there."

"Laycock?" he repeated, swinging his leg over the stallion's neck and dropping effortlessly to the ground.

"Yes, Laycock," she assured him wearily. "Listen, I know my accent must sound as strange to you as yours does to me, but we both speak the queen's English, don't we? You do understand what I'm asking?"

"The queen?"

He stepped close and peered curiously into her face. They were nearly eye-to-eye as Judy returned his gaze, aware, peripherally, that he was even better looking up close. If this guy ever gave up role-playing in the English countryside and auditioned for movies, Brad Pitt and Tom Cruise would have to watch their backs. He had thick, dark hair and even darker brown eyes that drooped a bit at the outside corners. He looked either sleepy or sated, as though he'd just awakened or just been laid.

But he was a kid, no more than early twenty-something, at least a half dozen years her junior. Judy hadn't time for the nonsense he was putting her through. Damn it all! He could stop acting long enough to give her directions to Wixcomb—*the* Wixcomb, not this replica constructed for tourists.

"Forget the queen. I'm telling you I have to return to Laycock Inn. Is it that way?"

She raised her hand and pointed. For the first time since feeling the rumble of pounding hooves reverberating under her feet, she faced the hills she had recently descended. At the top of the highest, most distant rise, the mists had lifted to reveal a sight that nearly stole her breath away: a castle surrounded by a crenelated wall. It looked in perfect condition, not the least bit rotting or crumbling.

Slowly, Judy dragged her eyes back to the matinee idol beside her. Meeting her gaze, he said simply, "Laycock."

Swallowing with a throat that felt as though it were lined with sandpaper, she asked, "Laycock Castle?"

"Nay. 'Tis merely a keep, though a substantial one."

Thank God! Judy smiled weakly and began, "I thought—for a moment, I thought—"

But she couldn't admit what she had thought, not to this perverse stranger. She could barely admit to herself that, for a second, she'd entertained the very real fear that the town to her left and the fortress above were the selfsame Wixcomb and Laycock Castle she'd been seeking.

"Some, though," the actor continued, "call it Laycock Castle."

Judy refused to faint, though blacking out seemed like a really comforting thing to do. She had surely fainted last night, and look at the consequences. Not again. No way.

"I am Lord Laycock."

"What?" She snapped her head around to study his face again. He wasn't Lord Laycock, not Carla's Lord Laycock. They were both dark, in hair color and complexion, and they shared a similar, athletic build. But this guy was too young, and with those bedroom eyes, he was definitely too handsome.

"Andrew of Laycock," he elaborated. "Son of Thomas and Lady Ardith, brother of Robin and Elfred."

"I—I met a Lord Laycock yesterday," Judy told him, aware she was beginning to babble. "I never caught his first name. I'd guess he was in his thirties."

"There are no other Lords of Laycock except for my sire, my brothers, and me. None of us encountered you yesterday. Had we, we would have spoken of it."

Judy recalled another fragment of information she had gleaned yesterday. The Laycock manor house had stood empty for some years until Carla's Lord Laycock inherited the place and turned it into an inn. Mrs.

Haversham had said there were no other surviving Laycocks except for "his lordship." No sires or sons, just the one computer guru.

"Behold!" Andrew pointed, and Judy followed the line of his extended arm. Emerging from beneath the iron-toothed gate in the wall came two riders, decked out like Knights of the Round Table. "My brothers," he announced.

By then, Judy's heart, if not her head, suspected they were not actors. Neither the princely fellow beside her nor the peasants in town. Yet they had to be! Her mind warred with her intuition until, looking around, she found herself distracted by something else alarming. The landscape didn't look autumnal. The leaves hadn't turned, the grass was neither brittle nor yellow. Quite the contrary, the trees in the vicinity appeared to be budding, and wild flowers dotted the high ground.

"Tell me something," she whispered, holding herself stiff, knees locked, hands clenched. "Is it springtime?"

"Aye."

She swallowed hard. "And the year...?"

"'Tis the sixteenth year of King John's reign."

Judy was no history buff, but in the extended company of Carla Whittaker, she'd acquired, by osmosis, a few random facts. A particular scrap of information leapt to the fore of her mind now: Only one King John had ever ruled England, and he'd succeeded his brother, Richard Lionheart, in 1199. That meant the early morning sunshine warming the English soil beneath her feet did so on a spring day in 1215!

She might easily have protested, calling Andrew a liar. But Judy said nothing, watching mutely while the pair of horsemen trotted down the slopes directly toward her. As the sound of shod hooves crescendoed, she gave up resisting.

She fainted.

Three

As Judy came to, her heart seized in fright. This time the world wasn't just upside down, she was, too. It took a few seconds to orient herself, but she finally realized that Andrew of Laycock had slung her over his shoulder, like a sack of potatoes, and set off on his horse. Though Andrew's arm gripped her thighs, holding her securely, the rigid bone in his squared shoulder was ramming her belly with every hard, bouncing stride the horse took.

"Let—" Oof. "Me—" Oof. "Down!" she demanded, pounding her balled fist against his back.

Andrew ignored both her assault and her command, yet as they rode beneath a portcullis' iron spikes, Judy was glad he did. The brothers Laycock rode too fast, too hard, to have made her dismount and landing anything but treacherous.

Suddenly, however, Andrew did halt. Belatedly and quite abruptly, he acceded to Judy's wishes. Sliding her off his shoulder, he grabbed her waist and set her down without warning. It seemed to Judy that he let go while her feet still dangled a few feet from the ground, because she landed hard, her knees buckled, and she had to brace herself, hands in the dirt, to keep from tumbling onto her backside. Robin and Elfred—Judy didn't know who was who—watched her with expressions of curious disdain as she pushed herself upright. Neither offered assistance.

"Where's my tote?" she demanded, slapping the dust from her hands. She felt a bit anxious, fearing that Andrew had left her bag behind in the road where someone could make off with her laptop, gadgets and personal necessities. But she was far more angry with these men, whoever they were, whatever their time, for daring to make off with her. Why, they had all but kidnapped her! Yet, in light of her bizarre and unfathomable circumstances, Judy decided it might be prudent not to get in their faces, New Yorker-style. So, instead of voicing her outrage over their treatment of her, she merely demanded, albeit testily, "Where did you leave my tote?"

"Eh?" He squinted, appearing confused. Then he muttered, nodded and gestured to one of his supposed brothers. That one produced the black nylon carryall and tossed it to Andrew.

"This satchel, do you mean?" He dangled it from the strap, allowing it to swing, and examined both sides. "I have it here," he told her. "Now, come."

"It's mine!" Judy tried to grab it from him.

"For the moment, 'tis mine." He tucked it under one arm, in the manner boys always carry their schoolbooks. With his free hand, he gave Judy a forceful nudge in the small of her back. "Inside with you," he commanded.

She had no choice. She went inside.

Climbing a tall, cement staircase, they passed through an entryway and stepped into a cavernous, stone-walled chamber. The hard floor had been strewn with grass, and a cluster of high-backed chairs were arranged beside a fire pit. Pushing her much harder than Andrew had, one of the other knights urged Judy toward the chairs. He muttered something she presumed meant, "sit," so she sat.

Servants shuffled into the room, brief conversations ensued, then the servants hurried off. Within a minute, though, the men were given pewter mugs. When the servant seemed to hesitate in front of Judy, she grabbed the remaining mug he'd been holding and held it up pointedly, until he filled her cup with the same beverage he provided the others. Judy sniffed and sipped. Wine. Not bad, but a little strong for this early in the day. Well, not this particular day. Nothing could be strong enough.

Andrew and his cohorts also drank, but they remained standing. They moved about, gesticulating—frequently pointing at Judy.

She chose not to watch them, not to listen. It wasn't as though she could understand a word they said. The men all spoke French, which Judy suspected was not the French she'd suffered through for two years in high school. Their French sounded as strange as Andrew's English. The difference was, she could at least comprehend his English. The Laycocks' French would have been beyond her scope even if she'd passed her foreign language class with better than a "C."

Instead, Judy emptied her cup, waggled it discreetly, and smiled encouragingly when the servant came to attend her. When her mug had been refilled, she tippled and looked around idly. This room, a true "great hall," dwarfed Laycock Inn's main chamber. The ceiling loomed high, and what passed for windows were merely chinks in the stones with no glass of any sort to bar the elements. Which proved a good thing, since the fire blazing in the pit, along with the flaming wall torches that attempted to ward off the chill and the gloom, smoked horribly. Were it not for those narrow slits, the smoke would have had nowhere to go.

Judy noticed decorative tapestries and banners hanging on the walls, as well as weapons on display—broadswords, shields, maces, and implements she could not name and prayed she'd never know the business end of. On a raised platform at one end of the enormous chamber, sat a long, plank table and several more carved chairs. When she craned her neck, she glimpsed, in a corner behind her, the lower stone steps of a staircase that spilled out onto the floor.

Two springer spaniels suddenly bounded through the archway near the keep's front entrance. Judy had a start. For a second, she thought they might be Duke and Duchess. If only they'd been! If only they'd bounded over the hills last night, hot on her trail. Then everything that had happened to her this morning would be somehow explainable, and she'd prove that the people she had encountered were merely cruel, stubbornly holding to their oaths to live and behave as though this year were nearer the last millennium than the pending one.

But the dogs weren't Duke and Duchess—they had long tails, and one had a scar on his side where no fur grew. When they leapt at one of Andrew's compatriots, he spoke to them familiarly. The dogs understood his command better than Judy could, for they promptly sank back on their haunches, awaiting further instructions.

The three men then turned as one, compelling Judy to look at them as they strode toward her chair and halted. Without doubt, these men were brothers, so they could not possibly be performers unless they were a family of actors like the Baldwin boys. One had Andrew's eyes but a lighter complexion and sandy-colored hair and beard. The other had blue eyes, but everything else about him, from his dark locks to the angle of his clean-shaven chin, appeared the same as Andrew's. And though each stood at a different but somewhat modest height, the trio had identical builds, even identical strides!

The blue-eyed man—Judy thought he seemed the eldest, probably only slightly older than herself—thrust out his arm, pointing at her. The tip of his finger nearly touched her nose, and she flinched, pressing herself against the back of her chair. He barked at her in his sharp, incomprehensible language.

Judy hadn't a clue as to what he had said. But she heard herself respond with the only French phrase that remained in her vocabulary ten years out of high school: "Je m'appelle Judith."

Judith. God, how she hated her given name, or at least she had as a teenager. But Mademoiselle O'Flynn, her tenth grade French teacher, had insisted she use it in class. So that's what came out now. *I am called Judith.*

The man scowled but continued to address her. Judy remained bewildered, and she'd used up her entire repertoire of conversational French. So she sat there finishing her second large mug of wine and fighting the urge to bring her legs up under herself and curl into a protective ball.

"She doesn't speak French, Robin," Andrew announced. "She appears only to speak English, though not very well. If you wish her to understand, speak slowly in that tongue."

"You have no Norman French and speak English badly?" Robin asked Judy with a frown. "Where are you from, wench? And do not lie, I warn you."

She refrained from announcing—haughtily—that she hailed from America. Andrew hadn't been very impressed with that information. And if she really had traveled back in time, America did not yet exist as a country. If she named it, this man, Robin, would believe she lied. Since he had warned her not to, she hedged.

"A faraway land." *In miles and time.*

The thought made her wince, and she swallowed back tears. When the servant with the jug appeared again, unobtrusively topping off the men's tankards, she held out her own for refilling. As soon as she could bring the cup to her lips, she swallowed back more wine.

"Your family. What are you called?"

"Lam—"

Her history, not surprisingly, failed her. Judy didn't know what the situation between England and Italy might be. Was there an Italy? Weren't they all city-states with petty kings to rule them? Did the Pope and King John get along? Were these English nobles Catholic or Protestant? When had the Reformation occurred? Judy couldn't remember, if she'd ever known. Her head hurt, so she gulped the dregs from her cup, hoping to dull the pain.

Fortunately, she found herself spared having to provide her surname, which sounded so obviously Italian to anyone with an ear, because Andrew commented, "Judith Lamb. A fair enough name. Indeed, an English name."

The third brother—Elfred, she presumed—reached out and roughly tucked up her chin. "Aye, a fair name and a fair face. But why is her hair unseemingly shorn? And these clothes." He lowered his hand from her chin, grabbed her wrist, and yanked her to her feet. "What manner of garments are these?"

Judy's metal mug clattered to the floor as she lost her grip on the handle. It rolled toward her tote, which Andrew had set down a few feet away. Immediately Judy stooped down, as though to pick up her tankard but actually to retrieve her bag. Unfortunately, her head swam and she wobbled, allowing Robin a second to perceive her intentions. Moving more quickly than she, he scooped up the tote and stepped beyond her reach.

"Give it back," she cried, lurching as she stood upright. If Andrew hadn't caught her about the waist, Judy thought she might have sunk to her knees.

Cradling the tote in one arm, Robin attempted to open it with his free hand. He had no success. "There is no string," he observed, "no tie. 'Tis sealed."

"How can a satchel have no opening?" Elfred asked curiously as he leaned forward to peer at the bag in Robin's hands.

"No doubt it's been sewn shut," Andrew surmised, taking the tote from Robin.

"It is not sewn shut," Robin declared with authority. "I examined it."

"Then 'tis a mystery I will solve."

"And what will you do with the wench here?"

"She is a mystery I should also like to solve."

Robin made a scoffing noise. "What? You've naught to do otherwise?"

"Nothing except protect those who remain here after you and Elfred leave." Andrew gestured with a broad sweep of one arm to include no one at all.

"You needn't mock me, Andrew. Though 'tis true Mother and our sisters are away at a wedding, and Elfred and I will soon be joining our sire near London, you are needed to protect the demesne, our servants, and the town's folk of Wixcomb."

"I mock no one, Robin," he insisted, though Judy heard a hint of sarcasm in his tone. "Why should I resent being left behind, still again, to watch over the babes and the aged when I have such a comely wench to amuse me?"

Robin tsked, and Elfred said testily, "You could do other with your life, Andrew. You could do as I do, and ride the circuit with other knights, competing in tourneys that earn us good, solid coin."

"Is that where you are going? To compete for money?"

"Nay, I—"

"Elfred is coming with me, as you certainly know," Robin put in. "He asked to join Father, and I decided he could."

"But I asked, and you said nay," Andrew pointed out.

"Damn you! For a brother I love well, Andrew, you try me sorely! What do you think, that we are joining our sire and the other English barons to tryst with comely damsels and drink ourselves into sweet dreams? This business with King John is serious. If Lackland fails to concede to our demands, there will be war!"

Judy jerked, and Andrew tightened his hold around her waist. His hand actually slid upward so that his splayed fingers pressed against her ribs, and the edge of his thumb grazed the underside of her breast.

Under other circumstances, Judy would have extricated herself from his embrace. Certainly, she'd have given the groper a good tongue-lashing. But Robin's bellowing had the same effect as someone beating a kettle drum—she flinched and her lashes fluttered. So Judy remained anchored by Andrew's arm, deciding that staying on her feet was preferable to falling down, even if the man who served as her anchor copped a feel.

"Grow up, little brother," the blue-eyed knight urged. Judy felt sure that he and Andrew had had similar conversations before, and that Robin had grown tired of them. "There is slim chance that Elfred will ever rule Laycock, and none at all that you will. Elfred accepts his lot; you must, too. For now, enjoy your days as lord of the keep, while Father and I are away. Mayhap the experience will enable you to oversee your own fief wisely, should you obtain one."

"I shall bear your advice in mind, Robin. And I shall most surely enjoy my authority, fleeting as it is, by entertaining myself however I like."

Robin glanced at Judy. "Aye, that you will, I'm sure," he said before turning to Elfred with a shrug. "Let us be off. This curious wench has delayed us, and we've no time to dawdle. I must join Father as soon as I'm able."

"You can't mean to leave that—that urchin here with Andrew!" Elfred sputtered.

"Aye. Why not? She appears harmless enough, and she seems to amuse him. At least, she soon shall."

"Robin, you cannot be serious! We should take her with us and, at the very least, leave her far away from Laycock Keep."

"Why should you do that?" Andrew demanded.

"Because she is not one of us," Elfred explained. "She speaks no Norman French."

"That only marks her as a common peasant. Do you fear the humble folk who work our land?"

"She doesn't work our land, nor is she wedded to a man who does. She doesn't even dwell in Wixcomb—

she could be anyone from anywhere! In these troubling times, 'tis not a risk I think we should take." Elfred paused but continued to scowl at Andrew. "What ails you? You cling to her as though she were your lady love."

"I thought we determined she is no lady."

"I sure as hell *am* a lady!" Judy announced indignantly, snatched from her languor by the insult.

In the boozy state that, like Demerol, dulled Judy's senses, she'd been content to try to understand as much of the conversation floating around her as her drink-addled mind and their curious accents allowed. She had even permitted Andrew's subtle groping without too much indignation. But she would be damned if she'd allow these ghosts, or whatever they were, to insult her. There, she drew the line.

To emphasize her assertion, Judy belatedly grabbed Andrew's offending hand and threw it off. Unfortunately, dignity failed her when she tried to step away and stumbled, nearly falling.

Again, Andrew seized her. This time, when he caught her, he hugged her to him. He even gave her a speculative smile before raising his chin to gaze over her head at his brothers.

"Did you hear that, Elfred? The damsel here insists she's nobly born. Mayhap 'tis true, despite her questionable use of English and her appalling attire. If it is, I should locate Lady Judith's kin. It might improve my lot if her sire, or her husband, could reward me for my efforts."

"Lady Judith!" Elfred sneered contemptuously. "Not in a thousand years."

"If she be not a lady, it matters naught to me." Andrew made his eyebrows dance.

"You are ailing," Elfred insisted, shaking his head in disgust, "if a female in chausses and a child's short tunic heats your blood. Have your way with her, if it pleases you. But if she proves to be a spy working for our enemies or—or a witch, your swiving will cost us dearly."

"A spy? A witch?" Andrew sneered. "I am not ailing, Elfred, but your wits are addled!"

"Be still, both of you," Robin snapped. "Indeed, Elfred,

you speak foolishly, and I've no time for it. I am leaving now. Join me if you wish, or go joust, or stay here and keep a wary eye on Andrew and the girl, whichever you will. Father and I have serious matters to attend to."

He turned and strode away.

Elfred hurried after him. "What of that sack she carried?" he asked Robin. "It has no seams, it must be enchanted. And what of the wench herself?" Without missing a step, Elfred turned back and pointed to Judy. "Her speech is neither true Saxon nor English. Her clothes are all male. And her hair! She is too foreign and curious to shelter anywhere but the scullery. 'Twould be better if she be disposed of."

Disposed of. A pang of fear permeated the alcoholic haze still cocooning Judy, and she whirled within the circle of Andrew's arms to call out to his brothers.

"I—ruined my clothes!" she announced, barely thinking up the lies before they spilled from her lips. Yet her explanation caught Robin's and Elfred's attention, for they halted at the archway near the door and turned around to face her. "I—I caught my hems on fire. Luckily, a boy—a lad—offered me these garments he'd outgrown, or I'd be naked. As for my hair—"

"What of your hair?" Elfred prompted.

Judy recalled a scene from one of her authors' manuscripts, a period story, a historical. "I was ill with fever not long ago," she informed them. "They—they shaved my head."

"There!" Andrew said. "A fever and deliriums could well explain why this damsel—mayhap a noble damsel—was wandering about unescorted."

"She was lost?" Robin asked, peering at his brother with narrowed eyes.

"Aye," Andrew replied. "When I first encountered her, she asked me for directions."

"To where?" Robin had drawn closer, and he spoke directly to Judy now. When she failed to answer quickly, he pressed, "From whence do you come?"

The Twilight Zone.

"What place do you seek?"

Another dimension.

Robin's handsome face turned ruddy, and Judy knew

she had better say something quickly. "London," she told him, naming the first city Americans thought of whenever they thought of England.

"London! No matter where you began your journey, be it within or beyond England's borders, to find your way here when looking for London, you surely traveled far out of your way."

"You don't know the half of it."

He transferred his scowl from Judy to Andrew. "What is it she said?"

"I told you, she does not speak English properly."

"Then how is it you understand her strange tongue so well? And what language is it that she does speak properly?" he fumed. "Latin?"

"Not even close," Judy remarked with a snort. Then, peering into Andrew's tankard and discovering it still held wine, she decided not to let the grape go to waste. Taking the mug, she hoisted it, threw back her head, and downed the contents. It was, she determined, much easier dealing with these horrors smashed instead of sober.

"God's tears, the waif is drunk," Elfred observed as he retraced his steps to stand beside Robin.

She definitely was that, and knowing it, Judy grinned. So far today, it was the best thing that had happened to her.

"'Scuse me," she apologized with a hiccup, covering her lips with her hand and closing her eyes.

That proved a mistake. The moment she did, she felt nauseous. Even when she snapped her eyes open again and tried to focus on Robin's face, he and the room beyond him whirled. Judy's stomach churned as she fought the urge to vomit.

"Aye, she's drunk," Andrew confirmed, slipping an arm behind her thighs and lifting her like a baby. "Don't fret, Elfred. I doubt the wench can do much harm. Even I should be able to handle her."

Though her lids felt heavy and remained nearly closed, Judy detected the leer in Andrew's chocolate-colored eyes when he glanced down at her. She'd visited enough singles' bars to recognize the gleam and to understand that "handling her" was precisely what he had in mind.

"See that you do, Andrew," Robin advised. "Use her 'til you're sore, and if you determine where she belongs, send her back there. But I remind you, little brother, you do have duties at Laycock which you'd best not neglect."

"I'm fairly confident I can manage all of them and Judith as well," Andrew returned. "Farewell, brothers! Rest easy in the knowledge that Laycock Keep shall still be standing upon your return."

With Judy still cradled in his arms, he strode across the hall and began to climb the exceedingly narrow, winding staircase to a floor somewhere above. "Where...are you taking me?" she asked.

"To bed."

Oh, bed. That sounded nice. A mattress and covers to cuddle up in.

Damn! Judy went rigid in Andrew's arms when, a heartbeat later, she recalled his true intentions. Her mouth dropped open in startled concern as he kicked open a door, banging it against an inside wall, and dropped her roughly onto a bed. When he jumped onto the bed and stretched out beside her, Judy finally found her voice.

"What the hell do you think you're doing?"

"If you don't know, I shall teach you. I'm told I'm rather good at it."

Oh, geez. She didn't need this. What she needed was a good, long nap—and a seat on H.G. Wells' time machine.

"Listen, I—"

Andrew kissed her, open mouth on open mouth. His lips felt soft and warm, and when his tongue darted between her lips, Judy felt a tremor of sexual excitement. The heat in her belly flared when he began nibbling her lips and his thumb gently stroked the line of her jaw.

Oh, God. Her reaction to him went beyond anything rational. It was worse, even, than her fleeting attraction to Carla's Lord Laycock. Was there something about the Laycock bloodline that heated her blood? By all rights, she should have been slipping into madness, wailing and pulling her hair. Instead, this obnoxious *boy* in a knight's costume sparked a fire that could have melted her insides, if she let it.

I am going insane, she decided. Yet there remained something oddly comforting about Andrew's attentions, base as they were. Judy, however, had no intention of giving in to him. Of all the women she knew, she was the least likely to sleep with a man she'd just met. Having never done so in the past, she did not propose to do so now. Most certainly, she did not intend to sleep with a ghostly stranger who'd been dead in his grave at least 700 years!

That last idea made her head whirl. The impossible events of that morning swam through her mind in a blur of dizzying images. Judy lost her ability to make any kind of choices, rational, determined, or otherwise. She pulled away, leaned over the side of the bed, and threw up noisily all over the floor.

"Jesu!" Andrew leaped to his feet. "How much did you drink, woman? Shite." He stomped toward the door and pulled it open. "Bridget! Sally! Someone, come here and clean up this room!"

He turned back to Judy, who peered at him from a precarious angle—to her, he seemed to be standing on his head.

"You may have put me off for the moment," Andrew conceded, "but there are many days and nights to come. You'll be mine yet."

Hell, she'd never been anyone's before, and Judy didn't expect to belong to anyone in the near future—*or past,* she added perversely. She would certainly not belong to a medieval knight who only wanted her for a quickie.

"I've got more pride than that," she mumbled to herself before retching again most piteously.

Four

After falling into a restless sleep, Judy woke again late in the afternoon with a heart-pounding start. For the briefest moment, she thought she might be in a Pullman car, because she found her bed enclosed by draperies. But then all the events of the past eighteen hours or so came back, and she felt sick. Not nauseous, just miserable.

Dry mouth, headache. She had a hangover! And when Judy's stomach grumbled, she knew she was starving as well. She'd have killed for a few aspirin, a Virgin Mary, and some crisp, buttered toast.

Knowing there was little likelihood of satisfying her cravings, she parted the curtains and climbed out of bed, wincing as she pressed a palm to her throbbing forehead. Looking around the room, she noticed details that had escaped her when Lord Andrew Laycock had, like some caveman, carried her up here. Now she saw that the stone walls boasted a few decorative hangings and the stone floor was strewn with grass. Not grass, rushes. Yes, Carla had mentioned rushes just the other day. And there was a window, a crude, uncovered opening like those downstairs in the great hall. But this one seemed considerably larger. Near it, in a small pit, burned a woefully inadequate fire. Judy walked toward it, warming her hands over the glowing coals.

Geez, hasn't anyone thought of fireplaces yet, the sort with chimneys?

Judy decided not, as she watched the smoke drift to the window. She drifted in that direction herself, and, leaning on the sill, stuck her head outside for a gulp of fresh air.

The scene in the yard below amazed her. It appeared that the protective walls surrounding the keep also housed a village. She saw buildings, people, animals...it looked very much like Wixcomb, at least the Wixcomb she had visited that morning.

Was that rapping at her door? Judy whirled around just as a voice beyond called, "Milady?"

Am I "milady?" Judy didn't know, so she didn't

respond. Yet the door opened, and a girl, probably in her late teens, entered carrying a covered tray.

"Milady!" she said, seeing Judy at the window. "You did not answer. I thought you still asleep."

"I just woke up."

"Lord Andrew said you would be waking soon. He ordered these victuals brought to you." The girl set the tray down on a small, utilitarian table.

"Victuals?" Judy repeated, peering at the wooden platter cautiously.

"Aye."

The servant whisked away the cloth, and Judy quickly learned victuals meant food. Eagerly, she picked up a small loaf of warm bread and broke off a piece. It tasted as heavenly as it smelled.

"What's that?" Judy asked as the girl poured amber liquid into a goblet. The last thing Judy needed was more wine.

"Beer."

Beer! Something else with an alcohol content.

Judy shook her head. "Do you have anything that's not fermented? Juice, milk, water?"

"Oh, aye. Mulberry juice. Would that do, milady?"

"Yes. Please."

The girl turned to leave. Judy stopped her. "Excuse me. What's your name?"

"Bridget."

"Bridget, could I get a bath?" She looked down at her sweater and gestured. "I'm really filthy."

"A bath? Oh, aye. If you wish, Lady Judith. It'll take some while, though."

"I don't mind. I've got time on my hands." *About 800 years' worth.*

With a bob, the servant departed. Judy sat on a three-legged stool and sampled the food on her...what was this? Not a plate. She explored the container with her finger. Bread! A hollowed-out bread crust. Not a bad idea. Anybody who was really hungry could eat their dishes for dessert.

Bridget returned carrying a cup of mulberry juice. Two men, who carried a wooden tub between them, followed. Though they seemed unperturbed crowding into the small room, Judy felt uncomfortable with the crush of bodies.

"Bridget," she whispered, grabbing the girl's sleeve. "I need to use the bath—the toilet. Where is it?"

Bridget frowned. Obviously, she did not understand. To convey the urgency of her request, Judy clasped her hands in front of her crotch and danced up and down.

"Oh!" Bridget grinned and giggled. "The jakes are in the corner."

"The jakes?"

"Aye. The garderobe," she whispered and then stepped through the doorway. When Judy followed, she pointed to a distant corner at the end of the hallway.

"Thanks." Judy headed down the corridor and slipped into an odoriferous cubicle with a hole in the floor. Not daring to peer into the shaft, she yanked her leggings off one foot, straddled the hole, did what she had to do, and pulled her pants back up. Damn! If only she'd had her tote, she'd have had facial tissue to use for toilet paper. Thank goodness the next item on her agenda was a soak in a tub.

When Judy returned, Bridget announced her bath ready and set out some folded linen rectangles she called drying cloths. Judy thanked her again, but instead of departing, the girl remained.

"Milady?" She looked at Judy questioningly.

"I'll take my bath as soon as you leave."

"I should assist you."

"No, thank you. I'm quite capable of washing myself."

Bridget looked doubtful. "Are you certain?"

"Very."

With as disapproving an expression as a servant dared make, Bridget left the bedroom again. Judy promptly stripped off her clothes and climbed into the tub.

The water felt heavenly, which briefly compensated for her lack of toiletries. But the small tub forced her to sit with her breasts squashed against her knees. Exasperated, she soon resorted to swinging her legs over the rim in order to dunk her head in the water, and by that time the initial pleasure had all but faded.

While wetting her hair and wondering how clean

she could get it without shampoo, Judy heard the door open and close. "Bridget," she said, "I told you I can bathe just fine on my own."

"Is that what you call what you're doing?" a masculine voice inquired.

"You!" Judy hauled herself upright and brought her feet back inside the tub. "What are you doing here?"

"Looking at you." Andrew cocked an eyebrow.

Judy spied her tote in his hand. "You have my bag. Please, give me my bag!"

"Why? Have you a magic wand in here or some other device to work black magic on me and mine?"

"No. I have soap in there, and shampoo."

"What is 'shampoo?'"

"Soap for hair. Special soap for hair."

Andrew approached the tub. "You may have your satchel, but only if you give me something in return."

She arched an eyebrow right back at him. "Fine. What?"

He sauntered over to the bed, still carrying the tote, and sat. As Judy watched, wide-eyed at his effrontery, he tugged off his shoes, unbuckled his belt, and pulled off his tunic. Wearing only hose and baggy drawers, he crawled between the sheets and drew the covers up as far as his waist. With a grin, he said, "Lie with me."

"Bite me!"

Andrew's smile vanished, and he flew off the bed. With two strides, he reached Judy. "That did not sound much like an invitation," he observed, grabbing the tub's rim with both his hands. "You'd do well to remember I am the master here."

"I thought your father was master here. And after him, your brother, Robin. And after him, your other brother—"

"I am lord and master when they're away, which I remind you, woman, they are! Andrew of Laycock is the only lord you need deal with. And...seek to please."

He smiled again, like a snake, and touched her cheek.

Judy drew her head back sharply. "You're a bastard."

"Nay, I am not. My parents were wed long years before I entered the world."

"I mean, you're an ass! A real slime ball. You have me alone, and you want to rape me!"

"Rape you? I've ne'er forced myself on any female, not even the village wenches or the servants." He straightened and backed away a step, looking righteously offended.

"You could have fooled me. We met only hours ago, and you're trying to get me into bed again. I'm not a slut. And I'm no village girl or servant, either!"

Judy nearly added that she was an important literary agent, intending to embellish her success and reputation, until she realized how unimpressive that bit of information would be to this medieval lord.

"Mayhap you are, mayhap you are not." Andrew leaned toward the tub, the muscles in his arms bulging and those of his belly taut and rippling. With that slight movement, he loomed over Judy threateningly. "One thing for certain, you are no local wench. So if I swive you 'til I'm tired of you and then break your long, slender neck..." He traced the column of Judy's throat with the tip of his finger, and she shuddered. "...None would be the wiser, eh? Consider that, wench, before you let loose your sharp tongue on me again."

He understood the situation perfectly. So did Judy.

But she refused to let Andrew intimidate her. Recklessly, she stood and wrapped a towel around her body as she rose from the water.

"You may as well kill me outright," she informed him. "'Dispose' of me is how your brother put it, didn't he? Because, Lord and Master Andrew of Laycock, you are never going to have any kind of sex with me unless I'm a corpse!"

She leapt out of the tub, splashing water. The soaked lower hem of her drying cloth dripped as well. Ignoring Andrew, she pulled her long sweater on over her head, removing the towel only after she was modestly covered and the sweater seriously damp. Then she reached for her dirty leggings. If she could just get her clothes on, Judy felt certain she could better deal with this brute who looked, with his shirt off, too much like a calendar pinup guy.

But she did not have the opportunity to pull on her

pants, because Andrew grabbed her from behind and carried her, flailing and screeching, to the bed. Again, he dumped her in the middle of it. Again, he climbed in beside her.

"No! Stop! I won't let you!"

Judy fought like a desperate, trapped animal. She kicked and clawed and slapped. Vaguely, she noticed that her sweater had ridden up, exposing her hips and belly. But modesty was her last concern.

She half expected Andrew to beat her, perhaps knock her unconscious, so that he could do whatever he wished whether she gave in or not. But he never so much as backhanded her. Instead he rendered her powerless by pinning her arms and throwing himself full atop her.

"I—can't—breathe," she gasped.

"Good. Then mayhap you'll cease your caterwauling."

"Why? Are you—afraid—the servants will overhear?"

He laughed. "I cannot imagine where you hail from, wench. But here, servants fear their masters, not the other way 'round. Still, I have no taste for women who claw and scream. I prefer willing wenches."

Willing wenches. Dear God, this was playing out like a bad movie! But it wasn't a movie. It was...real.

Judy let her body go slack as she focussed on more important matters. Being assaulted by a strange man, by any man at all, she would normally deem extremely important. But nothing about her current circumstances were normal. Why, then, had she been acting like they were? Anybody would have thought she had merely been stranded without her belongings in some resort hotel, the way she had preoccupied herself with her hangover, getting a bath, and finding something to eat. But an airline hadn't lost her luggage. She had, impossibly, traveled through time!

There was no point to fighting this man. Obviously, he could overpower her. If she continued to resist, he might beat her, even kill her. She couldn't risk death over a dubious degree of honor. It wasn't as though she were a virgin. And she needed time, time to find a way home.

Closing her eyes, she took a deep breath and

resigned herself to enduring the inevitable. When Andrew used her body, he would not be violating Judy Lambini. Judy Lambini did not exist. Tony and Nancy's baby girl wouldn't be born for nearly 800 years. And in just about 800 years, she'd be missing, having disappeared in England on a Halloween night, the presumed victim of foul play. The person in this draped bed, the one under Andrew, was no one. They called her Judith Lamb, but she had been born only hours ago, a grown woman with no past, no future, and apparently, not much of a present.

***

Andrew felt Judith go limp. He had expected her to respond to the pressure of his hands and his lips—earlier, he had felt her respond when she was in no condition to be amorous. But now she lay beneath him, lifeless as a sack of grain, so he rolled off her, feeling contempt.

Peering at Judith's closed eyes, her damp cheeks, he cringed and muttered, "Jesu! Are you crying?"

"I'm sorry you don't excite me as much as I apparently excite you."

Had this giant of a woman, nearly as tall as he, with her cropped hair and thick, dark lashes, ever excited him? Aye, she had. But those feelings, like his cock, had withered.

"Damnation! The only thing I hate more than a woman who fights is a woman who weeps—not that any woman I've had in my bed has ever done either," Andrew added.

"You're in *my* bed," she clarified, opening her eyes to slits and glaring at him.

"Not any longer." He stood up and pulled on his clothes. Andrew had never—never—had a wench reject his advances. High born or low, his first love, Lady Chandra, or one of Laycock's servants, they spread their legs eagerly, they giggled and they moaned. True, he hadn't had many women, compared with other knights his age. But he'd had a goodly number. So obviously it wasn't he who had the problem, it was she.

"What ails you?" he asked Judith suspiciously. "Are you made of stone? Have you no passion in your heart, no sensation between your legs? What sort of woman are you?"

If he had pricked her in the arse with the point of a lance, Judith could not have flown up off her back any faster. Sitting upright and leaning toward him, she screwed up her face and stared at him unblinkingly with wild, daring eyes.

"Don't you get it?" she shouted. "I'm a witch, just like your brother said!"

Before he could stop her, Judith grabbed her sack from the foot of the bed and somehow opened the top seam. Then she retrieved a black object from within, something no longer than the length of Andrew's hand. She pulled a stem from the top and proceeded to brandish it at him menacingly.

Andrew had never seen the like. "What is that?"

"A weapon! If I fire it, you'll die. Worse, you'll disappear, as though you never existed!"

Andrew considered the article in Judith's hand. Whatever the curious thing might be, it did not look dangerous—it had neither blade nor point. So he grabbed it from her, squeezed it, shook it, and waved it. When nothing happened, he laughed.

"If this be magic, it requires another spell to restore its powers. A rock would be far more deadly."

Judith's face turned pink. God's tears, if only he could arouse her ardor the way he aroused her fury! But as he could not, Andrew decided to tamp down her temper. Calmly, he asked, "What is this object, really?"

Judith sighed and shook her head. "I could tell you, but you wouldn't understand."

He scowled. "I may be young, but I am far from witless."

"I didn't say you were stupid," she insisted. "I just said you wouldn't understand. And you won't."

"Make the attempt," he ordered.

"I—I'd like to put some clothes on first."

"Have no fear, I shan't try to bed you again."

"Really? Not ever?"

God's teeth! The wench looked so damnably hopeful! Why did she feel no desire for him?

He glared at her, his mouth quirked to one side.

"Not anytime soon."

Judith glanced down at her tunic and then at her leggings, which remained on the floor near the tub. "My clothes are damp and dirty," she observed.

Andrew harumphed. "I'd not have deemed you a fastidious wench," he admitted. Then, quite graciously, he thought, he decided to supply her with fresh garments.

He left Judith very briefly, calling for Bridget as he strode to his private bedchamber. Ordering the servant to lend Judith one of her own tunics, he grabbed something from his own clothes trunk, something the wench could wear until Bridget brought her a suitable gown.

When Andrew returned to Judith, she no longer looked hopeful. She looked disappointed. Apparently, she'd been praying he would not return.

He bristled. "Bridget will bring you a tunic to wear. In the meanwhile, you may use this." He tossed his silk bed robe at her, and it fell across her bare knees.

Her lashes fluttered as she mumbled, "Thank you." And for an instant, she looked as comely and demure as any young damsel hoping to win a knight's favor. But even if she were the lady she claimed to be, Andrew was not the sort of knight whose heart a damsel hoped to claim. Women of noble birth rejected landless knights—those younger sons with neither power, wealth nor land—in favor of eldest sons and heirs. Chandra had rejected Andrew for just such cause.

Judith sat again on the edge of the bed, though now she was wrapped in the emerald green silk that enhanced her eyes. Andrew settled himself beside her and brusquely pulled her satchel into his lap. "You're not truly a witch, are you?"

"No."

"Nor are you in King John's employ, sent here to learn our secrets?"

She shook her head.

"Then what are you, Judith? A lady, a peasant, a—"

"—Wreck," she volunteered suddenly as a giddy laugh erupted from deep in her throat. "That's all I am right now, Andrew. Confused. Lost. Homeless. Scared."

Judith continued to laugh, sounding more and more mad. Jesu! 'Twas a good thing Elfred was nowhere about to witness this behavior. He'd drown her in the river if he heard such cackling.

"Stop! Cease!" Andrew grabbed her shoulders and shook her 'til she quieted. "I understand you've little or no memory, so of course you are befuddled. But your memory will return, and in the meanwhile, you're safe here."

"I am?"

By the saints! She sought another vow from him, another pledge.

"Aye. I shan't touch you again." *Did I say that? Did I truly say that?* Andrew gritted his teeth before demanding, "How did you open the satchel?"

"You were supposed to figure it out on your own," Judith reminded him. "You told your brothers you would."

"I tell my brothers all manner of things," he admitted. "I rarely mean half of them."

She smiled, and it was lovely. It seemed her first, truly genuine smile since she'd stumbled into his path. Andrew noticed that Judith had very good teeth, like his own. Few could boast having a mouthful, and almost no one had teeth that gleamed white.

"Here. See this little tab?" Judith asked, at last demonstrating the process by which she'd opened her bag. "You pull it one way to open the zipper, the other way to close it."

"The zipper?"

"That's what this fastening is called. I think because of the sound it makes."

Andrew pulled the *tab* himself. "I would have puzzled out its workings if I'd had more time."

"I'm sure you would have," Judith agreed. Andrew suspected she was being accommodating, not honest.

"This thing has teeth!" he observed aloud. "What creature grows so many tiny teeth?"

"No creature. They're not real. They're manufactured, made of plastic and nylon."

"Plastic? Nylon?"

"Materials. Like the silk this robe was made from." She fingered her sleeve. "Or the brass somebody fashioned into your buckle, here." She touched his belt.

Their eyes met. Andrew's thoughts no longer remained on his buckle. They had sprinted south to a particular part of his anatomy not far below his belt.

As though she'd burned her fingers, Judith drew her hand away. He wished she had not, but because of his pledge, he searched for another diversion. Abruptly, he upended the satchel onto the bed.

"Hey! Don't do that," Judith shouted.

"I would see what mysteries you carry in this enchanted satchel."

"It's not enchanted. It's just my gear."

"Gear?"

"Belongings," she explained impatiently.

"Show me," he demanded.

"No! These things are personal. Besides, you wouldn't understand what any of them are. They're nothing you could use."

"I shall be the judge of that." Simply because he'd decided to treat the damsel kindly did not mean she had any right to tell him what to do. In the end, she would do what he demanded.

"Fine," she conceded.

Or at least Andrew thought Judith conceded. She used the word as though it had another meaning than the one he knew.

"Here's another pouch with no opening, no strings." Judith picked up a small brocade purse. A flap folded over one side, and when she lifted it, the cover opened noisily.

"You've torn it!" Andrew said when he heard the ripping sound.

"No, I haven't. Look at this." Judith ran her fingers over the flap, sealing it in place again.

Disbelieving, Andrew took the pouch and imitated Judith's actions. To his surprise, the flap came away again intact. "How does it work?"

"It's Velcro." She showed him two black strips, one on the outside of the pouch, the other inside the flap. "The top here is made up of a million little hooks. On the bottom, there's just as many little loops. When you press them together, they latch."

Andrew found himself fascinated. Holding the small bag only inches from his nose, he studied the *Velcro* strips.

"Are these plants?" he asked, running his fingertips across the fuzzy surface. "Something that grows in the ocean, perhaps?"

"No. I don't know how, but they're man-made."

"So small...I would deem it impossible, if I saw this not with my own eyes. What is within?" he asked curiously, plunging his fingers into Judith's cache before she had the opportunity to explain.

"I told you, those are my personal things." She snatched the lumpy little purse away from him.

Judith owned so many fantastic possessions, Andrew decided not to interrogate her further about the small bag's contents.

"What is this, then?" He grabbed a box. It was shallow, wide, and quite heavy.

Judith's brow furrowed. She looked weary. "It's a machine," she informed him.

"Machine?"

"A device. It can do many things."

"What can it do?"

"Oh, Andrew, a whole lot of things. I can't explain it all to you now. It's just—too complicated."

He scowled thoughtfully before picking up the black object she had threatened him with. "This is no weapon, is it?"

Judith shook her head. "I just wanted to frighten you."

He grinned. She'd been so foolish. "I know."

She pursed her lips and made him wait a long moment before saying, "It's called a cell phone. Where I come from, people use them to speak to each other if they're far apart."

"Nobody shouts?"

"Sure, we shout plenty. Especially in New York. We use phones, though, when we're too far apart to shout and be heard."

He pounced on the information Judith had let slip. "York," he repeated.

"What?"

"You come from York. You said so but a moment ago."

"No, Andrew." She shook her head, but Andrew suspected the gesture was a weak attempt to make her denial plausible. "I'm not from York."

Damnation, the wench lied! Andrew intended to accuse her of prevarication, but before he could, a gust of wind blew in through the window. Judith gasped and shivered.

Impulsively, Andrew touched her damp head. "You should dry yourself," he informed her gruffly, actually glad to be diverted from their pending argument. He rose, went to the window, and tied a piece of tanned hide across the opening to shutter out the brisk breeze. "Warm yourself by the fire, Judith. Bridget should show herself soon with the clothing I asked her to bring you."

Surprisingly, the woman did as he ordered, approaching the fire with her arms stretched out before her. As she rubbed her hands together, Andrew headed toward the door. He could not resist her possessions, though. Impulsively, he scooped her belongings back into her satchel as he passed her bed.

"What are you doing?" Judith squealed.

"You can see well enough what I am doing."

"Don't! Andrew, please, my things are of no use to you."

She must be a lady, chatelaine of her own keep. She is certainly used to giving orders!

"I wish to examine all of them," Andrew announced. "Then I shall decide what's of use to me. You will not."

"You don't know what anything is if I don't explain it. Besides, most of it is girl stuff."

"'Girl stuff?'" He squinted at her. The phrase sounded disagreeable.

"Yes. Things—items, possessions—that only women use. Like your mother and sisters. Things a guy—a man—wouldn't be caught dead with."

"Scents?" he asked suspiciously. "Potions? Unguents? Materials you use when you have the flux?"

"Yes! Exactly."

Andrew tossed the black bag back onto the bed. He wanted nothing to do with the curious concoctions and accoutrements women used in private upon their persons. "You may keep it for now. But," he added, emphasizing that word, "I would have you show me everything your bag contains in due time."

"In due time. Sure, Andrew. Yes."

He deemed Judith quite appealing when she was obedient and obliging. He would have her obedient and obliging while he pumped himself into her and she writhed naked beneath him in bed. Why, by all the saints, had he promised not to touch her ever again? He had not meant it.

Somehow, this mysterious female had beguiled him. Chagrined at being a victim of her cunning, Andrew felt compelled to say in an imperious tone, "Wench, I am the master here. As such, you must always defer to me and address me as Lord Andrew."

Judith's mouth fell open, and her eyes glinted with fire—what he saw was no reflection from the nearby flames but her own temper flaring.

"You call me 'wench' and expect me to call you 'Lord Andrew?' I have a name, too! I think I should be addressed as Lady Judith! Because I am a lady, and you'd do well to remember it."

"I shall remember only what I choose to. Besides, I am far from convinced you are a lady. Until I am, to me you're no more than a wench."

***

Andrew quit the room and closed the door—just in time to avoid being pelted by Judy's cell phone, which she pitched in his direction with the force and speed of a professional baseball player.

That brief, spontaneous action seemed to relieve her last spurt of anger. She had too much on her mind to stay worked up over petty insults and youthful arrogance. Hell, she'd not only traveled through time, she'd nearly been...well, not raped, but forcibly seduced.

Judy picked up the phone. She had the wild idea that, with nothing to lose, she may as well try. So she punched the required buttons and then...felt afraid to put the phone to her ear. If it worked, if her call went through, she would know she had not gone back in time. If not asleep or delirious with fever, she'd have proof she had become the random target of a mean-spirited practical joke by performers who took their roles too seriously.

Warily, not daring to glance at the digital display, Judy brought the phone to her ear. Nothing. Dead air. She'd traveled out of range—by about 800 years.

Five

"Bridget? Bridget!" Andrew shouted as he made his way down the dim corridor.

"Milord, I was just coming to find you," she said as she reached the landing on the stairs. "Sir Philip's arrived. He's asking for you."

"And our visitor, Judith, is asking for some clean, dry clothes of which she's sorely in need. I thought I sent you to get her something of yours."

"I'm doing that, milord. I've been looking for shoes that might fit the lady."

"First give her a tunic to put on. Worry about shoes later."

Bridget nodded and scurried off.

Andrew took to the stairs. At the bottom, in the great hall, he spied his close friend, Philip of North Cross. Despite the ride from his sire's estate to Laycock, Philip looked, as always, impeccable. Not only did he wear the most fashionable clothes—today he sported a "mi-party" cotehardie and leggings, the opposite sides of each garment contrasting yellow and green—it seemed he repelled dust and grime. Only Philip could ride hard miles and appear as though he had recently stepped out of his bedchamber after a bath.

Glancing down at his own rumpled self, Andrew strode forward to greet his friend. "I didn't expect you," he confessed.

"But you're glad I've come, nonetheless?"

"Aye, of course I am, Philip. I see you already have a mug of beer to slake your thirst."

"And one waiting for you." Philip retrieved another cup from a nearby table and handed it to him. "Where has everyone gone? Bridget told me the whole clan is away, except for you."

"Always except for me," Andrew groused, sitting in a chair near the fire. When Philip joined him, he explained, "Robin and Elfred rode off to join Father and the other barons who've united against King John. If Lackland fails to agree to their terms, we'll soon be at war against the king. Surely your sire has gone, too?"

"Oh, aye. And my uncles and eldest brothers."

"But not you?"

"Nay, not I. If there is war, which I hope there shan't be, I'll of course be obliged to fight. But even I saw no need to loiter about while they negotiate terms." Philip sipped from his cup. "Where are your lovely mother and sisters? Surely they didn't accompany your father, Robin and Elfred."

"They left days ago to attend a wedding at Alnwick. They invited me to accompany them, which I declined. Of course, the idea that I join my brothers and my sire never once entered anyone's head, save my own."

"We're both youngest sons, Andrew. We cannot change the order of our births. I, for one, am glad. There's far too much responsibility that comes with being heir to a barony. I've no desire to rule North Cross."

"Then what is there?"

"For us?" Philip looked at Andrew with upraised eyebrows. "We could hire on as mercenaries. We've both earned our spurs."

Andrew chuckled, glad for the distraction his friend presented. "Even you might get dirty if you had to don armor and fight a battle or two."

"Don't even suggest such a thing." Philip grinned, his blue eyes twinkling as he feigned a shudder and shook his fair head. "I'd prefer to wed a comely damsel with a decent dower. I do not care to oversee an estate so large it requires all my time. But I'd like one rich enough to support me and my bride."

"Then you'd best spend more time seeking such a damsel, else your mother will be sending you to the bishop to have you made a priest."

Philip made a face. "Fie on you, Andrew! I came here to have a bit of sport—perhaps a hunt, at least some entertainment. And there you sit, describing all manner of gruesome futures I might face. What of you? Do you intend to hire out as a mercenary or join the Church? Or is it also your intention to find a bride? Since the lovely Lady Chandra threw you over for that rake from Normandy—what was his name? Jean-Paul du Lac—no damsel's caught your eye."

One damsel had, this morning in this hall. Andrew

hadn't thought much of her earlier when, like a witless mute, she'd stood directly in his path as he charged down the hill on his stallion. God's wounds! In truth he'd believed her to be a lad, because of her clothes and her height. Though he soon discerned she was female, after Judith began ranting in her unfamiliar dialect, his opinion of her had not very much improved.

Then she fainted, and Andrew had decided not to leave her in the dirt but to take her to the keep. Once he had her on his shoulder and had gotten a good feel of her round bottom and long, shapely legs, his opinion of the damsel began to change. His curiosity had been piqued, and that hadn't been the only thing that she'd aroused. Damnation! By the time the wench had drunk enough wine to be giddy, stumbling, and weak in the knees; by the time he had taken advantage of her condition to hold her close, to feel her curves and sense her heat, he'd wanted to bed the green-eyed wench with the soft cap of golden hair.

"Am I boring you already?" Philip inquired, rousing Andrew from his private reverie.

"You never bore me, my friend."

"Then answer my question. Has any wench at all, let alone an eligible maiden of gentle birth, caught your eye since Chandra became Lady du Lac?"

"We have a visitor," Andrew announced.

Philip frowned and cocked his head to the side. "Does that answer my question?"

"Nay. I choose not to answer your question. But you said you wished to enjoy a diversion of some sort, and Laycock's 'guest' may amuse you."

"Is this a female guest?" Philip asked, and Andrew nodded. "Tell me who she is. Do I know her?"

"No one knows her. Even she seems confused about her identity."

"How so?"

Andrew provided Philip with a succinct report on his morning encounter with the wench upstairs.

"How curious! Has she lost her memory, then? No recollections of either her home or even her name?"

"She has a name. Judith Lamb. And a brief while ago, she let it slip she hails from York. Yet when I questioned her, she denied she'd even mentioned that city."

"Intriguing! Mayhap she ran away to avoid a despicable marriage or something of that like. Now she's feigning memory loss so that no one will feel obliged to return her to her home and a situation she wishes to avoid. Silly of the wench to have provided her name, though. Now you can send word to Sir Peter."

Andrew started, splashing beer from his cup onto his knee. "Who is Sir Peter?"

"Peter Lamb," Philip explained. "You've ne'er heard of him? He has a reputation, though 'tisn't necessarily flattering. He is an alchemist. I know of him because he and my grandsire, the old lord of North Cross, were fast friends. They earned their spurs together. Despite the years and distance separating them, the two remained comrades, so he sometimes visited my home. Methinks 'twas a decade or more that they last stayed with us, Sir Peter and his wife. Shortly afterward, my grandsire died. I was about ten and two at that time."

"He sounds aged," Andrew commented.

"He is, certainly. But I mentioned his wife. I found myself besotted with Lady Sophie when she also stayed at North Cross." Philip grinned. "She was much younger than her husband, and as they had children together—this was mentioned in conversation, I never saw any of them—mayhap Lady Sophie is your visitor's mother."

Andrew digested this information. "Possibly. But surely there be other branches of the family with the same name."

"All from York?"

"You did not say the alchemist resides in York."

"Sorry. But he does. I put the name and the city together in my mind the moment you mentioned them. Tell me," Philip urged, "what does Lady Judith look like? Sir Peter's wife was dark. Hair like sable, eyes like jet."

"I did not say Judith is a lady. She claims to be, but she does not sound or look like a woman gently born. The wench has neither French nor Latin, but speaks English like a peasant from some unknown shire. As for her appearance..." Andrew paused, flashing for a moment on her naked thighs and belly, which he'd glimpsed when trying to have his way with her. "She is fair-haired, like you, and her eyes are light. A sort of grayish-green. Sea green, I suppose one might say."

Andrew recalled those eyes and the fan of dark lashes that framed them. He had never seen anyone with blonde hair and black eyelashes—the effect was striking. Judith was striking.

He felt glad he could say the girl looked nothing like Sir Peter Lamb's wife, Lady Sophie. Andrew didn't want Judith to be the daughter of nobles. He wanted her to be a peasant. Then, despite any vows to the contrary she had tricked him into making, he could take her at his whim. After all, he ruled here as master, while she had yet to prove herself more than a beggar.

"Ho, ho!" Philip chortled, tipping his cup to finish the last of his beer. "The way you describe the color of her eyes, it sounds to me as though you're smitten."

Heat flared under Andrew's skin, and he hoped his face had not gone red. "Nonsense."

"Is it, now?" Philip smiled. "When do I get to see this mystery wench?"

"Supper, I suppose."

"How long until we dine?"

"Not 'til evening." Andrew stood. "What should we do meanwhile?"

"Dice? Backgammon? Draughts?"

"Nay. My ride this morning ended prematurely, and I've been indoors since. I need some exercise. Is your arse too sore for a good gallop?" Andrew asked.

"A knight never gets saddle sore," Philip insisted, coming to his feet. "Indeed, I'll race you. What should we wager?"

That Judith Lamb is no lady.

***

Judy had done some washing after Andrew left her. First she shampooed her hair in the tub, then she laundered her sweater and leggings, hanging them off the edge of the table to drip dry. With no blow dryer, she resorted to toweling her hair. Pulling a stool closer to the fire, she sat beside the embers, running her fingers through her damp locks in an effort to dry them completely.

"Milady!" Bridget called from beyond the door.

Judy recognized her voice. "Come in."

The servant entered, her arms full of clothing. Depositing the bundle on the bed, she exclaimed, "It's growing dark. No one came to light your candles?"

"No. And I didn't think to do it myself. I guess I started daydreaming, sitting here."

Bridget tsked and grabbed a short, squat candle off the table. Lighting it from the fire coals in the pit, she quickly lit several more that sat in dishes and holders scattered about the room. Then she stirred the fire so that flames leapt and danced.

"You must be freezing in that light robe," the servant observed. "'Tis always cool in the keep, even in the warm months of summer. Though it be spring, the chill of winter lingers, especially in the evenings." Bridget smiled and gestured to the bed. "Please, milady. Let me help you select something to wear downstairs to supper."

Judy stood and considered the clothing the servant unfolded and laid out upon the bed for better viewing. The gowns looked far more elaborate than anything Bridget should have owned.

"I thought Lord Andrew asked you to lend me something of yours," Judy said.

Bridget scrunched up her face. "That he did, milady. But surely he was angry and ordered me to do so out of spite. He'd regret it, though, if I obeyed him."

"Whose clothes are these?"

"His sisters'. Beatrix and Camilla are not as tall as you, but I think their clothes will do. Besides, I only took items they have surely forgotten they own."

"I don't know if I should." Judy shook her head. "Camilla and Beatrix aren't here to offer them, and Andrew—Lord Andrew—didn't suggest I help myself to his sisters' clothes."

"They won't mind, truly," Bridget insisted. Lowering her voice, she added confidentially, "They're spoilt, they are, with more gowns to their names than either could ever wear. And I did not choose from among their favorites."

"This isn't someone's favorite?" she asked doubtfully, fingering a tunic of fine, soft wool that had been dyed a stunning shade of turquoise.

"Nay, it's not. The color doesn't flatter either of the girls the way it would you." Bridget smiled.

"You're sure Andrew—Lord Andrew—won't be upset?"

"He'd be upset if he saw you dressed as a servant, and though he would be responsible, I would get the blame. My lord could not have meant it when he told me to garb you in clothing such as mine." Bridget looked down at her dress, a dun-colored garment, serviceable but drab. "'Twould be an insult to a noblewoman."

"He doesn't believe I'm a noblewoman," Judy confided.

"Oh, he does. Of course, he does! He's just behaving badly. Lord Andrew often sulks and becomes quarrelsome, all because he resents being Lord Thomas' youngest son. As such, he's left out of important matters—or at least matters he feels must be important, because Lord Robin, and sometimes Elfred, are involved."

Judy considered Bridget with a new sense of appreciation. "You know the family well. And you're not afraid of Andrew, who is your lord and master—especially, as he pointed out to me, when his father and brothers are away?"

The younger girl giggled. "Nay. We grew up in this keep, he and I. Before I was old enough to work and Lord Andrew old enough to foster, we played together in the dirt in the bailey."

"The what?"

"The yard. Outside. Within the walls. The bailey."

"Oh. Yes."

"I remember when he used to wet his braies." Bridget chuckled, and Judy frowned, unable to comprehend the meaning of still another word. "His under garments," the servant explained. "So nay, I do not fear him, even though he's a man now and a knight. Lord Andrew knows I keep some secrets from our childhood. Besides, he's not a harsh master. None of the baron's family is."

"Good. Glad to hear it."

"Which gown do you prefer, Lady Judith?" Bridget inquired, returning to the matter at hand. "'Twould seem the turquoise is the better choice."

"The color's stunning, and the fabric is so soft."

"Aye. That's scarlet wool. Usually, it's dyed crimson more than any other shade."

"Scarlet *is* crimson."

"Indeed, milady. But that bright hue takes its name from the wool which is often dyed that color." Bridget narrowed her eyes and peered at Judy curiously. "May I ask where you make your home, Lady Judith? You seem unfamiliar with our ways. And your accent is, if you'll forgive my saying so, peculiar."

"I don't mind, Bridget. And I agree, my accent is quite different from yours. You have words I don't, and I have words you don't. But I'm from a place very far away. You'll never have heard of it. We do things differently there."

"Hmmm. Well? Should we get you dressed? I'm certain even in your homeland, ladies dress for supper."

That got a smile from Judy, who nodded her head in agreement. "Yes. Eating hot food in the buff could be risky."

Bridget did not seem to get the joke. She busied herself sliding Andrew's robe off Judy's shoulders and then bustled about, oblivious to Judy's nakedness. "On with this you go," she announced, holding a ring of gathered fabric above Judy's head. When Judy raised her arms, Bridget made sure her head and hands went through the proper holes. The soft, woolen cloth fluttered down to Judy's bare feet.

"I knew Lady Camilla was the taller so her gown might better cover you," Bridget declared.

Glancing down at the hem, which dragged on the floor, Judy would have guessed that Camilla was an Amazon. "I'll trip," she predicted.

"Nay, you shan't, milady. Not once we fasten the girdle about your waist. But first, we must do your sleeves."

The tunic had no sleeves, but Bridget slid two separate ones up Judy's arms and laced them through the eyelets in the fabric on her shoulders. The sleeves were embroidered with white and gold thread, which matched the belt she subsequently tied at the small of Judy's back.

"Let's hope either Camilla or Beatrix has the same

size feet you do." Bridget produced two pairs of slippers and gestured for Judy to sit. Judy felt like Cinderella's sister when she tried on the first pair—they were too small. But then, like Cinderella slipping on the glass shoe, the second pair slid on easily.

Judy stood and walked around. She felt naked without panties, not even a thong. And her breasts seemed to swing! But she thought, *When in Rome...*

Holding her arms out, Judy studied her sleeves. Bell-shaped, the back cuffs hung nearly as long as her skirt hem. She almost complained, but the style made her feel ridiculously feminine.

"Don't fret," Bridget urged. "You'll not have to do anything but eat and look pretty. If you had to do any serious work, we'd knot those sleeves to keep them out of your way."

"I know," Judy lied, hoping to sound as though she weren't completely ignorant of the customs of the day.

"Now, let me put your hair up, what there is of it, before you don the matching hennin."

"Hennin. Right."

Judy sat down on a stool. Bridget set to work, combing her hair and pinning it up off the back of her neck. Then she set some sort of hat on Judy's head.

Judy used her hands to explore it. A dunce cap! Tall and pointed, an attached veil floated down to her shoulders.

"I have to see this," she told Bridget. It was all too weird, but she felt excited in spite of herself. "I don't suppose there's a mirror around?"

"Oh, aye. I'll fetch you one."

Bridget dashed off and returned almost immediately. She carried an oval of polished metal the size of a dinner plate.

Judy gazed into the so-called mirror. She'd seen her reflection more clearly in top grade cookware.

"I have a better one," she announced. "I was hoping for something larger. I didn't think..."

Digging through her tote as she tried to explain, Judy found her mirror. About seven inches square, it had a fake tortoise shell frame made of plastic and an easy-grip handle.

"Sweet Mother Mary!" she heard Bridget gasp, and when she spun around to look at the girl, she found the servant crossing herself.

"It's just a mirror, but a very good one. Come, see," Judy urged.

Her curiosity overriding her reluctance, Bridget drew close. When Judy held the mirror before her face, Bridget gasped. And blinked. Then she touched her cheeks and nose as she studied her own reflection.

"How—how did you come by such a thing?"

"From home. These are our mirrors. You can find them in any size, from tiny little ones no bigger than coins to others that cover whole walls or ceilings. It's a lot clearer than yours, isn't it?"

Grasping the mirror's handle, Bridget flipped it over to examine the back. She shrieked and let it fall from her hand, though Judy managed to catch it before the glass hit the floor. All she needed was seven years bad luck on top of her current circumstances!

"It's a magnifying mirror," Judy explained, holding that side toward the servant. "It's nothing scary. It just makes things appear bigger than they are. Look at your eyes," she suggested.

Bridget did, blinking and squinting and making them wide. Then she peered over the edge at Judy and grinned hugely. "You're sure 'tisn't magic?" she asked.

"No, not magic. Just a good quality mirror. Someday, you'll have mirrors just like this right here in England."

"Not while I live," Bridget accurately predicted.

"Hold it for me, now," Judy urged. "I'll stand back. I'd like to see the dress. And the hat."

By directing Bridget to move the mirror higher and lower, to the right and the left, Judy managed to see a disjointed reflection of herself, a series of puzzle pictures she assembled with her mind's eye. "Oh, my God!" she said.

"What is it, milady? What's the trouble?"

Her face was the trouble. Sans makeup, she looked horrid, as plain as an old Amish woman.

"When is supper served?" Judy asked.

"Shortly. I'm not certain. Should I ask Cook?"

"No. Just leave me for a bit, Bridget. Thank you for

everything. But I have something to do on my own now."

"Very well, milady. I'll come for you when the victuals are ready."

As soon as the servant had gone, Judy sat on the bed and ripped open her brocade makeup bag. She knew she had to go easy. Imitating a *Cosmo* cover girl would have the locals tying her to a stake and burning her as the witch she'd claimed to be. But Judy Lambini didn't intend to go anywhere, not even to dinner with Andrew, without at least a little powder, a little blush, some subtly smudged liner around her eyes and, most important, a couple of coats of black mascara.

Six

The plank tables had been set up in the hall. The knights and men-at-arms of Laycock Keep were seated, drinking their cups of beer and ale while waiting to be served. At the high table, on the dais, Andrew and Philip sat alone, Andrew in his sire's chair.

Philip chided him. "Why do you sit in Lord Thomas' chair when e'er he and your brothers are gone, Andrew? As though you governed here as landed-lord and baron? You cannot desire Laycock anymore than I desire North Cross. Methinks you'd be in a quandary, and more than a little dismayed, should the keep, the demesne, and the town of Wixcomb fall to you to rule."

"Mayhap you do not know me as well as you think," Andrew shot back, glancing at the stairs and wondering what kept Judith.

"Nay, I think I know you better than you know yourself."

"Then what is it you think I desire, if it's not to reign as Lord of Laycock or master of another fief, be it large or small?" Andrew turned to peer at his friend.

"I couldn't say," Philip admitted. "But I know what I desire."

His gaze had wandered from Andrew to the corner of the hall. Andrew looked in the same direction and saw Judith Lamb standing at the bottom of stairs.

The damsel nearly took Andrew's breath away. She wore a gown and hennin the color of a twilight sky that suited her complexion as no other hue possibly could. Her hair lay hidden beneath the hat, exposing the striking contours of her neck and face. Such a face! Andrew narrowed his gaze to better contemplate her features. He'd never beheld the like on any woman, not even Judith herself earlier in the day. The arches of her eyebrows were defined, as were her eyes themselves—her lashes appeared even thicker and darker than they had been. Clearly, they were the longest, most ebony he had ever seen. And her lips, pouty and pink as rose petals, glistened moistly, as though she'd licked them in anticipation of a kiss. Her cheeks sustained a blush as well, as if she were flushed from lovemaking.

"And you said to me you believed her no lady?" Philip whispered out of the side of his mouth. "A peasant wench couldn't aspire to such beauty. This damsel is noble, if not royal, by blood."

Before Andrew could respond—before he could even get to his feet—Philip stood and strode between the tables and benches set up on the main floor. Knowing his friend would reach Judith before he possibly could, Andrew decided to remain on the dais. He stood, waiting for them to approach. Let Judith come to him.

Philip did not hurry. Reaching Judith, he spoke to her for some moments, annoying Andrew because he couldn't hope to overhear, not with all the knights' chatter as the servants brought out trays of food and set them on the tables. Finally, though, Philip took her hand and led her forward, escorting her to the dais.

"Here we are," Philip announced cheerily, pulling out the chair he had recently vacated so that Judith could sit. To her, he said, "I expect Andrew planned for you to sit at his other side. But then I would be forced to lean across him to converse with you. Better, methinks, that you sit between us."

Wordlessly, she glanced directly at Andrew. If she sought his permission, he could not give it. He felt he'd been struck dumb. Up close this eve, her countenance seemed as flawless as a statue's.

He managed a nod. When Judith sat, he sat.

"More wine, milord?" the steward inquired as he paused before the high table with his jug.

"Aye," Andrew managed gruffly, holding out his goblet.

By the time the man had finished replenishing Andrew's cup, Philip was holding out Judith's empty one. Andrew realized he had been unmannerly and a contemptibly thoughtless host not to see the lady served before himself. But it was too late. Besides, he reminded himself stubbornly, he remained unconvinced she was truly a lady. More likely she belonged in the scullery eating with the servants, not at a baron's high table.

"Lady Judith, you are so quiet," Philip observed,

smiling at her kindly. "Are you ill at ease to find yourself the only woman dining among so many men?"

She glanced at the whole of the room, at the many knights and men-at-arms eating gustily. Then she turned back to Philip and said, "No. More than once I've had the dubious distinction of being the only female in an old boys'... I mean to say, it doesn't bother me. The problem is—"

"What?" Her hand rested on the edge of the table, and Philip covered Judith's with his own.

Andrew wanted to fling it off.

But Judith seemed not to mind. She allowed Philip's fingers to encompass hers as though she enjoyed his touch. "We speak the same language," she said, "but differently. I have trouble understanding all the words you—everyone—speaks to me. And I think you have trouble understanding when I reply."

"I comprehend you perfectly," Philip insisted. "We'll speak slowly, though, shall we? I would wager there'll be no problem communicating if we don't go too fast."

Andrew watched Judith nod. She appeared so damnably grateful to Philip. As if *he* were responsible for her enjoying this fine repast. The hospitality of Laycock Keep. That beautiful gown she wore.

By all the saints! Where had she got it? Not her satchel. There had been no clothes in that bag of hers. And he'd told Bridget to get Judith one of her spare tunics. Andrew knew full well the serving maid could own no fine garments such as this one. It belonged to his mother, surely. Or one of his sisters. How dare Bridget defy his orders? The wench would know the feel of his fist before the eve was done. It mattered not that he'd never hit any woman, with open hand or closed. There could always be a first time, and Bridget had certainly provoked him to it.

"Andrew?" Philip addressed him, leaning forward to peer in his direction.

Andrew blinked but otherwise failed to acknowledge his friend. He watched, though, as Philip rolled his eyes at him before speaking to Judith.

"My lady, allow me to help you select the fare you wish to sample. Laycock's cook is indeed a good one.

You would never know it, for she's skinny as a reed. Most cooks are fat, are they not?"

Philip chuckled, as though he'd told a fine joke. Andrew snorted in contempt and began filling his own trencher.

"Here we have partridge," Philip explained, as if Judith would never have seen a partridge before and could not recognize it. "And carrots—they are in a sweet glaze, very tasty. Would you like some of the fish? The white sauce is excellent. I've had it many times here. You must also try this honey bread."

Andrew sneaked a surreptitious look at Judith. Philip was now selecting food for his own trencher, but she had not begun to eat. Did she expect the handsome, virile lord of North Cross to feed her as well, as though she were a babe?

"What's amiss?" he asked her curtly.

"I—" Startled, she raised her eyes to his. Judith appeared truly helpless, so much so that Andrew felt a keen need to fix whatever she found wrong.

"Aye?"

She glanced at his hand, the one clutching his eating knife. "I have nothing to, ah, spear my food."

"'Tis no crime to use your fingers."

"Nonsense!" Philip, from her other side, declared. "You've no eating knife of your own, milady? Then use mine. I shall eat with my fingers."

He should have done that himself, Andrew realized, scowling at the knife in his hand.

"Why haven't you one of your own?" he inquired, deciding it was Judith's own fault that she did not. "In that sack of yours, you carry more possessions than an entire village of people might have. Yet there's no eating knife?"

"Actually, there isn't. Where I come from, utensils—spoon, knife and something we call a fork—are set out on the table for each meal."

"Inconvenient, that," Philip observed after swallowing a mouthful of food. "What if you must eat elsewhere, perhaps while traveling on the road? Or what if you simply wish to peel and eat an apple from an orchard?"

"I probably wouldn't peel it. I'd just take bites right through the skin until I reached the core."

"I like that!" Philip smiled at Judith. "Simplicity is always best. Still, I insist you keep that eating knife. Here is the sheath." He handed it to her. "Tie it to your belt, and you'll always have it handy."

"I couldn't."

"Of course you could," he insisted. "I can easily replace the blade."

"Well...thank you." Judith nodded and turned her attention to her trencher.

Andrew kept picking at his meal, but he had no appetite, not even after the hard riding he and Philip had done that afternoon. Usually, the smell of Cook's fine fare made his mouth water. But not this eve. Suddenly, he knew why. He couldn't smell the food! Not the fish, the fowl, the fruit. What he *could* smell was Judith, and she smelled sweetly intoxicating. Like flowers—specifically, roses.

Closing his eyes, Andrew found himself able to filter out even a hint of other scents. Hers alone enveloped him. He imagined himself turning toward her, lowering his face to that swan-like neck of hers. With his lips on her flesh, he suspected he would grow absolutely drunk on her fragrance.

Opening his eyes, he decided to get absolutely drunk on wine instead. Finishing the dregs in his cup, he called for his steward and demanded the jug be left on the table.

"What's wrong, Andrew? Not hungry, this eve?" Philip questioned.

"Nay, I am not."

"You are thirsty, though."

"Aye, that I am."

Philip dismissed Andrew with a casual glance and ducked his head toward Judith's. "Andrew tells me he found you wandering this morn, that you were lost."

"Yes, I was. Very lost."

"He also tells me you're from York."

Judith snapped her head around and stared at Andrew with wide eyes. Sea green eyes.

"Did he?" she asked as she turned back to Philip.

"Did Lord Andrew also tell you I was dressed like a boy, in leggings and a sweat—a tunic, and that I was dirty and damp?"

"Why, nay, he did not. Dear lady! Did you have a terrible mishap? Did you lose your escort?"

"I had no escort. I set out on my journey alone. I did not intend to. It—just happened. Suddenly I found myself here—that is, on the road outside the village."

"Wixcomb," Philip supplied.

"Yes, Wixcomb."

"'Tis good, then, Andrew found you and brought you to the keep."

"He did not exactly find me." She glanced narrowly at Andrew. "What he did was nearly run me down with that huge horse of his."

"Andrew, you cur," Philip chastised him, shaking his head.

"I did not nearly ride her down," he protested in his own defense. "She should have got out of my way. As it was, Zeus and I cleanly avoided her. She's not damaged, is she?"

"I'm not a thing, an object, that could be damaged," Judith snapped, turning to face Andrew directly. "I am a person, a woman, a *lady* who could easily have been injured, even killed. But not damaged."

Andrew did not appreciate her censure. He should have sent her from the table, even locked her in her chamber. Instead, he muttered, "'Tis probably the difference in our dialects. As you said, Judith, we have different words, not merely different pronunciations. And you have no French at all."

"I do not live in France. I never saw the need to learn."

"Very good, Lady Judith." Philip had the audacity to applaud her conviction. "England is not Normandy, Anjou or Maine. I agree with you—we should speak the language of our ancestors, just as our servants and tenants do. Saxon served our people well before William conquered. Do you know what I think?"

As Andrew observed him, his best friend leaned so close to Judith, his nose nearly brushed her cheek.

"I believe that one day the language of the common

man will again be the language of the country. Not even Latin will prevail for the courts."

"I believe that, too," she returned emphatically, making no move to put the slightest distance between herself and her golden-haired champion.

"Surely your father and mother speak French," Andrew felt compelled to say.

Finally, Judith looked at him, giving the back of her head to Philip. "My...father?"

"Aye. Peter Lamb."

Her lashes—her long, thick, ebony lashes—fluttered.

"Sir Peter Lamb," Andrew elaborated. "The alchemist. Philip, here, deduced that he may be your sire. Is he?"

Judith moved her head. Andrew couldn't tell if she were nodding or shaking it, confirming or denying.

"If not your sire, mayhap your grandsire?" Philip asked.

"I—I—" She turned back to him. "What makes you think this...knight...is my father—my sire?"

"You share the same name, and you both hail from York."

"Oh."

"Is he your kin?"

Judith failed to reply to Philip's question. Instead she urged, "Tell me what you know of him."

"As Andrew said, he is an alchemist. A friend of my own father's sire, he visited North Cross when I was a lad. Though Sir Peter is now aged, I recalled he was wed to a much younger woman. Andrew and I surmised she may be your mother and he your sire."

"I see." Judith nodded, though a tiny, vertical line creased her brow directly above her small, straight nose. "You call him an alchemist. Does that mean he tries to transform other metals into gold?" Judith asked.

"Aye." Philip nodded. "And he fashions new implements to make men's tasks go easier. He is an inventor as well, you see. I recall as much because I found his work fascinating. Flight most especially intrigued him. Sir Peter eternally searched for a means by which man might fly, exactly as the birds do."

Andrew felt taken aback. Obviously, Philip had failed

to relay to him all that he knew about Peter Lamb. If the ancient lord were an inventor who created new and clever tools, mayhap even talking devices, Judith might well be his daughter. 'Twas the only reasonable explanation for the possessions she carried in her sack.

"Is he your father?" Andrew asked again when Judith looked his way. His tone was sharp, though he hadn't meant it to be.

"I don't know," she replied.

"We should send word to him," Philip declared. "I understand your mind is not completely clear, milady, mayhap because you were recently ill with fever. But if we wrote to him, made inquiry, we could surely confirm that you are Sir Peter's missing daughter."

"Does he have a daughter who's missing?" Judith asked Philip.

"We will not know that 'til we receive a reply, and that could take a little while. If you wish it, instead we might ride to York straight away," Philip volunteered, his eyes alight with excitement.

"I don't think—" Judith began.

"Nay, absolutely not!" Andrew interrupted. How dare Philip concern himself with Judith's welfare, offering to escort her home? She had stumbled into Laycock, not North Cross. "Philip, you know full well I cannot leave the stronghold, not with the rest of the family gone."

"I could escort the lady myself. I would bring my squire. There's no need for you to come with us."

So this had been Philip's intent all along. "She cannot go," Andrew insisted, glaring at his friend and now, apparently, his rival. "The damsel was, as you know, recently ill. And she surely traveled a far distance, arriving here not on horseback but on foot. She is not well enough for another journey. Not so soon. You do agree, do you not, Judith?"

His gaze met hers as he willed her to concur. Andrew felt enormously relieved when she muttered, "Yes. I'm afraid I do."

"Then perhaps we'll compose a letter for Sir Peter later this eve, or first thing in the morn, shall we?" Philip suggested. "Now, having eaten so fine a meal, I am in the mood to take a stroll." He stood and held out his hand to Judith. "My lady, will you accompany me?"

Andrew put his hand on Judith's thigh to restrain her. None could see; the table hid his action.

Judy stiffened, as though her hollow body had been filled with quick-hardening cement, when she felt him place his hand on her leg. The audacity! The gall! Turning slowly, she gave Andrew the most withering glare she could muster.

And yet...the discreet caress seemed more sensitive than rude, more possessive than imperious. It implied something between them, something potent and private. But there was nothing between Andrew of Laycock and her. They'd shared no intimacies. Intruding on her bath and attacking her in bed hardly amounted to a personal relationship.

She escaped outside with Philip, glad he did not invite Andrew to join them, happy to be free of all those raucous, unmannerly men in the hall. Knights, they were, to a one. And knights of old, not like Paul McCartney or Andrew Lloyd Webber, but the sort who wore armor and carried broadswords. God Almighty, the world had gone mad—or she had. Judy preferred to believe the world was the culprit.

The shock when Judy first came down the stairs, had nearly sent her scurrying. The great number of people and the noise—from their chatter in an unfamiliar language to the clatter of dinnerware—and the scents, from the aroma of cooked food to the stench of smoking torches, had hit her hard. It felt much like opening the door on a wood stove only to be blasted in the face by the fire's searing heat. The only reason she hadn't bolted was that she'd known similar experiences in her own time: power lunches, departmental meetings, contract negotiations with men, all older, all with more experience, who attempted to use their maturity and their finesse to intimidate and outwit her. But Judy had dived headlong into those situations. Flying by the seat of her pants, she had learned, she had adapted, she'd acquired her own maturity and finesse.

So she resolved to plunge into her medieval dinner in a medieval keep with medieval warriors, and she felt sure she would have held her own even if the handsome, blonde, blue-eyed gallant had not waded through the tables of boisterous knights to collect her. But thank heavens Sir Philip of North Cross did. His help, his attention, his companionable conversation had given Judy the confidence she may otherwise have lacked, enabling her to ignore that ass, Andrew. At least until the end, when he'd purposely touched her thigh.

"My lady?" Philip turned to her and spoke softly. They had been walking together silently, side by side, in the enclosed yard Bridget called a bailey. "Do you wish to continue? We could sit, if you'd prefer."

"Walking's fine." Judy smiled at her handsome escort. He stood shorter than Andrew—if she'd worn heels, he'd have stood shorter than she. But, geez, he was easy on the eyes and helpful, too.

"Are you chilled? Take my mantle," Philip offered, whisking off his cape and placing the wrap on Judy's shoulders. "I should have called for a servant to bring you your own before we came outside. Evenings are always chilly, no matter the season. You must forgive me for being so thoughtless."

"It would not have mattered if you had sent someone after my—my mantle." She spoke slowly, avoiding contractions and enunciating clearly. "I do not have one."

"That's correct! You explained that you arrived in boy's clothes, a simple tunic and leggings. I presume, then, your gown is borrowed. But Andrew found no cloak for you among all his mother's and sisters' possessions? He is the thoughtless one, I must say."

"Oh, he has plenty of thoughts." Judy sighed. "But none of them have to do with my comfort."

"If you were staying in my home at North Cross, your comfort would be my primary concern."

Philip halted; Judy did, too. He smiled at her as though he adored her.

Judy quickly resumed walking. She'd never had a man look at her with such open admiration. She didn't know quite how to handle that behavior from a veritable stranger.

A little nervous and eager for distraction, Judy glanced around. Starlight and torchlight illuminated the yard well enough for her to see. "What are all these buildings?" she asked, gesturing with her arm. Though curious, her question was prompted by an urgent need to fill the silence with words. "Do...do people live in them?"

"Only in the barracks, which houses the guards who protect Laycock. The other structures all serve one purpose or another—there's the armory, the stables, the wash house, the mews. Of course, the buttery's in the keep, beneath the great hall."

"The buttery?"

"Where the stores are kept."

"Stores?"

"The foodstuffs, and the wine and ale." Philip paused again and this time, turning to Judy, he frowned. "Surely you have such things where you come from, in York?"

"Oh, sure. Yes. At least, I think so. I don't truly remember." Judy shrugged. "And as I explained to you at dinner, your accent—the way you speak—is sometimes difficult for me to understand. Our words are not quite the same. But of course, we have butteries," she lied. "Do Laycock's servants all live in Wixcomb?"

"The laborers do. But the servants live at the keep."

Philip grabbed her elbow. The action startled Judy, and for a second, she thought he intended to make a move on her, same as Andrew. But then she saw that he had kept her from tripping over a dog nursing a litter of puppies. Philip bent down and picked one up. The puppy was a tiny, liver and white spaniel. Again, she was reminded of the viscount's dogs. But these were more closely related to Thomas Laycock's hounds than those who would one day belong to the software designer.

"Would you like to hold it?" Philip asked.

"No, that's okay. I have always been more of a cat person."

"There are plenty of cats around here, too," he assured her, returning the puppy to its mother's side. They watched as it promptly squirmed in among its siblings and set to suckling the bitch's teat. "Without them, we'd be overrun with rats and mice."

"Yuck!"

"I beg you pardon?"

"I'm terrified of rats and mice."

"You need not be terrified." Philip smiled. "But I agree, they aren't likeable creatures. They fight us for our food."

"That isn't why they scare me. They're so dirty. They carry disease."

"Carry disease?"

"You know," Judy insisted before suddenly realizing Philip didn't know. Should she tell him? Should she explain about germs and fleas and blood contamination? "If they bite you," she elaborated, "you can get sick and die."

"If any animal bites, the victim may fall sick and die."

"I suppose that's true," she conceded. "What's this?" she asked, approaching a stone circle rising up from the middle of the yard. "A well?"

"Aye. The bailey walls always enclose the well, so that if enemies lay siege, the people within shan't die of thirst.

"Lady Judith," Philip continued, pausing as he leaned one elbow on the edge of the well, "you seem unfamiliar with the most commonplace things. Have you lost nearly all your memory?"

I wish I had. "A lot, certainly."

"Then you do not recall an old man, an alchemist?"

Heck, I was glad I knew what an alchemist was! I guess I absorbed more in school than I thought. "No."

"At least you remember your name, your home. Even should Sir Peter prove not to be your sire, I feel confident we shall discover where you belong."

But can you get me back to where I belong?

"Andrew is right, it's not reasonable for him to leave Laycock when all else are gone away. But if you would like me to escort you—if you feel well enough, that is—I should be delighted to make the trip," Philip volunteered again.

"Maybe—maybe later."

Judy wondered why she declined. Of course, she knew that a trip to York, a visit with the alchemist, would prove fruitless. But she also knew the excursion would remove her from Andrew's proximity. That would be a blessing in itself. So why did she hesitate?

Philip pushed himself away from the well and stood straight. The toes of his shoes and Judy's touched.

"Are you not curious to know if you are wed?" he asked. "You may have a husband and children who are missing you. Would you not like to know?"

Though Philip phrased his comments as though he felt concern for any immediate family Judy might have, she recognized a man on the make. This fair and handsome knight only wanted to know whether or not she was available.

Judy felt flattered. What would it be like to date this guy? An honest-to-goodness knight, handsome, virile, young—well, too young, really. A few years her junior, same as Andrew. But she sensed a maturity in him that Andrew seemed to lack.

Philip seemed unlike Andrew in other ways. True, she hadn't known him long enough to make final judgments, but she hadn't known Andrew any longer. Judy sensed the differences between them lay not only in the obvious, the one being fair and the other dark. Philip was also mannerly while Andrew was boorish, and he seemed genuinely concerned for her, not intent on using her body for his own pleasure.

"I think I would know if I were married," Judy allowed. "Surely, I'd know if I had children. I'm quite certain I do not."

Philip didn't move his feet, but he angled his head slightly and leaned forward so that he seemed to stand even closer to Judy. "I agree that you would do well to trust your instincts. You appear a maiden to me, also. You manner is not that of a married lady. But still, 'tis important you learn the truth. If you've no husband, you surely have parents who miss you and may fear you are dead."

An image of Judy's folks, Tony and Nancy Lambini, at their house in Queens, filled her with sudden despair. By now, they knew of her disappearance. By now, they feared her dead.

"Do not cry," Philip urged softly, flicking a tear from the corner of Judy's eye with the pad of his thumb. "In due time, we will locate your kin. You shall all be reunited. And though they are surely concerned at this moment, when you return, they will be overjoyed."

Maybe yes, maybe no. Philip, despite his confidence, had no means of locating the Lambinis and reassuring them that their daughter lived. And she certainly didn't. With no idea how she had arrived here, Judy had no idea how to get back to where she belonged.

"I think—I think I should go inside."

"Very well." Philip turned, placed his hand lightly in the small of Judy's back, and escorted her into the keep.

"What's happened?" she asked, puzzled by what she saw when they stepped through the archway into the great hall. The tables had all been removed, replaced by people lying on the floor as though they intended to sleep there. "Is something wrong?"

"Those would be my questions," a familiar voice, behind her, said. "What's amiss? Did something happen...that should na' have happened?"

Judy whirled around to face Andrew. His face looked flushed, and he reeked of booze.

Philip, who turned more slowly to confront his friend, countered, "What would cause you to ask that? There has been no trouble."

"You two ha' been gone quite a..." Andrew hiccuped... "while. The servants ha' sought out their pallets in the hall."

"Judith and I merely took a stroll around the keep."

Andrew said something to Philip in French, and Judy saw Philip flush with anger.

"What did you say?" she demanded of Andrew. "Speak English so that I can understand."

He stepped closer and explained, "I merely asked if you two had sought out pallets. Or if you'd lain in the hay." He reached out and pulled Philip's mantle off her shoulders. "Nay," he mumbled, his face so near Judy's that his pungent breath made her recoil. "No bits o' straw that I can see."

"Andrew, you're drunk." Philip grabbed his cloak away. "Otherwise, you'd never dare suggest such a vile thing about us." He continued speaking, but as Andrew had done, Philip lapsed into staccato French.

"Oh, aye?" Andrew returned with words Judy comprehended. "Ask the *lady*," he sneered, his dark eyes flicking to hers, "whom she had in her bed this afternoon. She, without a stitch o' clothes on!"

What Philip might have said didn't interest Judy in the least. It was her host's retort that concerned her, incensed her. What he had attempted earlier in the day had been reprehensible. And she *had* had clothes on, at least her sweater! To refer to his own lecherous assault as though she'd encouraged his advances, participated in them, enjoyed them...!

Judy's indignant fury caused her to do something she had never before done in her life. Drawing back her hand, she slapped Andrew smartly across the face.

He sobered instantly. Judy saw it in his eyes. But he made no move to retaliate, physically or verbally. He merely stared at her for a long moment and then turned on his heel, leaving her to Philip's care.

Seven

For a week, Andrew kept himself scarce, though Philip visited Laycock frequently. Philip came to see Judy, not Andrew. She was glad of it, for he eased her loneliness and enabled her to forget, for a little while anyway, the horror of her predicament. And the more time she spent with Philip, the more she admired him. Judy sincerely doubted the same would have proved true if she'd been forced to endure Andrew's company for any length.

Today, walking with Philip beyond the bailey walls, Judy found herself returning again to the place she'd awakened that first morning to discover she had been hurled back through history. If Philip wondered why she frequently led him to this precise spot, he did not ask. His questions all had to do with York and the old knight called Peter Lamb as he attempted, not too subtly, to help Judy recall her past. Yet she never let on that she remembered her entire life in vivid detail anymore than she ever revealed the accoutrements in her tote bag.

"My lady?" Philip spread his cloak on the ground in a Galahad gesture. Joining Judy as she sat, he stretched out his legs and crossed his booted feet at the ankles.

"Have you had any word from your father?" she asked him, fairly certain that Andrew had no word from his own.

"Aye. One of my brothers returned home briefly, and he caught me up." Philip plucked a blade of tall grass and chewed on it. "King John balks at the conditions the English barons propose, but in the end, he knows he must accept them."

"Why?"

When Judy asked questions, Philip answered eagerly, even patiently. Through him, she had already learned a great deal about everyday matters in this year of 1215—also of greater, more political ones.

"John lost all his French fiefs when King Philip declared him a feudal felon many years ago. He has known little but defeat in his attempt to reclaim or expand his holdings. Five years past, he had some success in Ireland. But last summer, he found himself retreating from the French at Bouvines. Here in England, most noblemen are dismayed and disgusted by his unsavory character, his endless greed. So the barons have decided he must not be allowed to put himself above the law any longer. If John does not agree and sign our written conditions, he'll find himself murdered before he can rule another day."

He smiled at Judy and considered her thoughtfully. "'Tis unusual that a woman, especially one so young as you, is intrigued with politics. Most damsels I know are more concerned with home and heart."

Judy quelled her impulse to protest. She could have lectured Philip for an hour, but that not only would have been presumptuous, it would be pointless. The edicts and expectations of her lifetime did not apply to his. So she bit her tongue and smiled back at him instead. "I've always been different."

"Is that so?" Both Philip's eyebrows shot up. "Are you remembering this, Judith?"

"What? No. It's...just something I sense. My instincts, I suppose you'd say."

"Ahhh." He glanced around and reluctantly changed the subject. "What say you we visit the village?"

"No." Judy avoided going into town. It wasn't the Wixcomb she wanted it to be. Worse, she didn't care to return there and relive her initial experiences of that first morning, when she'd foolishly presumed the hamlet to be little more than a theatrical set. "I like it here."

"Why?"

Because it connects me to my past. It's where I fell that last night in my own time, and where I woke again in yours.

"I don't know. It's peaceful and pretty."

"Aye." Philip nodded as he gazed at the forest that consumed the land to the north 'til it reached Laycock's postern walls. "All England's pretty, I suppose, if you like trees."

"Don't forget the meadows," Judy added, turning around and gesturing toward the grass-covered hills that separated Laycock Keep from Wixcomb, to the south. "They're pretty, too."

Judy supposed they really were, to people who liked

that sort of scenery. The prettiest thing she could imagine seeing would be the corpulent, bristly-chinned hot dog vendor, Maurice, who worked the corner near her office. Judy could envision his aluminum cart with its frayed, cockeyed umbrella, and she could almost smell the kraut and onions, too.

"Are you sure I cannot persuade you to walk to the village?" Philip persisted. "There are artisans living there as well as farmers. I'd buy you a trinket."

"Philip, you don't have to buy me presents."

His eyes met Judy's. "But I would like to. I should also like you to visit North Cross someday soon. Will you?"

"Perhaps."

Judy didn't want to go anywhere too far away. Here was where she'd landed after her initial time travel. Here was where she certainly had to depart if she ever managed a return trip.

Yet she felt guilty refusing Philip. As Wixcomb was only a stone's throw away from "her spot," she pushed herself to her feet and agreed belatedly, "I suppose a walk into town would be nice after all."

Just as Philip rose to join her, a startling static charge of energy shot through Judy, making her sway as though she were standing on the deck of a ship that sailed through rough waters. The electricity didn't emanate from the air, as though a thunder storm threatened, but pulsed instead from the earth. For the briefest moment, the hair on her arms rose. Abruptly, and as suddenly as it came, the sensation vanished.

"Judith? Are you well?" Philip grabbed her shoulders and searched her face.

"I—I'm fine. I probably stood up too fast. Got a little light-headed for a second, is all. Let's go." She turned, extricating herself from Philip's grasp. But with her very first step in the direction of Wixcomb, Judy tripped on the hem of her skirt.

He tried to catch her, but his fingers only clutched air as Judy stumbled onto her knees. "Judith!" Philip followed her down to the ground so fast, it seemed he also fell. Suddenly, they both lay sprawled across his cloak.

"Methinks you are not destined to walk to the village today." He chuckled and shook his head, grinning at Judy ruefully. Then his smile vanished. "Mayhap you are destined to be here...in my arms."

Reaching out, Philip grasped Judy's waist and tugged her closer to him. Their noses nearly touched, and she could see flecks of black in his cerulean blue eyes.

Philip kissed her expertly, and Judy offered no resistance. This was the stuff of which young girls' fantasies and chick flicks were made—handsome knights wooing beautiful damsels in the grass under a cloudless, blue sky. All right—knights wooing damsels, period, Judy amended. Considering how tense and unpredictable her life had become, she deserved whatever respite came her way. A little romance...who would complain?

Philip began exploring Judy's parted lips with his tongue. She responded in kind—it had been a long, long time since she'd been thoroughly kissed, and Philip was one great kisser. He seemed to interpret her enthusiasm as permission to press his knee between her thighs. Gaining purchase above her, he maneuvered Judy onto her back.

Boy, this guy was slick. He knew just how much pressure to apply with his mouth and how far to go with his hands so that she wouldn't feel threatened. Philip could give lessons, Judy found herself thinking.

He began to fondle her breasts through the fabric covering them. Judy sighed as her nipples hardened. She knew her body was primed to respond to Philip's expert touching, and briefly, she envisioned full carnal congress with this golden-haired knight. But the image disappeared when Judy realized she could think about her situation as though it were happening to somebody else. Obviously, she hadn't given herself up to the moment or been swept away in a tide of passion, so she reversed her original inclination to let things escalate. If she didn't feel crazy with desire, she didn't want to make love. She'd been there, done that. The morning after was the pits.

"Philip, no. Stop. Cut it out!"

Immediately, Philip ceased. Pulling away, he looked

to Judy for some explanation or, perhaps, for further direction.

Geez. Handsome, one hell of a lover, a gentleman to boot, and I'm telling him no. Judy really hated to cut him off, but she had to.

"I'm sorry," she apologized. "I just don't—"

"I understand," he interrupted. "You do not know who you are or if you belong to someone. Thus, 'tis I who should ask forgiveness. I had no right to take advantage of you, Judith. I vow, it shan't happen again."

"Well, leave a girl a little something to hope for," she said, hoping to sound glib while trying to ignore the heated flush crawling up her cheeks. "My feelings, my status, could change by next week—or even tomorrow."

Philip gave her a heart-stopping smile, but Judy's heart didn't skip a beat. "Then I will hope also."

The two of them fell into companionable silence as they rearranged themselves on Philip's cloak. Finally, side by side and sitting upright, their hands clasped over their knees while they gazed idly at the landscape, he spoke as though there had been no pause in their conversation. "Judith," Philip said, "when we know, in fact, who you are and that you remain an eligible maiden, may I—may I court you?"

She had thought that's what he'd been doing. "Do you mean you want to ask somebody's permission to see me? Someone like my father, my—my sire?"

"Aye, exactly." He nodded.

"Well, sure. That is, you may," she agreed, refusing to dwell on the fact that in his lifetime, Philip would never be able to meet Tony Lambini and ask for his daughter's hand.

"I look forward to it." As he spoke, Philip leaned toward Judy. By the time he had uttered the last word, his lips again melded to hers.

"Excuse me!" another manly voice boomed.

Philip leapt to his feet, and Judy almost fell onto her back. They both glared at Andrew, who stepped out of the trees, leading his horse behind him. He looked so dark and dangerous that Judy's pulse quickened. Immediately, she reached up to Philip and took his hand. When she'd gained her feet, she kept her fingers twined through his.

"I did not mean to intrude," Andrew insisted, though he'd clearly intended to do just that.

"You didn't." Judy hoped she sounded cool. She really wanted to smack the obnoxious lord of Laycock.

"If I did not, then my old friend here has lost his touch." He smiled—no, he sneered, his gaze on their clasped hands.

"Andrew, 'tis good to see you," Philip told him. Judy suspected he sounded polite rather than sincere. "You always seem to be away of late, when e'er I come to Laycock."

"I may be the youngest son, but when I am the only son remaining home, I have responsibilities." Andrew halted before the couple.

"Speaking of your duties, Andrew," Philip continued, "what of the messenger you agreed to send to York? I would think that by now we might have had some word."

"You offered to write the missive. Did you?"

"Well, nay, I did not. I presumed—"

"If you wrote no letter, there was naught to send."

Philip exhaled an exasperated sigh. "Then we'd best attend to the matter immediately. All this time I've been waiting—" He inhaled a quick, noisy breath. "Judith needs to reassure her kin that she is well. She should be reunited with them."

"I agree. But do we know her kin?" Andrew cocked an eyebrow as though issuing a challenge.

Philip looked as annoyed as Judy felt. "Sir Peter Lamb," he ground out. "You know good and well 'tis he that I speak of. My grandsire's old friend seems the likeliest prospect."

"A prospect is not a verity. Besides, I thought we agreed Judith is not yet well enough to travel."

"Sending a message on her behalf would not exert the lady at all."

"Then I shall send out a rider if you write the damned message." Andrew moved his head slightly and addressed Judith directly. "If it is your desire, my lady."

Such a simple, reasonable question, yet it infuriated her. Did he dare to hint that she might prefer staying with him rather than returning to her family? Judy felt like the Prisoner of Zenda confined in the keep with Andrew Laycock!

"Please," she snapped. "Go ahead. Whatever you think best."

With a wave of her hand, she turned and stomped away. But both men caught up with her, flanked her, and kept pace.

"When we return to the keep, I'll write the letter," Philip announced. "When you determine who will ride to York with it, Andrew, do send him on his mission straight away. There remains several hours of daylight yet."

"Very well. Straight away. Rest assured," Andrew muttered peevishly.

Judy knew why Philip felt annoyed. She knew why she did, too. But she had no idea what had ticked Andrew off. Oh, he had been sulky and sullen since she'd slapped him—though he had absolutely no right to feel that way. If any man had ever deserved a woman's full fury, it had been Andrew. But Judy presumed the incident would have lit a fire beneath him. By all rights, Andrew should have been moving heaven and earth to try to locate her family. The sooner he did, the sooner she'd be gone and out of his hair. At least, in theory. Because Andrew didn't know any effort he made would prove fruitless. Only Judy did, and she wasn't telling.

"You know where the bailiff's chamber is," Andrew said to Philip as the three of them entered the keep and clamored into the great hall. "He'll have parchment and brush so you may compose your missive." He turned to a servant. "Jock, find me, ah...Louis. Aye, he's a fair rider. Find Louis, and have him come to me promptly."

"Milord." The manservant, Jock, gave his master a quick nod and then dashed from the hall.

"It shan't take me long," Philip advised Judy. He squeezed her hand reassuringly and then took to the stairs, leaving her alone with Andrew.

"Forgive me," Andrew mumbled as he poured himself a goblet of wine from a jug left on the high table.

Judy was very nearly floored by the unexpected apology. "For what, exactly?" she asked suspiciously.

"For interrupting you and my friend. 'Twould seem I

kept you from getting a good swiving from the most popular lover in this shire."

If she had been a bomb, she would have exploded. "You—you cockshead," Judy screeched. She'd heard the word bandied about and thought it seemed the perfect epithet for Andrew Laycock.

He whirled. "How dare you, you—"

"Watch what you call me, mister!" she warned, waggling a finger at him. "I've had about all the insults, neglect and unconscionable behavior from you that I'm going to take."

"Uncon—?"

"Forget that you've left me to my own devices the entire past week. Forget that I have nothing to do, no one to speak with, except for Philip, if and when he visits here. But do try to recall that you attempted to rape me not once, but twice."

"I never attempted to rape you," Andrew insisted, stomping toward Judy. "Why would I—*I*—have to force myself on a wench? Women come to me begging, do you hear? Begging!"

"Geez, Louise, you're arrogant," she returned. Andrew sounded like every boy she'd known in high school—all boasts, no conquests. "Begging? I don't think so."

"What would you know?"

"I know that I rejected you. And you know I might want Philip. That ticks you off, doesn't it?"

"You—you rejected—me?" Andrew sputtered, shaking his fists. "Nay, 'twas I who scorned you. Had I wished to bed you, I would have had you wet and wriggling beneath me. But I did not, do you hear, I did not. 'Tis why it bruised me not at all when I vowed to leave you chaste. Despite my early intentions to take my ease with you, once I had a closer look, I saw you had no appeal."

Judy's mouth fell open. She couldn't even think how to respond to such an aspersion. In that moment of quandary, she took a step toward Andrew so that they stood very close. So close they were nearly eye to eye.

"I have no appeal, huh?" she finally returned, knowing that comment had not been worth her furious thinking. "Then why does it annoy you that Philip and I were kissing? Because, really, if you don't desire me, why would you care that he does?"

Andrew exhaled a long breath, let his hands drop to his sides, and uncurled his fingers. Evenly, he replied, "I care only about Philip. We have been friends, closer than brothers, since we were young lads. I'd rather he did not sully himself with the likes of you before he recovers his senses."

Judy saw red. "Liar! You're jealous! The only women who'll lie down for you are whores or peasants who fear you because you're sometimes lord-and-master of Laycock Keep. When I rejected you, you were stymied. You'd never put the moves on a woman with any standards before. Now you're mad as hell that I refused you."

"Stymied? What is that?" Andrew inquired scornfully.

"A really good word you're too ignorant to know."

"Me? Ignorant?" He inhaled deeply, which expanded his chest. "You, wench, are the ignorant one. You cannot speak French; you hardly speak English. You do not know your kin or where they are from. Damnation, you were on your way to London when you found yourself at Wixcomb—they're not at all alike, Judith. No one else would confuse the one for the other."

"You—" She raised her hand. She didn't know how Andrew managed to provoke her so easily when none of the men in her previous twenty-seven years had ever brought her to the brink of violence even once, let alone twice.

But she could not follow through with another stinging slap. Andrew caught her wrist and held it in an iron grip.

"Would you like the truth, wench? You've no appeal because you've the body of a boy, not just the hair and clothing. Naked, 'tis obvious you have no hips, no buttocks, hardly enough bosom to notice. By the saints, you stand as tall as most of the men in England. No real man could be aroused by a lofty, lanky figure the likes of yours. If Philip seems intrigued, 'tis only because he finds you uncommon. But his interest will soon wane."

Judy sucked in her breath. Never had anyone insulted her so thoroughly, so painfully, as Andrew of Laycock just had. He hadn't condemned a singular attribute, but the whole of her person. His cruel criticism should not have affected her—Judy knew enough to consider the source. But for some reason, the source of the insult made it sting all the more.

Her mind raced. Andrew didn't find her attractive? Hot damn, but she would *make* him find her attractive, make him pine for her, drool over her, and want to kill himself for not being able to have her. No butt, no boobs, no way! She worked out at a gym, she had tight buns and a flat stomach. In the right ensemble, with her hair just so and her feet balancing in precariously high, stiletto heels, Andrew would willingly crawl through a nest of vipers to reach her—and surely die from snake bites before he ever did. But where would Judy get the right clothes, the right style? She couldn't go to a salon for a complete make-over. She couldn't have her hair, face and nails done. She couldn't pour herself into some tight little designer number that showed her legs and her cleavage.

And why would I want to? Judy nearly screamed aloud. She didn't have enough to contend with, living in an antiquated time in a foreign country, all by some force of magic she could neither control nor understand? Dear God, she had to be going mad to think, even for half a minute, of ways to get this idiot *boy* to lust after her. She didn't even like him—she sure as hell did not want to sleep with him. She liked Philip, and he already had the hots for her. Maybe she would sleep with him. But, if there truly was a God—and Judy believed in her little Catholic heart there certainly was—He would see she got home to her own time, her own country, before very much longer. What any medieval knight thought of Judy Lambini would prove completely irrelevant.

Judy glared into Andrew's dark eyes. His anger made them glint, so that they shone like hard, dark chips of obsidian. "I hate you," she spat.

"Do you?"

Still grasping her wrist, Andrew skimmed her cheek with the knuckles of his other hand. He barely touched her—his skin grazed hers as lightly as a gentle breeze. Yet it melted Judy's bones, as though she'd been skewered with a blazing bolt of lightning.

Despite her resolve, she shuddered and went soft, but so did Andrew's eyes. As she watched them unblinkingly, Judy saw those orbs liquify and lighten from a shade of black to the color of chocolate.

"Judith!"

Philip called to her from the stairs. Unwittingly, he saved her from herself.

"Y-yes?" she returned, whirling around to face him.

At that instant, Philip appeared on the lower steps. Hurrying forward across the great hall, he waved a small sheet of stiff paper in his hand. "Judith, I have the letter for Peter Lamb. Andrew, where is your rider?"

"Give that to me." He snatched the parchment from Philip's fingers. "Jock hasn't returned with him yet. I'll go and find Louis myself."

***

Andrew took a deep breath the moment he stepped outdoors in an attempt to control himself, to gather and harness his feelings. Any appearance of calm he had exhibited in the hall had been an illusion. Inside, his stomach roiled. He felt primed to explode, like fermented spirits that erupted from their containers.

"Milord, you wished to speak with me?"

Andrew snapped his head around at the sound of Louis' voice. The guard, in mail, looked flushed and sweaty. He had been training on the practice field.

Glancing down at the bit of parchment in his hand, Andrew shook his head. "Nay, Louis," he said as he crumpled the paper into a ball. "'Twas a mistake. Go back to what you were doing."

Eight

"Milady!" Round-faced, button-eyed, pug-nosed Sally opened Judy's door and poked her head inside. "Milady, there's someone to see you below, in the great hall."

"Thank you," Judy said, and the servant retreated, closing the door again.

It had to be Philip. He hadn't been to Laycock for a visit in two whole days, and Judy sorely missed his company. Actually, she missed his protection. When Philip was near, Andrew was not. But during Philip's recent absence, Andrew had kept close to the keep. He didn't seek out Judy's company. In fact, he barely seemed to tolerate her presence when they shared meals at the dais table in the hall. Nor did he speak to her unless absolutely forced to. Worse, Judy sometimes felt him staring at her, studying her, whenever they were in any sort of proximity. His scrutiny made her nervous. What was he thinking? What were his intentions? After that fight they'd had...

But Philip had finally returned. With him to amuse her, to help make the time pass more pleasantly, Judy wouldn't have to think about Andrew Laycock.

She bounded down the stairs and jerked to a halt. The man she saw wasn't Philip at all, but a stranger. This unfamiliar knight, she realized with a pang, could only be a messenger, one who carried word from the old man, Sir Peter-the-alchemist-and-inventor. Damn! The news he brought wouldn't serve her interests at all. Once Andrew learned she wasn't related to this fellow, he'd boot her out on her ear. He wouldn't start looking for some other family connection in some other place. And even if Philip made good his invitation, if she visited North Cross, how far would she be from that place outside the bailey walls, her launch and landing pad to and from the future?

Judy glanced furtively about, relieved Andrew was nowhere in sight. Maybe she could lie to the messenger, assuring the man she'd pass the news along to Andrew so that he needn't bother. Or, maybe not. Because in all likelihood, he had already reported to Laycock's current lord-and-master. Still, she might have a few minutes left to her. She could make a run for it. She could hide in the woods...

Oh, *that* was a plan, Judy thought with disgust before nodding at the knight, resigned to hearing his news.

He spoke French. Judy interrupted, insisting on English, and he began again. "My lady," he said, "Lord Philip wishes to advise you that he has been sent away on business for his mother, Lady Edwinna of North Cross. He shall be gone as briefly as possible, and if you'll allow him to, upon his return he shall call upon you immediately."

Closing her eyes, Judy exhaled an audible sigh. When she blinked her eyes open again, she nodded and smiled. "I see. Well, thank you. And—and of course, he may call upon me. I will be looking forward to it."

The messenger turned to leave, and Judy hesitated. *Now what*? Sure, she'd been granted a reprieve to remain living in this tense sort of limbo awhile longer, but so what? She felt as though she'd been condemned to solitary confinement while the keys to her cell hung on a ring just beyond her reach. The tedium and the frustration were driving her insane!

Andrew's nowhere around, a voice in her mind repeated. It was true. Judy decided to escape, at least from the confines of this fortress and her bedroom, and perhaps all the way to the future. If her luck continued to hold, she wouldn't encounter Andrew along the way.

She ran upstairs again and retrieved her tote. When she returned to the great hall, she found it as empty as when she'd left it. She also noticed, on the high table, an array of assorted utensils. Using a little sleight-of-hand, Judy made a U-turn on her way to the door and strode past the table, sliding an object into her bag.

Ten minutes later, she stood on that infamous plot of land outside the bailey walls. Nothing happened. She felt nothing at all, not even a breeze, certainly not a static charge of electricity. So after a time, she gave up in defeat and returned to the bailey.

Near the wash house, where cauldrons used to boil woolens stood empty and dusty, Judy flipped over a wooden pail and sat down with a heavy sigh. Ignoring her, laborers and servants bustled around doing whatever it was they did. Judy envied them. No matter how menial or endless the peasants' chores, at least they had something to do. She, on the other hand, found herself treated like a princess, or someone with severe mental deficiencies, by all the household staff. Bridget or Sally helped to dress her every morning and undress her every night. Cook prepared meals twice a day, which were served to her either at the high table or in her room. In between, she had nothing to do, no purpose at all, which sometimes felt more strenuous than grueling, forced labor. On occasion, she'd felt so fatigued by boredom, she'd considered asking Bridget if she had any chores she could help with. But Judy had bitten her tongue before making the offer, sure that if Andrew found her toiling around the keep like a common laborer, he would conclude she was no better. She didn't intend to let Andrew Laycock believe that Judy Lambini, literary agent with the Edwin Grant Agency, was nothing more than a lowly peasant!

Oh, how she missed her life as a career woman. Not just the big stuff, the cool stuff, like parties, receptions, or the thrill of negotiating a really big sale. She missed the everyday things—long phone conversations, harried taxi cab rides, breakfast and lunch conferences, quick trips to the deli, the dry cleaners, or the newspaper stand. But they were lost to her now.

Temporarily. Judy refused to accept she might never return home. Maybe, the next time she went to "her" spot behind the bailey walls, all those weird sensations would quicken again, just as strong as they'd been the night she had flown through time. And she would fly right back—or forward—into the future. Of course, there remained the strong possibility that she might have to wait until next Halloween to do a time travel encore. But at least she wouldn't have to wait another whole year for that holiday to roll around. Springtime blossomed all around Judy, which meant it could only be six months or less 'til All Hallow's Eve and—what had Ian MacCoombs called it? Samhain, yes, that was it. Samhain.

When Judy did go back to her own time, she anticipated making headlines, and not only in the tabloids. To ensure the experts took her seriously and no one called her a crackpot, she had to have proof of her adventure. To that end, she had recently begun collecting artifacts. Just before she'd left the keep, she had confiscated a malleable pewter goblet. Already, in a box under her bed, she had stashed a bit of decorative sewing and a scrap of parchment she'd found lying in the yard, discarded in a crumpled ball. These items could later be identified as authentic.

But filching odds and ends from the castle didn't require the time and perseverance of a scavenger hunt. Judy needed something to occupy herself so that she wouldn't think about the knight who'd gone away or the one who hadn't.

Despite her best intentions, Judy glanced at the keep. Her mind promptly played the pink elephant trick: Andrew's image popped up in her head and refused to disappear, no matter how she fought it. Though she attempted to recall every nasty, arrogant, insulting thing he had said to her, especially during their last argument, what she remembered, instead, was the way he'd touched her. The look in his eyes, too. Recalling either would have made her sigh with longing. Recalling both made her feel warm all over, especially between her legs.

"Damn!" Judy swung her head back and again surveyed the yard. This time, she willed herself to pay attention to the laborers' occupations. The workers appeared quite efficient despite the limitations of their world, and more amazingly, they seemed totally oblivious to the animals underfoot. If Judy found the situation fascinating, it occurred to her others would as well—others of her own time.

Pulling a notebook and pen from her bag, Judy began scribbling down her observations. Though she loved books and had a passing familiarity with the process of writing nonfiction, Judy couldn't be sure she had any real writing talent. But now seemed the perfect opportunity to take a stab at it. God knew, she had the time.

***

Andrew remained in the shadows of the stable, watching Judith. He had been observing her since he sent Sally to her room to announce she had a visitor. He knew Judith expected Philip, for he'd seen the anticipation in her expression when she entered the hall. He had also seen the disappointment written on her face when she spied the messenger awaiting her instead. Damn Philip of North Cross! What was it about that fair-haired knight that made damsels swoon? Philip himself seemed unaware. So much so, he had been searching for a bride, as though it required a bit of effort.

At least, for a change, Philip's mother, the lady Edwinna, had inadvertently helped Andrew's cause instead of her son's. Whatever business she'd sent Philip on would keep him away from Laycock and Judith. Since Andrew's family remained away as well, he would use this time to get what he wanted. What he wanted was Judith Lamb. Andrew hadn't forgotten his promises to her, those she'd tricked him into making. But she'd offered no certain proof of the gentleness of her birth, and until such time as he found himself presented with fact, Judith remained fair game. Andrew wouldn't force her, nay. But he would, by God, seduce her.

He approached her now, making no effort at stealth. But when he stopped beside Judith and said her name, she jumped, nearly dropping the book she'd been hunched over. Standing, she rounded on Andrew and glared at him. Her frown bespoke both fear and fury, but even before she opened her mouth, Andrew knew which emotion she would unleash.

"What do you want?" she snapped suspiciously.

"To join you, if I may." He kept his tone level, polite.

"You own the place, more or less. I can't stop you." With a flounce, Judith sat down again while Andrew took another pail to use as a stool for himself.

"I understand a messenger recently came to Laycock," he said casually.

"Philip sent him," Judith volunteered far too quickly. "He wasn't from that alchemist who lives in York, the one you—we—think could be my father. So there hasn't been any news about my family connections."

Andrew canted his head to one side and considered the wench thoughtfully. If he didn't know better, he would suspect she didn't wish to have news from Sir Peter. Why not? Had she lied about everything, especially her loss of memory? Had she run away from her father or her husband? Or was she, as he suspected, a peasant who had fooled the younger lords of Laycock?

"I am very aware of the news the messenger from North Cross brought," Andrew assured Judith. "'Tis my business, as lord and master, to know. Yet you must realize that any word from York would come by my own man, the selfsame one I sent with Philip's missive." *If I had, indeed, sent Louis to York with Philip's missive.*

"Oh. Right."

She nodded and crossed her legs. The top one bobbed violently beneath her skirt. Judith seemed rather distraught, and Andrew could think of only one reason for her distress. "Are you upset because Philip's gone away?"

"Upset?" Judith made a face as she turned to him. "Don't be—" She broke off, and suddenly her eyebrows went up. Rather sweetly, she exclaimed, "I mean, yes, of course! Oh, I'm very upset. When a day goes by that I don't see Philip—"

"Enough!" Andrew snapped, unable to listen to more, be it truth or lie. "He'll return. You shall see him again."

"I'm counting on it." Judith graced him with a catlike grin before raising her chin a notch, turning aside, and gazing across the yard.

Andrew had an impulse to grab her and kiss her so hard, she wouldn't worry if she saw his friend soon or not at all. He didn't, though, because he feared he wouldn't see the result he desired. Why didn't he have his friend's power over women? And what were those powers exactly?

"You think highly of Philip," Andrew observed evenly. "You're not alone. Females he has barely glanced at and never spoken to faint in his wake. What is it about him that so appeals to damsels like yourself?"

"That's easy." Judith continued looking away. "He's the opposite of you."

"What!" She might just as well have slapped his

cheek with a leather gauntlet. "I fear you are quite wrong. Philip and I are both barons' sons, and the youngest sons at that. We were even born the same year, so we are both now a score and two. We are also both knights who have earned our spurs. Philip and I are very much alike."

"Ha!" Judith barked a short laugh and deigned to appraise him, starting at the top of Andrew's head and working her way down to his shoes. He thought her bold gaze lingered overlong somewhere below his belt, and to his chagrin, he felt self-conscious. "Not a chance, Andrew. Philip is blonde and blue-eyed, extremely handsome. You're dark and—you're not." Judith turned away again.

Andrew suppressed another violent urge to grab her. But this time he felt no desire to kiss Judith. Instead, he wished to shake her hard. God's wounds! He never used force against females—why did this mysterious woman spark his fury and oblige him to throttle her?

"I see," he managed to grind out between clenched teeth.

For a long moment, silence reigned. Then Judith announced breezily, "I heard you had a grand passion for someone called Chandra. Then she dumped you."

Andrew didn't know that phrase, but he understood the gist. Though his urge to throttle someone didn't wane, suddenly Philip became the object of his fury. He'd have joyously strangled the blackguard, had his erstwhile friend been present to do so. Why, by all the saints, had Philip told this curious nomad, who claimed no identity beyond her name, all the sorry details of his life? Chandra had made a fool of him, marrying that landed lord from across the Channel without even advising him of it beforehand. The incident wasn't something Andrew cared to recall, let alone have spread hither and yon, and sung as a sad ballad. Why would Philip dredge up and confide the particulars of old, painful events?

Andrew's pride suggested an answer. "How did you hear of Chandra?" he asked. "Did you inquire about me and my women?"

Judith flushed darkly, the blush creeping up to her

cheeks from her throat. But she did not reply.

Andrew smiled. "I was much younger then," he explained casually as he locked his hands over one knee. "Chandra is gone now, and good riddance. But what of you? Have you known a great love of your own?"

"I couldn't say." Her words were clipped. "I don't remember anything about my life before."

"But now...?"

"Now, nothing."

Judith's foot still bobbed. She seemed more annoyed than anxious. Perhaps, Andrew considered, she was not so keen on Philip as he had presumed or she had implied.

Sitting straighter, Andrew put his shoulders back and inhaled deeply to expand the breadth of his chest. He didn't think now was the time to try to woo Judith with honeyed words. But perhaps a conversation in a neutral vein would make her warm to him. He asked, "Have you sisters or brothers?" On the heels of his query, he realized his mistake. She had no memory.

Yet she responded almost immediately. "Sure. I have a brother, Gary—"

Abruptly, Judith broke off, turning to Andrew with her mouth agape.

Andrew pounced. "You remember him? You recall your family?"

"No!" Judith shook her head vehemently, and she stood. "I—I don't know where that came from. Sometimes things just pop out of my mouth, but I don't know what they mean. Really, I don't."

He eyed her speculatively because, despite her pleas, she did not quite sound sincere. Andrew knew if she were lying, he should be angry with her. Yet if she lied, the chances were she was no lady. If not a lady, she could only be a peasant. Being female in the bargain, that meant Judith had no connections, no value. If so, Philip wouldn't want her, but he, Andrew of Laycock, could have her for as long as she intrigued him.

He smiled, and Judith demanded, "Why are you grinning? What's so funny?"

"Forgive me, my lady."

"Why do you call me that?" She backed away,

insisting, "You don't believe I'm a lady at all, though I've told you I was raised as one."

"Nor do you consider me your lord and master, though you are living on my charity."

"Hey, I'll work for my keep if you want me to. Or I could—I could leave."

She blinked. It seemed Judith's suggestion surprised her as much as it did him. Then her lashes fluttered, and her eyebrows came together in a worrisome frown. Obviously, she did not really wish to leave Laycock.

Andrew stood and grabbed her wrist gently. "There is no need for you to leave, Judith."

"Well, when word comes from—from my sire, from Peter Lamb, I'll have to—"

"That will be awhile, surely. York is not over the next hill."

Judith looked relieved. Her shoulders relaxed, and she nodded. Andrew seized the moment by changing the topic. "Please," he asked, "will you show me what you have in your book?"

Judith looked at the tome she clutched in her arms. Then she raised her eyes—her smoky, green eyes—to his. "Okay. If you want."

Though reluctant, she had agreed—and all because Andrew had spoken gently and met her glance with an imploring gaze. Thank the saints he had not reminded her of his earlier demand that she show him all her possessions in due time. Jesu! He had stumbled upon Philip's secret. That knight impressed women, be they little girls or old crones or any age in between, with kind words and longing looks. Now, so too would he!

Drawing Judith down to her makeshift stool, Andrew sat beside her again. She opened her book, but she pushed the pages bearing script to one side of the spiraled wire that bound the parchments together.

"By the saints, that is fantastic!" he said, too impressed not to admit it.

"What is?"

"The parchment. 'Tis unlike any I've seen before."

"It isn't parchment, just plain old paper." With a casualness that shocked him, Judith ripped off a clean sheet and handed it to him for inspection.

"God's tears!" He could not help cursing her carelessness with something so dear. "What did you do? You've damaged it!"

"I have not. Oh, it is kind of shredded along the edge, but that always happens when you rip out a page. It's no big deal."

"No 'big deal'?"

"Right. It's...not of any major consequence. There's plenty more." Judith used her thumb to fan through the remaining pages.

Andrew scrutinized the fine, rectangular sheet marked with pale, evenly-spaced lines. The paper looked almost as sheer as a veil, so that the sunlight made shadows of his fingers splayed behind the page.

"Jesu! 'Tis so thin and so very smooth. This is surely not made of skin?"

"No, it's made from wood pulp. Maybe rags, too."

"I have heard of that process," he told her, remembering something his tutor had disclosed. "The Spaniards invented it, or they brought the knowledge back to Iberia from elsewhere. But you have so many sheets bound together, they must be worth a king's ransom. The paper I've seen has been painstakingly produced, each page formed in a frame."

"I don't have a clue how this paper was made," Judith admitted. "I think, probably, it's made in huge rolls and cut to size, but I couldn't say for sure."

"Your father did not explain?"

"My father?"

"Peter Lamb."

"Oh! I don't know. I—I don't remember. Remember?" She flashed him a flickering smile.

Andrew reached over Judith's lap and flipped back the pages she had written on so that the top one lay face up. "What language is this?"

"English."

"'Tis not."

"It is," she insisted. "I know it looks different from anything you've probably read, but it's just another version of the language we're both speaking. You and I have different accents, different ways of saying the same word. Well, we make our letters differently, too. We don't use the same spellings, either."

Andrew considered Judith curiously. "We?" he repeated. "Who is this 'we' you refer to?"

She hesitated. "I'm not sure, Andrew. I told you, things pop out of my mouth, but in my head, I just don't know. I guess I'm referring to people who speak like I do, who read and write like I do."

"And these people, you've no idea where they live?" Andrew pressed.

"No."

"Judith." He uttered her name sternly, like a parent warning a child.

"I don't. I really don't."

"You may not," he conceded. "But though it has been a long while since I last visited the city of York, methinks they speak not very much different than I."

"I never claimed I came from York. You did. Philip did."

"You were the first to mention York. I recall it well."

"No, I—" Judith looked frustrated and very near tears. "If I did, I don't remember it now."

She grabbed the handle on her satchel. "I think maybe I should go inside now."

"Nay," he commanded as he grabbed her arm. Then, releasing her, he asked more gently, "Why do you wish to leave now? The sun is shining..."

"The sun is hot. I would really love to take off this heavy old dress, put on shorts—"

Again, she looked aggrieved at having spoken. Again, Andrew's instincts hummed. "You would prefer to don what?"

The color in Judith's face heightened. "They're an item of apparel I do recall wearing," she explained, almost daring him to question her dubious memory. "They're much cooler, much more comfortable to wear in warm weather than a long dress with long sleeves."

"Mayhap my sisters have such a garment in their clothes trunks," Andrew suggested, knowing full well they did not. But he had to say something to distract himself from the vision that had come into his head, a vision of Judith stripping off the cotehardie she presently wore to reveal her voluptuous naked body.

"Your sisters don't have any shorts in their wardrobe. Trust me." Judith sounded fatigued. She sighed but released her grip on her satchel.

"Write something for me," Andrew urged quickly.

"No, I'm tired of writing." Then, surprisingly gracious, she offered instead, "Maybe you'd like to write something? You could use my pen."

Andrew accepted the object Judith handed him as though she'd given him the cutting edge of a sharp knife.

"It's not going to bite you," she assured him with a laugh. Her unexpected giggle sounded high and girlish. Andrew imagined hearing her laugh in just such a manner while cavorting with him in bed.

"See the little silver lever at the top? Click it down with your thumb, like this." Judith demonstrated. "Did you see? The point comes out the bottom. Press the point to the paper and write."

Helpfully, Judith put the whole sheaf of bound paper under Andrew's blank sheet so that he had a solid surface to work on. Gingerly, he began to form meticulous figures, using the lines to guide his script.

After writing only one sentence from a verse of the Holy Scriptures, Andrew held up the paper and sucked in a breath. "Sweet Mother of God! Where does the color come from? How does it work?"

"Here." She took the implement, broke it apart, and dumped the innards onto the book in Andrew's lap. Picking up one piece and then another, she told him about "ink" and "points" and "spring loads." Andrew did not really comprehend her explanation, and when she reassembled the object to return it to him, her intimate touch sent a jolt through his fingers and hand.

"Ink," he repeated, trying to focus.

"Yes, the stuff that makes the lines on the paper."

"Soot and water?"

"Not exactly, but I suppose that could be a kind of ink."

"And you write words with this—"

"Pen," she supplied helpfully.

"Pen," he echoed. "But it has no brush, no fibers."

"Right again. I showed you. The ink's in the tube, and it rolls out on that little ball at the end of the cartridge."

Andrew dropped the writing implement, the *pen*. As it fell into his lap, both he and Judith reached for it. The pen got away from Andrew, and the only thing Judith managed was to graze his crotch with her fingers.

Andrew very nearly covered her hand with his and kept her fingers pressed against his manhood. He would have regretted that brazen move had he succumbed to instinct. Judith had to be wooed the way Philip wooed women. Fortunately, Andrew found himself prevented from doing anything crude because Judith yanked her hand away and sprang to her feet.

He glanced up at her to see that blood had rushed to Judith's face once more. He had never seen her blush so furiously when in Philip's company. Did this prove a good sign or ill?

Andrew bent over to retrieve the clever writing tool and discovered blood had rushed to a different part of his own anatomy. He jumped to his feet as well, so that his tunic hung loose over his groin and disguised the desire Judith inspired.

"You can keep the pen," she offered briskly when he attempted to return it. "I have more."

He swallowed hard and found his voice. "You do? I presumed there would be only one in all the world."

"Nope. There are at least three, because I have two more."

"Thank you."

"Take a few more sheets of paper to write on, too," Judith suggested. Her words came out in a rush as she tore several pages from her book and thrust them into Andrew's hands. "I really should go inside now."

Andrew let her go, gladly. He had never dreamt a conversation with a woman could be so difficult, so tiring, so delightful! He felt as though he had run up and tumbled down a dozen high hills. His pulse raced and his brow was damp with sweat. He felt elated and exhausted.

Yet as he watched her walk away, Andrew sighed. Whether or not she knew it, Judith Lamb was surely

Sir Peter Lamb's daughter. Only a clever inventor could have created the fine writing paper and writing implements Judith claimed. Her possessions alone proved close kinship between herself and Sir Peter, while her ability to read and write proved she'd been highly educated. Only royals and nobles were educated, and only an aged eccentric would educate a daughter to the extent Judith had been tutored.

Andrew looked down and kicked the dirt. He didn't want her to be a lady! He wanted Judith to be unassuming, the daughter of a crofter, a freeman, or a servant, but not the daughter of a knight and his lady. Andrew couldn't have his way with a lady, not unless she were already widowed, intended to take holy vows, or had accepted his offer of marriage. As yet, he had no reason to believe Judith had either been widowed or on her way to join a nunnery. And he certainly had no intention of proposing marriage. Besides, he had made those damnable vows not to try to bed Judith. Such a pledge meant little if made to a peasant. But it meant much, if made to a lady.

God's bloody tears! I may as well find Louis and send him to York straightaway. There is no longer any reason for me to keep the wench near.

That is what he thought. But that is not what he did.

Nine

Judy came awake before opening her eyes. As she did every morning, she steeled herself for what she would see when she looked around. Always, she longed to find herself in her bed, in her room, in her rent-controlled New York City apartment. At least, she hoped to find herself back at the Wixcomb inn. But when she peeked, she inevitably discovered herself, as she did this morning, lying on a straw-stuffed mattress in a bed topped with a canopy and surrounded by closed curtains. Not in the States, but England. Not in Laycock Inn, but Laycock Castle. Not in the twentieth century, but the thirteenth.

Hardly surprised and not as keenly disappointed as she used to be, Judy swung her legs off the bed, pushed aside the curtains, and stretched her arms overhead. Her back ached and her head hurt a little. Stepping out into the room, she found—again, no surprise—that the stone floor felt cold beneath her toes. Shivering, she hopped around and grabbed the silk robe Andrew had never reclaimed, covering her nakedness. And just in time, for Bridget, at that very moment, opened the door.

"Good day, milady!" she chirped, far too perky for any human being at this early hour, but most especially for a servant in medieval times. "I expected you'd want a bath again this morn. Elmo and Jock are bringing the tub. Mayhap I ought to leave it in your chamber?"

"Yes, maybe you should," Judy agreed. It had to be a pain to lug the thing from wherever they stored it.

Bridget set out Judy's bath towels. "As you won't be wanting me to assist you, I've other things that need doing, milady. Sally's bringing up your morning meal—the victuals should be here shortly."

"Thanks."

Judy swallowed a couple of aspirins and washed them down with water. She poured more cold water into a bowl and, after splashing her face, she quickly brushed her teeth. The men had just arrived with the tub when she felt an urgent need to relieve herself, so she grabbed her tote and hurried down the hall to the toilet.

On the facial tissue she used for another purpose, Judy spied a pink stain. Her period! That explained her aches and pains. At least she had a supply of tampons. Judy unwrapped one from the box she found in her tote, wondering if she'd have enough to last. *'Til when?* When would she be going back to her own time, her own world, her own home? She kept returning to the spot outside the bailey walls where she'd awakened that morning weeks ago. But except for a feeling she could neither interpret nor explain, it offered no clues and no real hope for finding a way into the future. The present—the countryside, the keep, even the people who populated it—seemed so authentic, so substantial... It was beginning to feel to Judy as though her real life had all been a dream. Sometimes she thought the easiest thing would be for her to accept that, and, from this day forward, proceed as though she were a woman born of the Middle Ages. Then, at least, all she'd have to worry about was Philip.

He had been absent longer than she had expected him to be, and so many dangers existed out there. He could have been attacked by outlaws, or gored and left for dead by the kind of wild pig she'd heard endless stories about when the knights in the hall told tales after supper. Philip could have fallen from his horse and broken his neck or been wounded in a sword fight—who knew? She didn't. So she worried...

...When she wasn't thinking about Andrew. It embarrassed her. It irritated her. She found spending time with him extremely uncomfortable, as they vacillated between being adversaries and friends. Yet when he wasn't around, it seemed almost worse. Then, Judy kept looking for him, not to dodge his presence but because she actually hoped to see him. Which only led her back to the sort of encounter that kept her off kilter and made her totally unsure of herself.

She didn't like being unsure of herself. She didn't like dealing with Andrew, she didn't like thinking about him. But, upon her return from the jakes, she stopped cold outside her bedroom door, which hung ajar. Within, she spied Andrew standing beside her tub holding a bucket. When he saw her, he scowled at her angrily.

She could ignore him, snap at him, or play it casual. Judy decided upon the latter tack. "What's up?" she inquired.

In reply, Andrew slammed the bucket down, sloshing water across the floor and into the rushes.

"What was that for?" Judy stepped into the doorway and leaned against the jamb.

"I might better ask, what is *this* for?" Andrew countered.

Since he gestured to the tub, Judy responded, "My bath."

"Another bath."

"What do you mean, 'another bath?' I only have one a day." She walked into the room and set down her tote.

"One a day," Andrew shouted. "Are you mad?"

"No." Judy clutched the edges of her robe tightly across her bosom and squared her shoulders. She didn't want to fight, but if he did... "You are obviously mad, though. And I don't have the vaguest notion why."

"Me? Mad?" Andrew fumed, taking a step toward the door and kicking it shut with one thrust of his long, muscular leg. "If there's anyone gone mad around here, 'tis you, not I!"

Belatedly, Judy understood the confusion. "I didn't mean you were crazy, just angry." She couldn't resist adding, "But you are acting crazy."

"Crazy?"

"Mad!" Exasperated, she also shouted.

"Don't berate me, wench," Andrew warned, grabbing her sleeve. "You've neither cause nor the right to do so."

"I don't?" His anger was contagious. She pulled her sleeve free of his grasp with one quick yank and backed away from him. "You lurk in my room, waiting around to chide me for having a damned bath, and I don't have a right to yell? I sure as hell do!"

"None, even I, would begrudge you an occasional bath. But one, every day for two sennights?"

"Two what?"

"Two sennights. A fortnight."

"A fortnight?"

"Two weeks," he explained, grinding out the words.

Andrew's voice rose again quickly as he continued, "Even if you are in truth a lady, do you think the people of Laycock Keep are all your personal servants? Do you think that they've no work to do other than attend to your frivolous needs?"

"Of course not. I only wanted—"

"God's teeth, I care not what you want, Judith!" Andrew took a step toward her so that they nearly touched. But he kept a few inches between them, placed his hands on his hips, and glared at her. "I do not want the keep's servants occupied toting water from the well, heating it, and carrying it up the stairs—for you! They have work to do. A lot of other work to do. Work my sire and my mother, chatelaine of this keep, expect to be done. Work I must ensure is done. Work that is not being done if the servants are spending all their time seeing to your damnable baths!" Andrew dropped his arms and tilted his head back. With narrowed eyes, he looked Judy up and down. "Good God, woman! No one can get so begrimed so fast, especially not a female who has no chores to do. You don't dig in the garden, you don't dye cloth or brew beer. By the saints, Judith—what do you do all day?"

Judy had never in her life been accused of laziness. The injustice of his criticism, the indignity of it, floored her—until she remembered she did do very little except try and while away the time.

"I—I'm a guest. It's my understanding guests are not set to work."

"A guest, are you? Did someone invite you to Laycock Keep?"

"No! You carried me here when I was out cold. I had no choice in the matter."

Andrew crossed his arms over his chest. "Do you think yourself a prisoner, madam? If so, let me assure you, you are not. Go—take yourself off to London, if that is where you were truly headed when you stumbled into Wixcomb."

"Fine!" Judy screeched the word but then failed to move, making no attempt to gather her belongings, dress and get out. She had feared this moment, and yet she'd brought it on herself.

Andrew continued to glare at her. "Well?" he said finally. "Are you leaving or nay?"

"I'm leaving. But not 'til I've had my bath. It's foolish to waste it, especially when I won't be having another one for a long time to come."

"Get in the tub, then."

"Not 'til you leave."

"Then you shan't be bathing, because I am not leaving. This is my family's home, and while the others are away, I'm the—"

"—Lord and master here," Judy finished for him, singsonging the familiar phrase.

"God's teeth! I *am* the lord and master here—don't you forget it."

Andrew strode toward Judy and she retreated, still facing him, until she felt the bed brush the backs of her thighs. Because he seemed to keep coming forward, she sat down with a plop before he knocked her down.

He did halt, straddling Judy's knees and bending slightly at the waist so that they were nearly nose to nose. "I told you before, you should seek to please me, not anger me."

"What did I do to anger you?" She really didn't know. She wasn't sure she cared to know.

But she wasn't about to find out, either, because Andrew did not say. He simply glowered at her menacingly, his face flushed and his breathing noisy. Judy could actually feel his breath brush her cheeks. It smelled minty, and despite the certain fact he failed to bathe as frequently as she, he smelled...good. If a fashion icon bottled the fragrance to sell at Bloomingdale's and Macy's, the cologne would be called "Andrew"—a musky, masculine perfume concocted not from flowers and oils but mined from men's pores.

Dear God, what is wrong with me?

Even as part of her mind objectively evaluated—and condemned—her own wayward notions, Judy felt and fought an impulse to reach up, twine her arms around Andrew's neck, and pull him down against her so that they both sprawled on the mattress, their arms and legs tangled together.

"You needn't leave," he told her suddenly, his voice

dropping an octave. “I care not if you stay ’til your dearling Philip returns, or we have word from Peter Lamb. I do, however, care that you cease bathing every damnable day of the week. If you need to wet yourself all over, there is a stream some little distance from the keep. Go there. Jump in. *Drown,*” he bellowed.

Flinching in the face of his verbal assault, Judy instinctively closed her eyes. In that brief second she couldn’t see, she felt Andrew’s lips touch hers. Shock pried her eyes open, and when she looked, she found herself gazing into his dark, molten eyes. A frisson of pleasure, of delicious desire, coursed through her limbs and into the pit of her belly. The feeling was incited not only by his kiss but by his own heavy-lidded eyes studying hers. He did not only scrutinize her face—he seemed to be searching her soul.

That’s it! Falling back so that the rumpled bedclothes pillowed her head, Judy drew up her knees and rolled away. She promptly jumped to her feet, backed away from the bed, and commanded, “Get out! Now. My bath water’s getting cold.”

Andrew straightened, turned and stared at her, the thoughtful expression on his face tightening into a grimace. “I will not,” he countered, his words clipped. “I have the right to be anywhere in this dwelling while you, who have yet to prove you hold any rank at all, have no right to order me about.”

“Very well. Stay. But I’m not passing on my bath.”

Judy wasn’t sure she had made the right move. Ideally, Andrew would storm out of the room. But Andrew was anything but ideal. The possibility loomed large he’d remain, forcing his presence upon her during what should have been, by all inalienable rights, a time of deserved privacy.

Judy retrieved her shampoo and body wash. Setting them on the floor within reach, she kept her back to Andrew as she opened her robe and stepped into the tub. Carefully, with a precision that would have impressed Gypsy Rose Lee, she shed the robe precisely as she lowered herself into the water, allowing nothing to be seen that shouldn’t be seen by the leering lord.

Andrew remained, as he had insisted he would. Judy

attempted to ignore him, concentrating on using her lavender puff to suds her arms, legs and chest. After the fact, it occurred to her she should have shampooed her hair first. But she hadn't thought of that because she'd been thinking about Andrew lounging against one of the bed posts, arms crossed over his chest, one ankle crossed over the other, his sultry, sable eyes trained on her overexposed body. Now she'd have to wash her hair using the pitcher and bowl, which wouldn't be easy. Damn him!

Covering her breasts with her arm, she attempted to grab the corner of one of the drying cloths Bridget had set out. Unfortunately, she hadn't thought to put them on the floor near her other supplies, so they remained on the table. Unluckily, too, Sally had brought in her trencher of food while Judy had been in the jakes, and she'd pushed the towels even farther away from the tub. The only way Judy could reach them now would be to stand up and give Andrew a big show.

"What are you attempting there, wench?" he asked curiously. All trace of rancor had disappeared from his tone.

She took a deep breath. "To grab a towel."

"What of your hair? Do you not wash it every morn as you do the rest of your body?"

"Normally, yes. Not today."

"Why not?"

"Because I don't like an audience," she snapped, turning to glare at him. "Also, because it's damned near impossible in this tiny little tub."

"Tiny? I bathe in that tub."

"One toe at a time?" she sneered.

"Nay. But then, I do have assistance. I do not insist on trying to bathe alone."

"Where I come from, we bathe alone. But we also have tubs big enough to stretch out in."

"Do you?"

"I don't know!" Geez, she had to watch what she said. "I think so."

"But we do not, so why don't you allow me to help you? I could wash your hair," Andrew volunteered, already approaching.

Judy froze, clutching herself. Why did he do this? Nasty one moment, helpful the next. A minute ago, hollering, but now picking up a stool and setting it down behind her, insisting on washing her hair. What next? Would he clip her toenails?

"I thought servants did that kind of thing," she said. "Not the lords and masters of fine keeps."

"Lords and masters do what we will. And I will wash your hair if it amuses me to." He grabbed a plastic bottle off the floor. "Is this your special soap?"

"Yes. Shampoo."

"Aye. Shampoo."

"What are you doing?" she asked in concern. "Andrew, this isn't going to work! My hair has to be wet before you put the shampoo in, and then it has to be rinsed. You can't—"

Judy shut up when Andrew tugged on her hair, forcing her to drop her head back over the edge of the tub. Next thing she knew, he poured a cascade of warm water into her hair from the bucket he'd set aside earlier. She expected water to splash onto the floor, running everywhere, but she heard it trickling into an empty bucket.

"How much of this concoction do you use?" Andrew asked, sitting down on the stool.

"Just a dab."

"A dab?" He leaned over her, looking into her face with a questioning expression on his own.

Judy smiled thinly, nervously. "Yeah," she said, "a dab. A very little bit. Squeeze out a dollop about the size of the end of your thumb."

Raising her own hands to demonstrate, she encircled one thumb at the knuckle with the finger and thumb of her other hand. Immediately, she realized she'd completely bared her breasts and that Andrew had a clear view of them. With a squeal, she quickly covered herself again.

He chuckled but said nothing. Judy could hardly believe it—Andrew Laycock was smiling, actually laughing! She hadn't ever seen him smile quite that way or laugh aloud before. And no one would guess that they'd been screaming their heads off at each other a little while earlier...most especially if they saw Andrew massaging her scalp as he lathered her hair.

Oh, what a delight! This was a favorite pleasure of Judy's. She always looked forward to having her hair washed before Vittorio trimmed it. Now, she closed her eyes and succumbed to ecstacy.

"Your hair is two colors," Andrew commented.

Snapping open her eyes, she almost pulled away and sat upright. Instead, she held herself still and asked tensely, "What do you mean?"

"Two colors," he repeated. "More than one hue."

"I got that part," she assured him tartly. And though she already knew the answer, she asked, "Where are there two colors?"

"Most of your hair is fair. But near your scalp, 'tis considerably darker. Why is that?"

Because my roots need to be done! "It just is, that's all."

Closing her eyes again, Judy found she had lost the delighted feeling, and she couldn't relax. All she wanted to do was get out of the water, now growing tepid, and take a good, long look at her roots. She had been so overwhelmed by her circumstances, she had completely forgotten how long it had been since she'd had her hair touched up. Though black roots should have been the least of her worries, vanity suddenly pushed them nearer the top of her list of troubles.

"Could you rinse it, please?" she begged. "I'm getting cold."

Andrew stood and poured more water through her hair. He used the hem of his tunic to dab a stray rivulet that trickled down her face. Grabbing a towel, he wrapped it around her head before offering another cloth to Judy.

As she accepted it, she asked, "Could you turn around?"

He gave her a look, the kind that would have compelled her to give out her personal phone number had it been on the face of a man she'd encountered at a party, in the elevator in her office building, or even in the produce section of the grocery store. Then Andrew turned away.

Judy didn't take the time to dry herself very well

before stepping out of the tub and shrugging on his robe. He made her crazy! First she wanted to wring his neck, then she wanted to kiss him. Hell, she *had* kissed him, or at least she'd kissed him back.

Why were they kissing, anyway? If she kissed anyone, she ought to be kissing Philip. He was the better man. He never tried to jump her bones, he stopped when she said no, and he wanted to court her. Didn't that mean he wanted to marry her? Besides, Andrew, here, had promised not to try to "bed her" ever again.

But if he did, Judy knew she'd be tempted to let him. Only she couldn't, because she had the curse. And, she noted with chagrin, he hadn't tried. Oh, he had kissed her, sure enough. But she suspected he'd been as surprised about that as she had been. Now, he reverted to being gentlemanly—at least as gentlemanly as Andrew Laycock could ever be.

Damn him.

"On the morrow, the stream," he reminded Judy as he opened the door to leave. Then he was gone, just like that.

***

Andrew fairly ran down the stairs to the great hall. Shouting at the first servant he encountered, he waited impatiently 'til the man brought him a cup and a jug of wine. Pouring his own badly needed spirits, he splashed wine on the high table and did not even move his feet when he felt the liquid dripping over the edge and onto his shoes.

He could have had her! Andrew had not expected such an opportunity, not when he had gone to Judith, furious at having learned she bathed each and every day. But it seemed his temper served to fuel his lust, and Judith— appeared to react the same. Jesu! When he'd kissed her, it had been all Andrew could do not to force the damsel onto the bed and climb above her. But she was a damsel, he had reminded himself, a lady. He could not defile her. He could not break his vow.

So instead he had done what—washed her hair? Whatever had possessed him to volunteer for a servant's duty? But he hadn't felt like a servant. He had felt like a lover, and he yearned for all the privileges being a lover would bring him. But again, he had restrained himself. By all the saints, he must be mad.

He refilled his cup and emptied it once more, wiping the trickle from his chin with the sleeve of his tunic. Attempting to expel Lady Judith Lamb from his thoughts, he glanced idly about the hall until his eyes rested, not on something there but on something gone—the dice that should have sat atop the backgammon board.

Striding over to the small game table, where last he had played with Philip several sennights ago, Andrew examined the board. And the stools. And the floor beneath the table. He even stooped down and ran his fingers through the rushes, searching for fallen dice. But his eyes had not deceived him, the bones truly had gone missing!

He whirled again, and immediately his glance settled on the chair his sister, Beatrix, normally used when she was in residence. She had embroidered a tiny pillow that she tucked behind the small of her back when sitting there. Always, it remained at the ready in that very chair. But not now, not today. It had vanished.

Andrew closed his eyes and rubbed his forehead with two fingers and his thumb. Could Bea have taken it with her? Nay. He had seen it often since she went with their mother to Alnwick. In fact, he had seen the pillow as recently as yesterday.

Of course, a servant might have removed it to his sisters' bedchamber, but Andrew more than doubted that possibility. Someone had made off with the pillow, just as someone had made off with the dice.

Laycock's servants did not steal. Those who served here today were the descendants of those who had served here a hundred years past. Well-provided for by the ruling baron, their loyalty only grew from generation to generation. Nor had anyone visited the keep recently, not even Philip, who certainly was no thief. That left only one reasonable suspect, one stranger, one guest whose identity had yet to be verified, whose behavior seemed strange, and who had access to the furnishings in this stronghold.

Judith Lamb.

Ten

"Andrew! Andrew!"

Hearing his name, he interrupted his conversation with Laycock's bailiff and turned to see who called him. He saw Philip approaching on horseback, bearing down on Andrew and his man as they stood in the middle of Wixcomb's main road.

Before he quite halted, Philip leapt from his saddle. "Arnulf, in the tower, told me you'd gone to the village. Why so?"

"I could delay holding court no longer," Andrew explained. "God Himself only knows when my family will be returning, yet our people had disputes that needed settling. Jesu, but I hate being called upon to play the magistrate and mete out justice. Surely I made some error in judgment."

"I'd wager your father fears the same of you. But the peasants are none the wiser—are they, Jonathan?" Philip quipped, glancing at the bailiff.

"I suppose not," Jonathan agreed. "But Lord Andrew doesn't give himself enough credit. He performed admirably."

Philip wrapped a friendly arm around Andrew's shoulder. "You're finished, then?"

"Aye. Court has been adjourned. God willing, Father will be back at Laycock before it need convene again."

"Lord Thomas is still away, then? And your brothers as well?" Philip asked as he and Andrew walked toward the eastern edge of the village, Philip leading his steed behind them.

"Aye. And yours?"

"I presume so. They are all determined to be at hand during the negotiations—I doubt my sire will return much before yours. Unless, of course, the talks don't go well. Then he'll be back, readying all our forces to attack King John's holdings."

"You haven't been home to North Cross, I take it?" Andrew asked.

Philip shook his head and brushed a long hank of blonde hair off his forehead. "Nay, I came here straightaway."

Andrew tensed. "You've come to see Judith?"

"Of course. She is always in my thoughts. Now, most especially."

"Why now?"

"Andrew, there is much I must tell you. But, first—has your messenger returned, the one you sent to York?"

"Nay." Having reached the spot where he had left Zeus in the care of his squire, Andrew took the horse's reins. Purposely, he turned his back to Philip. "'Tis soon, yet. We should hear something any day."

"What do you mean, 'tis soon? Your man is long overdue. I've ridden nearly the same distance and returned, yet I departed well after he did."

"What does it matter?" Andrew climbed into his saddle and waited for Philip to do the same.

"I'll tell you, old friend—it matters a good deal, because that business my mother sent me on had to do with finding a wife."

"For you? How is that?" Andrew asked, kneeing his horse and walking the animal slowly out of the village. Secretly, this turn of events buoyed his spirits, which had plummeted at the very sight of Philip.

"There is a damsel, eligible and dowered, whose mother is eager to see her wed. My mother bid me to go and see the maid and ask for her hand. She hoped the girl would prove convenient, if not all I might desire in a wife."

"Is she—convenient?"

Philip screwed up his handsome face. "Aye. A bit young, mayhap. Just ten and six years. But comely. And, fortunately, she has a small estate that would suit me well."

"What's the problem, then?"

"God's wounds, Andrew," Philip complained. "You know what the problem is. I'm bewitched by Judith."

He clenched his jaw. "Are you?"

"You must know that I am."

The men turned their horses off the main road while Andrew's squire followed behind, and they took to the hills leading to Laycock Keep.

"I had thought so. But were you truly smitten, I

wouldn't think you'd ride off to pay court to another lady."

"I had no choice. Mother insisted. She doesn't want me serving other lords as a mercenary or serving God as a priest."

Andrew knew there was no chance of that. Why didn't Philip? "Has this lady a name?" he asked, turning to his friend.

"Penelope. Penelope Winfield, daughter of the late Lord Graham and his widow, Lady Vivian."

"How did it go when you met her? Was she taken with you or nay?"

Philip exhaled, fluttering his lip. Grudgingly, he admitted, "She seemed to like me well enough."

"Ha! I'll wager she did."

"Be quiet, Andrew. I'm attempting to explain. I wasn't alone, you see. Several other young men also came to pay court. Her mother had a banquet, there was dancing..."

"And?" Andrew arched an eyebrow curiously.

"I attempted to be circumspect. I thought, if she took no particular notice of me, I could tell my own mother truthfully that naught had come of the venture."

"But Penelope fell for you madly, despite your best efforts."

"That's the God's truth," Philip wailed, as though he were both surprised and disappointed. "She told Lady Vivian 'tis me she wishes to wed. Now I find myself in the most damnable position."

"Why? Did you ask for Penelope's hand? Are you two betrothed?"

"Nay, of course not." They had reached Laycock's gate and ridden through it into the bailey. "But I've no good reason to turn down a damsel—and a dower—the likes of which Penelope presents. Not unless I've another prospect equally as attractive."

Andrew knew that no matter how fair of face the Winfield girl might be, she could be no match for Judith. But he also knew Philip didn't refer only to physical attractiveness. "I am sorry we've had no word from Sir Peter," he lied as he dismounted. "If we hear nothing soon, I'll send another messenger."

"Nay." Philip scowled as he climbed down from his

steed. "If you've no word by nightfall, I'll escort Judith to York myself. We need learn the truth about her as soon as possible."

"What if the truth is not what you hope? What if she's no kin to Sir Peter? Or, if she is, what if she has no wealth of her own?"

Shaking his head as he tilted his face to the sky, Philip said, "I pray it isn't so. But..."

"What?"

"I don't know. I truly don't. Yet there's no purpose in fretting over circumstances that have yet to occur."

The squire led both their horses away. Philip and Andrew walked to the keep's steps and paused. "Is Judith inside?" Philip asked.

"I believe so. Why don't you go in and see her? I've things to attend to. With everyone away, my duties never end. I shall join you two later."

"Very well." Philip nodded and climbed the steps.

As soon as he disappeared through the doorway, Andrew spun on his heel and sprinted toward the gate. "Arnulf," he called up to the guard standing watch in the tower. "Is Lady Judith at the stream?"

"Aye, my lord. She left only a brief while ago. Nigel followed her."

"Arnulf, if Sir Philip asks after the lady, tell him you've no notion where she is."

The guard grinned. "Aye, Lord Andrew. I've no notion where she is—or where you've gone, either."

It irked Andrew a little that Arnulf understood his motives so well. But they were all men, all knights—they thought of women with a single mind.

***

The stream cut a swatch through the forest. In the summer, it appeared little more than a bubbling brook. But now, in springtime, swollen with melted snow, Andrew saw that it had grown wide and deep. Judith bathed in the stream because he had forbade her the luxury of those excessive morning ablutions in her bedchamber. But since he issued that edict, she had come here infrequently. He chuckled—no longer did the lady seem eager or adamant about taking excessive baths. But then, a trek through the woods and a plunge into a freezing stream was bound to stifle anyone's penchant for daily dousing.

Though he had arranged for a man to follow and guard her so that no harm might come to Judith, Andrew had yet to observe her himself. Still, he knew where to find her because a footpath led directly to the banks near a particularly deep place in the stream, one that proved excellent for both wading and fishing.

He walked that path now. Just as he presumed he would, he saw Nigel standing in the foliage a short distance off the pathway. The man had pressed his back to a tree trunk so that he would not be noticed easily. But Andrew noticed him, and as well he noticed the big, stupid grin on Nigel's face.

Andrew hurried forward, diverting from the path only a few feet before he would have broken from the cover of the trees. Immediately, he spied Judith and understood why that fool knight behind him looked like a happy dimwit. Any man would feel giddy and mindless seeing the vision his own eyes beheld.

Judith stood waist-deep in water, soaping her hair. She glistened, smooth and shiny as alabaster. By the saints, the wench did not even have fuzz under her arms! Yet she owned breasts far more glorious than most damsels claimed. They rose high and taut so that droplets of moisture trickled down their slopes, clinging to nipples that had peaked in the chill. Andrew licked his lips, savoring the urge to taste the plump flesh that looked as firm as ripe apples. And he felt his cock grow hard.

Abruptly he whirled, pounded through the trees, and caught Nigel by surprise. As he gripped the guard's neck with his arm, he hissed in Nigel's ear, "How dare you look at Lady Judith that way."

"In—what way—my lord?"

"You are leering at her."

"N-n-nay, I am not, Lord—Andrew! I—was told—to guard her. To—keep her—from harm."

It was true, as true as Nigel's ogling had been obvious. Releasing the knight, Andrew said gruffly, "Go now. Henceforth, I will accompany the lady if she need come to the stream to bathe."

Nigel nodded with jerky motions and hurried away while Andrew decided that Judith could resume bathing in the privacy of her chamber. Outdoors, many people other than an assigned guard could have the opportunity to view her naked charms, be they travelers or town's folk. He should have thought of all this earlier. Now, he would not permit it to continue.

***

Judy pushed herself off the bed of the stream after crouching to rinse her hair. She sprang into the air, spraying water everywhere. Shaking her head to clear her ears, she thought she heard rustling in the trees. She stilled, covering her naked breasts, partially because she had no wish to be spied on and partially because she felt so damned cold.

She scoured the bank with her gaze but detected no movement. Perhaps she'd never heard anything in the first place. If she had, it might have been a deer. It was probably a deer. They roamed everywhere in the woods, and her presence encroached on their territory, not the other way around.

Because of that damned Andrew, Judy fumed as she caught her nearly empty, plastic shampoo bottle floating on the water's surface. That he forced her to wade in a creek instead of letting her take a bath in a tub of warm water, well... To be fair, Judy realized he had a point. Plumbing didn't exist, so she couldn't turn on a tap and draw a bath without assistance. She did need all those people to haul water from the well, heat it in a fire, and then drag it upstairs to her room, one bucketful at a time. That wasn't very considerate. She wouldn't be too happy doing it for someone else. But, once in a while, at least. On occasion, the "lord and master" of Laycock should let her have a hot bath in the privacy of her room.

Shivering, Judy hurried to the side of the stream and climbed up the sandy bank. She grabbed her towel and dried herself briskly, hoping the friction would warm her. Actually, the day seemed mild enough. But the trees blocked much of the sunlight, and she figured another degree or two colder and the water would be ice.

She stepped into her thong and smoothed the hip band over her belly before drying herself some more. Boy, it was chilly! Hurrying to get dressed, eager to get her borrowed gown on, Judy retrieved her bra from her tote. The freedom of going without had lost its appeal. She liked the support of an underwire, and besides, nobody would notice her unusual lingerie beneath a loosely belted tunic.

The mint-green satin brassiere, which matched her minuscule panties, clasped in front. Leaning forward, Judy swung her breasts into the cups and then clipped the plastic hook. As she straightened, adjusting the shoulder straps, she again heard crashing in the trees. The sound came from very nearby. Whatever thundered through the woods seemed to be heading for the stream, coming straight toward her. Gasping in fright, Judy clutched her towel to her bosom and stared at the tree line.

***

Andrew had been enthralled by the sight of Judith standing on the stream's sandy bank. She appeared like some mythical sea creature who had transformed itself into the epitome of womanhood after leaving the water to emerge on the shore.

Then he noticed the strip of iridescent green fabric that circled her hips and formed a tiny triangle at the apex of her thighs. He knew Judith was formed as well as any other female at that particular juncture. He had seen her tuft of maidenhair when she'd struggled with him in bed and her tunic rode high. That she covered her woman's flesh with just enough material to suffice intrigued him. That garment cupped her sex as he would, if he caressed it in his palm.

Andrew wanted to groan but kept silent. As he watched, Judith dried herself with a cloth. She touched her flesh as he wished to touch her flesh; it made him light-headed with desire. Then she turned to open her satchel, which sat on a large bolder, and presented him with her backside. The sight of those twin globes, blushing pink after her frigid bath, would have inflamed his lust all on its own. But when he saw that scrap of undergarment nestled in the cleft of her buttocks as it stretched upward to join the band at her hips, Andrew actually felt his manhood move. His cock jerked upright, demanding attention.

To ease his agony, he clutched himself and closed his eyes. He hoped he did not breathe so loudly Judith would hear him panting in the trees. Resolved to controlling his burgeoning passion, Andrew opened his eyes again. Judith was now donning some other apparel. As he watched, she leaned forward and dropped her breasts into cups fashioned of fabric the same hue as the strings girding her loins. When she stood, she had covered her breasts in much the same fashion as her sex—completely but minimally.

The effect proved evocative, tantalizing. Though she stood before him nearly nude and very nubile, his stolen, secret scrutiny no longer satisfied him. Andrew keenly aspired to strip her of those cloth scraps so that he might view all her essential femininity.

No longer did he think or reason. Propelled by instinct and primitive desire, Andrew walked forward without weighing the possible consequences. Fast and direct, he headed toward Judith.

"Andrew," she shrieked when she saw him. Though initially surprised, she seemed to recover quickly. "God, you scared me. I didn't know who you were, what you were."

He halted directly before Judith and took the drying cloth from her hand, dropping it on the ground. "By all the saints, madam. You are the most exquisite creature I have ever seen."

She did not respond, and he did not have the voice to say more. Instead he touched her, reaching out with sure but gentle hands. With purpose, he gripped the straps on her shoulders and ran his fingers up and down their length before sliding them down her arms.

The cups on her upper garment sagged a bit. Just as purposefully, Andrew slipped a finger inside the top of each, stroking the swell of her breasts. Judith did not pull away. In fact, she seemed to lean forward a bit, giving him better access.

He tugged on the cups. The curious garment slipped down her ribs, just a little, and her nipples popped out, exposed. He palmed them, swirling his hands over the hard, pink nubs.

"Ummm." The sound Judith made brought his eyes up to hers. Her eyes were closed. Still watching her face, he pulled the unique, useless garment down to her waist, freeing her arms as the straps slipped off her wrists. He bent his knees and lowered his face to her bosom. Finally, he began to suckle those nipples that had so enticed him earlier.

Andrew tongued them, nipped them, drew on them. Judith made another noise, deep in her throat. The mere sound, indicative of her mounting passions, made his cock throb. Yet he still moved as slowly as a cat stalking a bird. Lowering himself to his knees in the damp sand, he skimmed Judith's ribs with his fingertips as his lips heated a trail toward her navel.

Judith cast aside the garment from which Andrew had nearly freed her. As his kisses drew lower, she leaned forward even more and clutched at his hair. He raised his head again; her breasts bobbed temptingly directly above his face. What could he do but stretch upward and grab first one, then the other, in his mouth?

"Andrew," Judith breathed, and beneath his hands on her hips, he felt her begin to undulate. He could not resist slipping his palms around her backside and clutching the smooth, round halves of her bottom. He squeezed them, kneaded them, and Judith increased the tempo of her swaying.

If he did not get his cock out of his braies and into Judith soon, he felt sure his cod would explode. He'd heard tell of men dying of bursting cods. He did not intend to meet his own demise because of unsatisfied carnal need.

Drawing his fingers up along the cleft of Judith's derriere, he brought them forward, along the band encircling her hips. Then he slipped his fingers between the fabric and her skin and tugged, intending to lower and remove the flimsy barrier that presently kept him at bay.

"No!" As though startled and completely unprepared for his actions, Judith suddenly pushed at Andrew's shoulders and stumbled backward. "Andrew, don't. I—

can't."

He did not respond straight away. To be rebuffed at this late stage came as a shock. Though his mind grasped the obvious, that the course of events had been abruptly altered from what he had envisioned, his body had not yet acknowledged the same facts.

Breathing deeply, he purposely reined in his passions, praying his ballocks would remain intact. Then, gritting his teeth, he looked up at Judith, who, faster than he could have imagined, had put on her scanty breast binder and proceeded to draw her tunic on over her head.

"Why not?" he asked, his voice nearly unrecognizable. "Are you married? Did the memory of a husband only now come back to you?"

"No! No, that's not it." Shaking her head as she sat on the boulder and tugged on her shoes, Judith assured him, "I'm not married, Andrew."

"Then you are angry that I broke my vow to you."

"Your vow?" She looked confused at first, then she arched her eyebrows and said, "Why, yes, Andrew. You did promise not to try to—you know. But you did anyway." With a scowl, she added, "I thought knights of old took their pledges seriously."

"Knights of old?"

"Forget it."

"I don't understand you," he admitted, feeling frustrated. "Are you afraid of men, of me? I would ne'er hurt you."

"I know you wouldn't. I think. And I'm definitely not afraid of men. It's only—"

"What?" Andrew demanded as he came to his feet.

"Philip—"

He felt a flash of anger. "You know he's here, don't you?"

"Philip's here? At Laycock?" Judith feigned surprise.

"Aye, he's at Laycock. Surely you saw him riding in." Andrew narrowed his gaze as he considered Judith suspiciously. "I suppose you did all this—" He gestured with a sweep of his arm to the stream. "—To entice him. And I happened by instead."

"I did this—" She mimicked his gesture. "—To entice Philip? Damn you, Andrew Laycock, you're an idiot! As if I feel like some hot babe when I'm freezing my buns off washing in an icy stream in the middle of a forest. And listening to animals rustling through the woods, wondering if they intend to attack. Or worrying that maybe they aren't animals at all, but some dirty old men spying on me. Right! That's it. I came out here to impress Philip. Who, for all I knew, was somewhere hundreds of miles away doing something for his mother."

Grabbing her black bag, Judith began stomping up the footpath toward the keep.

Andrew watched her go. He felt furious, not only because he'd been denied the full pleasure of Judith's body, but because she dared to be angry with him. She had no right, no reason. She had got her way again—she'd kept him from making love to her. What had he got? A tremendous ache in his loins with no possibility of sweet release. He should be angry. Only he had the right to be angry.

He hurried after Judith. Catching up with her, he grabbed her shoulder, forcing her to spin around and face him.

"You are not to bathe in the stream again unless I accompany you," he informed her.

"The hell I won't! It suited me just fine until you showed up today."

"Do you think you were alone before? You were not, Judith. Before, like today, one of my men stood guard."

"Stood guard?" Her green eyes grew round. "You had someone *watching* me?"

Andrew nodded. "For your protection."

"For his enjoyment, you mean. And yours."

Again she spun around and headed off. Again, he grabbed her.

"Damn you, Judith Lamb. You will do as I say!"

"Damn you, Andrew Laycock! I will never do as you say!"

He narrowed his gaze. "But you'll do whatever Philip asks of you, I suppose?"

"Maybe. Because he asks nice."

Eleven

Judy muttered beneath her breath as she stormed up the hill toward the bailey. Her behavior with Andrew had been completely idiotic. No wonder he thought all bets were off. After the way she had acted, any man would. It sure hadn't been fair, her trying to blame him for what happened at the stream. She knew full well she'd been as just as responsible as he'd been. That she had yielded to his moves that way...

But they were smooth moves—no longer the abrupt, abrasive kind of groping Andrew had attempted when she'd first arrived. Any normal, healthy girl would have succumbed. It wasn't as though he were ugly or anything. Yet he had promised not to touch her anymore, and if he hadn't touched her, nothing would have happened. Heck, he didn't know of the fantasies spinning out in her head or the yearnings that churned somewhat lower. He had no excuse for breaking his pledge.

There was more that was worse. Not only had Andrew failed to live up to his word, he had manipulated her. The rudimentary psychology he'd used on her had been child's play—act aloof so that she'd want his attention. The galling thing was, she had fallen into his trap like some naive, high school girl. She had never been played so easily by a '90s guy. That Andrew, a veritable youth with little sophistication or finesse had "gotten her number," as Judy's mom liked to say—made her furious. With herself.

What man wouldn't play it any way he could to get what he wanted? That she'd fallen for his antics was the pathetic part of today's episode. But, what an episode!

Judy shivered remembering it. His lips on her skin, the way he had touched her. It might have been hopelessly romantic if he had wanted her, Judy Lambini, for herself. But, no. He wanted Judith Lamb for a quickie. Maybe a couple of quickies. And she needed more than that. At the very least, she needed the potential for more than that. It didn't matter that she was a visitor from another country, another century, whose time here would (please, God!) be short. Andrew didn't know her true circumstances. He didn't suspect she might disappear as quickly and mysteriously as she'd arrived. Yet he still desired her for only a moment of lovemaking. No, a minute or two of sex. Hot sex. Torrid sex. But meaningless sex, just the same.

He wasn't going to get it from her. Philip, on the other hand—

Philip! Andrew had said he'd returned. Why hadn't he come to find her at the stream? Judy felt sure her response would have been the same if it had been Philip removing her bra and kissing her breasts a little while ago. He was no Frankenstein, either. And he had other, admirable qualities—his admitted intention to date her—no, court her—properly. The promise of permanence, of marriage.

Judy stopped cold. Did she want to marry Philip? God, she had never thought about marrying except as an abstract, way-in-the-future sort of thing. But that thinking had been done in the modern, late, twentieth century. Maybe she needed to rethink the topic right now, in the ancient, medieval thirteenth.

Plunking herself down in the grass, Judy pondered. She approached the subject methodically, dispassionately, considering the facts and conjecturing possible and probable consequences. All in all, things did not look good for her if she failed to marry anyone. In this world, women needed to be attached to a man in some fashion, be it a father, a guardian, or a husband. Without one, she had no means to earn a living, no place at all in society. Especially if she hoped to remain a member of the upper class, such as it was. Judy didn't like to think of herself as conceited. But honestly, if she found herself doomed to stay in this time, she certainly intended to stay among the nobles. Life as a serf held no allure.

"I will get home," she told herself. *But what if I don't? What if I only had a one-way ticket, not a round-trip one?*

She wouldn't know for sure, not for a while. In the meantime, it could only be in her best interests to cultivate a prospective husband. The choicest man she knew was Philip of North Cross. If she gave in to Andrew's attempts at seduction, she would blow her one, slim chance for security. Well, Judy thought with conviction,

Andrew Laycock would not be tempting her anymore. She'd grown wise to his ways. Henceforth, she'd be on the lookout and avoid his wily lures.

Judy resumed her trek to the keep. When she entered the bailey, it puzzled her to find the activity more chaotic than usual. Laborers and servants scurried about while strange, saddled horses stood in the yard. Judy didn't think even Philip's recent arrival could have precipitated that much activity.

"Judith!"

She heard him call and turned to see Philip hurrying toward her. Geez, he looked perfect. Not only his face, but his clothes—A handsome, saffron-colored tunic edged in black at the cuffs and hem, black leggings, and black boots. He'd have made a great cover model for this year's *Gentlemen's Quarterly*, she found herself thinking.

Catching Judy up in an embrace, Philip said, "I've been searching everywhere for you. Andrew told me you were in the keep."

He did, he? "I went to the stream. When did you arrive?"

"Not very long ago. I came here directly after returning from my errand because I was gone so much longer than expected. Now, I'm doubly glad I did."

"Why?"

"Haven't you heard?

"Haven't we heard what?" Andrew demanded, intruding upon Judy's reunion with Philip. "What is happening here?"

She turned to look at him. Judy had seen Andrew only minutes earlier, but she hadn't been thinking much about his appearance. Now, she took it in. Unlike his friend, Andrew was disheveled. His longish, dark hair looked tangled and uncombed, and his whiskers needed scraping. And—she sniffed discreetly—he actually smelled. His scent should have offended Judy's sensibilities, but it didn't. Somehow, she found the odors of manly sweat, leather and horse rather intriguing, almost appealing.

With a determined blink, Judy focused on Andrew's attire. He wore something they called a gambeson, a heavy, quilted shirt that served as armor. It hung shorter than Philip's tunic, revealing more of Andrew's muscled legs. He had great legs and broad shoulders. The sword on his hip, anchored not only by a belt around his waist but a leather strap that crossed over his chest and back, gave him a swashbuckling air. They didn't grow twenty-two-year-olds like this back home. Andrew could never have been a college senior. He looked, instead, as though he could lead Hannibal across the Alps.

Judy shook her head to clear it of such frivolous thoughts and concentrated on the men's conversation.

"Your brothers have returned to Laycock," Philip was telling Andrew. "They say my father's back at North Cross. Negotiations with the king have not been going well."

"Then war is inevitable?" Andrew asked.

He shrugged. "Everyone fears for their lives and property. We cannot let Lackland's men destroy us as he has so many barons who opposed him in the past. Jesu! He murdered his own nephew, Arthur of Brittany, because the lad stood in his way. A man who could do that could do anything."

"Who—" Judy began.

But Andrew spoke, interrupting her as though she were not present. "Has my sire also returned?"

"Nay. He remains in London, advising those who sit at the bargaining table. Lord William Marshal and the Archbishop of Canterbury also remain. Those two have become the key negotiators representing the English barons."

"I suppose you'll be heading immediately back to your home?" Andrew asked.

Philip replied with a quick nod and an equally quick glance at Judy. Then he said, "I would speak with Judith briefly before I go."

"She's not my chattel," Andrew pointed out with a casual shrug. "Fare you well, my friend. Let us hope we see each other again before we find ourselves on the same battlefield."

"Wait! Andrew, about the matter we spoke of earlier. I pray you send another messenger if you don't hear from the first before day's end. 'Tis important to me."

"If my man is lost or waylaid, I shall definitely send

another," he promised before clapping Philip on the shoulder and jogging up to the keep's entrance.

Judy had a dozen questions she wished to ask. But the effort it took to remind herself this business really was happening, that the flurry of activity portended bloody battles waged with swords, staffs and maces, prevented her from formulating her questions into words. She merely stood there, staring up at Philip, her mouth agape.

"Come," he urged, tugging on her sleeve and leading her out of the way. When they reached the shadow of the keep's walls, he placed both his hands on her shoulders and looked deep into her eyes. "Are you well, Judith? Does Andrew treat you kindly?"

"Yes."

"Have you remembered anything? Your family, your home...?" His blue eyes studied hers. His queries were not casual.

"No, Philip." Judy had told the lie so often, her concocted amnesia story had begun to feel like the truth. "I still don't recall any particulars, so I don't know if that man who lives in York, Sir Peter Lamb, is related to me. I'm sorry."

"Sweet Jesu, so am I." He shook his head and furrowed his brow. "Judith, would that I knew you were a free damsel, neither unwed nor betrothed."

"I'm sorry," she mumbled again softly. It never occurred to her to confide in Philip, to tell him the truth. If she did, if she admitted to knowing in fact that she remained single—no live-in "significant other" or anything—then she would have to confess the rest. And Judy could not confide those details to Philip. Somehow, intuitively, she knew he could never accept them. When—if—they married, he had to believe her a woman of his own time.

"Andrew was correct, Judith. I must hasten away immediately. No one has managed to make a priest of me yet," he said, smiling, "so I shall have to fight in this barons' war against the king."

"When, Philip? When will the actual fighting begin? Will it be—here?"

"Nay, sweetling. Do not fear. There's little chance battles will rage here at Laycock or North Cross. We will attack, not defend, and we will attack John's fiefs. But there is still time to hope the tide shall turn, and that self-serving cockshead we call our king will put his hand and his seal to our terms. In the meanwhile, though, we must prepare."

"And you must go."

"Aye. But I shall return, I promise."

Drawing her to him, Philip kissed Judy full upon the lips. Though she attempted to kiss him back, she never raised her arms from her sides, so her effort lacked a certain enthusiasm. Judy felt wiped out, as though Andrew had earlier drained her of all passion.

***

Andrew sat with his brothers at the high table. While they ate and talked with their mouths full, he nursed a goblet of wine and watched the door. Where, by all the saints, was Judith? What were she and Philip doing together so long?

Suddenly, Andrew spied Judith at the entrance to the hall, looking around and clutching her satchel to her chest. When she saw the company at the dais table, she began making her way to the stairs, avoiding not only the servants but the cavorting hounds and their puppies as she clung to the shadowy walls, attempting to be inconspicuous. *Clever girl.*

"God's wounds, 'tis the wench! Why...?" Elfred pointed at Judith but turned to Andrew questioningly.

Judith froze and Andrew responded. "You knew she remained when you left."

"Aye, but that was some time ago. Surely you've tired of her charms, if she had any."

Andrew held his temper in check, saying only, "I have attempted to contact her kin."

"You know who they be?" Robin asked, leaning forward to rest his arms on the table as he looked curiously at Andrew.

"Philip does. He says she's the daughter of a knight called Peter Lamb."

"You've sent word to him, to this Sir Peter?"

"Philip wrote a missive, aye," Andrew hedged.

"Why is she wearing our sister's clothes?" Elfred demanded.

"Because she had nothing suitable of her own. Don't

take such offence, brother. They belong to Camilla, not to you."

Andrew saw Judith take another, small step in the direction of the stairs. So did Robin, apparently, for he ordered, "Come here, wench."

Again she halted, but after spinning on her heels, she strode purposefully toward the dais and stopped directly before Robin. "I am not a wench," she informed him. "I am a grown woman, and I have a name, as you well know."

Andrew held a short breath and glanced at his eldest brother sidelong. But Robin merely raised his eyebrows and drawled, "Forgive me, Lady Judith."

"Lady!" Elfred said. "Because Philip of North Cross thinks she's kin to some knight I've never heard of does not make it so. How can you even address her as such in jest? Look at her, Robin. Our sister's gown fails to transform her. She still resembles a peasant, a rain-soaked one at that."

"I do not," Judith countered, and Andrew slid down in his chair, half covering his brow with one hand. "Andrew—Lord Andrew—denied me permission to bathe in my room." She leaned forward, toward Elfred, and sniffed, as though she could smell his body's scent and found it offensive. "Since I am prone to personal cleanliness, I chose to bathe in the stream. My hair is wet only because I just now returned from there."

"He forbade you, a fine lady, to bathe in the keep?" Elfred repeated, considering Andrew thoughtfully. "You no more believe she's gently born than I do, eh, brother?"

"I do not disbelieve she is gently born."

Elfred chortled. "Sweet Mother Mary—is the wench *that* good between the sheets?"

Andrew sat straighter and clenched his fist. But the taste of Judith's skin, her shoulder, her breast, burst on his tongue. For the briefest moment, he found himself distracted. He did not hit Elfred, he did not say a word.

"Whether or not I'm gently born may be in question," Judith conceded. "But it's obvious none of you are gentlemen."

"Woman, watch your tongue," Robin warned.

She bit her lip but turned her head to glare at Andrew

as she complained in a low voice, "It's bad enough your brother insults me. But you let him."

He had, indeed. Judith owned a right to feel angry. But even if a lady born and bred, she had no right to speak to him and his brothers in that manner.

"Look at her!" Elfred said, giving Andrew a start. "Look at her eyes! Methinks she's casting a spell on you, Andrew."

Judith's green eyes blazed. But Andrew understood she cursed him only with silent expletives, not with incantations. Still, he knew no good would come from anything she might now say. So he stood, intending to lead Judith out of the great hall before Robin sided openly with Elfred.

He had yet to round the table and reach her side when Judith thrust a finger at Elfred and countered in a threatening tone, "Nay! I am casting a spell on *you*."

Andrew's brother nearly toppled off his chair and the dais.

"Elfred, must you always behave the fool when in this woman's presence?" Robin chided. "Whether the girl is the get of a baron or a crofter, she is naught but female. Surely she can do you no harm."

"God's bloody wounds!" Elfred scowled darkly at Robin. "Am I the only one among us three with all his wits? She is, if naught else, a stranger who has managed to get herself inside our home during these troubled times. Andrew thinks only with his cock, letting her have free rein at Laycock, well beyond the bed he shares with her. And you, Robin, credit her not at all. You believe her no more harmful than a fly, though with her magic satchel, she stands before us conjuring."

"Conjuring, am I?" Opening her bag, Judith retrieved some implement and gripped it tightly in her fist. Andrew saw Judith flick her thumb, and suddenly—magically?— a flame appeared. It looked as though her hand were ablaze.

Andrew found himself gasping nearly as loudly as his brothers. But he felt amazed, not frightened, and he did not cringe as he saw Elfred doing, staring in undisguised horror at Judith's flaming fist.

She leapt onto the dais before Andrew realized her intent. As she did, the flame went out. But Judith grinned at Elfred, looking purposely evil. And she asked, "Would you like to see it again?"

With another flick of her thumb, the flame reappeared. She used it to light a pair of candles on the table.

"I am a witch," she informed Elfred gleefully. "So you had better stop insulting me and suggesting I am one nasty thing or another, or I'll— turn you into a toad."

The bearded knight crossed himself and looked to his elder brother. "Robin, do something!"

"Andrew?" Robin said, turning to him.

"She is not a witch," he insisted, wishing to God his brothers had not returned here, even briefly. Joining Judith, he whispered in her ear, "And you're a damnable fool for saying you are." Then he grabbed the device she had kept concealed and held it up—a curious black tube about as long and as thick as his finger. "Look," he told them. "'Tis a tool of some kind. Surely Judith's sire, who is known to be an alchemist and an inventor, fashioned it."

"He made a stick that bursts into flame upon command? That cannot be." Elfred shook his head.

"You saw it with your own eyes, did you not?" Andrew asked him. "How can you question what you've seen with your own eyes? This thing exists. It makes fire. Show them, Judith."

She glowered sullenly.

"Do you want to be drowned before your father can claim you, before you are reunited with your family?" He spoke softly but looked at her sharply.

Judith sighed and took the smooth, shiny tube from him. Andrew observed her flick a thumb against a tiny wheel and the modest flame leaped up still again.

"Your sire crafted that fire-maker?" Robin asked Judith.

"I guess."

His dark eyes met Andrew's, so like his own. "This Peter Lamb must be clever in the extreme. He must also lay claim to great wealth, for a fire-starting implement such as that would be sought by any and all. I know I would pay a great sum to own one."

Andrew nodded. "Judith's sire must have great stores of riches. And a rich man would surely reward any who cared for his lost and homeless daughter, don't you agree?"

He nodded thoughtfully, but Elfred resumed his protest. "Mayhap her sire is a wizard, a sorcerer. Methinks he is, and that the fire-starter was created by unearthly methods."

"If so," Andrew asked, "what matter?"

"It matters because all magic is evil. You know the Church repudiates all wizards and witches, along with their enchantments." He turned to Robin and pleaded, "Send her away."

"Nay." The baron's eldest son shook his head emphatically. "'Tis in our best interest to wait for word from the alchemist. He may, as Andrew suggested, wish to reward us for taking care of the wench during her time of misfortune."

"But it is Beltane! If she be a witch, not a simple knight's daughter—"

"Lock her up," Robin told Andrew, interrupting Elfred's lament.

"Lock her up? She is a guest," Andrew returned.

"Mayhap she is a guest. Mayhap she is a peasant who's deceived you so that she may live in comfort for a while. Or mayhap, as Elfred fears, she is a sorceress. Until we know which she might be, she should be confined in her chamber."

"I won't do it."

"Andrew, dare not defy me," Robin warned. "'Tis only for the night, for Beltane."

"What!" Elfred said in dismay. "Only this eve? What if she means us harm?"

"If she meant us harm, she would already have wrought her evil spells and brought us low, don't you think?"

"But—she threatened to turn me into a toad."

"A simple enough task, certainly."

Andrew bit back a grin at Robin's quip. But Elfred continued to remonstrate. "What if her sire—should that alchemist Andrew mentioned indeed be her sire—fails to claim her before we depart again? What if then..."

Andrew heard no more of his brothers' conversation, for he was escorting Judith quickly to the stairs. Already they had climbed enough steps to be well beyond hearing the discourse at the high table.

"Slow down," Judy demanded. "I'm coming. You don't have to drag me!"

"Be still," Andrew snapped, nudging open her bedroom door before pushing her into the room. "You are such a fool!"

"Me? A fool? What did I do?"

"You know very well what you did. You baited Elfred, declared yourself a witch, and then—" He held up the tote by its handle. "—Then you showed him another of your fantastic devices. Do you wish to be cast out? Or worse, drowned?"

"I always thought witches were burned at the stake."

"Don't be frivolous!" Andrew said, slamming the door closed.

"I'm not frivolous, I'm angry. Your idiot brother insulted me, and you didn't say so much as a word in my defense. You forced me to defend my own honor, so while I was at it, I decided to scare the pants off old Freddie."

"'Old Freddie?'" Andrew made a face and shook his head. Then he said sternly, "I am deadly serious. Have you no concern for the consequences of your behavior? Or do you seriously believe Philip will come to your rescue in some fashion?"

"He will. He won't let anything happen to me. He—cares for me," Judy informed him, unsure herself whether or not Philip actually loved her. "He wants to marry me, not just jump my bones."

Andrew's dark eyes seemed to bore holes into Judy's until she had to look away. But she heard him say softly, "Woman, you deceive yourself."

"Are you saying he doesn't?" she demanded, meeting his gaze again.

"Nay. But what Philip wishes to do and what he will do may not prove to be the same thing."

Judy's confidence ebbed. She felt herself skidding down the high she'd enjoyed while frightening Elfred so easily. Yet she stubbornly accused Andrew of jealousy. "You're just saying that because you want to get laid. You want to have your way with me, even though you promised not to try it again. And you did try again, in case you weren't aware," she added petulantly.

"You did not seem unreceptive to my advances."

She blushed. "What would you know? Besides, I didn't let you get what you were after. I wouldn't do that—to—Philip."

It seemed Andrew's turn to flush darkly. "You take great risks, Judith," he said finally. "I hope you know what you're about. I hope, despite your insistence otherwise, that you do recall your home and family and know, in fact, that you are an eligible maiden with wealth and land of your own. Because if you are not, Philip of North Cross will never have you as his bride."

That's okay. I'm not planning on sticking around long enough to really have to marry anyone. It's just plan B, and you're...you're...

Judith couldn't think anymore. Andrew had maneuvered himself directly in front of her. He stood there, looking down into her face as though he could read her mind, which, thank heavens, had gone thoroughly blank. And now— he reached up his hand. Did he intend to touch her cheek? Judy braced herself for the whisper of his fingertips against her skin. She didn't want him to touch her. Like a shell filled with the sounds of the sea, she found herself saturated with the echoes of his earlier touches, his fingers, lips and tongue against her skin. No, she didn't want him touching her. She couldn't take it if he did.

Andrew flipped his hand over, palm up, exposing the disposable lighter he had been clutching all this time. As he moved past Judy and sat on the edge of her bed, he asked, "How do you keep it burning?"

With jerky steps, she sat beside him and concentrated on her explanation. Talking with Andrew about a disposable lighter would keep her from thinking about kissing, stroking and doing the deed—she hoped.

"That tab beneath the wheel," she said. "Hold it down, and the flame will stay 'til you let go again."

Andrew followed her directions and kept the flame alight. He smiled, pleased with himself, with the toy.

"Your strange implements fascinate me, Judith. The paper is so plentiful and fine. The—what did you call it? The pen makes writing so easy. And this fire-starter is a marvel. Spontaneous fire, even a flame as small as this, could change the lives of everyone in the world.

"But the mere fact these exquisite articles exist and you own them would surely frighten more people than Elfred. They would want you locked away for more than just Beltane." He paused and met Judy's gaze. "What does Philip think of these enchanted objects you possess?"

"Beltane." Judy leapt on that second reference, ignoring Andrew's question. "What is it?" she asked. "Why do your brothers want me under lock and key tonight?"

"Elfred fears you are a witch. But a witch who does not know Beltane?" Andrew chuckled, smiled, and flicked the lighter again. A new flame wavered in the air as he explained, "Beltane is the first day of May, the beginning of spring. The Scots, the Irish, and many Saxon peasants believe Beltane is a mystical time. They think ordinary souls can work magic, and that people can even slip through time. 'Tis foolishness, but some respect the old ways, just as I admire the new." He upended the lighter to examine the bottom.

Beltane. To Judy, it sounded much like Samhain, at least the way Ian MacCoombs had explained that historic holy day. According to legend, then, souls could slip through time on both those dates. According to personal experience, Judy knew people could slip through time on All Hallow's Eve—maybe she could slip through time again on May Day.

Oh, God! She needed to be outside tonight, not locked away in this cold chamber high up in the keep. She needed to go directly to that spot outside the bailey wall and hope for the energy charge as she willed herself to travel forward through the centuries to her own world. Then she wouldn't have to worry about how inappropriately Andrew made her feel, or whether or not Philip's intentions toward her were sincere. She sure wouldn't have to worry that Elfred of Laycock would convince his elder brother to cast her out because he believed her to be some kind of sorceress. Home again, in her own time, her own country, Judy could once more be herself, a modern woman not beholden to any man at all.

"Are there celebrations?" she asked curiously. "Rituals?"

"What?" Andrew stopped playing with the lighter and peered at her. "Oh, aye. Some of the peasants light bone-fires to keep the *spoorns* away."

"Bone-fires? Spoorns?"

"Aye. They burn animal bones to frighten the spoorns, the evil spirits. And they will pass their children through the flames because it is said 'twill better the youngsters' futures and fortunes. But mostly, what the people do on Beltane is make merry and make love. On the following morn, they can blame the fairies and too much drink for their wanton behavior." Andrew snorted. "There are always quite a few babes born just before the new year, all conceived on Beltane."

Judy barely listened. She turned to look out the window and saw the top of the bailey wall. Beyond it lay her freedom, even the road home. Certainly she could manage to slip out of the keep later, after darkness fell. No matter that she would be locked in, she'd get out—she had to.

"It sounds exciting," she said, trying to tone down the excitement, the anticipation, she felt. "I'd really like to see it."

"Would you?" Andrew toyed with the lighter, rolling the plastic tube between his fingers.

"Um-hm." Judy leaned toward him, attempting some manipulation of her own, and rubbed her cheek on his shoulder. Her heart did a little flutter, so she willed herself to feel nothing. She had a purpose in coming on to Andrew, and that purpose was not to get laid. "I'd like to see the bone-fires. I'd like to dance and...drink."

"And make love?" Andrew turned his face toward hers. The dark bristle on his chin scratched her smooth skin, yet she found the sensation pleasant despite her resolve to feel nothing.

"Yes," she answered, vaguely promising him something she never expected to give.

"We need not wait 'til evening to roll about in the damp grass." Andrew turned more fully toward Judy, embraced her, and pushed her down on her back. When he lay down beside her, he mumbled in her hair, "We could make love here in this nice, soft bed."

Oh, yeah. "But...it wouldn't be the Beltane celebration."

"We need no peasants to celebrate." Andrew kissed Judy's ear, her throat, her chin. He moved one hand down her chest, cupping her breast.

Her insides were turning to pudding. She had to stop him before she couldn't stop herself. "This isn't right," she announced, forcing her limbs to go stiff. "I—I can't."

"Oh, aye, of course you cannot." As though in full agreement and understanding, Andrew calmly slid off the bed and found his feet. "You must save yourself for Philip, eh? Mayhap he'll come 'round and take you off so that you may both enjoy the dancing, the drinking, and other...pastimes...by the Beltane fires. Because I surely will not."

"Andrew!" Judy rolled to her knees and called to him as he opened the bedchamber door.

"What?" he snapped, pausing to glance over his shoulder.

Judy refused to beg. She had never begged anyone for anything, and she certainly did not intend to start with Andrew Laycock, junior lord-and-master of this medieval keep. Besides, she didn't need him. She would do what she had to do on her own.

"My lighter," she said primly, holding out her hand. "My fire-starter. Give it back."

"Why?"

"Because it's mine, not yours."

Andrew hesitated, glancing at the object in his palm. Then he looked up at Judy and said, "I never take what is not offered freely," and tossed the lighter back to her.

She caught it as he exited the room. Immediately, she scrambled off the bed and tried the latch on the door.

He'd locked her in.

Twelve

Nobody fed Judy that evening. It seemed they intended to let her go hungry rather than risk opening the door. What did they think, that she would overpower anyone who dared bring her supper into her room?

In fact, Judy had been planning ways to do just that. But—having glanced at the digital timepiece secured to the leatherette cover of her daily planner—she knew it was hours past mealtime. Damn! The Laycock brothers treated her as though she were a female Hannibal Lechter. If only she had the powers that Elfred feared and Robin suspected. If only she'd come from even farther in the future, she could vaporize her huge, heavy door with a laser gun. She'd hurry downstairs, then, and outside, and straight to that place of power where the winds of time would carry her away.

Place of power. Wow! That's what Ian MacCoombs had called those spots he'd come to explore, which he insisted were numerous in the Wixcomb area. That's what lay beyond the bailey wall, where she occasionally had that weird, undefinable sensation and where, that first night, she had felt as though she'd exploded into a million sparkling particles.

The mystery of Judy's time travel suddenly began to come together in her mind. Ian had spoken of yin and yang, had said that some places of power were masculine and others feminine. Some, he had explained, filled a person up while others dissolved or dispersed energy. Judy felt certain she had dispersed in some fashion, probably the way the crew of the *Enterprise* did whenever Scotty beamed them up. She had traveled centuries, nearly a thousand years, unencumbered by her body, only to reassemble as the woman she was in an age where she wasn't meant to be.

"I have got to get out," Judy muttered with renewed determination. Again, she attempted to open her door as she had fifty times already. Failing once more, she frowned pensively as she walked to her window.

Rain had begun to fall softly, the gentle mist

glistening as the moisture drifted to earth. But Judy spied no human activity, heard no singing, saw no bone-fires. In spite of the lateness of the hour, full darkness had yet to fall—they had incredibly long daylight hours, here in the England. So perhaps it wasn't time yet. Perhaps they had to wait for night to descend. Or, perhaps, the rain forced them to cancel their revelry.

Judy began to sink into despair. Then she roused herself, demanding aloud, "What am I thinking?" She didn't need company. She had no plans to bring human exhibits home with her to 1998. Her travel plans could only be solitary; tonight, she would make her journey alone.

***

Judy had broken four of ten fingernails. For hours, she had pulled, tugged, even rammed her door with her shoulder. She had attacked the hinges and called to anyone she thought she heard passing in the corridor. She had even lain on her stomach and peered through the slim crack between the door and floor—for what purpose, even she hadn't been sure. Now her hands looked rough and raw, and her arms hurt. Yet still that damned door refused to budge.

Faint music drifted to her ear, not from below but from beyond. Rushing to the window, she spied in the blackness a huge, smoking fire on a distant hill. The revelers had proved heartier than she'd presumed. Despite the rain, they had ventured outdoors and climbed the hills to celebrate.

Judy panicked and felt the urge to pace. Resisting that compulsion, she took a deep breath instead and sat on a stool. Clearing her head, she forced herself to calmly consider the door again and analyze its configuration. There had to be a way to open it based on...physics? Some laws of nature. Some principles that people of this time did not know but she, a college graduate, had to have tucked away in her brain. Once the knowledge came back to her, Judy would breach the barrier and escape.

But it wasn't coming to her, the way her little bit of French had surfaced when she needed it, and all that darned history she hadn't realized she knew just popped out of her mouth.

***

Judy wiped the perspiration from her brow. Why was she sweating? It wasn't that warm, and she surely hadn't overexerted herself physically, not for some time. Had to be nerves.

Okay. If she couldn't unlock her door or break through it, she would trick someone else into opening it from the other side. Deciding on this new tactic, she grabbed coals from her fire and dropped them into the earthen bowl she used for washing. Though she used a towel to pluck the glowing chunks of wood from the pit and toss them into the basin, she still burned the pads of her fingers, which immediately began to redden and blister.

Her flesh stung, but she didn't care. Music and voices continued to drift to her window from the peasants' celebration, and it spurred her to action. She had to get out *now*. Carrying the bowl to the door, she set it on the floor and then scurried back to the table, where she wet her towel and wrung it out. Then, like an Indian sending signals, she lay the damp cloth over the coals till they smoldered and smoked. Fanning the gray, acrid fumes toward the door, she hoped they would seep below and between the banded boards.

"Fire!" she cried dramatically. "Help me, please. Fire!"

Footsteps pounded up the stairs. "Eeeyesss!" Judy made a fist and pulled it toward her body in a triumphant gesture. Her ruse had worked! When they opened the door, she would fall against whoever stood there, startling that unwary person and knocking him aside. Then she'd run like mad down the stairs and on outdoors. God willing, she wouldn't trip and no one would catch her. She had to make it through the gate in the bailey walls to that place of power.

The gate. Would the portcullis be raised or lowered? Up, she had a chance. Down, she was doomed. But stuck in this room high up in the keep, she knew she couldn't even make a grab at freedom. So she decided not to worry about the portcullis. Her immediate and only concern remained the chamber door.

She kept fanning her towel and blowing, encouraging the smoke to billow and swirl around her. This didn't seem like such a hot idea after all, she reconsidered, coughing and rubbing her itchy eyes. Where had the people gone whom she'd heard coming up the stairs? Why didn't they open the door and let her out?

"Hey! You! Whoever's in the hallway, let me out! I—I'm suffocating!"

"Witch!" Judy recognized Elfred's voice. "You used your magic fire-starter to set your room ablaze. Now use other magic to put out the flames."

"I didn't. I—I can't!"

"You can," Elfred insisted.

"But the keep. It'll burn down."

"Nay, it shall not. 'Tis made of stone. Only the furnishings in your room will be destroyed, if you fail to put out the fire."

"But I'll die," Judy wailed.

"That may be true," he conceded. Elfred sounded not at all displeased at the notion. "Witches die when set to flame. You should have thought of that before—"

"Where's Andrew?" she interrupted, putting the wet cloth over her mouth as she dragged in a gulp of air. Andrew would let her out. He wouldn't let her die, even if she were near to dying, which she wasn't.

Elfred laughed. "Nowhere about," he informed Judy. He said nothing more after that, not even when she spoke to him. Though she hadn't heard retreating footsteps, she knew he'd gone away.

Damn him! Squinting in order to see through the smoke and the tears welling in her eyes, Judy grabbed the pitcher of water off her table and dumped the entire contents into the bowl of glowing coals. She knew the fire would go out, but she did not anticipate the volume of smoke and steam that hissed upward, directly into her face. The hot fumes sent Judy staggering back to the window again.

Fighting for air, she hung out the window, gasping. By the time her breathing came without huge effort, she realized the night had gone still. The festivities, whatever they might have been, appeared to have ended. Perhaps the damp weather had forced a premature conclusion to the burning of bones, the wanton sex, the ceremonies designed to frighten goblins and ensure good luck. Or perhaps twelve o'clock had come and gone. She didn't know if the witching hour of midnight had any significance in pagan rituals, but she suspected it might. Dates turned over from one to the next at that moment. For all she knew, the first of May, Beltane, could now be yesterday.

Frantically, she dove toward her bed and the tote on top of it. She scrabbled with her fingers, searching the contents by feel until she found her daily planner with its little digital clock. When she saw the numerals blinking up at her from the notebook's cover, her heart sank. Midnight had indeed come and gone, at least as people measured time in her world. As they also counted days, the date, revealed in a tiny square in the upper corner of the clock, read 12:12:98.

"God, no."

As though she'd been struck a painful blow to the side of her head, Judy held her cheek in her hand. Cringing, she slid to the floor 'til she sat with the bed bracing her back. With one hand, she dashed away tears before wiping her runny nose. And finally, she absorbed the full impact of what that date meant to her, to her family, to her friends.

By December 12, 1998, Carla Whittaker had certainly given up searching for her or even waiting on her return. She had flown back to New York, probably saddened by Judy's disappearance but resigned to getting on with her writing, her work, her wedding.

Her parents had to know that she was missing, had surely been living with that knowledge for weeks. Had they traveled to England, spoken to Lord Laycock, Mrs. Haversham, and even Ian MacCoombs in their efforts to discover what had happened, where she had gone? Of course they had. They had walked where she had walked, seen what she had seen.

She wept, cradling her head in her arms now as she leaned against her bent knees. Pitiful, heart-wrenching scenarios played out in her mind, as the Ghost of Christmas Future tortured her with images of her own parents' holiday, the one they would attempt to celebrate while believing their only daughter dead.

The Edwin Grant Agency. She brought her head up as she thought about her work place. Had they already replaced her? Did somebody new handle Carla and all her other writers? Did her coworkers and clients miss her, or had no one skipped a beat, settling right in with the agent who now occupied her office?

Misery washed over her like a cold, ocean wave. It knocked her flat, nearly suffocating her, and left her chilled and shivering. Despairing over her losses, succumbing to her defeat, she dropped her head into her arms again and wept until her tears ran dry.

***

Judy hiccuped as she looked out her window. Did she detect the faintest hint of light beginning to overlay the evening clouds? No. It couldn't be. She saw not the slightest suggestion of dawn. She had time, yet. Time.

She placed one foot on the end of the wire she'd ripped from her spiral notebook. With both hands, she rubbed out the remaining kinks, pulling hard, drawing it as straight as she could while she worked it from one end to the other. Examining the funky-looking wire, she knew it would never be any straighter than it already was. But it still might work—it had to. She could spare no more time for refinements.

Sometime during the night, she realized she hadn't been confined with a padlock. The mechanism that held her imprisoned was no more than a latch, simple and primitive. She only had to lift the latch to obtain her freedom, easy as that.

And complicated as that. The door had been fashioned of heavy boards, as thick as young tree trunks. It fit the framing stones securely—only an inch of space kept the wood from dragging on the floor when it opened and closed. The remaining three sides, including the top, fit snug as a puzzle piece. On the latch side, the space in the seam would allow nothing wider to pass than a sheet of paper or a piece of straw. And neither of those items would prove sturdy enough to flip the iron latch on the outside of the door.

But a wire would. Judy had scoured the contents of her tote, considering and discarding pens, pencils, and a rat-tailed comb before landing on the idea of the wire. All she'd had to do was rip off the paper and straighten the curly-cued metal.

The task hadn't proven quite as easy as she'd anticipated, but she had done it. Now she knelt on the floor and put her eye to the space between the wood door and the stone wall. Then she slipped the wire through that space directly below the latch.

One single thrust upward, that's all it took. Yet the rush of wild happiness she felt was tinged with annoyance and anger. She should have thought of this much sooner. If she had, she might be home by now. But she hadn't the leisure for self-recrimination. Hearing the latch flip, she eagerly leapt to her feet and levered the inside door latch. When she pulled, the door finally swung open.

Freedom!

Giddy with relief, delight and anticipation, she whirled around, grabbed her tote, and ran into the hallway—only to stop, catch her breath, and press herself against the wall.

She couldn't be brash. It was late, very late, a perfect time to escape because the servants wouldn't be moving about yet. And their masters, the lords of Laycock, must be in their beds as well. In this era when people went to sleep as soon as the sun set, even those nobles with candles to burn could not still be awake, debauching women and drinking wine. Yet she couldn't be brash.

She tiptoed carefully down the stairs, holding her breath and inhaling only sporadically. As she picked her way through the snoring, snorting bodies and left the keep through a rear exit, she could not contain a smile. Though she hadn't succeeded yet, she just knew she was going to make it. Very soon, she would be home.

***

A hound using Andrew's foot as a pillow made a sound barely loud enough for him to hear. Yet he did hear it, and he woke. Opening his eyes to mere slits, he peered through the gloom to try to see what had snagged the spaniel's attention. He felt no concern. Laycock was well-protected, and even the dog sensed no danger. But still, it proved unusual for anyone to be moving about at this hour of the night.

It was Judith! By all the saints, she had gotten out of her room. Now, as he watched, the damsel stepped over servants and guards who lay sprawled haphazardly across the great hall's floor. Where in damnation was she going?

He didn't ask. He didn't call out to her or even sit up straighter in the chair where he'd drifted to sleep after a long night in Robin's company. But after she had slipped from the hall, he rose silently, nimbly circumventing the prone bodies in his path as he followed her outside.

Stepping into the bailey felt like stepping into a tomb. The blackness seemed palpable, and the air was damp and chill. He was glad he had failed to remove his mantle upon returning to the keep earlier. Now, he hugged the woolen cape close about his arms as he watched Judith dart straight toward the bailey wall. She melted into the shadows, a black figure fading into a black abyss. Yet, as she made her way toward the front gate, he glimpsed her periodically when a faint halo of light cast by a flickering torch illuminated her fair tresses.

She slipped beneath the iron teeth of the raised portcullis, clinging to one of the stone towers that flanked each side. As he followed several paces behind, he noticed that she continued to hug the outside of the wall just as she had the inside. This surprised him. He'd half presumed she would dash down the hills toward the village. He never expected her to purposely hide from the guards pacing the crenelated parapet above.

Gaining speed as she made her way around the stronghold's perimeter, Judith broke into a run when she neared the postern side. He quickened his stride to keep pace with her, no longer concerned that he remain unnoticed. She proved herself oblivious to him as she abandoned caution for recklessness.

Who is she meeting? he wondered, caught between curiosity and suspicion, concern and dismay. Had Judith planned to rendezvous with Philip? Had their scheme been thwarted by Robin locking her in her room?

Andrew knew relief that she had been restrained and almost felt grateful to his brothers, who had insisted upon her confinement. They, after all, would leave soon to rejoin their father, and Judith would again be free to roam at will. But because of Elfred's fears and Robin's discretion, she would still remain with him at Laycock. She could not run off with Philip. Even if his friend continued to wait for her, Andrew would never allow him to take her.

Abruptly, Judith left the cover of the high wall and dashed off, surprising him. To him, it seemed as though she had spied her lover's welcoming arms and rushed to embrace him. But there was no lover, not even Philip, and no ready arms to catch her. Judith fell to her knees on a little patch of sparse grass a short distance away. Andrew stopped, remaining undetected standing near the wall, and watched her in puzzled confusion. She huddled alone, clutching her satchel in her lap and rocking back and forth.

The wench broke his heart. Judith Lamb had never looked more pathetic nor more vulnerable than she did at this moment. He yearned to go to her, to take her hand and lead her back inside the keep where he could hold her safe. But she startled him with a wild, demented cry, and he froze where he stood.

Judith threw back her head and wailed plaintively, pleading unintelligibly with the starless heavens. Even as she shouted into the night sky, she clawed at the ground with one hand, grabbing clumps of grass and fistfuls of damp soil. To Andrew, she seemed to be desperately clinging to the earth as someone who lost his footing on a wall might clasp the ledge.

"Please, please, please," she shouted. "Home, home, home! Take me home! Take me home!"

The sound of her muted cry, muffled by the heavy, damp air, gave him the sensation of spiders crawling down his spine. If Elfred saw her now, a virtual madwoman invoking the forces of Nature, he would insist Judith was a witch and Andrew could not gainsay him. She appeared to be a witch, a sorceress, or a magician, though not a very capable one. For whatever forces she implored, they answered her only with an onslaught of hard, pounding rain. Though Andrew ducked his head and visored his eyes when the downpour descended, he saw that she continued to leave her head thrown back, exposing her face to the needling raindrops.

"Jesu," he muttered, finally running to her and gathering her into his arms. "Judith!"

"No, no. Let me go! *Let me go!*"

She fought wildly against his embrace, but he refused to release her. "You are not going anywhere, Judith, except into the keep. Why, in the name of all things holy, are you out in this storm shouting at the sky?"

"I—I—I—" She ceased flailing and blinked at him, as though only now recognizing him. Then she shook her head, offering no explanation for her escape from a locked chamber or her baffling rampage at the night.

He didn't care. Judith was neither a witch nor a wraith but merely a woman. His woman, by default if not declaration, for everyone else seemed to reject her. Even Philip, whom she trusted, perhaps adored.

"You're shivering," he observed as he scooped her up and held her close, carrying her back toward the fore of the bailey and the huge iron gate. "You foolish, obstinate wench. You've probably caught your death out here in the rain."

"Good," Judith muttered. "Good."

Thirteen

"What in damnation do you mean, there was a fire in her chamber and you did naught to release her? You endangered her life and the lives of all those who live in the keep!"

Standing in Elfred's bedchamber shouting at his brother, Andrew clenched and unclenched his fingers. He wanted nothing so much as to beat Elfred senseless. But that would only serve to rouse Robin's ire, and besides, he wanted to hear an explanation, outrageous and unacceptable as it might be.

Elfred threw back his covers and climbed out of bed. Reaching for his robe, he insisted, "How dare you burst in upon me before dawn has even broke? I endangered no one's life. The keep cannot burn, and neither can witches, if they be not tied to a stake!"

"You bastard! Judith Lamb is no witch!" Glad Elfred had donned his bed robe, Andrew grabbed him by the fabric covering his chest.

"She is something unholy," he insisted.

"Why do you believe that? The fire-starter's a clever tool, is all. And we know her sire is an inventor. 'Tis he who created the damnable thing. 'Tis hardly magic."

"So you say. As you say her sire is that alchemist, Peter Lamb. But you've no proof, Andrew. You've no proof at all."

"That gives you the right to let her die—to...to kill her?" He pushed Elfred away with a hard thrust, so that his brother stumbled into a table at his back.

"What is going on here?" Robin demanded, appearing unexpectedly in the open doorway.

Andrew turned around to face him. "When we were gone from the keep last eve," he explained, "Elfred kept Judith locked in her room despite a fire that could have killed her."

Robin frowned at Elfred. "Is this true?"

"Nay!" Again, he repeated his contention that Judith could not die because of her sorcery. "Besides, 'twas she who set the blaze as a ruse to get out of the chamber so that she could work her magic on Beltane Eve," he added.

Calmly, Robin glanced at Andrew with both his eyebrows raised. "She is not dead, after all. Mayhap Elfred is correct."

"He is not correct. Jesu, but if Judith possessed unearthly powers, would she need a ruse to get free of her chamber?" He sneered at Elfred. Then, facing Robin, he insisted, "The girl was merely fortunate. Bridget told me what went on here last eve while we were making merry. Judith screamed and begged for release as smoke billowed from beneath her door, filling the hallway. Yet Elfred prevented Bridget from unlocking the door."

"I would see the chamber myself," Robin declared, turning to go. But Andrew grabbed his sleeve.

"Nay. Do not disturb her. The damsel's tired."

"But not dead," Elfred added.

"Keep quiet, I warn you!" Andrew whirled and glared at him threateningly.

Sighing, Robin said, "No serious harm has been done, then, eh? Let it go, Andrew. Elfred will be leaving here with me this very day, as we must visit other demesnes to ensure the barons' efforts against King John are organized. Then we shall rejoin Father near London. There shall be no more incidents involving the wench."

"The lady," Andrew corrected.

"Aye, then. The lady. Surely, by the time we all return, either to go to battle or because the king has at last agreed to our demands, Judith—Lady Judith—shall long since be reunited with her kin."

Andrew nodded.

"Speaking of ladies, I've had word from Mother," Robin continued. "She and our sisters have gone on to visit other relatives. They shan't be returning to Laycock for some weeks yet. 'Tis a good thing, I believe, that they not be in residence while we ready ourselves for war." He cocked an eyebrow at his youngest brother. "You will prepare to command our men, aye? Sir Roland is an excellent captain of the guard, but should Father send word that our knights are needed to attack the king's fiefs, a lord of Laycock should lead them to the site of battle."

"It should be me," Elfred grumbled. "I am Andrew's elder."

"You were the one who wished to join Father and me, and now he has other tasks for you. Cease your complaining and get dressed," Robin ordered before quitting the room and taking Andrew with him.

In the corridor, he said quietly, "The girl should go. I do not believe her a fey creature, but even you must admit she is most unusual, in both appearance and demeanor. If this knight, Peter Lamb, is indeed her sire, he has done his daughter a great disservice." Robin shook his head, his expression troubled. "Mayhap, in a small society of students of nature, Judith is deemed an asset. But she can be naught but an outcast among gentility, as the daughter of a Jewish moneylender would be among good Christian people."

Andrew clenched his jaw, yet he nodded silently.

"Mind my warning," Robin urged. "Get her gone from Laycock Keep before Mother returns."

***

"Where is Lady Judith?" Andrew asked Bridget as he sat down at the high table to partake of the evening meal. He had not clapped eyes on her since Beltane, not since before his brothers rode off. "Have her join me."

Bridget frowned. "Milord, she remains abed."

"Still?" The wench had been abed for two whole days and the evening between. He had surmised that she was avoiding him purposely, but perhaps she had fallen ill with something more than mere exhaustion. "Why?" he asked the servant brusquely to cover his rising concern. "What ails her?"

"I fear I know not."

"She's not dead?" he demanded, jumping to his feet.

"Oh, nay, milord. I saw her returning from the garderobe once yesterday and again today. But she's eaten nothing that I've noticed, and she sleeps the days away. Methinks she has a fever, milord."

"Why did you say naught?" He stomped off the dais and headed toward the stairs.

"You've been occupied, Lord Andrew." Bridget hurried after him. "I did not think you'd wish to be bothered."

"As you did not think I'd wish to be bothered when my cockshead of a brother left her to burn to death in her chamber?" He glanced over his shoulder and glowered at the young woman who had once been his playmate.

"I—I did not know where you and Lord Robin had gone," she explained. "Besides, Lord Elfred was quite unyielding. He forbade me and anyone else to unlock Lady Judith's door."

The two of them reached Judith's room. Andrew pushed the unlatched door open and walked directly to the bed.

He felt a start. Sweet Mother Mary, but she looked sickly, so pale and drawn. Her closed eyes seemed bruised and sunken.

"God's blood, Bridget!" he said in a harsh whisper. "We must do something."

"I know not what, milord. Mayhap if she wakes and tells us what is wrong—"

"Judith!" he interrupted, speaking directly to her. "Judith, do you hear me? Please, sweetling. Open your eyes. Speak to me." He shook Judith's shoulder gently and touched her face. She didn't move, and her skin felt hot and moist with perspiration.

"The lady is burning up. Bridget, bathe her with cool water. Now! Try to bring her fever down."

As he stood by watching the servant tend Judith, he wondered if he had been prophetic when he told her she might have caught her death in that cold rainstorm. But he had merely meant to chide the wench. He hadn't truly believed what he said. The damsel was too substantial and too robust, too youthful and too vigorous, to succumb to what—a damnable spring rain? Judith couldn't die from getting wet!

But she could will herself to die. With an abrupt feeling of dread, he suspected she actually *wanted* to die. This illness might serve as the method—the excuse—to be released from a life she no longer wished to live. The other evening, on the hillside beyond the bailey, she had been imploring God to take her. Now, God would take her—if Andrew let Him.

But he didn't intend to let Him. God could have her one day. He would have them all one day. But not today, nor tomorrow, nor any day soon. Now, Judith was here. And if she belonged to anyone, she belonged to Andrew of Laycock.

Bridget wrung out her rag and set it aside. She looked at Andrew helplessly. "Mayhap, if we got a bit of water into her? The lady's lips are parched."

Agreeing, he gave Bridget a nod and replaced her at Judith's bedside. Taking the cup she handed to him, he raised Judith's head and touched the rim to her lips.

"Judith." He tried to tip some liquid into her mouth. "Judith, drink."

It seemed more dribbled down her chin than down her throat, but he hoped she took a little into her stomach. "Leave us," he told the servant as he laid Judith's head back against the pillow. "I'll call you when I must leave her room. Then, I shall want you beside the damsel at all times. If she soils herself, clean her. If she can drink more water, give her broth for nourishment. Do you understand?"

"Aye, milord," Bridget assured him, though he did not even turn to look at her before she left the chamber. He looked only at Judith's face, his innards twisting in fear as he watched the illness begin to ravage her beauty.

Suddenly she thrashed, startling him as she began to break out of her lethargy with a violent energy. Attempting to keep her still and comfort her, he grabbed Judith's shoulders and held her close until she finally fell quiet. When he released her, he found she'd turned her face away.

He touched her chin, drawing her face back toward him. "Sweetling, listen to me. You've been asleep for days now. You must awaken. Do you hear? Awaken!"

Nothing. The wench again lay still as stone. Regretting it before he did it, he slapped her cheek lightly with three fingers of one hand. Judith mewled like an annoyed feline and rolled away, burying her face in the covers.

He grabbed the bowl and cloth, and drenched the rag in water again. He knew Bridget had already bathed her, but he felt a need to do something. Touching Judith's chin so that she lay looking upward, he clumsily placed the sodden cloth full over her face.

"No!"

"Aye," he countered stubbornly, relieved to hear her protest. He rubbed the cloth roughly over Judith's face, as though she were a dirty child who needed scrubbing. He hoped she would protest some more.

"N-n-n-n..." she muttered, grabbing blindly for the rag.

Andrew let her catch it and toss it off. It heartened him to see her blink her eyes again. "Who am I, Judith?"

"I don'..." She breathed heavily. "Drew. An...drew."

His heart leapt at this small accomplishment, this mumbled response.

"Aye! I be Andrew. And you be Judith. Judith?"

"Don' yell... My head...hurts. Hurts!" She closed her eyes again, grimaced and touched her hand to her brow. "As...pirin. Gimme...aspirin. Please."

"Ass-brin?" he repeated. "What is ass-brin?"

She didn't reply. Her eyes remained closed, and her hand dropped to her side. He feared she might be slipping away again.

"Nay, Judith Lamb, do not drift off! Stay with me, do you hear? And tell me!" He leaned over and shook her shoulders one more time. "What is ass-brin?"

"You...know."

"I do not know! Tell me!"

"Please...don' shout. My head..."

"Where do I find this thing you want? In your satchel? Is it in your satchel?"

Her eyes opened only to slits, and she nodded almost imperceptibly.

A moment later, he had her tote perched on the edge of the mattress. Unzipping it, he pulled the sides apart and stared into the abyss.

"What does it look like, Judith? For what do I search?"

"Pills. In a...a bottle."

He had no idea what "pills" or a "bottle" might be. Taking the tote to the unoccupied side of Judith's bed, Andrew spilled most of its contents across the wrinkled bedclothes.

God's toes, what a clutter of indescribable objects! Which among them might be ass-brin?

"Judith? Here. Look. Tell me what item you desire."

She resisted him. After a time, either because she wanted ass-brin more than she did sleep, or because she simply wanted to be free of his pestering, Judith managed to roll onto her side and run her hand over the collection of debris beside her. He watched as she felt with her fingertips first one object and then another, discarding each without looking at any.

Finally, she clasped a small container in her hand and held it toward him. He marveled at the remarkable vessel. He could actually see into it and its contents, which appeared to be a great number of flat, white pebbles.

"Open," she mumbled.

He tried. He failed.

"Line up the arrows...the triangles. One on cap. Other on neck."

He peered at the *bottle* and finally made out the emblems. Rotating the cap until the minute figures matched, he managed, on this attempt, to pop the lid off.

"Two. No—three," Judith told him.

He tapped three of the pebbles into his hand and gave them to her.

"Water. I need...water."

He brought her the water cup, and she tossed the pebbles into her mouth. She swallowed much more liquid to ease them down her throat than she had sipped earlier. Then, as though the effort drained the last of her feeble strength, she fell back against her pillow and closed her eyes.

She appeared to be asleep again already. But as he straightened the coverlet, tucking it beneath Judith's chin, she mumbled, "Three. Every...hours."

Judith said something between "every" and "hours," but he couldn't make it out. He decided to give her three of the pebbles every Church hour. Terce had just passed. He would give her more at Sext, when the sun rode high in the sky.

***

Andrew had carried a high-backed chair into Judith's chamber. He sat in it now, near the foot of her bed.

Tired, he fought to stay awake. All day he had busied himself with preparations for war. The burden of leadership had not wearied him, but his gnawing concern for Judith stretched his raw nerves taut. Never completely out of his thoughts, whenever he heard the priest ring the bells at Sext, None and Vespers, Andrew interrupted what he was doing to go to Judith's room and force the pebbles into her mouth. He could have instructed Bridget to feed her the mysterious disks. But Judith trusted him to do it, so he did.

It seemed that her head no longer hurt so violently as it had. She slept peacefully, without thrashing. If the ass-brin could make a headache vanish, he hoped the ass-brin could cure whatever else ailed Judith.

A short while ago, at Compline, he had given Judith three more of the...what? Not pebbles, he decided as he sat examining two of the small, white circles in his palm. Earlier, he had broken one apart with his thumbnail. It appeared to be powder, not rock. As it crumbled into his hand, he thought it might be flour, a bit of dried bread, a piece of holy wafer, mayhap. Then he gingerly put his tongue to the white dust and found it tasted bitter. No wonder Judith preferred to swallow them whole. What had she called these things? *Pills*. He would have to remember her word, because he had no word of his own for them.

His eyes flicked to the form lying so motionless in the bed. Did Judith's stillness portend good or bad? Her quiet state could mean her health improved and that, no matter what her desire, she was growing stronger. But perhaps her stillness indicated only that she slipped nearer to death.

Impulsively, he pushed himself to his feet and went to her bedside. Noticing a cup of broth still sitting on the table, he retrieved it and tried to force a bit between her lips. Much of the liquid dripped onto her sheets, but he saw her swallow. And then, suddenly, she began to choke. With a mutinous cry, she knocked the cup from his hand, sending it spewing broth as it tumbled to the floor with a clatter.

He chuckled, laid her down again, and wiped both her chin and her neck with a rag. Judith could not be so near death after all, if she could force her will on him with such vehemence!

Bending down to retrieve the cup, he noticed a casket hidden under the bed. He pulled it out and opened it. Inside lay his things, his family's things! Beatrix's embroidered pillow, a goblet, and his own bone dice. He had known Judith had taken them—but why? Could she be a common thief, a poor peasant who had tricked them into letting her live here like a noblewoman? Were these the spoils of her clever victory over her betters, who thought themselves educated and wise but whom she considered easy foils?

Nay. Judith was many things, but common wasn't one of them. Certainly, she could be no petty thief. He would, in fact, have given her these paltry household items if she had asked. But she hadn't asked.

He shook his head firmly before returning the casket to its hiding place. Despite the evidence, he could not believe she was a thief anymore than he could believe she was a witch.

He sat down in his chair. Beside it, near his feet, lay Judith's satchel. Because he had been thinking of all her fantastic possessions, he pulled the bag into his lap, opened the *zipper*, and began to examine the items carefully, one at a time.

Judith did indeed own more than one writing pen. He discovered two. Again he came upon the fire-starter, which erupted so handily with a spontaneous flame. He also fondled the brocade pouch with the fasteners she had called *Velcro*. There were other containers like her *pill bottle*, too, some large, some small. A few contained salves, and others held more pills of different shapes and colors. However, he found Judith's sheaf of bound pages had gone missing, though the paper she had written on remained, folded in half and clasped together with a curious device of looped metal.

He toyed with a hefty tube that seemed to be capped with a big, shiny eye. When he moved the lever on the side of the tube, the eye burst into light. He exclaimed, swearing furiously, and flung it away. Then, feeling foolish and glad no one had seen his cowardice, he retrieved the device. When he thumbed the lever up and down, a cool, steady beacon, too white to be fire, appeared and disappeared, though he could find neither a wick nor a flame inside. What a marvel! Had Peter Lamb created this device and all the others? If so, the inventor should be ruling the world, or at least be the wealthiest man in all Christendom. What other men, even kings, would pay for these things!

He discovered a small box. Flipping it over, this way and that, he couldn't even guess what it contained, what its function might be. He did see tiny written words: P-L-A-Y. R-E-W-I-N-D. He knew the words "play" and "wind" but could not fathom why they, and others, had been sketched onto the box. The biggest word he saw, S-A-N-Y-O, meant nothing to him at all. It was another of Judith's words, one from her odd-sounding English.

"Shite," Andrew swore. The next item he pulled from the bag he had not seen before—it must have been caught beneath something heavier when he'd dumped the satchel onto Judith's bed. Now, for an instant, he felt terrified all over again. He would have flung the object, as he had the illuminating eye, except his fingers felt as though they had melted around the handle.

Cautiously, he looked at the thing in his hand. Breathing deeply, he willed himself to stay calm as he peered at himself and saw his own face looking back at him. God's blood, he beheld a mirror! No polished piece of metal this, but something else altogether. The surface felt smooth and cool beneath his fingertips, almost like ice. But the veneer wasn't ice that dripped as the frozen water warmed and melted. The object remained solid.

And his reflection remained perfect. He couldn't help staring. God's teeth, but he was not a bad looking man! And he looked much more like Robin than he'd ever thought he did. But then, he had never seen himself before, not in such clear, precise detail. It seemed as though another Andrew of Laycock had materialized, an Andrew of Laycock with neither bulk nor depth who proved to be his identical twin.

When he flipped the mirror over, he had another surprise, but he quickly came to terms with that uneasy feeling. He understood that this surface had been designed to distort his reflection, more so than the ripples in a pond or the uneven plane of a piece of polished metal. Jesu! He had never been so intrigued by anything as he was the pores and the whiskers on his face.

After a time, he gave up his personal examination because he had saved the most intriguing item for last. From the satchel, he finally pulled a mysterious, flat box and set it on his knees. Examining the edges, he soon puzzled out how to open it. And, with a quick intake of breath, he did.

He did not know what he expected to find inside. Something blindingly brilliant, perhaps. Something truly magical, at least. Or, perhaps, a vast amount of gold and jewels. Something valuable, precious, even holy.

But there seemed to be nothing inside. The underside of the lid appeared flat and smooth as the mirror, though its surface looked dim. The bottom half, in his lap, had been carved with an array of raised rectangles, each marked with a symbol. They were—aye—letters! Pleased he recognized them for what they were, since all had been queerly fashioned and some were missing, he understood these symbols formed the written word. But it perplexed him, since he found nothing to write with in this box—no paper, no brushes, not even one of Judith's pens.

He closed the box and latched it. As he sat back in the chair, watching Judith sleep, he felt confident that one day she would explain its purpose because she would recover. He would see to it. He would not let her die.

But what then? She would leave—she would leave him! He could not delay contacting Peter Lamb indefinitely. When they discovered he had sent no messenger to York, Philip, if not Arthur, would send a man to question the alchemist. And Andrew knew what the old knight's response would be: Judith was his missing daughter. Not only would she be welcomed home, Philip would then court her in earnest. Nay, he would promptly ask for her hand and quickly wed her!

At least Philip would wed her if Judith fulfilled his requirements for a bride. If she failed in that matter,

Philip would instead marry Penelope. Such a union would please Andrew as much as it would please Lady Edwinna. But what if Philip chose the other damsel over Judith not because she proved to be poor, but because she proved to be already wed? The idea that Judith might have a husband made Andrew's stomach queasy. He had never expected Judith Lamb to come into his life, but now that she had, he couldn't imagine living without her. By the saints, he could barely *remember* living life without her!

He decided not to speculate. As he gazed at her slumbering form, he knew Judith was going nowhere for a long time to come.

Fourteen

Judy had been drowning in a murky, turbulent sea. Deep currents buffeted her, tugging, pushing, pulling, while tentacled monsters imprisoned her with their limbs, squeezing the breath—and life—from her. Sometimes, it seemed to Judy she broke free and swam away. She even reached out to grasp a hand, a hand attempting to draw her to safety. But then light, sounds and other intrusions dismayed and disturbed her. So she allowed herself to sink down deep again, so deep, the dense, numbing darkness cocooned her. If dangers remained present, she hadn't sensed them.

Today, though, that strange sea coughed her up, and she could not resist opening her eyes. Like any shipwrecked sailor, she felt too weak and exhausted to do more than contemplate her surroundings from the same spot in which she'd awakened. To her chagrin, she found no white, sandy beach beneath her, only dingy linen. No brilliant blue Caribbean sky above, only the heavy fabric that canopied her bed. No swaying palm trees, only the cold stones of her room at Laycock Keep. And no chattering monkeys and birds, only the servant called Bridget dozing in a chair.

She remained in this time, *that* time, nearly eight centuries before her own. When would it end? When would she be back where she belonged in New York City, U.S.A.? Would she never put another disk in a computer, never pull another contract draft off a fax machine? Would she never hail another taxi, go to a restaurant, or drink a cappuccino? And what of her family? Was she destined never to see her parents again, or her brothers, or her friends? Had that last heart-to-heart with her old college roommate, Sarah, proved to be the final midnight gabfest she'd ever have on a telephone?

Sucking in a noisy, woeful breath to try to keep from bursting into tears, she inadvertently woke Bridget. The servant's head snapped up, and her eyes snapped open. Finding her awake, Bridget leapt from the chair and hurried over.

"Milady, are you truly awake?"

"Mmm-hmmm." Judy sniffed and dabbed at her eyes with the backs of her hands, glad she'd kept any tears from falling.

"Oh, Lady Judith, Lord Andrew will be so pleased!" Bridget clapped her hands together.

"Why?" Her voice sounded more like a frog croaking than a person speaking.

"Why?" Bridget repeated. "Because he's been fretting himself near to death over you, milady. He's sat in that chair watching over you most every night."

"I don't—"

"Let me get you something to drink," the servant interrupted, turning aside to ladle water into a cup.

Grateful for the cool liquid that would soothe her parched throat, Judy gulped it down until her greediness resulted in a coughing fit. As Bridget slapped her back, the maid warned her, "You must be careful, milady. You've gone so long without decent nourishment, you won't be able to hold much down."

"I—I'm okay. Fine. Thank you," Judy rasped as she sat back, propped by the pillows Bridget had plumped behind her.

"What was it you were saying, milady?"

"I wouldn't think Andrew—Lord Andrew—would care much that I'd been...ill. I seem to recall he...locked me in this room. And when it filled with smoke, he didn't come...to...release me."

"I'd know nothing about that, milady," Bridget insisted. Yet Judy understood from her manner that she knew *all* about it. "What I know, as I said, is that Lord Andrew took a keen interest in your well-being. He's had me at your side since the moment he learned you'd taken ill."

"Where...is he now?"

"No doubt he's with the bailiff or the captain of the guard, doing what the lord and master of a keep must do."

Judy snorted. *Lord and master*. Some things never changed. "I thought—I thought his older brothers had returned."

"Aye, they did, Lady Judith. But they left again. That worrisome business with King John, and all. We be praying it goes well, that there's no war."

Bridget did a little bob. "I must find him and tell him you're awake and talking. I'll ask Cook to make you something that will sit easy on your stomach. You need to eat. You're thin as a reed after all these days."

"How many days?" Judy asked as the servant retreated.

"Nearly five, milady. Five days."

Five days! Beltane had come and gone nearly a week ago. Of course, it had been over by the time she'd gotten herself out of this room, out of this keep. She should have known even then it was too late to try to get home as dawn of the following day encroached.

But she had been so hopeful. She'd felt that—that *feeling*—when she'd reached the place of power. She had been so sure the winds of time, or whatever the heck they were, would carry her back, forward, whichever direction it was, to 1998. But she had traveled nowhere, absolutely nowhere.

When could she hope to try again? Samhain? Halloween! Dear God, that was still nearly six months away. Judy knew she would never last that long, not here, not at Laycock Keep near her special place of power. Elfred would stone her or burn her at the stake for having magic powers, magic possessions.

She should have died. She didn't know what she'd come down with, or even how she had caught it—probably some bug that people of her own time never encountered and had no immunity against. But considering the people of this age had no knowledge of anatomy or medicine, she should have succumbed to the illness. *Why am I still living, here or any other place?*

No sooner had she asked herself the question than she noticed her bottle of aspirin on the table. Had she been taking aspirin? She could not have gotten out of bed and found the bottle in her bag, not of her own volition. But who? Who would know she even had the medicine, let alone what it was used for and that it might possibly help?

She shook her head and scratched her stomach. She didn't have the answers, not to any of her questions.

"Lord Andrew. Lord Andrew!"

He halted mid-sentence in his conversation with Roland and turned to look at Bridget. When he spied the servant running across the bailey, he felt his heart seize. *Judith. She's dead.*

"What is it, Bridget? What's happened?"

"She's awake, milord. Lady Judith's awakened."

"Are you certain?"

"Aye, milord, I'm certain. We spoke for a bit. I told her I was coming for you, and that I'd have Cook make her something to eat."

"Do that. Now. I'll go to her directly."

Andrew dismissed the captain of the guard and took off toward the keep. He had to restrain himself to keep from running. It wouldn't look good for the baron's son to be seen sprinting to the room of a stranger, a ragtag wanderer who had happened to stumble into Wixcomb. Certainly, it hadn't looked fitting that he'd spent so much time in the sickroom of a woman Elfred had proclaimed, loudly and vehemently, to be a witch.

But Andrew couldn't resist. He finally took off running, up the tall stairs to the keep's front portal and then up the narrow, spiral staircase to Judith's room.

"Judith," he exclaimed as he opened her door. Andrew thought he had never seen so welcome a sight—Judith Lamb sitting up in bed, her green eyes focused and clear.

She blinked at him, startled, and clutched the sheet higher over her bosom. Then her eyes narrowed, and she said accusingly, "Where were you?"

"Where? I was here." Closing the door quietly, he approached the bed.

"Bridget told me you were here, while I was sick and sleeping. I—I meant that night. Beltane. There was a fire in this room, and Elfred wouldn't let me out."

"I know. I heard. I'm sorry."

Judith's lips curled down in a tremulous pout as she gazed up at him with huge, teary eyes. "You should have let me out. I needed you, Andrew, but you didn't help me."

Her mournful accusation broke his heart. Why, by

all the saints, had he gone to the bone-fire with Robin? Because Judith had angered him, that's why. She'd tried seducing him for reasons other than desire, and instead of taking advantage of the opportunity she'd finally given him, he had stalked off in a huff, his pride bruised, his feelings hurt. Then he had accompanied his brother, seeking to satisfy himself with other wenches when only one could satisfy him. And she, he had left in harm's way, nearly losing her forever.

"I believed you were safe, Judith." He glanced around the room, though he had previously inspected it and found none of the bedclothes, nor any of the furnishings, burned. "How did the fire start?"

She scowled and looked down at her hands, folded in her lap. "I don't know. It—it doesn't matter. I put it out."

He smiled. "You're very resourceful. I have always known that about you." He sat. "How do you feel?"

"Pretty lousy. But a lot better than I have been, obviously."

"Once I realized you'd fallen ill, I watched over you the best I could. I had Bridget sit with you when I could not, and I made certain to give you three of those ass-brin pills every hour."

"Every hour?" She looked up at him, surprised.

"Aye. When e'er the bells rang—Sext, None, Vespers."

Judith's brow furrowed. "How many Church hours are there?"

"Eight."

"Thank God." Her forehead smoothed, and she looked relieved. "Otherwise, you might have poisoned me. But, Andrew, how did you know to give me medicine? How did you know what aspirin is?"

He explained, and she nodded thoughtfully, scratching her head. Suddenly, though, her scowl returned. "I don't know whether or not to be grateful to you. I'd probably be better off dead, if I have to stay locked in this room."

"Jesu!" After all they'd been through—after all *he* had been through, fretting over her—the wench came awake for scant few moments and already she pricked his temper. Jumping up, he pointed out, "'Twas only one damnable eve. But you could not accept Robin's single command. You had to do things your way."

"Robin's command? You were the one who locked my door!"

"And you escaped, only to make yourself ill by going outside in the rain. What in damnation were you attempting, Judith? You looked like a mad woman, ranting at the sky. If Elfred had seen you, God only knows what he'd have done."

"How I—how I looked is irrelevant," she insisted. "You had no right to imprison me. I haven't done anything but get lost and wind up on your doorstep. I'm no criminal."

"Nay? You're not a thief?"

Judith's mouth dropped open. "Me? A thief? How dare you even suggest such a thing."

"How dare I?" he repeated, perversely glad for an excuse to fight with her now that he knew she'd recover. Hunkering down beneath the bed, Andrew retrieved the casket he'd inadvertently discovered. Opening the lid, he held up, one at a time, the various items Judith had removed from his household, ending with his sister's pillow, which he placed right in the middle of her lap.

Judith blushed guiltily but insisted, "I didn't steal those things. Not really. I just never thought you'd miss them."

"Whether my family missed them or not doesn't make your taking them any less thievery. Why, Judith? Why did you steal from those who took you in and provided for you?"

Her eyes met his. For a moment, she stared at Andrew. Then she blinked, looked away, and admitted, "To prove I'd been here."

The explanation so surprised him, Andrew didn't know how to respond. He felt a horrible, sinking feeling in his stomach. She was not a sorceress, but could she possibly be engaged in intrigue?

"Judith, are you in someone's employ? Were you sent here to gather information against us?"

"You mean for King John or his people? No, of course not."

"Then why would you need to prove you'd lived among us?"

Squeezing her eyes shut, Judith shook her head and hugged herself. Within moments she was scratching, raking her uneven nails up and down the length of her arms. "I swear to you," she vowed, opening her eyes again, "I'm not employed by anyone—at least not in the way you suspect. I'm not here to spy on your family, to find out how many soldiers your father has or if and when he plans to attack the king's...what-do-you-call-them? Fiefs. Geez, Andrew." She shook her head impatiently. "Even if your enemies wanted to know your secrets, do you really think they'd send a lowly woman to do the job? Not!"

What she said sounded reasonable. Yet he suggested, "There is one way a woman could learn many more secrets than a man ever might."

"How's that?"

"Through seduction."

Judith's mouth dropped open. "Me? Seduce you? I'm the one who threw you out of my bed, remember? Besides, you're the low man on the totem pole. If I was here to seduce some man in your family, it would be your father, if he were around. Or at the very least, Robin. Next in line—" she made a face— "would be Elfred."

Judith reached behind her neck and scratched some more. She looked sad, but she chuckled. "You know, if I had come here to find out what you people were up to, I'd have had the good sense to show up looking like a princess, dressed to the nines and smelling wonderful. I would not have arrived wearing damp, dirty clothes and then stood around in the road, just hoping you or someone else from Laycock might try to run me down with a big, fat horse."

Judith's argument seemed as logical as any man's. She had convinced him, but before he could tell her, she asked distractedly, "Do I have the measles, by any chance?"

"What?"

"The measles. Oh, hell, I can't have. I had German measles when I was a kid, and I was vaccinated against the regular kind. I must be allergic to something—I'm itching like crazy!"

"Allergic?" he repeated.

Judith ignored him. Instead, she asked for her bag, which he gave to her. Digging inside, she pulled out the exceptional mirror. "Maybe I do have something like measles," she muttered tiredly. Then, when she spied her reflection, she gasped in horror.

"Oh, my God! How could you suggest I might be a seductress? Were you being purposely cruel? I have never, ever looked this awful before in my entire life! How can you stand to look at me?" She glanced up at Andrew as she shoved the offending mirror back into her bag. "I look like death warmed over. And this god-awful itching...!"

Judith grimaced as she squirmed and reached beneath the covers to scratch somewhere hidden. "I don't remember itching before. What's causing this?"

Andrew had a passing familiarity with a woman's vanity—he had sisters, after all. He knew Judith did not look her best. But who would, after the days of dire illness she had just endured? Still, he leaned toward her and peered at her face, looking for blotches, something that might indicate the reason for her discomfort. Seeing nothing visible, he suddenly knew the cause of Judith's distress had to be nearly invisible.

"Be still a moment," he urged, parting the lank strands of Judith's multi-hued hair to examine her scalp. As he had suspected he might, Andrew immediately spied a little creature scurrying across her head. "'Tis naught to fret over, Judith. You itch because you have lice."

"*Lice*!" She shrieked so shrilly, Andrew took a step backward. As he moved away, she stumbled out of the bed, dragging the top sheet with her and wrapping it around her torso. She weaved dizzily as she cried, "There are bugs on me?"

"Only very small ones." Andrew grabbed her arms so that she wouldn't lose her balance and fall.

Judith's face puckered, and she wailed. "Only very small ones! Oh, God! Oh, God!"

Her wobbly legs gave out, and she sank directly to

the floor. With a vengeance, she began clawing at her scalp.

"Cease. Cease, now," Andrew told her, scooping her up and sitting her down on the bed. "It sometimes happens. 'Tis naught to be upset about. I'll have your bedding changed, and you can bathe."

"Indoors? In a tub?"

"Aye. Indoors, in a tub. In my room, so the servants may clean this chamber."

"But the lice. Are they going to drown in the water? I thought you had to have a special shampoo, something medicinal..."

"I'll give you strong soap, Judith, so strong, you'd best take care or it shall remove a layer or two of your skin."

"Now," she commanded, apparently never too weak to give orders. She grabbed his arm with one hand and held the sheet modestly in place with the other. "Now, please. I can't wait. I can feel them crawling all over me!"

"Very well. Straight away," he assured her in what he hoped was a calm, soothing tone. By all the saints, he'd never seen anyone grow so frantic over a few silly lice. "Come with me to my bedchamber."

Nodding, Judith insisted on walking but leaned on Andrew as he helped her to the door. Suddenly she stopped and reached out. "My tote!" she said, pointing.

As Andrew grabbed the satchel, Judith gathered some clothing. Then they quit the room together.

"Sally!" he barked as they entered the hallway.

"Sally's elsewhere, milord." Andrew recognized Elmo's voice as footsteps clamored up the stairs. "How may I serve you?" the manservant inquired when he reached him and Judith.

"Elmo, I need a bath in my bedchamber. A hot one, very hot, and extra water, left in buckets. I also want strong soap, the strongest we have. See to it immediately."

"Aye, milord." Elmo turned and sprinted back down the stairs.

Though Judith managed stubbornly to keep on her feet, Andrew caught her up in his arms again and carried her most of the way. When they entered his room, he settled her into a chair.

"I shouldn't," she muttered. "The little buggers are going to jump off me and all over your things." She looked at him. "You already probably have them on your clothes!"

"Don't fret. I'll bathe when you're done. Now, drink this." Andrew poured Judith a glass of strong, red wine—when she swallowed it down, she made a face. Immediately, he regretted serving her spirits when she'd gone without food for so long. Belatedly, he worried that she might puke.

"Milord?" Bridget pushed open the door and presented a tray. "Elmo said you'd be here. I've brought Lady Judith's victuals, and the men'll be here shortly with the tub and the water."

"Good. Set the food down, and then you may go. If we need you to assist, I'll call."

"Andrew?" Judith said when the servant had gone.

"Aye."

"When the others come, would you please hide me? I'd rather no one else saw me looking like this."

He couldn't help pitying her as he watched Judith scratch and squirm, hating that she felt so miserable. But she was alive! She hadn't succumbed to that awful fever.

"Judith," he said gently, "I know you're distraught over your appearance. But, truly, you look—"

Wonderful. God's blood, he had almost said "wonderful!" He had no business saying any such thing, and he knew she would only scoff at the compliment. So Andrew amended, "You look as well as anyone could expect, after so many days abed with a raging fever. Besides, Elmo, Bridget and the others are merely servants of no consequence. What they see, what they think, matters not."

"It matters to me."

Andrew saw that it did, though it puzzled him why a lady would concern herself with the opinions of lowly servants. Yet when the men brought the tub to his room and others toted in the buckets of hot water, he did as Judith requested by standing in front of her chair to shield the damsel from their prying eyes.

He tested the temperature when the tub was filled. "It's hot, but not too hot," he assured her, drying his fingers on his tunic. "Have you finished eating? You'll want to get in, now, before the water cools."

Judith set her trencher aside, though she had consumed next to nothing. "Yes, I've eaten plenty. But I prefer to be alone when I bathe."

Andrew did not want to leave her alone. She'd been very sick and remained quite weak. And she hadn't eaten enough to fortify a louse. She could faint, fall, hurt herself. But he didn't wish to antagonize her, either, so he reluctantly agreed. "Very well. But I shan't be far. If you need me, call."

"I will. Thanks."

***

Judy waited until Andrew left the room and shut the door behind him. In her whole life, she had never felt so vile. And she looked as bad as she felt! To think that once upon a time she'd actually called in sick to work because she'd had a bad hair day... She had been clueless then, absolutely clueless.

Dropping the grimy sheet and glad to be free of it—the linen probably teemed with lice, too—she opened her tote and retrieved the mirror. She felt a sick temptation to gaze at her reflection again, the sort of urge people had to look at car wrecks as they drove by. Instead, she dug through her belongings, looking for her comb and scissors.

It took awhile—she panicked, thinking she'd left the scissors behind, either at the London hotel or Laycock Inn—but she found it tucked safely away in a zippered pocket sewn into the tote's lining, the same pocket where she kept her wallet secure.

Next, she steeled herself to examine her hair. Avoiding any glimpse of her face by angling her head just so, she peered into the mirror she propped on Andrew's table. Carefully, she parted her hair and combed her greasy, lice-infested locks. Dear God, but her roots had to be two inches deep! And her ends seemed split to infinity. How long had it been since she'd visited the hairdresser's? Too long, obviously.

That hardly mattered now. What did matter was cutting off this smelly seaweed clinging to her scalp. So Judy did, attempting, as best she could, to emulate what she had seen Vittorio do fifty times.

When she finished, it was apparent she hadn't her hairdresser's training or skill. In fact, she suspected she looked worse than when she started. Her only consolation was the knowledge she had most certainly left a lot of those awful buggers on the floor along with her badly shorn locks. If she needed to, she'd wear one of Beatrix's pointy hats or Camilla's scarves every waking hour of the day to hide her shaggy coiffure. After all, it wasn't as though she had a meeting scheduled with an editor anytime soon, now, did she?

Armed with her dwindling supplies, she soaked and scrubbed with the soap Andrew provided, starting at the top of her head and working her way down to her toes. When every inch of her flesh glowed rosily, she doused her hair with conditioner and wrapped her head in a towel. While the emollients soaked into her follicles, she shaved her legs and underarms. Then, using the clean water Andrew had ordered left in extra buckets, she rinsed not only her hair, but her entire body.

After toweling herself dry, she donned her own under things and pulled on her powder blue leggings. Purposely, she'd grabbed her own clothes from her room instead of a borrowed gown, because she felt sure her sweater and pants had less chance of being bug-infested. Yet it felt too warm for a thick, ribbed sweater today, so she decided to borrow something from Andrew. Rifling through his trunk, she found what she needed—an old linen tunic, one obviously well-worn and a bit frayed at the hem. Using her scissors, she cut it short and put it on as a shirt, which she belted.

"Judith! Judith, are you faring well?" Andrew called through the closed door.

"I'm fine," she assured him. "I'll be done in just a little while."

She returned to her mirror, surprised that she had the strength to continue. But determination energized her. With the speed and expertise she had acquired since discovering the wonderful world of makeup in her early teens, she smoothed foundation over her face, dusted her cheeks with powder and blush, and lined her eyes with kohl. Lastly, she dabbed thick coats of black mascara on her lashes.

"Judith? May I enter?"

"In a minute!" *Do they have minutes—on sundials, maybe? Does Andrew know what a minute is*? "In a moment. Please, give me just a little more time."

Her hair remained damp, especially with the mousse she had worked into it. She couldn't tell what it would look like when dry, but she crossed her fingers, hoping she'd appear more like an actress playing Peter Pan than a biker girl or a punk rocker. She also hoped the strands that remained visibly bleached would look more like frosting than an old, growing-out, dye job. Not that anyone here knew what "frosting" was, or Peter Pan. But she did. It was what she thought that mattered.

"Judith, I must see—"

Andrew flung open the door and Judy realized, as she turned to him, she'd been lying to herself. What Andrew thought mattered, too.

As he burst inside the room, he left off his explanation. The look on his face when he stared at her transformation made her uneasy. His expression reminded her all too much of his brother Elfred's, just before that idiot declared her a witch.

Maybe she had gone too far, even for him. Maybe Andrew wouldn't think she looked nice at all. Just bizarre. Like a...witch.

Fifteen

Andrew did not know what to make of Judith. She wore her own clothing, the leggings and shoes in which he'd first seen her. The tunic, however, seemed rather too familiar. He suspected he owned the garment, though Judith had cut it to a size she apparently preferred—a child's size. As well, she had cropped her hair and changed its color anew. But her miraculous recovery overshadowed that shock: No longer pale, her eyes sunken deep, Judith's skin had reclaimed its flawlessness, and her cheeks glowed a robust pink.

He felt relieved, elated. Still, all he said was, "Your hair."

Judith's lips turned down. "It looked awful. It probably doesn't look much better now, but at least maybe some of the lice went with it." She motioned to the pile of clippings on the floor.

"Some did, no doubt," he agreed. Reaching out, he gingerly touched the blonde and brown fringe skimming her brow. "I thought your tresses short before. Now, they be shorter than mine."

"Where I come from, women often wear their hair short. Some women even shave their heads."

"Good God—why?"

Judith shrugged. "To make a statement, I suppose."

"A statement?"

"To be different. To prove that they are persons in their own right, and that they don't care what other people think."

"Do you care what other people think?"

She hesitated, revealing her reluctance to reply. "Yes," she admitted. "I don't want Elfred—or you—to think I'm here to cause you harm."

"Yet you purposely declared yourself to be a witch, and you brandished your fire-starter to prove it," he recalled with a smile.

"I was mad. Angry. And your brother's such a twit!"

"A twit, is he? Am I a twit?"

Andrew's hand lingered near Judith's cheek. Her lashes fluttered as she looked up at him. "No. You're not a twit."

"And you are not a sorceress. I never thought that of you, Judith."

"What...do you think of me?"

He dropped his hand, but remained in the spot where he'd been standing. The fabric of their clothes brushed—another half a footstep, and he knew he could feel Judith's body, sense her heat. And then he would tell her exactly what he thought of her, wanted of her, needed from her.

"I think..." He cleared his throat. "...You are most unusual. A woman like no other."

"Ha!" She laughed and looked down at the floor. "I'm a dime a dozen."

"You're what?"

"That's an expression," she explained, peeking up at him through her wealth of ebony lashes. "It means I'm ordinary."

"You are not ordinary."

"Well, I'm not special." She moved, switching her weight from one foot to the other. His clothing finally grazed hers, and he felt the substance, the roundness, of her breasts as they skimmed his chest.

He inhaled a sharp breath. "To me...you are special."

No longer able to resist, he stepped closer. Judith's bosom plumped against him, and she took a breath as she lifted her green-eyed gaze to his. He hadn't noticed the golden flecks in her eyes before. She looked lovely and vulnerable.

"You only think I'm special," she responded, "because I'm different from the people you know."

"You are special, Judith," Andrew insisted, leaning toward her, very subtly, to avoid frightening her. "Not because your speech is odd and your clothing peculiar, but because you...are you."

He pressed his lips to Judith's forehead. Her skin felt warmer than he had expected, but he hadn't a moment to consider that fact. His thoughts hurried elsewhere as he felt her lean her weight against him while she settled her cheek against his chest. "Judith, I—"

She slipped. Her legs gave way. Before she could

crumple, Andrew caught her in his arms and hugged her to him. "Judith?"

Finding her feet again, she extricated herself from his embrace. "I'm sorry. I didn't mean to—to—"

"You're not well yet," he announced, surprised and sorry to know it was true. "You're still running a low fever. You should return to your bed."

"No!" Judith scowled. "I'm not going back to bed. I just had a bath and finally put on clean clothes."

"The servants have surely replaced your linens by now."

"Uh-uh." She shook her head stubbornly. "I would like some fresh air, though."

Judith feared another infestation of lice, that was obvious. He wondered how to tell her what he knew. "I could take you outdoors," he suggested. "'Tis very warm today, and there is, uh, something we might wish to do out there."

"What?"

He exhaled a loud breath before plunging ahead. "You still have nits in your hair. I can see them. But I can pick them out."

She blushed to her roots. "I still have bugs on me? And you want to go outside and nitpick, like a couple of monkeys?"

"I do not understand what a 'monkey' is, but if you fail to come with me, the eggs will hatch."

"Eeeuuuwww!"

She made a face that made him smile—he very nearly chuckled. Without requesting her permission, he gathered Judith up and headed for the door. "Let's do it and be done," he said. "I know you shan't rest easy if there remains the slightest chance you are home to a louse."

"But people will see!"

"Let them. 'Twill not shock anyone, as they've all been in your place one time or another. Many, no doubt, share your problem even now."

"Geez," she muttered miserably as he carried her down the stairs to the great hall, "little kids get lice. Dirty people. Not ladies."

"That isn't so. You're a lady, aye? And you have them.

But not for long," he promised, smiling at her confidently.

With a resigned nod, Judith wrapped her arms around his neck and clung to Andrew—like a monkey.

***

In the yard, Judy watched as he located a stool and a bucket. He sat her down on the upended bucket, which was lower than the stool, which Andrew took for himself. Strand by short strand, he examined her hair, plucking whatever nits were, exactly, and flipping them onto the ground.

"Won't they just hop right onto someone else?" Judy asked.

"They're eggs, Judith. Eggs don't hop. And I'm...preventing them from ever hatching."

This situation ranked as the worst thing that had ever happened to her—except, of course, for flying through time. But on the mortification scale, having her hair nitpicked by an English lord rated eleven on a scale of ten. Having it done more or less in public, where all the people who worked at Laycock Keep could see what Andrew was doing, probably pushed it up to a score of fifteen. Her only consolation was that these people certainly picked nits, lice, fleas and what have you quite regularly. Besides, in her own time they had all been dead so long, they did not remain even as dust. So, maybe this episode retained the rank of eleven in the humiliation competition.

Judy had to admit that it felt rather nice having someone toy with her hair, nearly as nice as having it washed. And Andrew certainly provided a more comfortable seating arrangement than a beautician's chair. True, the bucket beneath her left something to be desired. But not his muscled thighs, upon which she rested her arms. Or the warmth of his crotch at her back. She could feel all of him there, behind her. *All* of him. She suspected some of that *all* seemed to be growing.

"I'm finished," he announced, drawing her abruptly from her contented musings.

"Are you sure they're all gone?" she asked, twisting around to face him.

"Aye. Fairly sure."

She saw his gaze flick upward. Immediately, she touched her hand to the top of her head. "What is it?"

"Your hair is dry now. 'Tis much darker than before, though some of it remains fair. How did you manage that?"

"Magic."

"Watch what you say, Judith," Andrew advised. "You should not make such a jest, especially if Elfred's near."

"He isn't near. He and Robin left Laycock."

"Who told you that?"

"Bridget. You're in charge again, oh lord and master."

He arched an eyebrow as the corner of his mouth quirked on a smile. "You make still another jest?"

Judy grinned. "I guess so, because nobody's my master. Don't need one, don't want one."

Andrew's smile faded before it quite took hold. Gazing over her head, he asked, "Not even him?"

Curiously, Judy turned around. "Philip!" she said, seeing the fair-haired knight cantering into the bailey.

"Judith! Judith, is that you?" He reined his horse in and leapt off.

"Yes, it's me." She stood as he approached, less wobbly on her feet now.

"Why have you made yourself to resemble a lad?" he asked.

Judy bristled. "I do not resemble a lad."

"She doesn't, Philip. Admit it." Behind her, Andrew also stood. She felt his hands as he braced them on her shoulders. The gesture comforted her.

"Nay, of course she does not," Philip conceded. "You are beautiful, Judith, as always. But...I've ne'er seen a damsel with hair so short. And in boy's clothes!"

"They're not boy's clothes." She glanced down at her legs and feet. "Except for the shirt. It's Andrew's, but I cut it shorter to fit. I had to make sure everything I put on was fresh and clean."

Philip frowned at Andrew, seeking some explanation.

"Judith has been very ill most of the past sennight. We feared she mightn't survive. But she's nearly recovered now."

"Sweetling, how terrible! I'd no idea!" Philip grabbed both her hands in his own. "That is why they cut your hair again? The fever?"

"Actually, this morn Judith discovered—"

Judy ground her heel into Andrew's toes. He ceased his revelations immediately.

"I mean to say, Philip, you are precisely right," he amended. "Now tell us, how do you come to be here? I thought you'd ridden out with your sire."

"I did. But before we drew near to London, we had word that King John had begun to balk once again. The cur and his men have apparently renewed their veiled threats against us, so Father sent me home to help make ready for war."

"Then why are you at Laycock instead of North Cross?" Andrew inquired.

"Because I've not seen Lady Judith for so long, and because I wondered if your messenger had returned with good news."

Judy knew immediately which messenger Philip referred to. She also wondered if he'd returned to Laycock Keep with *bad* news.

Freeing her hands from Philip's, she turned around to look at Andrew. "He must have come back by now. What did he tell you?"

Andrew's dark eyes met her own. "He hasn't returned. We have had no word."

"What!" Philip said so loudly that Judy whirled to face him again. "Andrew," he complained, "you pledged to send out another man if the first did not return the same day I was last here. Surely something's happened to that messenger. Why did you not send another?"

"Because I had more pressing concerns than confirming Judith's noble lineage, that is why!"

"Naught is more pressing to me," Philip confessed. To Judith, he said, "Excuse us, will you, my lady? I would speak to Andrew privately."

She nodded, helpless to do otherwise, and both men stepped aside. They needn't have, because they proceeded to converse in French. All Judy could do was watch, attempting to interpret their body language.

"Andrew, why are you thwarting my efforts to confirm Judith's status as daughter of a knight?"

"I am not," Andrew insisted.

"You are. And you know I must verify her bloodlines, lest I am forced to ask for Lady Penelope's hand. That matter cannot be delayed much longer."

"Then ask for Penelope's hand. Naught prevents you from doing so."

"I'd prefer Lady Judith to be my wife."

"If, indeed, she is a lady," Andrew pointed out. "What if she's not? What if she's no kin to Peter Lamb? What if there remains the possibility she's as gently born as she claims to be, but 'tisn't your grandsire's friend to whom she is related? What then, Philip?"

"I know not, Andrew. I fear I could not wait 'til her true family is located. But from what I know of her, I am certain Sir Peter is her sire."

"Then offer Judith marriage!" Andrew said so loudly that he glanced around and, spying Judith looking at him, smiled and nodded apologetically.

"I cannot do that, not until I am certain she remains unwed and—"

"—Comes into the marriage with an estate large enough to support you," Andrew finished for him.

"Jesu," Philip hissed. "You make me sound like a greedy bastard, when you are in the precise same position as I!"

"Not exactly," Andrew amended. "I am not balancing the fates of two women, trying to determine which I shall love and hold dear based on the weight of her wealth."

"Talking to you is senseless," Philip declared. "As I am the one most keen to know Judith's true circumstances, I shall ride to York."

"But you said your father sent you home to North Cross to prepare for battle. How can you set off across England when you have responsibilities at home?"

"Unlike you, Andrew, I have many brothers. I did not return alone. Guy, Bertrand and Charles can prepare our forces without my personal assistance."

"Your father, Lord Cecil, will be angry that you disobeyed his orders," Andrew predicted.

Philip laughed sharply. "'Tis my mother, Lady Edwinna, I fear more than my sire! She is intent on having me make a good marriage, and she favors

Penelope. Should I lose that young lady's hand and then discover Judith is not suitable, she will personally send me to the bishop to have me ordained."

"You should not go to York," Andrew insisted. "I will send another messenger. You can send a messenger."

"I can go, and I will go. 'Tis you who cannot," Philip observed, gesturing with one hand to the bailey and the keep, over which Andrew ruled for the duration. "There's the rub, isn't it, Andrew? You want to know who Judith is, same as I."

"Nay, I care not." He shook his dark head. "The only reason for my interest is so that I may return her to her proper family. I am not the one hoping to wed her."

"You speak falsely, friend. Since we were lads, I've always known when you are lying."

"Damnation, I am telling you the truth," Andrew exploded. "Do you want to know why there's been no response from Sir Peter? Do you want to know why my messenger has failed to return with any word? Because I never sent a man to York!"

The yelling worried Judy. As she watched the pair, Philip squinted at Andrew as though in disbelief.

"I would have an explanation, Andrew," he said, his voice low. "You want her for yourself, don't you? That is why you've sought to delay finding evidence of her rank and eligibility. Unable to wait, I would be forced to pledge myself to Penelope Winfield, leaving Judith free. Then you could take her to wife. I'm correct, am I not?"

Andrew said nothing.

"I shan't allow you to manipulate me any longer. I will know the truth before I settle on Penelope, if it comes to that. And I will take Judith with me when I ride to York, so that you cannot court her, or seduce her and steal her from me while I am away!"

Andrew snorted contemptuously. "You think I haven't seduced her already?"

Judy saw Philip flush ruddily as he turned and stomped in her direction, Andrew following close behind. "What is it?" she asked him as both men halted beside her.

"My lady, tell me true," he begged in English. "Have you and Andrew...been intimate?"

What the hell has he been telling Philip? "No!" she responded firmly, answering his question but glaring at Andrew.

"Has he courted you in my absence?"

Judy met Philip's gaze. "No. As a matter of fact, he and his brothers locked me in my room. There was a fire, and he didn't even come to let me out!"

"You cur," Philip shouted at Andrew. Then he took Judy's arm and said, "You'll come home with me to North Cross, where you'll be welcome. On the morrow, we shall ride out together to York and visit Sir Peter Lamb. I'm sure you'll be glad to be reunited with your father and all your other kin."

Oh, hell. She didn't need this. Living at Philip's place wouldn't be bad...he was the one who wanted to marry her, after all. She had to have some protection until she found a way back home, or, failing that, made some sort of life here in medieval times. But riding on horseback to York, wherever that was, didn't sound like a hot idea. Besides, once they got there, the old man would tell Philip she was no relation of his. What would he think then? What would he do?

"Philip," she ventured softly, "I would like very much to accept your hospitality. I'd like to...meet your family. But as for going to York." She paused before bluntly plunging ahead. "What if this knight, this old alchemist and inventor, isn't my father after all? What if he doesn't know me? Do we really have to go traipsing all over the country to try to find where I come from? Does it really matter that much?"

"It matters, Judith." He set his mouth in a tight, solemn line

She wished Philip had said it didn't matter at all. Even more, she wished Andrew hadn't thrown their tentative friendship in her face by telling a bunch of lies about their relationship. Bad enough he picked lice from her hair in front of an audience, but to tell his best friend that he had slept with her? *What a jerk!*

"Does it matter to you, too?" she asked him.

Andrew shrugged. "'Twould seem that it matters to everyone, Judith. At least in this world."

He hadn't meant anything in particular with that

last remark, and Judy knew it. But suddenly it all became so clear to her, the great dichotomy between her world, late 20th century America, and theirs, medieval England. In her own time, her daily problems usually came down to catching a cab in the rain, while her pie-in-the-sky dream was to become a successful, maybe famous, literary agent. Here, the commonplace problems proved far more basic—getting rid of lice. Finding a man who could provide for her would prove her only major, long-term goal.

Her head swam. Either she was still sick, or she'd made herself ill by relinquishing the very essence of herself to curry favor with a man who might, hopefully, solve all her problems. How low she had sunk in such a brief time, to need a man to survive, a man who wouldn't even have her unless her parentage proved worthy. What an irony, what a joke! Back home, guys were terrified of women who wanted them to meet their families. Here, a female had no worth except as an extension of her parents.

She swooned. Andrew caught her, as always, just in the nick of time. While he cradled her in his muscular arms, she heard him say, through the ringing in her ears, "The lady is not traveling anywhere, most assuredly not with you. Did you think I spoke false when I said she has been gravely ill? Did you think I exaggerated when I said she nearly died? If so, that intuition you claim to have has failed you, Philip, for I spoke true. Judith is far from fully recovered, and 'til she has regained her health, she is going nowhere but back to her bed."

Andrew strode off, clutching her to him. As the distance between them and Philip grew, she heard the North Cross lord call after them, "I shall return for her, Andrew. When she is well, Judith and I will ride to York and confront Sir Peter!"

Sixteen

Judy sat in the solar. Because it was the highest room in the keep and no enemy had a hope of scaling the walls to this height, the solar laid claim to the stronghold's biggest window. She came here now because, after so many days lying in bed recovering, she yearned for a semblance of the bright outdoors. Basking in the warmth of the sun-washed room, she reflected upon the darkness of people's lives before the advent of electricity. Not only did the poor souls—herself now among them—find themselves basically blinded from nightfall to sunrise, their homes, whether cottages or castles, remained gloomy places even in daytime, lit mostly by smoky fires and dim, greasy candles.

Though the solar provided a cheery atmosphere this afternoon, she sighed heavily. Before her, on the floor where she sat cross-legged, lay her dwindling toiletries. She didn't know what she would do when she used everything up. And everything would be used up very, very soon.

Already, she had nearly depleted all her travel-sized accoutrements. Her shampoo was gone, along with her toothpaste, and only a dab or two of hand lotion remained in the tube, while her alpha-hydroxy face cream had been reduced to a smear inside the frosted glass jar. She still had pain relievers, antacids and half a roll of breath mints. But her tampons were gone. Thank heavens, she had carelessly tossed a sample package of thin pads into her tote before she left home, so she would be set the next time she got her period. But what of the time after that? What did medieval women do for hygiene when they menstruated? She had no idea and no one she could ask. Even Bridget or Sally would think she was crazy to remain so ignorant at her advanced age.

She puffed out her cheeks and exhaled noisily. She had time before desperation forced her to make inquiries on that particular topic. In the meanwhile...

Eager for diversion, she looked at herself in her hand mirror and discovered the perfect distraction: a zit! A big, red bump bulging on her cheek. That's what she needed—pimples!

Like a surgeon called upon to perform an emergency operation, she opened her makeup bag. Dumping the contents on the floor with the rest of her personal care items, she rummaged through her limited selection of old cosmetics, the stash she always took on trips, until she found a well-worn cover stick. Speedily, she painted over the blemish and then opened her compact to add a pat of powder. It, as well as her blush, had a large, empty space where the metal container clearly shone through. The same held true for her palette of mini eye shadows. Judy's two lipsticks, a neutral shade and a colorless gloss, were as stubby as her liner pencils. Most frightening, however, was the state of her mascara. When she plunged the wand up and down inside the tube, she could feel it hardening and knew, in another couple of weeks, she'd have nothing to thicken and blacken her lashes. Judy's only ample item appeared to be a nearly full bottle of "Tea Rose" perfume. She spritzed some on, letting the cloud of fragrance drift into her hair and onto her shoulders, hoping the scent would somehow console her.

It didn't. Sniffing wearily, she asked herself: *What am I going to do? I can pluck my eyebrows forever, but my disposable razor can't be replaced. When it goes, I'll get hairy like Sarah did, our sophomore year at college. Geez, when they finally took her cast off, the leg she broke didn't just look withered, it looked like it belonged to a chimpanzee! I'm going to look like a chimpanzee*! All too vividly, Judy imagined long, dark hairs twining around her limbs, and her underarms full of fuzz.

She sat there feeling sorry for herself until a shout from beyond caught her attention. She climbed onto the window seat and looked outside. "Someone approaches!" she heard a guard on the wall announce again, and then a flurry of activity erupted in the yard below.

She watched, fascinated by the precautions everyone took these days as they half-anticipated an attack or a siege. The dashing and scurrying, the women and children flying inside the keep, reminded her of her parents' stories about people ducking into fallout shelters back in the '50s whenever air raid sirens blared.

The Laycock laborers also fled for no reason. Soon another guard confirmed that the man rode alone, and then the approaching visitor was identified as Philip of North Cross.

Philip! Whirling away from the window, Judy's hand went to her heart. He had come for her, as he said he would! He intended to take her to York. But she didn't want to go to York. Besides it being a waste of time and the prelude to her being booted on her rear, she simply didn't want to spend all that time with Philip. She wanted to stay here with—

Andrew. The solar door swung inward and he stood there, filling up the portal. He breathed heavily, winded from running up the stairs. But though he failed to speak for a moment, his gaze held hers.

"Why were you not resting in your bedchamber?" he demanded finally, sounding thoroughly annoyed.

"I was bored. I wanted sunshine. I knew you wouldn't let me go outside, so I came up here instead."

He walked toward her. "You should have asked me."

"Why? You're not my lord and master, no matter how often you tell me you are."

"I might have let you go outside."

"Right."

"Wrong. I would not have. Judith, you need to rest 'til you're fully recovered. You are not fully recovered."

"I am," she insisted. "I don't know what I had, but I don't have it anymore. My appetite's back; I've been eating like a pig."

He reached out and grabbed her upper arm. "You're thin as a needle."

"I am not!" She pulled her arm free.

Cocking his head to one side, Andrew peered at her suspiciously. "Are you only saying you are well so that I will let you leave with Philip?"

Boy. I've blown it. "No. No, of course not."

"Then you do not wish to go with him to York?"

Again they locked gazes, only now the floor of the large solar no longer separated them. She could almost see her reflection mirrored in Andrew's dark eyes. She had an urge to step closer to him in order to see more detail. But if she stepped closer, she'd feel him, his bulk, his strength. And she'd end up telling him the truth. She couldn't do that. Andrew had been a real jerk, letting Philip think something had been going on between them. Because there hadn't been. Not a thing. Nothing at all.

"I didn't say that," she snipped. "Why wouldn't I want to go to York? You're sure my family lives there. If they do and I see them, the truth will come out. Then you'll all know for a fact I'm a lady, and you'll regret how badly you've treated me."

"How badly—I've treated—you?" Andrew ground out the words as his eyes widened, in surprise or outrage, she couldn't be sure which.

She took a step backward, reminding him, "You locked me in my room!"

"On Robin's orders."

"You didn't let me out when the place caught fire."

"I wasn't even home! I knew naught about the fire 'til much later. Besides, you set it. Elfred was right. You set it yourself in a ploy to get free."

"Maybe I did, maybe I didn't." She crossed her arms over her chest and tapped her foot. "The point is, I am free now. Free to go to York with Philip."

"Then you do wish to accompany him."

"Why wouldn't I? He hopes to reunite me with my family because he wants to marry me. I need a husband, Andrew. I'm sure I don't have one, so I guess I'd better get on the stick and find one. You know as well as I do, a woman alone is a woman under suspicion. Besides, Philip would make a great husband. And once he meets this Peter Lamb person, whom you and everyone else believes is my father, then we can get married."

Judy listened to herself, hardly believing what she heard. She had to be losing touch with reality; she sounded too convincing, as though she actually believed what she said. But she knew none of it was true. Her father was Tony Lambini, and he lived not in York but in New York. Nor was she a lady with a capital L, like Fergie, Duchess of York. And Philip of North Cross would never marry her, not only because she lacked the right lineage but because she, Judy Lambini, wouldn't marry him even if he asked.

Until that very second, she hadn't realized she had no intention of marrying Philip for convenience or any other reason. But Andrew didn't know what she knew, and he could just rot, damn him!

"Very well. He's here," Andrew informed her. "By now, he's seated below in the great hall, awaiting you. Go! Ride off with Philip. Wed him, share his bed, and bear his children."

"Fine," she snapped, "I will. Just for you."

"What do you mean, for me?" His heavy eyebrows met above his nose in a scowl.

"It's not as though you want me here. You know you don't." She pushed past Andrew, so distressed she didn't even think about collecting her tote, let alone picking up the debris she'd left scattered on the floor. Tears filled her eyes—hot, hurting tears that nearly prevented her from seeing the door.

Yet before she had taken more than a few, quick steps, she felt a hand clutch her own. Then she flew backward, whirling into Andrew's arms. She gasped as he clutched her close, and she moaned when he kissed her hard.

She kissed him back. Wrapping her arms around Andrew's neck, she kissed him as though they had never kissed before and might never kiss again.

"Damnation, Judith," he muttered when he released her lips to rain kisses on her forehead, her eyes, her cheeks, her jaw. "I have always wanted you. 'Tis why I brought you to the keep."

"But...you only wanted to sleep with me."

"Oh, aye. I wanted to lie with you. But I wanted more of you, Judith. You make my heart glad."

You make my heart glad. Her heart soared as though it had wings when Andrew's lips reclaimed her mouth and his tongue sought hers. While his hands roamed her back and her backside, she felt a strong yearning to wrap her legs around his waist. She wanted him to take her there and then.

But they couldn't make love at that moment. Both of them knew it, and both of them reluctantly pulled away. "What about...Philip?" she asked softly.

"You may be blunt with him, or you may be kind. Which do you prefer?"

"Well, kindness, certainly. I may not want to marry Philip, but I don't want to hurt him."

"Then, come. Back to bed with you. Until he leaves, you'll be ailing."

"Wait!" She pulled her hand free from Andrew's and began to pick up her toiletries, stuffing them into her tote. He assisted her until she had all her belongings secure. Then they hurried down the stairs.

***

"Lord Andrew." A servant accosted him just as Judy opened her door and slipped into her room. "Lord Philip is here. He asks to see you or Lady Judith."

"Tell him I shall be down shortly."

"Very well, milord." The man turned and retreated.

"Shut the door!" Judy whispered loudly when Andrew finally followed her inside. "Help me with these sleeves, will you?"

Handily as a servant, he loosened the laces that kept Judy's sleeves attached to her gown while she undid her girdle. Tossing them aside when she dropped the belt to the floor, he grabbed her tunic hem and drew it upward, pulling the dress off over her head.

Not until air caressed her nakedness did Judy recall she wore no underwear. From the look on Andrew's face, he, too, had been in such a frantic hurry that he hadn't anticipated her sudden nudity. But when he saw her unclothed, arms overhead because they remained caught in the tunic he still clasped in both hands, he threw the garment away. A second later, he had fastened his lips to one hardened nipple while he kneaded her other breast with his fingers.

"Oh." Judy threw back her head as he fondled her and kissed the column of her throat. "Andrew!" She hooked one leg around his hip, straining to feel the bulge of his sex against hers.

"Jesu," he muttered, grabbing her buttocks so that she could lift her other leg and twine it around him. "Sweetling, I want you so badly."

"I want—you," she breathed, smothering his handsome face with kisses.

"We—cannot." He turned so that she hovered over the edge of her bed.

"I—I know."

Andrew lowered her but followed her, so that Judy lay back against the mattress and he lay full atop her. "We really mustn't," he insisted, undoing his belt.

"There's no—time," she agreed, scrabbling at his tunic, trying to wrench it off over his head.

"Judith, are you within?" a man's voice called from beyond the closed bedroom door.

They both recognized Philip's voice, and they both froze. Then Andrew straightened, righted his tunic, and picked his belt up off the floor. As he fastened it in place around his waist again, Judy scrambled beneath the covers.

"Yes, Philip, I'm here," she returned breathlessly.

"May I come in?"

Andrew strode quickly to the door, kicking Judy's discarded clothes out of the way as he went. Then he opened the door and said, "Of course, you may enter."

Judy saw a scowl darken Philip's fair features. "I knew not that you were here as well," he told Andrew, stepping into the room.

"When I heard you'd come, Philip, I thought to learn whether or not Judith felt well enough to receive you. She thinks she is, though I do not."

"I can't go downstairs," Judy put in, still trying to catch her breath. "But I'd like you to visit." She punctuated the invitation with a wan smile.

"You do not sound well." Philip continued to frown as he approached the bed, though he now seemed more concerned than irate. "Are you congested?"

"No. Just weak."

He put a hand to her brow. "You are warm and flushed. Methinks you still suffer a fever."

Judy couldn't help glancing beyond Philip at Andrew, who remained near the door. Oh, she suffered a fever, all right. A lustful fever!

Philip did not sit. He stood, his hands clasped in front of him, and glanced back at Andrew before telling Judy, "I had hoped to take you to York. 'Tis a fairly long journey, and I haven't much time."

"Because you're preparing to go to battle against the king's men?" Judy inquired.

"What?" He blinked at her. "Oh, aye. That's it."

Yeah, yeah, that's the ticket, Judy added in her mind. He was such a liar! She hadn't expected that of Philip. And yet, she didn't care. If he didn't really have the time to drag her up to York, so much the better.

"I wouldn't want to keep you," she told him. The truth being that she couldn't wait for him to go, so Andrew would return to her, alone. "Besides, I think I need to sleep now."

"Forgive me, my lady." Chivalrously, he took her hand and bowed over it, kissing her knuckles. "I do not mean to tire you." Turning, he walked to the door and said to Andrew, "I need speak with you. Will you join me?"

"Aye. Judith, we'll leave you to rest." Andrew backed out of the room following Philip, but he awarded her a subtle look, full of promise, before he shut the door.

***

"God's bloody wounds," Philip muttered as they headed downstairs together. "I would suspect you of trying to keep me away from Judith, if I had not seen with my own eyes that she is ill."

"We've been friends our whole lives," Andrew returned as they paused upon entering the great hall. "Why would I thwart your pursuit of true love?"

Philip cocked an eyebrow. "I know not, except, perhaps, because you fancy Judith your own true love?"

He flinched but covered his reaction quickly with a merry laugh. Until that moment, Andrew had failed to realize feelings that Philip assessed so accurately. He did not merely wish to bed Judith; he loved the wench, short hair, sharp tongue, strange possessions and all! He wanted her at his side for decades to come, 'til they grew old and had raised a dozen children between them.

Yet he insisted, "I think not. My brothers are suspicious because she insinuated herself into our household with no endorsement. In these troubled times, they trust no one. And Elfred actually believes she's the daughter of a wizard or some such. Nay. I've no need to entangle myself with a damsel of dubious origin." He leaned an elbow on a table and peered at Philip. "Why do you?"

"I told you. I care for her. She intrigues and delights me. If her father is both knighted and wealthy, and she comes dowered through him or another source, I would gladly make her my bride. Certainly, she is more woman than Penelope."

"Penelope can be little more than a child. She'll grow into a woman, given time. Besides, she was certainly reared to be a landlord's wife and trained to run his home as a chatelaine. Judith was not. Though intelligent, mayhap even educated, she knows naught about a lady's place in our society."

Philip closed his eyes and shook his head. "She stirs my blood, Andrew."

If Philip hadn't opened his eyes the moment he spoke, Andrew would have punched him. But he did, unwittingly avoiding the attack.

"Then you must bide your time." He straightened, clapped a hand on Philip's shoulder, and began escorting him to the keep's front portal. "Mayhap all this business with the king will be finished soon. Afterward, you'll have the leisure to escort Judith to York. When you learn her true identity, if you still wish, you may wed her then."

"Damnation, Andrew!" Halting, Philip threw off Andrew's arm as he turned to him. "Do you not understand? 'Tisn't battle preparations that limit my time, 'tis Lady Penelope and my very own mother! They would have me go to Winfield and propose marriage promptly. I am running out of excuses to put them both off."

"Then proceed to York alone," Andrew suggested. "Verify that Judith is the alchemist's daughter, a noblewoman born and reared, and return with that information. Certainly, Judith will be pleased."

"What if she isn't?"

"Pleased?"

"Nay. What if she isn't Peter Lamb's daughter or any kin to him at all?"

Andrew shrugged nonchalantly. "Then I suppose you'll know the better choice for you is Lady Penelope."

"Obviously, I am not making myself clear," Philip conceded irritably. "Judith must be identified by her kin in the flesh. I haven't the luxury of leisure time, not with my mother and Penelope pressing me to make a decision. Riding alone to York, speaking with Sir Peter, returning here, and then escorting Judith back to York, would take too long now. If you had but sent your messenger when you promised—"

"I didn't," Andrew interrupted curtly. "So what will you do?"

"I don't know." He looked down at his shoes. "I must put off both Edwinna and Penelope longer still. Perhaps I can, because they will see the tensions between the barons and the king's men, as well as our preparations for war, as legitimate priorities. If only Judith recovers quickly now."

"Not for her sake, but for yours?"

"Damn you, Andrew," Philip exploded. "Judith cares for me, too, you know. She wishes to have me court and marry her as much as I want to."

He bristled. "Is that so? Then why don't you wed her immediately and let your mother and Penelope be damned?"

Philip set his jaw and narrowed his blue eyes. "Why don't you?"

"Because...I am not looking to marry. Chandra cured me of that notion. Besides, my family would ne'er welcome her. My brothers think her too fey, too strange."

"Ha! You care not what Elfred thinks, or Robin, or even your sire. You have no future here at Laycock, so you are free to go where you will, do as you wish. But you know you need a wealthy bride if you're ever to marry. 'Tis one matter to earn your living as a mercenary or even to take holy vows. But to risk marrying a cottar's daughter and being reduced to the life of a tenant farmer, as though you were born a serf? Never! You would no more take that chance than I."

Philip sounded so certain, but Andrew wondered. Would he? Would he risk everything to marry Judith?

"I don't know what else I can say to you, Philip." He shook his head and resumed his trek to the door. "You have your choices: Ask for the hand of either damsel immediately, or bide your time, hoping that Judith is dowered or, if she is not, that Penelope has waited for you. 'Tis your risk, your decision."

Philip nodded in agreement as they stepped outdoors. "You will send word when Judith is recovered, or if you learn anything about her situation that might concern me?"

Andrew nodded, too, but he did not say aye.

Seventeen

Andrew delayed returning to Judith's bedchamber. He could hardly believe he restrained himself, for the anticipation of making love to her heated not only his blood but his flesh— indeed, he felt feverish.

But he understood he'd arrived at a critical juncture in his life. Everything he did from this moment forward would have a lasting impact. No longer could he idle away his time, resenting his status as younger son but enjoying his family's indulgence, doing naught to carve a place for himself in this world. He'd lived two and twenty years already. He was a man, not a boy. He had to stop behaving like a youth and finally make a man's choices, living with the consequences, whatever they might be.

He poured himself some wine and sat in his favorite chair near the fire pit. Though he could only feel contempt for his friend's callousness, Philip was right when he insisted that the two of them shared similar circumstances and faced similar fates. Yet there remained a singular difference between them: Philip could wed Penelope, who would provide him with the privileged life he'd always known. If Andrew married Judith, he had no proof she could do the same for himself. Nor was he confident that he could provide adequately for her.

Finding his goblet empty, though he did not recall drinking the wine, he refilled it and sipped thoughtfully. Did he truly care whether or not Judith had land or money? Would he view her differently once he had proof she was a lady in fact or, on the other hand, if he found it impossible to determine her heritage at all? Andrew believed he would not. He hoped he was a better man than Philip and that living a simple life with Judith would prove superior to living in abundance without her. Yet it was one thing to sit in the comfort of his sire's keep and conjecture on the matter. It would be something else again to face being a landless pauper with a wife and babes to provide for.

Raising his cup to his lips, Andrew again discovered

it empty. He set it aside, annoyed. Getting drunk would solve naught. Nor would worrying about events yet to happen—that might never happen. The wise thing to do would be to take Judith to York as Philip had intended. The old knight might well claim her as kin and confirm that she remained an eligible maiden. And if it happened that Judith owned an estate, however small, which would come to Andrew through their marriage, then the two of them might live together happily without facing hard choices. So to take her to York, Andrew decided, was what he must do.

He took the stairs slowly, not eager to return to Judith's chamber, and entered her room without warning. She remained abed, no longer flushed but radiant. She smiled invitingly and held out her arms.

Andrew winced and glanced away. It took all his willpower not to accept her unspoken invitation, the one he had yearned for, dreamt of, and anticipated for so many weeks. Yet he managed to close the door and remain standing near it. He did not go to Judith.

"What's the matter?" she asked, her tone sharp as her smile disappeared. "Did Philip say something? Are you angry?"

"Nay." He shook his head. "Nothing untoward has happened, and Philip has returned to North Cross. But we did have a conversation that made me realize..."

"What?" Judith leaned forward. "What did you realize?"

"'Twould be wrong for us to make love now."

"What!"

Andrew couldn't hold his position. He strode stiffly to the bed, sat down, and took Judith's hand in his own. "'Tisn't that I've no wish to. By the saints, there is nothing more I want than to know the delights of your sweet body! But Judith, 'twould not be right for me to have carnal knowledge of you."

"Not be right...?" she repeated, blinking at him in obvious disbelief. "Andrew Laycock, you tried to have carnal knowledge of me the very first day I was here. Not once but twice, if I recall. You made another attempt that day you found me bathing at the stream. Now that I'm willing, you no longer can? What is this?" she demanded, her voice growing higher. "Do you only have sex with women you have to force yourself on? Do you get off on brutality or something?"

"Nay!" That Judith could suggest such a wicked thing appalled him. "I have ne'er forced myself on a woman. I told you that. By now, you should know me well enough to be sure I would not."

"I don't know you at all." She yanked her hands free from his and looked away toward the window.

"Judith." He turned her face back to his with a touch of his fingers. "Judith, I shall escort you to York to see your sire. I cannot present you to him with any honor if I've lain with you first. Even if he never knew, 'twould be a grave insult to him."

Her lashes fluttered. "Why do you have to escort me to York? I don't care if Peter Lamb is my father or not. I thought Philip was the only one who cared about that." She paused and met his eyes. "But I was wrong, it seems. You do, too, don't you?"

Andrew took a deep breath. "I shall escort you home for the purpose of reuniting you with your kin and, when we confirm your assertion that you are—" he almost said, "a gently born lady," but caught himself. "—Unwed, then I shall ask Sir Peter for your hand."

Judith's eyes narrowed. "You're saying you want to marry me?"

It took him a moment to try to form his reply. He did want to marry her, he already knew that. But he'd asked a woman to marry him before, and though Chandra had agreed, she'd run off and wed another man. It was not so easy for Andrew to propose marriage again.

"You take a lot for granted, pal," Judith sneered, and he knew he'd fueled her ire by hesitating overlong. "Fact is, I don't want to marry you," she added before throwing herself back against her pillows and drawing the covers up to her chin.

She had closed the conversation and dismissed him.

But he didn't leave. He stood, insisting, "Judith, you must come with me."

"No. I'm a little slow, but I finally figured it out. When you thought I was nobody, you wanted to jump my bones. But then you got to thinking maybe I was somebody, and it wouldn't be right to have an affair with a noblewoman, especially one who could have a husband somewhere. Now you want to find out, one way or the other, because you've decided to marry me so your best friend can't. This isn't about me. It's about your rivalry with Philip. But you can forget it, mister. Marry you—ha! Whether I'm related to one of those farmers in town or I'm King John's niece, you're never ever getting into bed with me." She gave him a narrow, steely glare. "Get out, Andrew. I'm not going anywhere, most assuredly not with you!"

He had tried to do the honorable thing, and now the wench turned on him. "You're going," he ground out, grabbing Judith's wrist.

"No."

"Aye!"

"Why?" She wailed her short query plaintively. "We could have had a wonderful time together, no complications, no strings. Why did you have to go and ruin it, Andrew?"

"Because we must both know your kin and your circumstances, Judith. Without a history, there can be no future. And I want a future—with you."

He finally brought her to silence. Judith stared at him with wide, green eyes shimmering with tears. When she blinked, one drop trickled from each eye, wetting her cheeks.

He wanted to brush the dampness off her skin, but instead he strode to the door. "We shall leave on the morn," he advised, his words clipped. "Pack what belongings you will, but be prepared to depart after sunrise."

***

As soon as he'd gone, Judy brought her hands to her face, pressing them against her eyes to thwart the deluge of tears. She had never been so humiliated in her life! Never before had she openly invited a man into her bed. Finally she'd risked making the overture, confident that Andrew desired her, and he had refused. Why? Because he wanted to *marry* her! Dear God, everything was so crazy in this world. Here, if a guy didn't give a damn about a girl, he was hot to get her between the sheets. But if he cared for her, loved her, then he wouldn't touch her...until she proved she was worthy of wife- and motherhood.

Well, she wasn't worthy, not by Philip and Andrew's standards, so they could both just drop dead. She didn't need either of them. Judy Lambini wasn't going to York, not now, not tomorrow. She was going home—*home!*—to New York. And when she left, she wouldn't be taking any irrational, impossible, medieval knight with her. No sireee.

***

Judy didn't know what to pack, but she had to pack. Andrew had left her no choice. Besides, she consoled herself, it would kill some time until the next Samhain.

After wrapping one of Andrew's sister's gowns around her nylon tote, Judy tied her bundle with a length of cord. Then, making sure she was put together, from her sweater to her leggings to her boots, she stomped down the stairs carrying her belongings over her shoulder like Santa did his sack of toys.

Andrew awaited her in the bailey. "Did you eat?" he asked solicitously, taking her bundle and securing it behind the saddle of a small horse that stood near his stallion, Zeus.

"Yeah," she replied, lying through her teeth. She'd had no appetite this morning. She didn't think she'd ever feel like eating again.

"Good. You need to keep up your strength." Andrew gestured toward the smaller horse. "Are you going to mount your palfrey?"

"My what?"

"Your palfrey, milady. The little mare."

"Oh. Sure." Taking her time and playing for more, Judy walked all the way around the spotted gray beast. Once. And once again. With her limited equestrian experience confined to pony rides as a youngster, she searched her brain for any knowledge that would help her now. Suddenly, she recalled a useful bit of information: A rider mounted from the left. She stopped beside the animal's left flank and gazed at the beast. It didn't matter that the mare looked a great deal smaller than Andrew's stallion, the horse still seemed damned tall.

"Is there a problem?" Andrew asked.

Judy snapped her head toward him. "No," she said, lying again. "I was just going to the proper side to climb up."

"There is no proper side, Judith. Left or right will do."

"Oh." That was news, she thought as she considered the stirrup. The darned thing came only to the middle of her chest. How would she get her foot into it? She wasn't a contortionist, after all.

"Oh!" she yelped as Andrew solved her dilemma without discussion. Grabbing her from behind, he tossed her into the saddle. Judy thought he squeezed her rump a little harder than he needed to as well, but she didn't comment. In truth, she felt relieved to have gotten onto the animal without incident.

"You do know how to ride, do you not?" Andrew inquired, climbing up onto his own horse.

"Do ladies know how to ride?" she shot back.

"I've ne'er known one who doesn't."

"Then I know how to ride." Lie number three.

"If you're ready, let us be off." Without waiting for her response, Andrew spurred his stallion so that the huge beast lunged toward the gate at a brisk canter.

Judy was not ready. For a brief moment, she wondered how to steer her horse to make the animal go where she needed her to go. But the mare took off on her own, mimicking the bigger animal's gait by lunging into a high-stepping canter. Judy squealed, wrapped the reins around one fist and grabbed the palfrey's mane with the other.

Andrew understood immediately that Judith did not know how to ride—her inexperience was obvious. But despite the tension between them born of bruised feelings and incipient anger, he could do naught but admire her. Amazingly, the wench managed, by perverse determination alone, to stay astride her palfrey—though she did bounce riotously, her delicious derriere jiggling tantalizingly in the saddle. Why, he wondered, had she chosen to wear chausses and not a lady's gown? God's teeth! He didn't think he could endure the whole journey with Judith displaying herself in such an alluring fashion. His cock had been turgid since they'd ridden out of the bailey—he might injure himself if the swelling did not go down.

To help quell his lust, he pushed well ahead of Judith. The road that meandered through the forest covering most all of England fairly disappeared beyond this point, and he needed to watch where he led her. Even more, he needed to keep Judith out of his direct line of sight.

***

Andrew didn't hear her. During many hours of pushing forward, riding hard miles, he had been absorbed in thought, worrying that he'd left Laycock Keep without a lord in residence. As well, he had fretted over what would happen when they reached their destination. Only belatedly did he realize that Judith's palfrey's footfalls no longer echoed his own steed's. Turning quickly in his saddle, his heart stopped cold when he discovered Judith nowhere behind him.

"Judith!" he shouted as he reined Zeus around and headed back along the narrow, trampled track that lay dark beneath the leafy canopy. "Judith!" he shouted again, kicking the stallion into a run.

The trail wended among the trees. Ducking and dodging branches as he raced along, Andrew's heart and the stallion's hooves pounded in syncopation. Beyond every bend, he expected to see her; when he did not, he spurred Zeus harder. Finally, coming around still another turn, he spied her. Pulling hard on his reins, he halted his warhorse before the animal careened into the palfrey and sent Judith flying out of her saddle. As it was, she appeared almost boneless, slumped in her seat with her chin on her chest while the mare munched grass sprouting among the ferns.

"Judith? Judith, you're not falling ill again, are you?" he asked, fearing the worst. She looked quite pale. Andrew knew he should not have pushed her so hard.

"No," she replied curtly as her head came up. Her eyes met his, and she pursed her lips. "I just needed to rest. I asked you to stop, but you didn't even slow down."

"Forgive me. I didn't hear you."

"I'll bet."

She remained angry with him, yet Andrew felt so relieved at finding her whole and well after fearing he'd lost her, he refused to return her disdain. Leaping down from his saddle, he reached a hand up to her and urged, "Come down, then. 'Tis almost midday. We can have a bite to eat."

"It's not even noon?" Judith wailed plaintively. "My God, I thought we'd been riding for ten or twelve hours already."

"'Tis difficult to see the sun, but it remains directly overhead."

"I believe you." She reached for him, but instead of merely using his hand to assist in her dismount, she collapsed, sagging toward him. Andrew caught her and hugged her to him.

She slid down his length until her feet reached the ground. Gazing at her upturned face, he realized how very much her short hair suited her. Even the dual hues of those shaggy tendrils framing her features seemed natural and most becoming. And those eyes peeking up at him through that thick fan of lashes, sea green and sparkling, like sunlight glinting off the waves...

He fought a tremendous impulse to lean forward and kiss Judith's suddenly yielding lips. He feared losing all restraint if he touched his mouth to hers. He did not wish to compromise her, not until he knew for certain he could call her his forever.

Yet—oh, Jesu, what was this? She leaned closer to him, pressing her thighs against his legs, her breasts against his chest. They were so near in height, it seemed all their parts meshed perfectly. And no longer did she offer her lips to him. Instead, she had fastened them to the hollow of his neck as she rested her head on his shoulder. He felt their heat as Judith moved slightly, leaving a fiery trail across his throat, up the underside of his chin, and then farther, along the line of his jaw.

"What...are you doing?" he managed gruffly, holding his limbs stiff and unresponsive though he knew his cock had gone stiff in a very spirited response to Judith's ardent attentions.

"What?" she mumbled, her reply muffled because she didn't pull away. She'd become preoccupied thinking about how good it felt to be in Andrew's arms again. His embrace was strong but gentle, not hard and painful, as everything about that crummy horse seemed to be. Besides, despite her justified anger, she had missed his arms around her. Now that they encircled her again, she felt as though she was where she belonged.

"I thought we had agreed to restrain ourselves until we've met with your father," Andrew recalled.

"Oh. Oh!" With a gasp, she belatedly realized where she was, what she'd been doing. Embarrassed and irate, she stumbled backward into the mare standing behind her. She knew her cheeks flushed hotly, so she covered her face with one hand before turning aside. "I—I felt faint," she said, deciding she wasn't lying outright. "I'm not myself today. I'm hungry and tired, and a little light-headed."

She attempted to stride off, but her knees buckled. As she wondered if she'd ever walk straight again, she felt Andrew catch her and lift her into his arms. Then he carried her to a nearby tree. After putting her down beside it so that she could use the wide, sturdy trunk to rest her back, he said, "I'll get us some food."

Judy felt just as relieved when Andrew busied himself elsewhere for a minute or two. She'd been so furious with him, so hurt! If he'd been a man of her own time, in her old life, she would never have returned his phone calls. Conversely, she'd have gladly returned any tokens of apology, whether candy, flowers or jewelry. But Andrew hadn't apologized. He had dragged her off on this trip despite her protests and for the last several hours, he'd put her through the tortures of the damned. But did she have any pride? No way. The second he had her in his arms, she kissed him!

There had to be some reason Judy Lambini, modern day woman, couldn't stay mad at Andrew Laycock. Once she was back in her Manhattan apartment, Judy intended to figure out why. Until then, she would just keep her distance.

By the time Andrew returned to Judith with a small bundle of victuals, he had regained his composure. He doled out the food and then offered her a sip from his wine skin.

"No." She refused adamantly.

"Nay? But you must drink as well as eat, especially when you're traveling. Already, the morning's ride has wearied you."

"No," she insisted, turning her head aside and chewing her bread as though it were leather.

Andrew sat back on his haunches and studied her. "Why not?"

"Because I'm afraid I'll—" Judy broke off her explanation. After a moment's hesitation, she decided honesty couldn't wound her pride any more than her heart had already been mangled. She admitted, "I'm afraid I'll fall asleep in the saddle. In case you didn't notice, I really don't ride all that well. I have enough trouble staying seated when I'm conscious. If I dozed off, I'd probably do a nose dive."

Another of her silly, incomprehensible phrases, Andrew realized. "A nose dive?" he repeated.

"I'd fall off the palfrey head first."

"Ah."

Judith eyed him warily. "Go ahead," she urged with a gesture. "Make a joke or something. A lady who can't ride, imagine that. I really don't care what you think anymore."

She did care, that was obvious. So Andrew decided to be gallant rather than truthful and said graciously, "I confess I didn't notice that your riding skills were lacking."

"Really?" Judith sounded dubious as she watched him through narrowed eyes.

"Aye. But if you wish, as we continue, I can instruct you. It may give you more confidence."

"Thanks, but there's no point. I doubt I'll be doing much riding in the future."

"Truly? Why not?"

"Because...peasants don't own horses." She challenged him with her gaze.

Andrew refused to pick up the gauntlet. He would not fight with her now. But he noticed that after she swallowed her bread, it seemed to stick in her throat.

"Would you like some water?" he asked.

"Yes, I would."

He straightened and turned, intending to retrieve the water skin.

"That's okay. I'm not helpless, I can get it myself," Judith insisted, sounding rather like a cocky page. "Where is it? In your pack on Zeus?"

"Aye, but—" Andrew looked over his shoulder and discovered, to his dismay, that Judith clung to the tree trunk as she dragged herself to her feet. Wincing, she brushed off her backside before taking a few wobbly steps.

He grabbed her elbow, but she shook her head as she pulled free. "It's all right," she assured him. "I may not be an expert rider, but I have been walking since I was only one or two. I know how to do that fairly well."

Judy knew she wasn't proving her point with her slow, crooked gait. Lord Almighty, but her legs felt like she'd just done twelve solid hours on a Stairmaster! Still, she had some dignity left, bruised ego and all. Under her own power, she made her way to the horses and the water.

Andrew let her go unassisted, smiling to himself as he watched Judith hobble over to Zeus. Damnation, but the wench was willful, stubborn and proud. Most men considered those admirable traits only in other men. But they suited a woman such as Judith just as she suited him.

Judith knew they were a pair, Andrew knew she did. When all this business was done, she'd admit it and fall into his arms once again. That's what mattered to him, not who her sire was, or if she had wealth. Only that he could hold her, and love her, and cherish her 'til his time on Earth ran out.

Eighteen

Judy made a contented sound and snuggled into her blanket where she lay beneath the ashen sky. "Snuggled" wasn't the most appropriate word, she corrected herself as the term came to mind. Snuggling implied cozy comfort, an altogether pleasant experience. If one of her writers had used "snuggle" to describe the way she felt in this situation, Judy would have suggested he find other, more accurate modifiers: atrophied, cramped, frozen, miserable, suffering, aching...

She and Andrew had ridden for what seemed another eternity after their lunch and bathroom break. Bathroom, ha! Judy thought she might be getting a rash on her bottom from using leaves for toilet paper, or maybe blisters from slamming against the saddle hour after agonizing hour.

Her thighs and her butt weren't the only parts of her anatomy that felt raw, inflamed, or so sore as to be nearly paralyzed. Her legs, feet, back and arms throbbed as well. All afternoon, as her anguish increased, she had longed for Andrew to announce they were stopping for the night. He didn't, though, and she didn't ask what his plans were. She would have died before begging him to pack it in for the day, and there were times she thought she was going to.

Of course, Andrew did stop, finally—still in the never-ending forest with no tavern, inn or even a crofter's hut in sight. She managed to climb off her horse unassisted, and then Andrew started a small campfire, obviously pleased as punch when he used the disposable lighter to ignite his little pile of twigs. Afterward, he set out with a bow and arrow, announcing his intention to kill some game for supper.

Judy supposed he had—the aroma of cooked meat still hung in the air. But she hadn't eaten anything. She hadn't even been awake when Andrew returned from his expedition. The moment she lay down on her blanket to wait for him, she went out like a light. Thank God.

Exhaustion had inured her to her various discomforts so that she managed to rest a while. Now, though, as birds began chirping to welcome the approaching dawn, she again found herself keenly aware of her personal miseries. Not only did every muscle in her body scream in torment, the earth she lay upon poked and prodded every square inch of her body. Bravely, she ventured to turn her head from one side to the other, risking excruciating neck pain.

She discovered Andrew lying beside her making little snuffling sounds as he slept. She found his light snoring kind of cute and rather endearing, but that was because of his proximity. When Andrew drew near, she fixed her sites only on him, while the big picture grew as fuzzy as an out-of-focus snapshot. But boy, oh, boy, it felt chilly, and Andrew was nothing if not a great source of heat. She could only hope that as long as he remained sleeping, she would be safe—from herself. Apparently Andrew intended to keep her safe from all other dangers by leaving one hand on the sword lying between them. She marveled, with an inner sense of delight, to know she had slept beside a knight prepared to protect her at all costs by brandishing his heavy steel blade. Yowza!

Yet a big ache throbbed in her chest so that she couldn't continue looking at him. She rolled her head away as the combination of Andrew's macho manliness and innocent repose tugged at her heart. Geez, Louise! Why did she put herself through this? She wasn't anymore right for him than a knight from the Middle Ages was right for a 1990's career woman. So loving Andrew—

I don't love him! What am I thinking? Love Andrew, ha! All she had actually wanted was a little romance, a fling, with an extremely attractive and available guy. But he'd quashed that plan. Now, she was only biding her time 'til next fall when she could make another attempt at time travel. Loving Andrew, for a bit or forever, would be just plain stupid. And Judy Lambini wasn't stupid. Besides, she reminded herself, despite Andrew's sex appeal, he could frequently be a great big jerk!

The object of her musings snorted and moved slightly. Her body tingled where his touched hers, so she inched away, putting more space between them. Then she propped herself on one elbow and, unable to resist, peered down at him again.

It was clear why he made her feel all gushy inside. Though she had spurned his advances on principle, she knew he'd caught her fancy the very first day she had met him. She had let him grope her while he argued with his brothers in the great hall. She had felt that spark of sexual heat the first time he'd climbed into bed with her, and when he'd grabbed her leg under the dinner table, too.

No man in her own time had ever excited her the way Andrew did. But then, she had never met, in her own time, someone like young Lord Laycock. He had a body like a lifeguard and thick, shiny, dark brown hair that sort of waved around his head, making Judy want to run her fingers through it. Andrew's eyes were even darker, nearly as black as his pupils, and they drooped as though their long lashes weighted down his lids. Bedroom eyes, if there ever were any.

She moved the arm much of her weight lay upon and yelped when a stone pressed into her flesh.

Andrew's eyes popped open, and his hand clenched the hilt of his sword as he sat upright, scouring the vicinity with a purposeful gaze. "What is it?" he demanded, turning to her after he'd apparently concluded they faced no danger.

"Nothing. I was lying on a rock or something. It hurt."

"Oh." Andrew pulled her arm across his lap and stroked it from wrist to shoulder.

He seemed to be trying to soothe her pain. It worked.

"How badly do you hurt?" he asked.

Judy chortled. "Badly. Very badly. How can you stand it, riding so long and hard?"

"I'm well-used to riding. I hunt, and I train with Zeus so that we're prepared to go into battle together. I vow, 'tis far more grueling to ride wearing chain mail and brandishing both shield and mace."

"I suppose. But knowing things could be worse doesn't make me feel any better."

Andrew shrugged his blanket aside and stood. "Let me tend the fire and bring you something to eat. Sweet

Mother Mary, but you must be starving! I dared not wake you earlier because you needed your sleep. But now you must put some food into your belly. Afterward, I can do something to ease your aches and pains."

Judy nodded gratefully, but she doubted anything short of a whirlpool, a masseuse, and a big dose of pain pills could ease her misery.

"What's this?" she asked dubiously when Andrew returned to her pallet and handed her something impaled on a stick.

"A hare."

Judy peered at her food more closely. Minus fur and tail, and cooked to a golden, crunchy turn, it remained, indeed, a rabbit, which she did not find particularly appetizing.

"Eeuuww!" With a grimace, Judy waved the stick at Andrew.

"What's wrong?"

"I can't eat this. It still has its head!"

"You needn't eat the head," Andrew explained patiently, sitting down on the edge of her blanket. "Nor the bones nor the entrails. Just the flesh, which is very tasty, even cold."

"I can't. It reminds me of a Guinea pig I used to keep as a pet."

"A what?"

"Another small animal, one I fed and played with but never cooked and ate."

Andrew narrowed his eyes. "Methinks you must be more than a lady—mayhap a spoilt princess. Well, let me play the servant and tear the meat from the bones for you. You must eat, Judith. Your foregoing drink and food is not an option."

Reluctantly, she agreed. Andrew held the stick and patiently peeled the meat away from the small carcass. He fed each morsel directly to her, holding it between his thumb and index finger until she took the food into her mouth.

"Hey, this isn't bad after all," she admitted. "It reminds me of something I've eaten before."

"When I travel any distance, I always carry a pouch with a special mix of herbs my mother combines together. The seasonings enhance the flavor of many meats, from fowl to fish, and they're easy to carry. Plain meat will always suffice to ease one's hunger. But why not make the victuals savory so that they are truly enjoyable?"

"Smart thinking," Judy agreed, wondering where she had eaten something so similar. It hadn't been too long ago, and she thought it must have been in England. At home, she tended to eat ethnic takeout or frozen entrees.

Her appetite aroused by the taste of food, Judy gestured for Andrew to give her another tidbit. Grinning, he complied, but she closed her mouth too quickly, accidentally capturing the tip of Andrew's finger between her lips. They both went completely still. He left his finger imprisoned, and she neither chewed nor swallowed. As their eyes met, she slid her lips farther down, past Andrew's knuckle, and sucked. A tremor ran through her as he inhaled a quick, startled breath.

Judy didn't breathe. Andrew's drowsy, molten gaze heated her own insides until they melted. Finally, she had to inhale or drown in the churning, liquid emotions bubbling inside her. Yet when she drew breath and Andrew reclaimed his finger, she choked on the meat that had been resting on the back of her tongue.

Andrew moved with quick efficiency, circling her until he crouched behind her. There, he slapped her full on the back until the passage in her throat cleared.

"Are you well?" he asked, concerned, as he sat down to face her again.

She nodded, unable to speak.

"Drink," he ordered, handing her the wine skin.

She obeyed, grateful for the cool, tangy liquid that soothed her spasming throat.

As she wiped tears from her eyes, she avoided Andrew's gaze. That proved easy enough, because he seemed to be looking anywhere but at her.

"I said I'd help ease your aches away," Andrew reminded Judith, wondering why he did so. God help him, but he didn't think he could touch her body without exploring all her curves and crevices. "Roll over."

"What?"

"Onto your belly."

She obeyed, tucking her face into her folded arms. He couldn't believe Judith deigned to heed his command now, of all times. She should have been insisting they gather their things and head out. But nay, she lay before him, patiently waiting for him to fondle her. Innocently, she trusted him to do naught but ease away her aches because he had insisted they wait to make love.

Fool! Andrew wondered which of them he called that name, himself or Judith.

Attempting to maintain a degree of indifference, he straddled her legs and began massaging her neck and shoulders.

"Ahhhhh!" she cried, her voice muffled by the blanket beneath her.

"'Tis that bad? Sweetling, you need more physical activity."

"I get plenty of physical activity," she grumbled. "Just not on horses."

"On what, then?" He pressed his fingertips purposefully against the knobs of her spine.

"Exercise equipment. I know you've never heard of anything like that. They're machines...implements...to work a person's muscles."

Judith was obviously recalling things as her memory fought to return, but he did not comment. He couldn't be sure that she was as aware of this fact as he. Casually, he inquired, "Where does one find such implements?"

"A lot of people own their own. Others, like me, go to special places where...I don't know, I guess you'd call them tradespeople, keep a great variety of exercise equipment. We pay money to use their machines."

"I see," he muttered, though he did not. People kept their bodies strong by working, riding, running, even swimming, but mostly by toiling at the tasks that kept them housed, fed and clothed. To have some sort of tools for that purpose sounded both impossible and impractical.

Andrew suspected Judith's lower extremities would feel more sore than her arms. Scooting down the length of her body, he began to knead the knots in the muscles of her calves and her thighs.

"If I go to heaven," she said on a sigh, "I want it to feel like this."

He smiled. He wanted it to feel like this, too, with Judith's body beneath him. Although he would prefer her face up or at least on her knees.

Shaking his head to clear it of such wayward, dissolute thoughts, he examined the fabric of her chausses as he ran his fingers over her calf. "Of what sort of material are your leggings made?" he asked. "I've ne'er seen or felt anything like it."

"I dunno. I think it's a combination of cotton and Spandex or something."

"What is that? How do you weave it so fine?"

"I don't weave it. I buy it."

"You purchase all your fabric for your clothing from merchants? You spin no cloth yourself?"

"Nope. My job...my work...is something altogether different."

He went still, though he peeked at Judith's profile. Her eyes were closed, and she seemed more asleep than awake. Cautiously, he asked, "What is your work?"

"I sell books," she responded without hesitation. "Not published books, but the manuscripts that are made into books and sold to the public."

"Explain" he urged, resuming his massaging of Judith's limbs.

"It's complicated. I don't know if I can." She paused so long, he wondered if she had drifted off to sleep. Suddenly, she asked, "Andrew, are you familiar with *Beowulf?*"

That, he knew. "Aye. 'Tis an ancient story brought to England by the Norse hundreds of years past."

"And someone wrote it down, hundreds of years past. *Beowulf* is the oldest story ever written in English." Judith rolled her shoulders. "Could I ask you to get my neck? It's really sore."

Andrew readily complied, and she continued, "The people I work with write stories—long, long stories. I take their stories to publishers, the folks who print them—"

"Print them?"

"Make many, many copies of them and bind the pages together," Judith clarified. "The publishers pay the writers for their stories, and I get part of that money for finding the publishers on the writers' behalf. Ummmm...Andrew, that feels so good." She sighed contentedly. "I know it doesn't sound like hard work, but it is. I swear, an agent works seven days a week."

"Thus, you have no time to weave your own cloth?"

"No. No time at all. I use the money I earn to buy cloth—actually, garments already sewn of cloth—and that's why I don't know how the material for my leggings was manufactured. Um—made."

Andrew considered what Judith told him. God's toes, but he had been to York, and he'd never encountered people whose customs seemed as strange as Judith's, or whose language sounded as foreign. He never saw *exercise equipment*, either. Did she reside within an exclusive society of some sort, one to which her alchemist sire belonged? Were they outcasts even among the people of that city?

Judy realized Andrew had stopped working his magic with his fingers. She rolled onto her side, delighted that she felt no pain when she did. "Andrew? Is something wrong?"

He looked up, meeting her eyes. "Nay. I was only thinking."

"About what?"

He considered her for a long moment before answering. "I notice that the day grows light. We should be on our way, Judith, for I've no time to spare. I left Laycock without waiting for my brothers or my sire to return and protect it. If war breaks out before I get back—"

"It won't."

"It won't?"

"There won't be any war, at least not any serious fighting, because King John's going to sign that charter your father and the other barons are drawing up. I didn't put it together at first, when Philip explained what was going on. But the other day, I suddenly realized—"

Judy broke off as though she'd been garotted. She stared back at Andrew, who stared hard at her. *What have I been doing?* she asked herself. Had she totally lost it, rambling on about health clubs, her career, and even worse, telling Andrew about the signing of the *Magna Carta* as casually as a psychic made predictions on one of those 900 hotlines?

"Jesu." As Judy watched, he crossed himself and muttered, "You have the sight."

"No." She scrambled up, shaking her head emphatically as she sought some way to distract Andrew from her stupid confessions. "It's just a hunch, that's all. Like I mentioned, Philip told me all about the negotiations those, uh, barons, Marshal and Langton, have been handling. There's no way King John won't sign the charter. Really. But if you're nervous, we can get a move on." She gathered up her blanket, trying to be helpful and eager. Then she paused and suggested, "Andrew, if you'd rather, we could go back to Laycock. We don't have to go to York. You know I'm not that keen on it. Besides, I wouldn't want you neglecting your duties to chase after my phantom family."

He stood, grabbed her shoulders, and looked deep into her eyes. Judy's heart raced as she feared he could read her mind, her heart, more easily than she could read a newspaper.

But then he shook his head and said softly, "Nay. I think we must go to York."

Nineteen

"Keep your back straight, Judith. Do not slouch. That's better. And remember your feet—heels down, toes up."

"Right. Got it."

She attempted to return Andrew's encouraging smile. In fact, his coaching had made her a better rider over the past few days—not that she could have done anything much but improve. But her mind wasn't on riding; she kept thinking about what—whom—they rode toward.

Surely they would reach their destination today. What other reason could Andrew have for insisting she wear the lady's tunic she'd brought with her, along with his sister's veil and chaplet? None that she could think of. Obviously, he expected to meet the alchemist in York quite soon. Obviously, he anticipated learning the truth about her circumstances.

She sighed, wondering why she kept going through the motions. Sure, this was a diversion, a way to while away the endless days. But was she only killing time, or was she killing herself by signing her own death warrant? When Andrew learned she wasn't the old knight's daughter, he'd not only abandon any thoughts of marrying her, he probably wouldn't even want to "keep" her.

Geez. Suddenly, she wanted to be a kept woman! Yet being Andrew's live-in girlfriend wasn't just a silly, romantic notion. Judy had no desire to endure the elements and forage for food while waiting for next Halloween to arrive. Laycock Keep might be cold and gloomy, but it seemed like the Plaza compared to the huts in Wixcomb. And those huts seemed like Holiday Inns compared to wandering homeless.

"Judith, look!"

She jerked, glanced toward Andrew, and discovered him pointing. She looked up ahead, expecting to see a medieval city's low skyline on the horizon. But she only saw a solitary house sitting in the center of plowed cropland. This couldn't be the alchemist's residence, not if the man lived in York.

"What is it?"

"A surprise." Andrew met her gaze with a kind smile. "This eve you need not sleep under the stars. This eve you shall have a roof over your head."

Shelter of any kind sounded wonderful. Judy had experienced one night outside in the rain, and one night was enough. She only hoped Andrew made reference to the house they approached, not a barn or a stable. "Whose roof?" she asked.

"Lord and Lady Ackworth's. 'Tis their house, straight afore us."

She smiled, enormously relieved. No York, today. No Peter Lamb. No losing Andrew or her means of surviving her medieval sojourn—yet. "Are they friends of yours?" she asked.

"Aye. Friends of my parents. They're like kin to my brothers, my sisters, and me."

"Then—then we haven't reached York yet?"

Andrew's brow creased, and he shook his head slightly. "Nay. There's a way to go. I'm sorry."

Judy wasn't. If she had felt a bit more confident, she would have kicked her mare into a trot, maybe even a run.

As it was, they made good time up to the house.

"Ho, there!" Andrew greeted a servant in the yard. "Is your master at home?"

"Aye, milord. I'll fetch him." He bobbed his head respectfully and hurried indoors.

Another man appeared in the doorway and called out as Andrew helped Judith dismount. He spoke French, but Andrew replied in English.

"Aye, 'tis me, Uncle Geoffrey," he confirmed, opening his arms and striding toward the middle-aged fellow heading down the front steps.

As they embraced, "Uncle Geoffrey" switched to the same language Andrew spoke. "And who be this comely lady?" he asked. "Don't tell me you've wed, Andrew."

Judy met Andrew's quick glance as he replied, "Nay, Uncle. I am not wed. This is—"

He broke off, glancing at Judy with a somewhat pained expression. She realized then that Andrew had no idea how to explain her. She considered identifying herself until she recalled the lord's presumption that she was a lady. After all, she looked like one. But she had neither the speech nor the manners, and she did not want to embarrass Andrew. So she kept silent and waited for his next move.

"This is Lady Judith Lamb," Andrew announced finally. "She has been visiting Laycock Keep, and now I'm escorting her home to York."

"Are you? Delightful, my lad, delightful. You will be staying with us for the night?"

"If you'll have us."

The stocky, gray-haired man took another two steps that brought him directly before Judy. He lifted her hand, bowed and kissed it. "A pleasure to have you here, my lady. I am your humble servant, Geoffrey Ackworth."

She nodded politely but, over the lord's head, gave Andrew a pointedly meaningful look. Judy had no idea if he could interpret all she tried to convey—she had quite a few things she wished to discuss with him in private.

Then, as though he read her mind, Andrew continued, "You must not take offense if Judith doesn't speak. She was ill for some time and lost her speech because of it."

"How dreadful!" Ackworth appeared sincerely distraught.

"She prefers we speak English. 'Tis easier for her to understand."

"I shall gladly comply. You look so robust and beautiful, my lady, I can only assume you are fast approaching a full recovery."

He paused, distracted by Andrew's horse. Admiringly, he ran his hand over the animal's neck, flank and hindquarters. "'Tis a beautiful beast you have here, Andrew."

"Aye. He came from Tuscany, from the stable of one of that country's best breeders. My father gave him to me some years ago, advising me that, as a younger son, my horse would not only prove my most faithful companion, but the means by which I might earn a living."

"Thomas is wise—and generous." Ackworth smiled at Judy. "Come," he urged, offering her his arm. "My wife, Lydia, is somewhere within. She'll be excited to meet you and to see Andrew again."

As the three of them entered the house at the second story—a tall flight of cement stairs enabled them to ignore an obvious stable at ground level—Ackworth strode across the firelit room to a short, wooden staircase. "Lydia?" he called out. "Lydia, we have guests!"

"Andrew!" the lady exclaimed from the top of the stairs before hurrying down to hug the young knight just as her husband had. "Where are the rest of your family?"

Andrew explained.

"Then who watches over Laycock and the village?" Lord Ackworth inquired.

"Our captain is loyal and dependable, as is our bailiff," Andrew assured him. "Also, I'm confident there is no chance we shall come to war. King John should be signing the barons' charter very soon."

Andrew's pronouncement came as a surprise, not only to the Ackworths but to Judy. He believed what she had told him without question. He trusted her, despite the circumstances of her unexpected intrusion into his life.

It seemed a greater compliment than any Philip had given her, couched in flowery phrases.

"You know more than I," Ackworth conceded. "Lydia, this is Lady Judith Lamb, a friend of Thomas' family. Andrew is escorting her home to York." He glanced at Judy. "May I present my lady wife, Lydia."

Again, Judy nodded, smiled shyly, and remained silent. Again, Andrew provided the reason why for Lydia's benefit.

"Having lost your voice doesn't prevent you from eating, does it?" Lydia asked with a smile and a sparkle in her eyes. "Supper is ready to be served. Let's sit, and eat, and catch up on things, shall we?"

***

Judy soon felt so relaxed, she actually began to enjoy herself. Because no one expected her to speak, she found herself spared the anxiety of worrying that she might say something inappropriate. Also because she didn't talk, Andrew anticipated her every need so that she wouldn't be forced to mime. He made sure she had plenty of food to eat and mead to drink. The mead didn't hurt, either—she soon felt a warm, contented glow. But that sensation, she knew, could also have been prompted by the anticipation of sleeping a foot or two off the ground, on a mattress, between clean, linen sheets. That, and the decided relief that she hadn't gotten all dressed up to confront Sir Peter Lamb.

"It may be fortuitous that you happened this way, Andrew," Ackworth suggested as a servant cleared away the remains of their meal.

"How so?"

"Let me show you something before I explain." He excused himself and went upstairs. When Ackworth returned, he carried a parcel wrapped in soft wool. "Look," he said, laying the object on the table in front of Judy and Andrew.

He peeled the cloth away and Judy gasped. It was the dagger, the jeweled dagger, that she had seen enclosed in glass at Laycock Inn! Before, she had barely glanced at it. But now, the dazzling, stone-encrusted hilt and ornately carved steel blade mesmerized her.

Beside her, Andrew exhaled a low breath. Asking for and receiving permission, he lifted the weapon gently with his fingertips. When he held it up and turned it one way and another, the numerous flickering candle flames ricocheted off every blue, red, and yellow gemstone. The effect resembled an expensive evening gown covered in sequins and beads that winked beneath the light of a chandelier. But these stones, though also minute, were semiprecious jewels that generated their own fire. No one in the room could take their eyes off them.

"'Twas bequeathed to me by my mother's brother," Ackworth explained. "He lived a long life, nearly eighty years, and died only recently."

"You are a fortunate man, Uncle," Andrew told him.

"Not so fortunate." He smiled ruefully and glanced at his wife, who sat beside him, opposite Andrew and Judy. "Like my own uncle, I am childless. But unlike him, I have no one at all to whom I may bequeath this weapon."

Judy watched Andrew. Everything in him tensed, every muscle, every sinew, every bone. "Aye?" he said tightly, staring across the table at Ackworth as though he were almost afraid to look down at the fabulous weapon.

"I've another problem. I am a landowner, but no great baron like your sire who has many men-at-arms to protect a demesne of that size. Lydia and I fear that someone may hear that this exquisite, precious dagger has come into my possession—"

"—And that we'll be murdered in our beds by thieves who wish to get their hands on it," Lydia added.

Andrew had been resting his hands casually on the table. Now, he clenched them. Yet his voice remained even as he asked, "What do you intend?"

"To sell it." Ackworth shook his head sadly. "An ornamental weapon such as this should not be hidden away as I must hide it. It should be a family's treasure, passed down from one generation to the next."

"What...do you ask for it?"

"I would like a destrier, Andrew, one from which I could sire many more to be trained for battle and sold for good coin."

Judy watched Andrew rub his thumbs against his fingers. He wanted that dagger more than anything, she could tell. And he would have it, because one day the innkeeper in Wixcomb would keep it on display, a family heirloom.

Abruptly, Andrew flattened his hands against the wooden table. "I confess, I wish I had your price, Uncle. But I do not."

"You have Zeus," Judy blurted.

"She speaks," Lydia exclaimed.

Almost—but not quite—regretting her outburst, Judy nodded and feigned a hoarse voice as she quickly added, "Not very well, I fear."

Andrew appeared to ignore the last exchange as he turned his head to frown sternly at her. "I cannot part with Zeus," he informed her. "He and I are one. A knight works years with a steed so he may depend on the beast when they charge into battle together. More often than you know, Judith, a knight's life depends not on the sword in his hand but on the animal he rides."

"But—"

"Geoffrey hoped to sell it to some young man he respects," Lydia explained, speaking to Judy but looking fondly at Andrew. "When we saw 'twas you who had come to visit us, we were of a single mind." She glanced at her husband and smiled regretfully before telling Andrew, "We love you as we would our own."

Andrew looked pained as he repeated, "I cannot pay your price," before leaning back and dropping his hands into his lap. "Besides, I am a younger son. If any of Thomas Laycock's children should acquire this knife, it should be Robin."

"But Robin is in London, and you are here," Ackworth said, pointing out the obvious.

"And you'll have children of your own," Judy promised him impulsively. Though she whispered, she knew she sounded far more certain than she was. That Carla's Viscount Laycock had descended from a direct line leading back to Robin seemed more likely than that he was a distant grandson of Andrew's. Still, the dagger belonged to the Laycocks well before, and well into, the 20th century. Surely it came to the family now, in the 13th.

Andrew's eyebrows met above his nose. Judy wondered if, finally, she had stepped over the line, forcing him to believe what Elfred believed. But then he shook his head, looked back at Ackworth, and smiled apologetically.

"I'm sorry. By all the saints, I wish that I could buy it from you, but I have no means."

Judy gasped. *This is wrong! Andrew has to get that knife.* She nudged him and leaned forward to whisper again in his ear. "Lord Ackworth wants a warhorse like yours. I understand that you can't give up Zeus. But what does Zeus do with his free time back at the Laycock stables?"

"What do you mean?"

"I'm asking if there are any baby Zeuses running around at home."

"Aye. Two. One foal is but a few months old, the other still less than a year. Neither is the animal Geoffrey desires."

"But both of them will be, right? It's just a matter of time?"

"Judith, I haven't time. Geoffrey wants to sell that dagger soon."

"I'd bet, if you offered him the other two stallions, the young ones, he'd hold that knife for you 'til they were old enough to go to him."

Andrew considered what she had said before facing their hosts and saying something to them in French. Then, tucking his head close to Judy's again, he spoke softly behind his hand. "I do not desire the dagger for myself, Judith. I need no such prize. If I could buy it, I would make a gift of it to my sire. 'Tis his 50th natal day soon. Surely, he would treasure it."

Judy wanted to hug him, but she didn't. She wanted to weep, but she blinked back the tears burning her eyes. Boy, he was turning out to be something she hadn't expected. Not even when she found she wanted him so badly that she'd invited him into her bed. First, the open trust he had displayed in her. Now, the selfless generosity on behalf of his father.

Andrew really, really had to have that knife. And Judy had to have her tote.

"Could you get my satchel for me, please?" she asked.

He looked baffled, but retrieved the nylon tote for her. When she had it in her hands, she turned around and gave both the table and the Ackworths her back. Then she set the bag on the floor between her feet and dug through her possessions. When she found what she was after, she hid it in the folds of her skirt and faced the others again.

"Lord Geoffrey, Lady Lydia, I have a proposition for you," she declared, speaking very, very slowly and enunciating every syllable. They had to understand. Judy needed to handle this negotiation herself without Andrew interpreting for her, or the presentation would not be as effective. Presentation was everything—it was the key to getting what you wanted.

"Andrew wants the dagger, but he cannot trade you Zeus for it. However, Zeus has sired a foal, a little boy horse—"

"A colt," Andrew interrupted.

"Yes. Aye. A colt. And he will give you that colt in exchange for the dagger."

Ackworth considered Andrew thoughtfully. "Nay. I'm sorry, but I need a mature stallion for breeding. The one I owned a score of years has been dead half a year already. I have good mares that go wanting even now."

"The colt will be ready to breed...when?" Judy looked at Andrew.

"The winter after next. Or possibly that autumn."

"Andrew, I fear I cannot wait that long," Ackworth said. "Nor can I hold this beautiful, damnable weapon that long, either. I dare not risk it."

"I wouldn't ask you to." He shook his head.

"Wait!" If they'd stop interrupting, Judy knew she could move things along. "Actually, Andrew's destrier has sired two foals. There is one even younger."

"I am sorry, my lady. I need a mature stallion now, not foals who cannot mount mares for several seasons."

"Hear me out," Judy pleaded, glancing at the sparkling hilt of the weapon under discussion. Andrew wanted it so badly, and she wanted it so badly for him, she felt as though she wanted it for herself. She felt exactly this way when holding out for more money for her clients.

"Andrew will let you take the babies, the foals, immediately." She glanced at him again. "They're weaned, aren't they?"

"One is."

"Okay. Very well. He will let you take them as soon as they're both weaned. We realize you cannot use either of them for breeding straight away, but..." She plucked the object she had been hiding in her lap, stood, and held it out to Lydia. "You may also have this."

The lady shrieked, in fear or delight, Judy couldn't at first determine. But she grabbed the fake tortoise shell handle right out of Judy's hand and lifted the mirror to her face. Lydia gaped and blinked. Then she grinned, exactly as the servant, Bridget, had upon recognizing her own reflection. Soon she was chattering in staccato French that even Mademoiselle O'Flynn couldn't have caught two words of. She flew up from her chair, flipping the mirror over to its magnification side, shrieked again, and then held it under her husband's nose—for a second, not long enough for him to take it from her. Lady Lydia was too busy examining her eyes, her hair, her teeth.

They struck the deal. Andrew drew up a note so that Geoffrey Ackworth could claim Zeus' offspring from the Laycock stables even if Andrew wasn't present to oversee the transaction. Lydia Ackworth had her mirror, which now appeared to be permanently attached to her hand. And Andrew had his engraved, jewel-studded, ceremonial dagger to give his father, Lord Thomas, ensuring that one day, centuries down the road, Viscount Laycock of Wixcomb, England, would inherit it.

Twenty

Judy no longer ached as she had the first couple of days on the road. Perhaps the pain had been dulled this particular night by the amount of alcohol she had consumed. More likely, she'd become inured to her discomfort because of her exhilaration. Wow, negotiating the dagger deal had been a high, a real toot! Judy hadn't felt this good since she'd wrangled Carla's last book contract.

But now, she confessed to her hostess, she felt tired, so she followed Lady Lydia upstairs to the floor beneath the vaulted roof. Judy anticipated an ancient, rustic version of her grandmother's attic guest room—something cozy and dry with a little bed tucked away in a corner. What she got was a narrow, lumpy mattress stuffed with straw lying on the rush-covered floor.

Gratitude quickly replaced her initial disappointment. Though a far cry from cozy, everything at least appeared dry. And, truthfully, she felt glad to have anyplace at all to lie down flat. So she kicked off her shoes, knelt down on the floor, and curled up on the pallet. Within minutes, she fell asleep.

***

"Judith." Andrew whispered so softly, her name was barely audible. With Geoffrey and Lydia sleeping only a few paces away in their private bedchamber, he had to be quiet. Yet he had to speak with her, had to thank her, had to convey how very much her efforts meant to him.

"Wha...?" Judith blinked until her eyes focused. Then a drowsy little smile quirked the corners of her mouth. "Are you sleeping up here, too?"

He wished he were. But as he drew a coverlet over her legs and up to her shoulders, he said, "Nay. 'Twould be unseemly to share your quarters. I have a pallet belowstairs."

She crinkled her nose. "I thought," she said, "I'd have a real bed tonight."

Damnation! Judith deserved a real bed after all she had done for him this evening. If he had realized her expectations, he would have gone into the woods and cut the timber to fashion her one.

"I am sorry," Andrew apologized. "Only the wealthiest landowners, the likes of my own sire, can afford to have unused beds in their homes. Most people would not think to do so even if they could. Many fine ladies and lords grow up sleeping on pallets with their sisters or brothers."

"I wasn't complaining. Just a little surprised."

"You surprised me, too."

"I'm always surprising you." Judith rolled her eyes. "Tonight I was afraid you'd finally decided I was some kind of mystic fortune-teller. You know—when I said you'd have children."

He wanted children. With Judith. "Will we?"

"We should," she whispered, fondling a hank of Andrew's hair that fell away from his face as he leaned over her. "We'd have only dark, swarthy sons and dark, sultry daughters. A handsome family."

He covered her hand with his own, drew it across his cheek, and then planted a kiss in the center of her palm. "Judith." The anguish and hope he felt in his breast nearly strangled him.

"What is it? What's the matter?" She came more awake as she sat up and studied his face in alarm.

"Naught." Brusquely, he put her hand down, tucking it under the covers. He couldn't touch her at all, or soon he would be stroking every inch of her body. "I came only to tell you how grateful I am for your assistance this eve. I'd ne'er have thought to bargain with Lord Geoffrey. The price he asked for the dagger was more than reasonable. Because I couldn't meet it, I'd have let the matter drop."

"But you wanted it for your father so very much."

"Aye. 'Twill please him greatly. I should like to please him before I go."

"Go?" Her eyes widened. "Where will you be going?"

God's blood! He hadn't meant to say that. But it was almost too easy to bare his heart to Judith. He wanted to share everything with her, his thoughts, his life.

But he couldn't explain. It would be easy enough to say that if she proved to be Sir Peter Lamb's unwed, dowered daughter, he would leave Laycock Keep to live with her on her own land. But Andrew had no wish to bring up the possibility that if she had no dowry, after they married he would have to leave her to earn their way with his horse and his sword arm.

So he said only, "Surely you understand my situation, Judith. A younger son cannot remain at his sire's keep for all his life. 'Tisn't done."

"Oh." She blinked slowly, and he felt her warm breath flutter against his cheek. The lingering scent of roses that always seemed to follow Judith teased his nostrils, and when he lowered his gaze, he found her lips so near his own, he could easily have touched them with his tongue.

"Judith." He leaned toward her, and she slid her arms around his neck. His body and hers melded together as he laid her down and followed after, crushing the blanket and her gown. But at least, at last, he again felt the curves of her limbs, her hips, and her breasts.

"Andrew." She rained kisses on his face as his hands roamed over her, exploring those curves. "Andrew, I want you."

"And I want you. Jesu, I want you!" He spoke against the column of her throat, so that his voice sounded muffled.

A voice from another chamber sounding clear and sharp startled them both into stillness. "Judith!" Lydia called out. "Lady Judith, is all in order?"

Rigid, Andrew continued to clutch Judith against him. As he held his breath, she replied in a normal voice he could never have managed, "Yes, Lady Lydia. I am fine. I was only...talking to myself."

"We're glad your voice is returning," the lady said, "but 'tis best you get some sleep now."

"I will. Good night."

I've gone mad, Andrew thought. He had as yet no claim to Judith—to have come to her bedchamber in another's home, where they might be discovered together and her reputation sullied...!

"Forgive me," he mumbled, releasing Judith and backing away. "I vowed not to touch you before I've seen you home to your kin. 'Twas wrong of me to lie beside you on your pallet."

"Andrew!" she said. "You hurt me terribly by rejecting me whenever I offer myself to you. I'll tell you a secret. Though I've sometimes been persuaded to go along, I've never offered myself to any man but you."

His heart clenched. "I am not spurning you, dearling. I would ne'er spurn you! But this is not the time or the place."

"It wasn't the right time or place at Laycock, either," she grumbled petulantly.

"Sweetling," he whispered, hoping to reassure her, "in only two days more, all shall be different. After we speak with your sire—"

"My sire," she gasped, staring wide-eyed at him. "We'll be arriving in York the day after tomorrow? Is that what you're saying?"

"Aye. If we ride hard." He pushed to his feet, damning himself for having come to her and damning himself for leaving her now. "Forgive my intrusion," he said stiffly. "Go to sleep. You need to rest."

"Andrew!"

He ignored her soft cry and left as silently as he had come. Yet Judy never fell back asleep.

***

When they resumed traveling the next morning, Andrew set a quick pace, encouraging Judy to alternately trot and run her mare so that they would make better time. Her head hurt and her eyes itched, and it seemed she was forever riding through curtains of spider webs spun between the trees lining the road. Besides plucking sticky filaments off her face and belligerent spiders out of her hair, she also had the worst case of morning mouth she had ever tasted. Of course, she had neither mouthwash nor flavored toothpaste to chase it away, so she was quickly sinking into a very foul mood.

Andrew's almost manic energy did nothing to lighten her spirits. Why, she wondered, was he in such a damned hurry all of a sudden? Didn't he have a clue what might happen once they talked to that old man? Was he stupid, or what?

As Andrew obviously had no intention of slowing

down, she decided to drag her own heels. Obstinately, she reined in her palfrey so that the animal would not take off after Zeus when Andrew kicked his stallion into faster speeds. She felt pretty cocky when she realized she could control the mare so well, and she enjoyed a perverse satisfaction in being able to force Andrew to travel at the slower pace she set.

Judy tried to ignore the fact that her efforts would make no difference in the long run. Instead, she wallowed happily in her churlish, silent tantrum and behaved like a kid balking at bedtime. Obviously, their confrontation with Peter Lamb would prove as inevitable as falling asleep. But for the time being, she clung to the notion that she could forestall it indefinitely.

***

Andrew couldn't fathom Judith's behavior. He'd known she was out of sorts since they'd cantered away from the Ackworth manse. Now, her delaying tactics were putting them well behind in their journey. Because she balked, sticking to a snail's pace, he could no longer be sure they would reach York on the morrow after all.

"Judith, are you ill?" he asked curtly as he hobbled their horses for the night. Though darkness would be long in coming, Judith had stubbornly insisted she could go no farther today, so he had reluctantly agreed to stop. Now he needed to be sure she wasn't suffering a relapse before he let his temper get the better of him.

"Why, do I look ill?" she shot back, hauling her bundle of belongings off her palfrey's rump.

"In truth, you look pale."

"I'm just tired."

"But you had better accommodations at Lord Geoffrey's house than we do on the road. Methinks you should have slept fairly well."

"Did you?" Judith dumped her sack on the ground, put one hand on her hip, and cocked an eyebrow at him.

"Not all that well," he admitted as he busied himself gathering twigs for their fire. He glanced at her surreptitiously, instinctively wary of her every move. He was glad he had no need to leave her to hunt small game for supper, as Lydia had provided food aplenty for their journey. Today, he would not dare risk leaving Judith unattended, else she might escape his watchful eye.

Escape! That's how she seemed today, like a prisoner intent on escape. But why would she wish to leave him? Only last eve she'd confessed again that she desired him most passionately. Surely those feelings hadn't cooled as the sun rose in the sky.

"Why not?"

Judith's query caught Andrew off guard. "What?"

"Why didn't you sleep well? You had a pallet and a roof overhead, same as I did. What was your problem?"

"I haven't any problem," he snapped, annoyed by her tone and annoyed with himself for succumbing to such vulgar emotion.

"The hell you don't!"

He threw the armful of sticks he'd collected down on the ground. Tight-lipped, he demanded, "Judith, what are you saying?"

"I'm saying you've got a problem. I'm your problem. I stumbled into your life, and you thought you'd get lucky and have a little fun. But it hasn't been much fun, has it? I've been nothing but a big pain in the butt since you met me."

"Judith."

"Don't interrupt," she advised, pacing back and forth, clenching and unclenching her fists. Judy knew picking a fight with Andrew would help nothing. But, damn, it felt good. She was going with it. What the hell.

"Let's face it, though I probably intrigued you at first, you've never known quite what to make of me. I'm not like anyone else you know, I don't fit in. I talk funny, I have funny things. I bet you're starting to think Elfred was maybe right about me."

"I have never believed you to be a witch."

"Then what is it you believe I am?" she demanded, striding forward and stopping a few paces in front of Andrew. "You don't know, and it bugs the heck out of you that you don't. You'll move heaven and earth to find out. Boy, was I wrong before when I said you and Philip were nothing alike. You're exactly alike. Neither of you can accept me for what I am, for what you know of me firsthand. No, I have to have credentials, people to vouch for my rank and status, to confirm my name is Judith Lamb and that they know my father, my friends, the place I was born, who my mother was, whatever. You can't just—"

She broke off abruptly. She had almost said "love," that Andrew couldn't love her for herself. Where did that come from? She wanted him to desire her, yes. To care for her, yes. But she didn't want him to love her any more than she wanted to love him. They had no future, at least no more than several months, until next Halloween. After that, she'd be outta here. Gone. History. Or future. Yes, she'd be the Future Girl, Judy added to herself with a wry, despairing chuckle. And in her future world, Andrew Laycock had been dead close to a thousand years, while in his, her oldest ancestor had yet to be born. They had no business even being together. Their time was stolen time. Eventually, the cosmic mistake that had caused their lives to intersect and overlap would be rectified. Then, this interlude would be snatched away.

Yet that intuitive glimpse at a future without Andrew clutched at Judy like a pair of icy hands. With a wavering intake of breath, she dropped her head and willed the painful sensation away.

Andrew felt something in his own chest, a pang of fear. What a self-centered fool he had been! The damsel had been ill off and on for months. She'd also trekked across half of England or more on foot, completely lost. Now, he'd been forcing her to ride horseback league after league, day after day, when she had no experience at it. Jesu, did he intend to cause her death?

He rushed to Judith, believing her about to collapse. But she didn't even stagger. When he approached, she spun around and stomped sure-footedly away.

The wench made him crazed! She was too volatile and mysterious a creature for any man to bear, let alone love. But he did love her. If he'd ever doubted it, the panic he felt at the thought of losing her swept those misgivings away.

"What?" he demanded. He shouted so loudly, a flock of startled birds fluttered noisily out of the branches of a nearby tree. "Tell me what's amiss, Judith, so that I may amend it. God's blood, but I've done all in my power to make things right for you, even neglecting my duties at Laycock to take you home to your father in York. What else—"

"My father doesn't live in York," she shouted, whirling around to face him and gesturing widely with her arms. "My father isn't Peter Lamb! My father's name is Anthony Lambini, and he lives in—"

"America."

Judith's sudden, wild outburst surprised Andrew, but not nearly as much as the foreign word that left his lips so matter-of-factly. Yet such was the place she had named as her homeland when he first met Judith on the road to Wixcomb. He had forgotten about it when he heard her mention York not long after. The memory had slipped further away when Philip claimed to know her kin. But it came back to Andrew now, as though she had told him of it only yesterday.

"Yes. He lives in America in a city called New York." Judith sniffed and gave him a teary-eyed smile. "So do I. My name is Judy Lambini."

He felt stunned, numb—his skin had gone cold, and his mind had gone blank. "Judy Lambini," he repeated.

"Well, actually it's Judith Lambini. Judith Rose Lambini. But I generally go by Judy." She struck out her hand, feigning bravado. *Dear God, let me get through this!* "Pleased to meet you," she said.

Andrew didn't know how to respond. He took her hand, and before he could do more, she pumped it up and down.

"That's how we say hello where I come from."

"This place, America."

"Um-hm."

"You never lost your memory, did you? Only your way."

"What? Oh, yeah. When I met you, I sure as heck was lost. And looking for Wixcomb. Not your little village, but a different Wixcomb. The rest, well...I didn't exactly lie. You and Philip kept filling in the blanks—providing answers to your own questions. I just went along with everything you two said because I couldn't tell you the truth."

He braced himself. They had set out for York to learn the truth. He wanted to hear it, needed to hear it, but he understood there was no cause for them to travel on in order for him to have his answers. "Can you tell me the truth now?"

Judith flung her head back and looked up at the azure sky that fitted the green meadowland like a tortoise shell dome. "Sure, I can. In fact, I'd like nothing better. Because, honestly, Andrew," she confessed as she brought her head down and met his gaze directly, "I've been dying to tell you the truth for a really long time."

Tentatively, he stepped closer to her. Firmly, he put one arm around her waist. Gently, he flicked away a tear that streaked down her cheek.

His insides clenched. He felt as though he faced dragons, for he feared that what he learned now might be worse than anything he had ever considered before. "Then tell me," he urged, his voice rough and low. "I shall listen."

"But will you believe?" Judith asked anxiously.

"I promise you, I'll believe," he said. And he meant it.

Twenty-one

They sat down together, side by side, their backs against a tree. Evening always took its own, good time in coming, so while daylight lingered, Judy began her fantastic confession.

"Let's see," she began. "I guess I should start with my trip to England with my friend and client, Carla Whittaker. She writes those long stories I mentioned the other day. Hers are mostly about people who lived and died a long time ago. The one she was working on was about King John."

"But John is alive."

"No, he's not. Not in my world, Andrew. In my world, he's been dead nearly 800 years."

She knew that news would hit Andrew like a bomb. It did, the explosion followed by a long, long moment of astonished, incredulous silence. But Andrew didn't protest. In fact, he said, "Tell me more."

She began to think maybe when she got home again she should see a shrink. What a relief it was to get everything off her chest! It would be worth $150 an hour to have someone listen so patiently while she droned on and on and on, completely self-absorbed and self-important. Once she got rolling with Andrew, describing her brief meeting with Viscount Laycock, Andrew's distant progeny, and seeing the jeweled dagger, she rushed to relate the events of that first morning. After she described awakening outside the bailey walls that weren't in ruin anymore, and how she had thought everyone was an actor in period garb, well, Judy just couldn't stop. Not until she covered it all, right up through this very afternoon when she'd realized she simply couldn't go through with facing the old knight in York who worked at changing base metals into gold. Which, she informed Andrew in an aside, couldn't be done anyway. Only then did she pause for breath and wait for Andrew to respond.

She saw by the look on his face that he didn't believe her. Despite his pledge and for all his quiet patience, he didn't believe her!

"Judith, mayhap you are no kin to Peter Lamb, but..." He shook his head and looked down at his lap. "You were sick, very sick. Mayhap you had wild dreams that seemed so real—"

"Damn you!" Judith flew to her feet and, as he peered up at her, Andrew knew the most painful regret. He had vowed to believe her, but he couldn't, and now she despised him.

"Listen to me." He stood and grabbed her wrists. "I care not if your name is Lambini or Lamb, if you hail from York or New York, if you're gently born or common. I shan't abandon you. I'll find a way to provide for you. I have no other obligations, Judith, and as I'm free to do as I will, I shall stand by you."

"Stand by me!" Her eyes narrowed to slits. If she'd been a cat, she'd have laid back her ears and extended her claws. "I wanted—I wanted more than that from you."

"More than my love?"

Her lashes fluttered. Oh, God. *Now* he told her he loved her? Andrew's timing was really off. She didn't want to hear about love now, not when he'd made it clear he didn't believe her.

"You don't love me," she insisted.

"Aye, I do."

"You can't! A man who can't believe me can't love me."

"How can I believe you?" he implored, feeling helpless in a manner no man, most especially a knight, should feel. "Your tale is too fantastic, Judith. 'Twould be easier to believe you have magic powers, as Elfred believes you do."

"Elfred can go to hell! So can you!"

Judith stomped away, and Andrew prepared to sprint after her and detain her. But she only went as far as her black satchel. Tearing it open, she began digging out her belongings, tossing most onto the ground at her feet. "I'm not from this world or this time," she grumbled, "and I can prove it. Look."

She had removed an item from the satchel Andrew had never noticed before—a leather purse of some sort. She opened it and took something from within, which she held out to him.

"These are photographs," she explained when he approached. "Bet you've never seen anything like them before, have you? They're pictures—likenesses—of my family. This one shows all of us in front of the Christmas tree two years ago. Those are my parents and my brothers, Gary and Jeff. This one—" She held another in front of Andrew's face— "is just my parents, Tony and Nancy Lambini. And these are my nephews," she continued, flipping another *photograph* on top of the last, "Adam and Jason, Gary's kids. Here's Melissa, Jeff's baby daughter."

In her fury and righteous pain, Judy flipped more pictures at Andrew so quickly, a couple fluttered to the ground. When he bent to retrieve them, she grabbed a fistful of paper money from her billfold. "See this, Andrew? This is our currency. Actually, this—" She waggled a couple of five pound notes in front of his nose— "is English money. This—" She pulled out a ten dollar bill. "This is American money. Never heard of paper money, have you? Didn't think so."

"Here's my driver's license. I am not even going to attempt to explain what it is or what it's for, but trust me—if you can," she sneered contemptuously. "This tiny rectangle is a legal document. It has *my* picture on it. Though it's a terrible picture, I think if you look, you'll be able to see it really is me. I suppose it's impossible for you to read the small print—the spelling and letters are not like those you're used to—but give it a try." She waggled the New York State driver's license under his nose until he snatched it away and peered down at it. "See my name there? Judith Rose Lambini. And the short series of numbers? 8-12-71. They refer to the eighth month and twelfth day of the year 1971. I was born August 12, 1971, Andrew. 1971!"

She dropped her hands to her sides and leaned forward, screaming into Andrew's face, venting all her frustration, unburdening all her secrets. "The year you are living in—hell, the year I'm living in at the moment—is 1215! I don't know what kind of calendar you people use, but the kind my people use designates this year as 1215. Oh, God." Feeling herself on the brink of insanity and complete despair, Judy paused, gasped, and held her forehead in her hand. "I'm not born until 1971," she repeated quietly. "That means I don't exist in 1215. So what the hell am I doing here?"

She raised her head and looked at Andrew, a fragile damsel in distress, the sort of female he, a knight, should have been able to protect. At least, he should have had the answer to her question. But he had no answer. He had barely begun to open himself to the mere possibility that everything Judith described she had truly lived, not merely dreamed. It couldn't be true, none of it could. Yet the things she had shared with him during the past weeks, and the things she showed him now, the *pictures*, seemed far too fantastic to be of this world, of this time.

Andrew picked up something Judith had discarded on the ground. The tube with the big, shiny eye that emitted a beam of white light. "It's a flashlight," she informed him before he could ask. "In England, they're called torches."

He ran his fingers over the casing. "What is it made of?"

"Plastic."

"Plastic?" he echoed, and she nodded, sniffing. "A material not of this world," he surmised.

"Oh, it's of this world, all right. It didn't come from outer space." Afraid she would lose Andrew when it seemed, again, that he might be willing to believe after all, Judy gestured with her arm toward the sky. "It didn't come from beyond the moon, is what I'm saying. Somehow—I don't know how—plastic is made from oil. But that's something nobody figures out how to do until sometime in the 20th century."

"In America."

"Yeah, I think so."

"Take me to America." He raised his head and his eyes met hers. He'd made a concession, issued a challenge.

"I can't."

"Why not?" Andrew's mind flipped through the information Judith had given him. "Even if you traveled through time on Samhain, you were in England in your own time before you arrived in the England of mine.

Thus, America exists now, during the rule of King John, same as it exists in your year of—what is your year, the year you met my descendant, Viscount Laycock?"

"1998," Judith supplied. She rubbed her forehead as though it ached and shook her head again. "You're correct, Andrew. America—the land—exists in 1215. Only nobody from Europe has discovered it yet. It lies way on the other side of the Atlantic Ocean, and right now the only people who live there are natives. The first Europeans who travel there in ships don't arrive until around 1492."

Andrew narrowed his eyes, computing in his head. He couldn't come up with the incredible numbers he searched for.

Judith supplied them. "Not for another 300 years, more or less."

His pulse began to race. Judith's tale sounded mad, absurd. But she was quite correct—if he didn't believe her, he didn't truly love her. And he did love her. Worse, if what she was telling him proved a deranged fantasy, she was mad. Or a witch. And that, he did not believe. Besides, her possessions served as evidence.

"You said I would have children because of the man you met in Wixcomb, the Wixcomb of your time," he reiterated softly. "And you said there'd be no attacks against King John's fiefs, that Lackland would sign the barons' charter. But you did not see into the future to make those predictions, did you? Instead, you recalled the past."

Judith nodded.

"If all you say is true, I would understand that you know something you experienced—your meeting with the Laycock lord who lives in your time, for instance. But how could you know what happened here, in England, so long before you were born?"

"It's history," Judith said with a shrug. "We learn about it in school because it's so important. Andrew, those conditions your father and his friends force King John to sign end up affecting not only English law, but law everywhere, all around the world! Eventually it will become known as the *Magna Carta*. The king signs it in a field called Runnymeade, somewhere near

Windsor." Judith smiled. "Geez, I didn't know I knew that. I have to admit, lately I've been amazed by what I know! Anyway, your descendant, the viscount, has some parchments written during the negotiations that my friend, Carla, came to England to see. I saw them, too, preserved under glass."

Judy held her breath and considered Andrew warily, hopefully. She felt as though her whole life hinged on his believing her, and perhaps it did. As she watched, his expression changed. She hoped—suspected—he was no longer dismissing her every word as madness. But did he believe her, really believe her?

"What did Philip say when you told him?"

His question caught Judy by surprise. "I—I never told Philip."

Her answer surprised Andrew just as surely. "Why not?"

"It never occurred to me. If it had, I wouldn't have dared."

"Why not?" He took her hand lightly, clasping only her fingers.

"Because Philip would never have believed me. You know he wouldn't."

"But he and I are very much alike. I explained our similarities to you once, did I not? So if you felt certain he'd dismiss your story as lunacy, why did you risk telling me?"

"Because you're not at all alike."

"And you felt sure I would believe."

"I did," Judy conceded. "Actually, today, I kind of counted on it."

Andrew's heart swelled. He pulled Judith closer and clasped her hard against him, rubbing his bristled cheek over her smooth one. No sane man could accept her story as true, but fortunately for him, he had obviously gone mad.

"I believe you, sweetling," he assured her. "I cannot fathom it, but I believe."

Judy's swollen heart burst open like the petals of a blossoming flower. She clung to Andrew, giddy with relief. "I love you," she admitted, no longer feeling brave, just glad to be able to confess everything, even her love. As she squeezed her eyes tightly shut and savored his strong, supportive embrace, she realized Andrew was a better person than she. If their situations had been reversed, she'd have called the cops and had him transported to the nearest padded cell.

"Sweet Jesu, woman," he whispered in her ear, "I love you also. No matter who you be, where you are from, or how you came to be here, understand I shall not be letting you go."

"That's okay by me." She smiled into his neck, glad Andrew couldn't see the blush she felt creeping into her cheeks. But it was okay, everything was okay, for she had no intention of leaving Andrew Laycock. Because really, when a girl traveled nearly a thousand years back in time to find her one true love, how could she let him go?

***

As the sun began to sink low in the western sky, gilding the verdant green landscape, Andrew laid Judy down in the grass. He kissed her tenderly, from her brow to her eyes, from her wrists to her fingers. The torture of his deliberate caresses proved agonizingly sweet. But the two of them had waited so long to be together, and there remained no reason to either delay their desires or restrain their ardor. Neither the constraints of her world nor his could force them to deny their passions anymore.

So Judy found herself responding with impetuous abandon, and soon Andrew's impatience became evident as well. It only took seconds for him to remove her medieval girdle, gown and shoes. When those layers had been tossed aside, leaving only her skimpy, futuristic underwear in place, she began fumbling with his belt, intending to discard his tunic, too. But Andrew forced her to pause as he flipped her bra straps off her shoulders, kissing the skin against which they'd lain.

"Damnation, woman," he whispered. "Since the first time I saw you in these brief and curious garments, I have longed to examine them."

"Oh, just take them off," Judy begged in a throaty whisper. "Please!"

Grinning, he obeyed, burying his face in the valley

between her breasts. Even as he kissed her, he worked the clasp between the bra cups and unfastened it so that her breasts sprang free.

Judy chuckled. "And you didn't even go to high school."

He ignored her comment. Andrew did not understand many things Judith said, but he intended to spend the rest of his life deciphering her unusual words. Now, however, he saw no need for talk. Instead he slid the garment that covered her breasts off her back and arms, and began to suckle her nipples. Each pink nub tasted sweet as a berry, and the soft, pebbly flesh against his tongue made his cock strain to be freed from his braies.

Judy peered down at Andrew, who gazed up at her through his thick, black lashes while his moist tongue teased her rosy aureola. A current shot to her groin so that she couldn't resist moving, rolling her hips against him.

He groaned and pulled himself higher against her length, until they lay face to face. Catching her lips with his teeth, he plundered her mouth with his tongue. Again, Judy rolled her hips and felt what she'd been longing for—his hardness, that ridge of masculinity which promised so much pleasure.

"Andrew!" she gasped, breathing his name into his mouth as she scrabbled at his leggings and undergarment where they tied at his hips.

Andrew didn't thwart her. He wanted his sex free to burrow into Judith's. Yet as she bunched his clothing up his chest and down his hips, he continued to nibble her lips, her chin, her throat. Finally, he finished what Judith had begun, tearing his tunic off over his head, and his chausses and braies off his legs. Naked at last, he crouched beside her and tongued a trail from her breasts to her navel. When his lips met the hip band of her nether garment, he kissed the smooth, shimmering fabric. Judith hissed, inhaling through her teeth, and thrust her hips upward again in an obvious invitation for him to take her.

"Lie still, sweetling," he urged, determined to love this woman as no man but he ever could, so that she'd not be tempted to leave him for another man, another time, another world. Spreading her legs, he knelt between them and slipped his hands beneath Judith's bare bottom. Raising her slightly, he nibbled at the tiny triangle of bright green cloth that hid her woman's flesh. His breath blew into the fabric, fluttering against the nest of curls they protected.

"Andrew, please!" Judith cried out. "You're torturing me!"

"Nay, dearest. I am loving you."

"Then love me, please. Completely. Now. I need you inside me, Andrew."

He considered delaying but knew there would be time later for more lovemaking. They would have all the time in the world, once he made this wench his wife. So Andrew said, "Your wish is my command, my lady," and drew aside the thin band of material that separated her legs and the globes of her derriere, exposing the moist pink petals of her sex. He ran a finger between those folds, and Judith bucked, crying his name.

He had never heard his name uttered with such intensity, such need, before. Judith's calling out to him nearly made him spend. But he managed to nestle the head of his manhood inside her cleft. Then he slid his sex home, knowing he'd come home, to his woman, the one he had been destined for, though she'd had to travel near a thousand years to find him.

Judy wrapped her arms tightly around Andrew's neck and twined her legs around his waist, cleaving to him, making them one for now, forever. She hadn't known sex could be like this, her nerve endings like a knot of severed electrical cables sparking and sizzling. No man in her own time had made her feel this way, not even close. Whatever she'd gone through, Judy decided, what ever lay ahead, would be worth it to have Andrew's love.

"Andrew! Oh, hon!" she panted, sensing she would soon erupt with a climax the likes of which she'd never had before, not with anyone, not even alone.

Judy climaxed. The feeling resembled the sensation she had experienced on Halloween, when it seemed she had burst into a shower of shimmering starlight. As she spasmed with her release, she felt Andrew spasm, too, spending himself, warm and liquid, inside her.

"Jesu," he whispered as he rolled off Judy and lay beside her, holding her close. "I never dreamed..."

"Neither did I," she returned. "Neither did I."

***

They were not hungry, so though Andrew made a fire, he and Judy merely sat beside it, talking. At first she presumed they would discuss their future. But then she realized there was no point. It had already been decided. She would stay, and they would be together. Besides, Andrew seemed curious about his descendant, the future Viscount Laycock, and Judy began wondering if she were related to Carla's English lord, herself as much a distant ancestor as Andrew.

"He seemed dark, like you," Judy told him. "A little gray in his sideburns. I'd guess he was older than Robin by a few years. Otherwise, I can't tell you much. He wore a cap—a hat—and glasses. I didn't bring any eyeglasses with me, not even shades, so don't ask me to explain what they are right now. Suffice it to say, they kind of covered his eyes, so I didn't see much of his face."

"You called him a 'goo-roo.' What is that?"

This, Judy explained as superficially as possible. And then, to help Andrew better understand, she retrieved her laptop from her tote. She hauled it out, set it on her thighs, and opened the cover.

"I did that earlier, when you were ill."

"You opened it? You didn't turn it on, did you?"

"Turn it on?"

"You didn't. Good, then there should still be juice in the battery. Here, let me show you."

Attaching the power pack, Judy booted up and demonstrated simple things, such as word processing. Andrew seemed captivated, reaching over to tap the alphabet keys and move the mouse by running his finger over the touch pad.

He attempted too much too fast, and the computer beeped.

"Holy mother of God!" he exclaimed, literally leaping off the ground.

Judy laughed. "Liked that, did you? Then you'll love this."

She turned off the laptop and closed the lid. Again, she began rummaging through her belongings. She wished she had a boom box or a disk player. But her old standby, her tape recorder, would have to suffice.

"Check this out." Judy yanked the headphones out of the device, glad her tastes ran to jazz, standards, and Broadway show tunes. If rap music or heavy metal blasted out into the still twilight, Andrew might have run off screaming. When she pressed the "play" button, only an orchestral version of "Funny Valentine" flowed thinly from the tiny speaker.

Yet the music seemed profound, almost huge, in the virtual vacuum of that medieval countryside. Though the horses lurched skittishly before settling down again, Andrew sat motionless, staring at the tape player in undisguised awe.

"Even coming from the future," he said finally, "this be magic."

"No, it's not. We simply have methods of capturing the sounds of instruments and singers so that anyone can hear them again and again, whenever they want to."

"Show me."

Judy stopped the tape, rewound it, and began the tune again. When Andrew looked up at her, she thought she saw tears glistening in his eyes.

"How can you give up such pleasures?" he asked.

"I don't have any choice."

"You could, Judith. You could choose to part the curtain of time again."

"That's not why I don't have a choice." She smiled and touched his hand. "I can't leave you. Ever."

Andrew grabbed Judy's waist and hauled her into his lap, where he kissed her as though he had only just found her after a lifetime of searching. He said, "At least you have your magic box. You can still hear your music here, in this time."

"For a while," she conceded. "Until the battery runs out."

"The what?"

Judy explained, and just as she finished, "Funny Valentine" stopped playing. Andrew glanced at her, alarmed.

"Don't worry. It still has power. The next song will start in a second." When the music began again, Judy stood and held her hand out to Andrew. "Wanna dance?" she asked, feeling like a brave girl at a middle school social, who dared to cross the cafeteria and approach one of the boys holding up the wall.

"Aye," Andrew answered gamely, taking her hand and coming to his feet. Judy wondered if he had any idea what she had proposed, but instead of inquiring, she placed his right hand behind her waist and positioned her left on his shoulder. Then, grasping his free hand, she swayed to the music and took a few, small steps, which Andrew followed quite easily.

The sun had disappeared some time ago, but its waning rays wrapped the world in a lavender cloak sequinned with the first of many flickering evening stars. In the English meadow, near a copse of trees, Judy Lambini danced with her medieval knight under a twilight sky. The song that graced their ears and underscored that blissful interlude, which she would remember and treasure forever, could have been no other: "As Time Goes By."

Twenty-two

Judy was married. She couldn't believe it. She wouldn't have believed it if everything had been typical, if she'd met Andrew at Zabar's deli a couple months ago and eloped with him. But that she had married a knight, a medieval knight, in a small, stone church in the north of England, and that the Mass following the brief nuptials had been performed by a dubious priest with dirty fingernails whom Andrew had paid to conduct the service, well...she just couldn't believe it.

But that's what happened, because Andrew had persuaded her they had no reason to delay. So, after a night of seemingly endless lovemaking on a blanket of grass as green and velvety as any chemically treated lawn Judy had ever seen in the suburbs of Connecticut, they had given up their trek to York and turned around. In a village near the Ackworths' house, bing-bang-boom, they'd gotten hitched.

It seemed impossibly romantic, a real live fantasy...at first. But now, with Laycock Keep again visible on the horizon, Judy began to second guess her actions. Marriage to a modern day Andrew would have required a huge adjustment. Marriage to the medieval Andrew required enormous sacrifices. Until just this moment, when she caught sight of the imposing stone structure that would be her home forevermore, she hadn't considered how devastating her concessions might prove to be. And without even thinking about them, she had willingly chosen never to return home to her time, her country, her family, her career. Why? Why had she so cavalierly made Plan B into Plan A? Her behavior might have been more reasonable if she'd known for a fact she could not return to her true home. But to consciously choose not to try to get back—what had possessed her?

"We're home," Andrew, riding beside her, announced.

She turned to him, felt the warmth of his smile wash over her, and had the answer to her questions. *He* had possessed her. For the love of Andrew Laycock, Judy Lambini had given up everything she had ever known.

Now, as he bridged the distance between them by reaching out and catching her hand, she again felt confident her losses could never rival her gains.

"Do you think your family has returned yet?" she asked him.

"I don't know. We'll see, soon enough."

***

"Lord Andrew!" Nigel greeted them from the guard tower when the couple approached the gate some minutes later. "Welcome home, my lord."

"Welcome Lady Judith home as well, Nigel," Andrew returned. "She is my bride."

Nigel grinned. "'Tis a pleasure indeed to welcome you home, my lady."

"Is any of the family here?"

"Aye, my lord. Your mother and sisters returned a few days past."

Judy said nothing as she and Andrew rode into the bailey, though she did feel relieved. She preferred to face the female contingent first. If she got them on her side, facing Andrew's brothers and his father, the baron, might not prove so difficult.

"Don't be afraid," Andrew urged as they dismounted, and he took from his bundle the jeweled cross, still wrapped in wool. "My mother shan't bite you."

"But how will she feel about you marrying? And marrying someone with no estate of her own, no money?"

"Mothers tend to want all their children wed, especially her daughters and lesser born sons. Besides, our marriage shan't affect her. We will not stay long at Laycock Keep."

Judy wanted to know where Andrew intended to take her, where they would make their home. She understood now that younger sons were expected to go off and make their way in the world without support from their families, that only the eldest, like Robin, had any right to remain. But she hadn't thought about being displaced when she'd agreed to marry Andrew. Life was hard enough in a castle. She couldn't imagine the trials of living elsewhere in this harsh world.

"Mother!" Andrew said when they stepped into the keep's great hall. Leaving Judy near the arched entrance, he opened his arms and strode forward to embrace a woman seated in a high-backed chair.

Oh, geez. Judy had always been aware of the universally negative perception of mothers-in-law. She'd told a few jokes along those lines herself. But she'd presumed the gripes were all good-humored foolishness—neither of her own grandmothers was a nag or a shrew.

So Judy wasn't prepared for the vision of her own mother-in-law—a middle-aged woman with horns! Honestly. Really and truly. The lady of the keep wore a headpiece with a sheer veil that framed her cheeks and chin, while from the top sprouted two lethal-looking horns!

Please, tell me she sings opera!

After a quick conversation in French, Andrew turned toward Judith and held out his hand beckoningly. In English, he said, "Mother, I should like you to meet Lady Judith, my wife. Judith, my mother, Lady Ardith of Laycock."

Okay, Judy thought. *I've survived the publishing business and dinners with knights and men-at-arms. I can get through this first meeting with my mother-in-law.*

"Lady Ardith, it is a pleasure to meet you." Judy debated curtsying and decided against it.

Ardith nodded. Then her glance flicked to Andrew and she said, "You are married?"

"Aye, Mother."

"Since Chandra's marriage, I'd no idea you were courting anyone, Andrew. Let alone Judith Lamb."

Judy nearly choked. Andrew frowned, asking, "Do you know her?"

"I know of her."

Ardith gestured to unoccupied chairs, and both Judy and Andrew sat. He put the cross on a small table beside him and demanded, "How do you know of her? She is a stranger here."

"She's no stranger to Philip, are you, Judith?"

Oh, hell. This woman was protecting her son. Horns like a bull and the maternal instincts of a lioness.

"Philip of North Cross and I are friends, my lady," Judy said. "That's all."

"Mother, when did you speak to Philip?"

"He's ridden here twice since your sisters and I returned. He told me he hoped to marry you, Judith," she explained, glancing at Judy with a nod. "Philip also voiced his suspicions that you two had ridden to York so that the lady could be reunited with her family there."

Judy wondered if she heard a veiled reprimand directed at Andrew for his having left the stronghold leaderless. "We didn't," she assured the woman, sensing the need for solidarity between her husband and herself. "When I first arrived here, I was lost and confused. I had no memories. Because of...because of my name, Philip felt sure I was related—that I was kin—to a knight who lives in York. But I am not related to him, so Andrew and I never went there."

"Why is everyone speaking English?" a female voice queried from the vicinity of the stairs.

Judy glanced in that direction and saw first one young woman, then another, descending the steps.

"Because my wife only speaks English," Andrew explained as he stood. "Judith, these are my sisters, Camilla and Beatrix. Sisters, this is my wife, Judith."

"Your wife! How extraordinary," the oldest of the two girls exclaimed. Beatrix resembled Ardith, with sandy hair and light blue eyes, while Camilla looked more like Andrew, her hair and eyes both dark as sable. "Welcome, my lady."

"Aye, welcome," Camilla echoed. Then she frowned and said, "That looks like my gown and circlet you're wearing."

"It is," Andrew confirmed. "When Judith first came here, she had naught to wear but the clothes on her back. I gave her some of your things. I knew you wouldn't mind," he added, arching an eyebrow at her.

"Oh, nay. Of course not. I never much liked that dress. It looks better on you," Camilla told Judy.

"Why didn't you have any clothes?" Beatrix asked curiously as she and her sister sat down.

"As I was telling your mother," Judy explained, "I found myself lost and quite alone. I had no memories of my past life, because—because I'd been ill with a bad fever. But now I recall most everything."

Andrew gave Judy a questioning look, raising both his eyebrows in tandem. She nodded slightly to reassure him and then proceeded to tell another fiction she'd lifted from one nameless manuscript or another. Judy said, "I come from a land very, very far away. So far away, you have never even heard of it. I was raised a lady, but when I was shipwrecked—"

Her husband blinked, startled, but Judy ignored him and continued.

"I found myself on England's shores with nothing but the clothes on my back. I hadn't a dime—I mean, a penny—in hand. I promptly fell ill, and when I recovered, I had no memory for a while. So I began to roam, and eventually my wanderings led me to Wixcomb. Andrew found me, and he and his brothers were kind enough to take me in."

"How extraordinary!" Beatrix said again as she clapped her hands together in delight.

Camilla added, "And you and Andrew fell in love and married."

"You married," a new voice shouted.

Judy and the others turned toward the archway to see Philip standing there. *Oh, God!* She sighed but felt all her muscles going taut as she watched the fair-haired knight approach Andrew.

"You took Judith off when that was my intention," Philip said accusingly. "You escorted her to York and confirmed her eligibility. And when you knew she claimed wealth of her own, enough to support you and spare you the life of mercenary or monk, you wed her!"

Andrew had risen to his feet and stood in front of his chair. Philip shouted into his face while his own face flushed ruddily. Judy found it amazing that she inspired so much emotion.

"I did none of those things," Andrew countered. "How dare you accuse me of marrying Judith for what she could give me! I'm not the one who had another eligible damsel, the lady Penelope Winfield, to embrace as second choice if Judith failed to meet my expectations."

"Aye, you did not," Philip agreed heatedly. "'Tis why you wooed and wed her, because Judith was your only hope. You stole her from me when I desired her more than Penelope. You never cared for her as I did, yet you betrayed me. How could you, old friend? When I think how I have been fending off not only Penelope, but her mother and mine."

Furiously, Philip took a swing at Andrew. Because they stood so close, he couldn't have missed. Andrew reeled, knocking over the chair behind him, but he still returned the punch.

Soon chairs were scraping over the stones as all the other women in the room backed away. Judy looked at them, surprised to discover they seemed prepared to watch the two knights pound each other senseless. She couldn't believe it. She wouldn't have it.

She spied the cloth-wrapped bundle still lying on the small table. It had skittered nearer to her when Andrew's chair flew over. She grabbed it, unraveling the length of cloth, while Philip and Andrew continued to brawl. Her husband, she noticed, had gone down. On his back for only a brief second, he began scrambling up again. Philip seemed on the attack, for he bounced on the balls of his feet, and his arm was drawn back, his fist balled.

Just as Andrew dragged himself up, but before he could retaliate and before Philip could sock him again, Judy threw herself between them, jeweled dagger drawn. With her back to her husband, she aimed the blade at Philip.

"Hit him again, and this pig-stabber will be sticking out of your shoulder," she warned.

"Judith!" Philip blinked at her in surprise. "How can you—"

"Because he's my husband. You're not." She waggled the knife point in Philip's general direction. "Are you going to stop fighting? Because there's something I think you should know."

He stood still, set his jaw, and scowled over Judy's shoulder at Andrew. "Very well," he agreed tightly.

"I don't know how long you stood in the archway, but you didn't overhear as much as you should have. I was telling Lady Ardith and her daughters that my memory has returned. I know for certain, just as I always contended, that I was raised to be a lady. Yet my homeland if far away, Philip. I'm not from York, and Peter

Lamb is not my father. In fact, I have no kin alive in this world, and I sure don't have any money or own any land.

"Andrew married me in spite of my poverty, my lack of noble family ties. You wouldn't have. You know you wouldn't have. So stop acting like a jilted lover and go propose to Penelope, whoever she is. I hope you're not too late."

Judy lowered her arm, clutching the jeweled hilt of her weapon with the point aimed toward the floor. Philip looked down at it, a frown creasing his brow.

"Forgive me," he said. Then, raising his gaze, his glance flicked between Judy and Andrew. "Both of you. I behaved selfishly, and none of my actions was based on true love." His eyes locked on Judy's. "I should very much like to know true love myself one day, but I fear I haven't the time required to search for it. I suppose I'd best hie myself off to Winfield and make do."

Flashing a sheepish smile, Philip took Judy's hand. "Forgive me, my lady. My only excuse is that I did care for you greatly. In truth, I still do. But I see now that Andrew loves you more than I ever would, because he's made a sacrifice I never could." He released Judy's fingers and looked up at Andrew. "You are indeed the better man."

They hugged, as men did in this time, not in Judy's. Then Philip wheeled toward the women who had returned to their chairs. "Forgive me, my ladies, for behaving so badly and disrupting your hall. The next time I visit, I vow I shall be better mannered, for hopefully, I'll have a new bride on my arm."

"You're forgiven," Lady Ardith assured him with a smile and a nod. "You are always forgiven."

Philip left quickly then.

Beatrix observed, "We seem to have missed a great deal while we were away. Who is Lady Penelope?"

"Never mind that now," Camilla said. "Wherever did that dagger come from?"

Camilla wouldn't let Judy rewrap the knife. She took it, admired the hilt, and passed it on to her sister.

"Judith helped me obtain that ceremonial blade," Andrew admitted. "She would make a fine merchant, the way she barters down a price. 'Tis a gift for Father on his natal day."

"It is beautiful. He'll be well-pleased," Beatrix predicted.

"Have you had word from him?" Andrew asked his mother.

"Reports are that matters with the king are proceeding smoothly. No doubt he should be returning soon." Ardith turned to look at Judy. "I see you are handy with a weapon, dear. How are you with a needle or a pot and a spoon?"

Judy blinked. She couldn't sew a button on that stayed put through one machine washing. Her culinary skills centered on microwaves and frozen entrees, though she could stir fry just about any combination of ingredients. But Judy suspected Chinese food rarely appeared on the menu at Laycock Keep.

"Mother, I have no land, no keep or manse," Andrew reminded Ardith. "Judith has, therefore, no need to learn the skills of a chatelaine."

"But she said she was raised up a lady," Beatrix recalled.

"The customs in her country are different than ours."

"What country is that?" Camilla asked.

"It's called America," Andrew said truthfully.

"You're correct. I never have heard of it."

"It doesn't matter," he insisted, and Judy sensed he felt as tense now as she had been earlier. "While at Laycock, Judith should be treated as a guest. When we leave—"

"When you leave," Ardith put in, "Judith will have to make you a home wherever you go. And she is in England, now, so while you are here, let me help prepare her for the duties of a wife wed to a Laycock lord."

"Mother, please."

"It's all right, Andrew." Judy put her hand on his arm. "I do have to learn your ways. I don't think we have any intention of returning to my homeland, do we?"

He gave her a look as Ardith said, "You're a wise woman, Judith. Now, come with me."

***

Judy stood over a cauldron in the bailey. She and Sally were stirring the family's woolens as they soaked in vats of water boiling over open fires.

She remembered envying the common folk who toiled as laborers at Laycock Keep. She had thought even their endless chores seemed preferable to the boredom she'd known. Boy, had she been wrong.

It never ended. From dawn to dusk and beyond, seven days a week, when she completed one task another demanded her attention. Or whatever she'd finished needed doing all over again. That old saw about a woman's work never being done must have had its origins in medieval times. Women who complained in her own era hadn't a clue what they were talking about.

And what was with this laundry? It had seemed to Judy, during those first weeks she'd lived at Laycock Keep, that the wash house sat neglected, these very cauldrons upended and dusty from disuse. Since Lady Ardith had arrived, the bottoms never had a chance to dry before they were refilled with water and clothing.

The belief that the aristocracy lived lives of pampered leisure was a crock, too. Judy noticed she was standing out here in the sun, stirring stinky, wet wool right alongside Sally. Except for their clothing, nobody could have discerned who was the lady, who was the servant!

She grumbled a profanity beneath her breath, wiping her damp brow with the back of her hand. She didn't know if the moisture was sweat or steam, but she knew she'd give anything to take a dip in that frigid stream that flowed through the demesne.

"Milady!"

She thought Sally intended to reprimand her for swearing. But when she glanced at the girl, she found her pointing toward the keep. "What is it?"

"The baron is home, along with Lords Elfred and Robin."

Judy shaded her eyes with her hand. Three men had indeed ridden into the bailey. They were dismounting and heading inside the keep even now.

"Give me that." Sally took the wooden pole Judy had

been using to stir her kettle of wash. "You'd best go indoors. I'm sure Lord Andrew will be wanting to introduce you."

"Oh, no! I look awful."

"Nay, you do not, Lady Judith. Just put your scarf back on." Sally handed her the discarded veil and the pounded brass circlet that would hold it in place. "Lord Thomas might find your shorn locks a trifle unusual."

"Great." Judy slapped the head gear on and arranged the gauzy scarf so that it draped the sides of her face, obscuring her short hair. Then, resigned but a little curious, she headed up to the keep.

Everyone had gathered in the great hall except for Andrew. Noticing his absence, Judy hung back, clinging to the shadows of the stone arch.

"Judith, come here," Ardith beckoned with a wave. Reluctantly, she crossed the room to the opposite end where the Laycock clan had settled themselves in a grouping of chairs near the fire pit. "Thomas, I've someone you must meet."

"You!" Elfred said, pointing at her. "You remain here?"

"Aye, of course she does," his mother told him. "Judith is Andrew's wife."

"Wife! He took the witch to wife?" He addressed his question to someone behind Judy.

"Damn you to hell, Elfred—Judith is not a witch," Andrew returned, shouting from the doorway. Then he stomped angrily across the room toward his family, halting only when he stood nose-to-nose with Elfred.

"Control yourselves, lads," Thomas of Laycock ordered sternly. "What is this your mother tells me, Andrew? You've taken a wife?"

The baron shifted his gaze to peer at Judy appraisingly, and she returned his perusal. Lord Thomas remained a good-looking man, straight backed and square shouldered, though he had more gray than brown in his hair and his beard. Judy realized that in 30 years, Andrew would look much the same.

"Aye, Father," he confirmed. "Allow me to introduce Lady Judith."

"Though a surprise, 'tis a pleasure." He nodded at her, his dark eyes alight.

"A pleasure to meet you, my lord," Judy returned.

"I did not expect this," Robin admitted, looking at Andrew.

"Nor I, last time we spoke."

"Then she is Peter Lamb's daughter?" Elfred asked, looking skeptical as he cocked one eyebrow.

"Do not speak of my wife as though she were absent," Andrew warned.

"Sit, please," the baron ordered, gesturing to Judy and Andrew.

They took the last empty chairs, and though Judy didn't know what the protocol was, she ventured to answer Elfred's question. "No," she said, "I am not related to Peter Lamb."

"I knew it! She's a sorceress who's bewitched Andrew."

Lord Thomas said nothing. He merely turned his head and gave his middle son a look that caused Elfred to clamp his lips shut so tightly, they bled white.

"Tell me where you hail from, my lady, and how you came to wed my youngest son."

Judy had her story down pat now. She related it again for the baron's benefit.

"Fascinating," he said when she finished. Judy wondered if he used that word as she used "interesting" when commenting on a manuscript she didn't care for.

Then Lord Thomas settled his gaze on Andrew. "Latter born sons usually wed women who have the means to support them, through wealth or land. Your bride admits having naught, Andrew. What do you intend?"

"My choices remain the same, Father, except I'd no longer consider the priesthood." He smiled at his own little joke. Then the smile vanished, and he said soberly, "Judith and I shall leave Laycock. I will hire myself out to some baron or landed lord who needs another good sword arm to protect his fief. Mayhap, though..." He hesitated. "Mayhap Judith could remain with you at the keep while I am away."

Judy felt as though she'd been sucker-punched. Andrew had married her, and now he intended to leave her to be one of those knights who dined in the hall and slept on the floor in some other lord's keep? "Andrew!"

He ignored her soft cry and said to his father, "Before we speak of this matter in earnest, I've something for you. 'Tis why Judith and I remained at Laycock awaiting your return."

Judy glanced at Andrew's lap. The cloth-wrapped dagger lay on his thighs.

"I've something for you as well, Andrew. I have a few drafts of the barons' demands, to which the king put his hand. Since he finally signed the charter itself, I thought you might be curious to read what we devised. Among you three—" Thomas glanced at all his sons—"you have always been the most curious."

Judy felt her heart skip a beat. If she were not so distraught over her husband's plans to abandon her to earn a living as a mercenary warrior, she'd have indulged in amazement. To think, Lord Thomas had just brought home the very parchments that would survive to her own time, when Carla would visit Viscount Laycock to study them for her book!

Andrew must have realized the same. He glanced at Judy sidelong, though he spoke to his father. "Thank you. I am keen to read them. But now, in honor of your natal day." He handed the knife to Thomas.

The baron unwrapped it and held the weapon up. A shaft of sunlight piercing the stone wall through the cross-shaped arrow slits hit the garnets and amethysts, the topazes and aquamarines, so that white light speared and flickered off the hilt. Those who hadn't seen the dagger before, Andrew's father and brothers, made soft sounds of awe and admiration.

Thomas smiled warmly as he raised his dark eyes to his youngest son's. "Thank you, lad, from my heart. I will treasure this weapon and see it holds an honored place in our family for generations to come. All should know 'twas you who gifted me with it."

Andrew looked as pleased as his father. Judy should have felt just as pleased—it was she who had helped engineer this moment. But she couldn't think of anything but Andrew leaving her. The worry crowded out all other thoughts and emotions.

Thomas himself returned to that topic. He said, "I

am a landed lord, a baron. I have need of trained men to protect my keep, my demesne, and the people in the village."

"You are offering a position to Andrew?" Elfred whined. "But he is your youngest. You've not offered anything to me!"

Thomas looked at Elfred. "I thought you preferred roaming the country with your comrades, entering tourneys and the like."

"I do. But—but I forewent such things to assist you and Robin during the negotiations with Lackland."

"Aye, you did. Well, Elfred, if you wish to be a permanent knight in my employ, you've only to say so."

"I do!" Elfred grinned. His smile turned rather smug, Judy thought, when he turned toward Andrew.

"For you, though, Andrew, I have another position in mind. One I've thought Laycock Keep has needed for some time. Would you consider becoming my seneschal?"

He didn't reply yea or nay. Impatient, curious, Judy whispered, "What's a seneschal?"

"A castle-keeper," Andrew explained. "Chief officer in a baron's household. Among other duties, the seneschal represents his lord in courts of law."

"Oh." It sounded impressive. Better, it meant Andrew would remain at Laycock Keep, and so could she. "Well, say aye, you'll be glad to," she urged.

Andrew's sisters giggled and Lady Ardith laughed. "Say aye," she prodded also. "'Tis best you learn to listen to your lady wife and heed what she says."

"Your mother is right," Lord Thomas confirmed.

Andrew glanced at them all, his parents and Judy. Then he nodded and said, "Aye."

Twenty-three

"Judith!"

She paused on the stairs, raised her sagging head, and turned to look down. There, Beatrix stood on a lower step just above the floor of the great hall. "Yes?"

"After the evening meal, Camilla and I will be sorting flowers, roots and leaves to mix into tisanes. If you'd like to join us, you're welcome."

"I'll think about it," Judy replied before continuing up the stairs to her room.

She'd lied. She didn't intend to think about sorting weeds for medicinal use, unless— No. Whatever they used in this era for a toothache could not cure the one that had been nagging her since the evening the baron had returned to Laycock Keep. The only procedure sure to eliminate the pain was a root canal, which Judy's dentist had suggested she attend to promptly, but which, of course, she had put off. Now she had no dentist! She was even running out of aspirin and ibuprofen, popping the pills as though they were breath mints. What, she wondered, did people born to this time do when their teeth hurt like hers did? Did they pull them? Judy wouldn't mind having her tooth pulled—by next week, she'd pull it herself, if she had to. But it wasn't the sort of tooth a person could yank by tying a string to a doorknob, and she didn't dare conjecture about any medieval methods for tooth extraction.

She shouldered open the door to hers and Andrew's room and stumbled inside. Long, late afternoon shadows streaked the walls, for which she felt grateful. God knew she needed peace, quiet, solitude and darkness.

Flinging off her annoying veil and chaplet, which she wouldn't have to wear if her hair was long enough not to shock the family, Judy crawled onto the bed and curled up in a fetal position. She wept, unsure whether the pain in her mouth or the agony of her days made her so miserable.

It could as easily have been the one as the other. Her cheek felt swollen, but so did her feet, for she'd been on them all day following Lady Ardith around the keep and the demesne. Good grief, the woman never sat still for a second! If she wasn't supervising the servants, she was seeing to the villagers, tending them in illness, injury and childbirth. Or she was making beer. Judy had never suspected Laycock Keep functioned as a homey, micro brewery. But now she knew more about barley fermentation than she cared to.

Oh, she'd forgotten that Lady Ardith did sit down sometimes—to spin wool, make thread, weave cloth, and then, for fun, to sew decorative needlework. Judy opened her hands in front of her face, glancing at her palms and her fingers. She had stabbed herself so often, she looked like she'd had acupuncture! Besides that, the skin had an unnatural, grayish cast. The color came from dying wool the day before yesterday, and the blue stain still hadn't faded.

"Judith? Are you here?" Andrew asked softly as he entered their room. "I looked for you with my sisters, but they said you'd come upstairs. Are you well?"

"Not really." Judy propped herself up on her elbow.

"Are you with child, perhaps?"

Yikes! I hadn't even considered that possibility. Please, God, don't let it be so. It's going to take years for me to be able to endure daily life here as anything but a bored and pampered guest. I couldn't take being pregnant, too. I doubt I could survive the delivery, after what I've seen of natural childbirth lately.

"No, I'm not pregnant," she assured him before admitting, "My tooth is bothering me a little."

"I'm sorry." Andrew sat down gently beside her. "I'll have Sally bring you something that will help. Now, let me see." He peered at her. "Nay, your face doesn't look swollen."

"No? It still hurts."

"I'm sure it does." He nodded sympathetically and kissed Judy's nose. "Why don't you lie back again? I'll tickle your arm."

Judy lay back down and couldn't help smiling. How sweet of him to comfort her when he probably had far more thrilling, masculine pursuits that he could be engaged in. Dragons to slay, or something like that.

"How was your day?" she inquired.

"My day?"

"Yes. What did you do today? Were you busy? Anything interesting happen?"

Andrew appeared so bemused by her query, she decided to let him off the hook. "It's all right. I pretty much understand what you do every day." She closed her eyes, savoring the feel of his fingertips gently raking the skin on her arm. "Andrew, do you ever wonder about my world? The time, so many centuries down the road, that I was born into?"

"Nay."

"Nay?" She opened her eyes and met his gaze. "Why not? After all, I know a great deal about your world, your time. I would think you'd be curious about mine."

"I am curious," he admitted, "but thinking about it wouldn't help me to know or understand. I like listening to your stories, Judith, but I cannot see into your mind or picture your memories. I can merely guess. Guessing about matters that can never be clarified is fruitless, don't you agree? Thus, I do not wonder. You're my wonder, my gift from that future age. Glad I am that you found your way into my world. My time. And to me."

He smiled and kissed her shoulder. How she loved Andrew's kisses, wherever he chose to bestow them. And his touch, so soothing on her arm. Yet Judy wanted to press him, to ask him if he'd risk attempting to travel through time with her to the future. Moistening her lips with the tip of her tongue, she frantically sought the right words to phrase her question, wondering why it was suddenly important to her. She shouldn't need to ask him, because she had already made her decision. She'd resolved to live in this foreign country in a bygone era that was barely recalled by her own people in her own century.

Yet before she could speak, Andrew said, "My day was full. And it is always satisfying to me, attending to both the major problems and the small details. It pleases me."

"Being your father's castle-keeper?"

"Aye. And your husband." He let his fingers drift up her shoulder and down her breast before retracing the route all the way past the bend in her elbow and back to her wrist. "I enjoy being an officer in my sire's household more than I would have enjoyed being a guard."

"But you're good at other things, like being a knight. All that jousting, sword fighting, and riding hard on Zeus. You like to do those things, and they're not required of a seneschal very often."

He tickled her neck and ran his fingers through her short hair before retreating again to her arm.

"I am skilled in the knightly arts, and I also enjoy them. Did I not earn my spurs? Yet I prefer..."

"Yes? What do you prefer?"

He sighed before speaking. "Working with my mind rather than my muscle. I'm not much like Elfred."

"Elfred wants to hunt witches." Judy blinked up at him. "In my time, Andrew, a lot of men use their minds, not their muscles, to earn a living." *In my time, you could, too.*

She wanted to add that, but she hesitated when he kissed her ear and paused to dip his tongue inside. For a moment, she found herself distracted from her questions, even from her toothache.

"Elfred's a dolt," Andrew continued, as though she'd made no further comment. "He's not a bad sort when you know him, but he is a bit simple and very superstitious. Now, though, he's found his place with Sir Roland."

"And you have your place as seneschal for your father." She held her breath for a few seconds.

"Aye."

Judy couldn't ask him. Not about trying to reach her world or attempting to live in it for a while. And there really was no reason to ask, she reminded herself still again. Andrew was right. She was here, she knew his world. He belonged here, and so did she. Beside him. Forever.

Andrew of Laycock was the love of her life.

His fingertips leapt from her wrist, lying against her side, and landed on her thigh. He began caressing her leg, moving ever upward.

Little sparks flared in the wake of the heat he imprinted on her skin. Seeking comfort, perhaps oblivion, in his embrace, she hugged Andrew close when his hand slid between her thighs. Feeling his fingers on her sex, she realized that her tunic hem had ridden up. She was glad nothing, even a layer of fabric, separated them. She reveled in her exposure, even her vulnerability. Right now, she needed to be consumed by her husband—his strength and his love.

"Sweetling, your lashes are not black today."

She stiffened. Andrew should have been in the crow's nest on the *Titanic*—he'd have spotted the iceberg with time to spare.

"They're never going to be black again."

"Nay? I rather liked them thick and sooty."

Taking a deep breath, she explained, "I used to color them. That's what women of my time do. But the color I brought with me is gone. I can't go to the drugstore and buy a new tube."

Andrew frowned. It was the look he always had when he didn't quite understand her. Then he kissed her eyes, forcing her to close them. "I love your lashes," he said, "light or dark. I love everything about you, Judith of Laycock."

He proved it, too, in the next half hour, by making tender love to her. She tried to lose herself in his ardor, but she couldn't keep his observation from her thoughts. There was, in fact, something between them, something far more difficult to breach than a single layer of fabric.

She did her best, so that Andrew would be satisfied and pleased with her. And she'd have had to have been a corpse not to respond to his lovemaking. Yet her mind's eye observed, and her senses recorded the details of this intimate interlude. It seemed there was a need to imprint it all on her memory.

When at last they found themselves sated and tired, Andrew fell asleep. Judy remained awake, however.

Her mascara had dried up. Her razor was just about dead, too. In another month or so, she wouldn't have any foundation, powder or blush left, either. Then she'd use the last of her eye shadows and lipsticks as well.

It shouldn't have mattered. Andrew would insist it didn't matter. Besides, none of the women around Judy, from Lady Ardith to her sisters-in-law and the female servants in the keep, wore cosmetics. Yet he'd fallen in love with a woman who painted her face. A woman who appeared different yet attractive, strange but alluring. And in a very short time, Judy knew she would no longer be that exotic-looking female. Then, her husband wouldn't recognize her as the woman he'd fallen in love with.

She felt a stab of pain in her back molar, worse than the dull ache she'd been enduring for some time. Cautiously, so as not to disturb Andrew, she crept out of bed and retrieved her aspirin bottle. Popping open the lid, she dumped three tablets into her palm. With a swig of water, she downed them. But as she went to replace the cap, she noticed only two pills lay at the bottom of the container. Two! How could she survive on a couple of aspirin with a tooth needing a root canal?

If she had been alone, she would have sobbed aloud. But because Andrew remained with her, she whimpered silently and crawled back into bed.

I'm being selfish. Andrew's so happy, and his family has accepted me. I'm a lady, for crying out loud! Considering what might have happened to me after flipping back through time, I've come out on top, anyway you look at it. I even found the only man in all the world, in all of time, I could ever love as much as I do Andrew. And he loves me—for now.

But now wasn't going to last. Not only would Judy stop looking like the girl he'd first met, she would stop being the woman she had been. *I'm a literary agent!* she screamed wordlessly. She wasn't the chatelaine of a keep. She didn't want to brew beer, or make sure the servants swept the old rushes out of the hall. She didn't want to learn to set broken bones or worse, deliver babies. She sure as heck didn't want to spend most of the rest of her life sewing!

"Sweetling, what is it?" Beside her, Andrew rose up on one arm. As he stifled a yawn, his eyebrows arched. "Judith," he observed soberly, "you're weeping."

"It's my tooth," she said, giving him a half truth, perhaps only a partial truth. "It really, really hurts."

He stood and righted his clothing. "I'll fetch a servant and have her bring you something. I don't suppose you feel like coming down to the great hall to eat?"

Judy shook her head.

"I'll send you up some victuals. Mayhap a bowl of soup and bread to sop the broth. Would you like that?"

"Sure."

"I won't be away long. I must speak with Father. But I'll return to you shortly."

"Andrew, you don't have to. I think I'd really prefer to be alone, if you don't mind."

A little scowl flitted across his brow. Yet he returned softly, "Whatever you wish," and bent to kiss Judy's brow before departing.

***

Judy might have dozed, she couldn't be certain. Then she heard Sally's voice and opened her eyes to find the servant leaning over her. "Milady, are you awake? I brought you something for your tooth."

She sat up and took the tiny, earthen bowl Sally held out. A dark, wet, unpleasant-looking substance sat at the bottom of it.

"Black alder," Sally explained. "Put a finger full on the tooth what ails you. It should help ease the pain, and if it's loose, the bark will tighten it."

"It will, huh?" Judy asked skeptically.

"I've brought you soup, bread and wine," Sally said, gesturing to the table as she moved about the chamber lighting candles.

Judy didn't feel very hungry, but as she looked around, it surprised her to find that day had given way to evening. "Is it late?"

"Midway between Compline and Matins."

She understood now that Compline was nine o'clock in the evening and Matins, midnight. "I must have fallen asleep."

"Aye, you did," Sally confirmed. "Bridget came up earlier but decided to leave you rather than wake you. Come, milady." Sally set the last candle on the table and gestured to the food. "You should eat, and the soup shan't bother your tooth very much."

Judy slid off the bed, sticking a dab of alder between her molar and her cheek as she walked to the table. But voices from outdoors snagged her attention. Veering toward the window, she looked outside. "What are they doing?" she asked.

"'Tis the summer solstice," Sally explained. "This eve the villagers and the servants will have another bone-fire. There shall be dancing and drinking, and all manner of carrying-on. Mayhap there'll be some magic, too."

Rigid, barely breathing, Judy asked, "What do you mean, magic?"

"Do not fret, Lady Judith. 'Tisn't the sort of magic Lord Elfred accused you of. We know you be no witch."

"Thank you, but that's not what I asked. What sort of magic?"

"Well..." The servant scowled and didn't explain.

"Well, what? Tell me!"

"There are certain nights of the year when queer things can happen. Samhain, Beltane, the summer and winter solstices. There may be more, but those are the most important of the lot. Not that we all believe, you understand, but we leave room for the possibility."

"Do—do people ever disappear on the summer solstice? Have you ever heard tales of someone departing this world without—without leaving a corpse behind?"

Sally nodded solemnly. "Aye. 'Tis said to have happened to my own mother's sister, afore I was born. My grandsire believed she be killed and buried in the forest. But my mother thought otherwise. She said my auntie went nowhere, that a storm came up. When the winds died down, she had gone, simply vanished. We rarely speak of it." Sally shivered and hugged her arms. "Frightens me, it does, just thinking of it."

"Then don't think of it," Judy urged, forcing a smile. "It's probably only a story."

"Will you eat something, milady?" she asked as she headed to the door.

"In a bit. Thank you."

Sally nodded and left the room. Judy went to her tote, deliberately removing all the things that most delighted Andrew, from her lighter and flashlight to her paper and pens. Her eyes filled with tears as she stacked them up on the table near the wall and topped the pile with her tape recorder. Andrew loved her things, her common, ordinary, everyday things. She got a kick out of watching him when she explained their functions and he attempted to use them for the first time. She always felt proud of him when he got the hang of anything and used it just as efficiently as she did.

But Judy had already shared everything she'd brought with her, everything that functioned without electricity, everything that hadn't been used up. She had nothing more to show Andrew.

Her breath hitched in her chest. She swiped at the tears blurring her vision and hunkered down beside the bed. A box lay hidden beneath it, the same box she had tucked away under the bed in her old room. It held the things she'd pilfered from the stronghold—dice, a candle holder, a cup. Judy put those items on the table as well. She didn't need them anymore. She wouldn't be telling her story to the media or trying to prove to the experts that she'd traveled through time to live and love in 13th century England.

Her story was a story of the heart, and that's where she'd keep it.

Her fingers brushed the paper she had laid out. Hesitating, she considered writing a note to Andrew. Hell, not a note, a book—a book about what he meant to her, about her dilemma, about the decision she'd been forced to make and how it killed her to make it.

Judy never picked up the pen. Her feelings were too huge to condense on paper. Besides, no matter what she confided, Andrew would inevitably feel as hurt and betrayed as she'd have if he left her.

Judy felt herself shutting down. People had to feel like this, she thought, when they were dying, letting go. She was letting go. And going numb. At the moment, she didn't even feel her bad tooth throbbing.

Purposefully, she moved about the room snuffing all the candles save one. Then she lay on the bed to wait awhile longer before she made good her escape.

An hour passed, and the door opened. Holding herself very still, through slitted eyes Judy watched Andrew's silhouette, backlit by the torch in the hallway. He hesitated on the threshold, and she wondered what she'd been thinking earlier. That he wouldn't come to bed all night? Of course he would. And now that he had come, could she still leave him?

She must. She could endure a lot of things, even the damned toothache, but not Andrew falling out of love with her. Better she live a lonely, loveless life without him than watch his love transform into indifference or disappointment.

"It's all right." Judy spoke up suddenly but kept her voice low. "I'm not asleep, Andrew."

"Are you feeling better?"

"A little," she lied.

He drew closer and stopped at the side of the bed. "Is the pain keeping you awake?"

"No. I've slept off and on."

"Did you eat?"

"I...can't remember."

He sat on the edge of the mattress. Judy inhaled through her mouth, which made her molar throb. The pain gave her the courage to say, "Andrew, I hate to ask this of you, but..."

"What? Anything, and I shall do it."

"Could I sleep alone tonight? If the mattress jiggles even slightly, my tooth hurts terribly."

"Of course." He stood. "Forgive me, dearling. I did not think."

"It's not your fault. Honest to God. None of it's your fault."

She felt tears pooling in her eyes and hoped Andrew wouldn't notice.

"I will sleep in your old bedchamber. If you need me, Judith, that is where I shall be."

He hadn't noticed. "Thanks," she whispered, looking up at him, trying to memorize his face. But the room remained dim, even with the light from the hallway, and her vision had become distorted with her tears. Barely able to make out Andrew's features, Judy wondered if that would be her fate, to recall her husband only as she saw him this evening, merely a blurred image fading into shadow.

He took her hand, kissed it, and turned to walk away.

"Andrew!" she called after him impulsively.

"Aye?"

"Remember that night at the Ackworths', when I bargained with Lord Geoffrey so you could have the dagger?"

"Of course. I shall never forget it."

"Andrew, that's what I do. You're a knight and a seneschal, so I understand what you do. I just—just wanted you to know what I do."

"Very well, Judith. Rest, now."

***

Andrew couldn't get Judith's words from his head—what a strange little speech she'd made. At first, he credited it to her pain and weariness. But later, he suspected something more lay behind it. His pulse racing and his heart thudding, Andrew ran to their chamber, throwing open the door.

Judith was gone. He saw immediately that she didn't lie abed, and a quick sweep of the room with his gaze assured him that she remained nowhere within. "Damnation!" he muttered. "The bone-fires, the solstice!" He whirled around and bolted back out the door and down the stairs.

Earlier, the evening had been warm and still, the sky sprinkled with stars. But now Andrew felt a breeze toying with his hair as he crossed the bailey on his way to the gate. The peasants' fire, high and bright and crackling upon a nearby hill, belched sparks as it licked the sky. Though he glanced at the blaze and saw many people thronged around it, he didn't head in that direction. He knew exactly where to go—to a spot behind the postern wall.

"Judith!" he shouted when he spied her sitting cross-legged in the dirt, wearing the tunic and chausses he'd first seen her in, with her satchel clutched to her bosom. "Judith why are you here?"

"Andrew!" She gestured, warding him off. But he grabbed her hand and clutched it, sitting on the ground beside her.

"You want to return to your own time," he accused her, understanding the truth now. "You want to leave me. Judith, why?" In the moonlight, he saw her tears. On his face, he felt his own tears.

"I don't want to leave you," she insisted, shaking

her head. "But I have no choice. I thought I could stay, but I can't. I can't!"

"You can." He came to his feet, crouching, and pulled her hand. But she refused to stand, refused to come with him. Instead, she wrenched herself free and clutched a fistful of grass, as though it would anchor her to the earth.

"I can't," she said again. "I don't belong here, Andrew. I tried to make it work, for your sake and mine, but everything's going wrong. I'm losing my sense of self, and if I'm not the woman I was anymore, I won't be the woman you love." She tilted her chin and blinked up at him, raising her voice to be heard over the noise of the nearby revelers. "I couldn't bear to watch you fall out of love with me!"

The wind gusted. It blew Judith's short hair away from her face and then back into it. For a moment, the world grew darker as a cloud scuttled across the moon.

"Ne'er would I not love you! For all my days, you're in my heart!" he insisted. He fought a wave of panic with a surge of fury.

"I'm not going to argue with you, Andrew!" Judith shouted, for despite their proximity, the wind had begun to roar and tear at the trees. "If I can make it, I'm leaving here. God willing, I'll return to a time and a place that I belong."

"No!"

"Oh, Andrew, please!" she begged. "I have to leave, I don't have any choice! Just—just remember me. The way I was, and how happy we were together. And find someone else to be that happy with again. Forever!"

He opened his mouth to speak but was silenced by a sudden awareness that the earth beneath him quivered, pulsing with an energy like the heat of the sun. Fearful, he again tried to drag Judith away, nearer the shelter of the wall. But she resisted, catching him by surprise with a purposeful shove. He lost his balance, fell and rolled.

Debris blew into his eyes, so for a moment, he saw nothing. But he heard her voice above the din: "I love you, Andrew Laycock!"

"I love you," he returned, unsure he'd spoken aloud

as he scrabbled back onto his hands and knees, looking for Judith.

She had gone. He was alone.

Twenty-four

Judy came to under a marbled gray sky. Since birds chirped in the trees, she sensed dawn was drawing near. That was all she sensed. Afraid to look around to see if her surroundings had changed, she didn't have a clue as to the time or the place.

Her chest felt like a chasm of despair. She had sacrificed so much. If her attempt to fly through time again had failed, Andrew would probably reject her for trying to leave him, for wanting to go. If, however, she'd succeeded, the next fifty or sixty years were going to prove agonizingly long, without him to live with and to love.

Andrew wouldn't have left me out here all night, not if were still there, in the 13th Century.

That thought jolted Judy upright. Before she lost her nerve, she turned to glimpse the castle wall. The oily shadows were dissipating with the rising sun, but she saw no wall—only stones, low and jagged, a ragged ruin of what had once been a tall, solid rampart.

Her breathing came in harsh little gasps, and she could feel her heart pounding. By God, she'd done it! She'd come home!

But what if she hadn't? What if it were another decade, or even another century, either long before or after her own? She would have lost everything then. Not only Andrew, but her life, her career, and her family.

The sky grew opalescent, lighter and more blue. Anxiously, Judy looked all around, not only at the remains of the keep behind her, but at the hills before her. Below, nestled within those low, rolling hills, she spied Wixcomb, all quaint and charming, just the sort of place people would visit to stay at an ancient old inn.

Hope surged in Judy's breast, but she tempered it with rational logic. It might be 1910 or 2150, she didn't know. She couldn't count on anything. She would only learn the truth if she got to her feet and hiked down the hills to the manor house. But apprehension held her in place. Not knowing for certain seemed far better than knowing for a fact she had aimed wrong and landed elsewhere in time. How did she know if her fervent thoughts last night, as the wind picked up and the starlight disappeared, had directed her to All Saints Day in 1998? God knew, she hadn't been able to concentrate as she'd left Andrew behind.

She hugged herself, though not because she felt chilled. In fact, the temperature seemed rather warm for autumn in England. Alert, she glanced around again. Tall grass grew in the meadows where sheep grazed lazily. The trees appeared heavy with bright green leaves.

She felt a sharp pain pierce her heart. She had missed the mark. This wasn't her time after all. *I've lost it! My God, I've lost everything*!

Dreading confirmation of her fears, she remained where she sat, clinging to her tote. Her tooth hurt again, though not as badly as in previous days. Maybe that black alder concoction had helped, after all. Hopefully, no matter what the year, she'd dropped herself down into an era where at least there were dentists.

Movement caught Judy's eye. It wasn't the sheep. No, it was a dog, a pair of dogs—liver and white spaniels, bounding up the hills toward her from the direction of town. And a man! A hiker, it seemed, wearing khaki shorts, tan boots, white crew socks, and a baseball cap. Judy couldn't make out the insignia on the cap, but as he drew closer, she saw that his white T-shirt bore the distinctive logo of a Hard Rock Cafe.

"Thank you, God," she muttered, realizing she'd returned to a time somehow close to her own. Heck, if she'd landed early, she would make sure to snatch up some Microsoft stock, Judy thought wildly, hoping to beat back that keen sense of loss still gnawing at her. How would getting rich ever compensate for losing Andrew?

Dabbing at her eyes because tears blurred her vision, Judy peered at the man approaching. Did he...? Yes. He wore a Cleveland Indians cap! He had to be Viscount Laycock.

She scrambled onto her knees, sitting back on her calves. And he broke into a run, the dogs romping before him and reaching Judy first.

"Duke? Duchess? Is that who you are?" she asked

the hounds, scratching their ears and deciding to become a dog person after all.

Then she looked up at the fellow who'd stopped abruptly a couple feet away. "Lord Laycock, I've never been so glad to see anyone in my life," she admitted. "I was afraid I—I'd missed...that I'd get stuck...Then I thought maybe I dreamed—Have I been gone very long? 'Cause I—I feel that I have been. I met someone, and we...well, maybe I didn't. I just don't know anymore."

She knew she was babbling like a nut case. Dropping her head, she covered her face with her hand, trying to get a grip. It seemed doubtful she ever would. How could she be so happy yet so miserable, so glad to be in her own time yet so lonely without her husband?

"Here." Stiffly, Laycock thrust his upturned hand beneath her face. In his palm lay two tiny, yellow pills. "For your pain."

"What?" Confused, she looked up at him again. The guy hadn't changed a bit, or had he? His shades were dark, not amber, his cap looked new. And was there a bit more gray in his sideburns?

"They're from my dentist. Wash them down with this." He handed her a plastic water bottle.

Bemused, Judy took the pills and popped them into her mouth. As she swallowed them down with a squirt of water, she had the most curious sensation that the viscount's hand seemed familiar to her touch. *Oh, no. Not more weirdness. I can't take anymore weirdness. And I sure as heck am not acquainted with Viscount Laycock's hands!*

"You always come this prepared?" she asked lightly with a smile, attempting to sound normal under these exceptional circumstances. "Because it just so happens, I have a major toothache."

"I was aware your tooth pained you sorely, Judith."

Her heart stopped. The world did, too, for an instant. Even the birds stopped chirping, and the sheep stopped bleating. "An...drew?"

"Aye. Aye!" He fell to his knees as he threw off his cap and yanked away his sunglasses. She saw the tears streaming down his cheeks just before he grabbed her, held her, and began kissing her face a hundred times.

Yet all those kisses weren't enough. She wanted more.

"Andrew? Andrew, how can it be you?" she demanded, afraid to believe what she saw, what she felt. He couldn't be here, he couldn't, not like this, not in shorts and a Hard Rock T-shirt! "While I flew through time, were you reincarnated or something into Carla's Lord Laycock?"

"Nay, wench." He held Judy's face in his hands and looked at her lovingly, adoringly, as he shook his head. "I am Carla's Lord Laycock—and your husband, too."

She took a deep breath, peering back at him. "But you're older, Andrew. You were older than me when I first met you, and younger back then, back when we were in your time."

"Indeed. I'm thirty-six."

"What!"

"Do you want the whole story immediately, or would you prefer to go to the inn?"

"I want to rip off your clothes and make mad, passionate love to you. But you'd better explain everything right now. I'm pretty shaken up, actually, and incredibly confused."

Andrew drew Judy onto his lap and held her close. "When you left on that summer solstice," he began, "I was furious with you. I told myself I hated you more than I ever did Chandra. For months, I sulked and brooded, or picked fights with strangers and family alike. But in time, I overcame my pain and anger. Gradually, I came to understand that despite our love, you couldn't live in my time because you had no purpose there. You'd been afraid you would become someone I couldn't love anymore."

"Judith," he continued, "I realized that I needed you beside me, or else I would be lost. Of course, I'd have been pleased had you stayed with me in the year we originally met, when I remained surrounded by all that was familiar to me. I didn't care," he said with a smile, "if you had blonde hair or dark, glossy lips or painted toenails."

"You don't think I left because of that!"

"No. I understand why you left. Though it hurt me terribly, I couldn't fault you for going.

"But I knew, too, I had to find a way to join you. Since I'd found myself so intrigued by the many gadgets you carried in your satchel, especially the laptop computer, it occurred to me I might fare far better in your time than you could in mine. Thus, on the next Samhain, I followed you. 'Twas no hardship for me to give up sword fighting." He grinned and rocked Judy in his arms.

"That night, I went to your spot and willed myself forward through time. With the magic of that celebratory eve, I very nearly succeeded."

"What do you mean? What went wrong?"

"Though I traveled ahead through the centuries, I didn't find myself in the precise year from which you'd come. I soon learned I'd arrived nearly a decade earlier."

"You've been waiting ten years for me?" Judy couldn't fathom that. For her, it had been minutes. For him, it had been a decade.

"Ten years, and more. While I waited for you and your friend, Carla, I set about learning everything I could about this modern age, most especially how to speak modern English." He winked. "I'd brought some things with me, valuable artifacts and antiques, so that I could sell them and support myself in your economy. As well, I hired a solicitor to prove I was the last Laycock heir. Tricky business, that, but I pulled it off."

"Did you bring your father's dagger?"

"No. That piece wended its way through the generations. I inherited it."

"Wow."

"Wow, indeed. I also inherited the manor house, which I turned into an inn. Then I learned computer programming and set myself up in business. As you already know, I'm fairly successful."

"Andrew, I can't believe this!"

"Now you know how I felt when you told me your story, that afternoon on the road to York. But it's true, every word. And though it had been a long time since I last laid eyes on you, Judith, at least I moved toward you with every passing year. I confess, I hired an investigator and kept track of you in New York. I knew when you graduated high school and college, and when you took that job at the Edwin Grant Agency."

"That's kind of creepy," Judy admitted. "I never had a clue."

He gave her a great, soulful hug. "How's your tooth?"

"Better."

"We'll make an appointment with my dentist straight away."

"Fine, but I want to hear the rest of your story," she urged impatiently.

"Eventually, I did hear from Carla. She e-mailed me. I cannot tell you how ecstatic I was that day! Then I had to wait for you both to arrive. Worse, I had to keep away from you when you did."

"Why? Why did you do that? Why didn't you tell me everything?"

"Judith, I knew you. Damn, I knew you as my wife! But you didn't know me at all. You'd never met me before, let alone married me. This time-traveling business gets a bit confusing, but you understand, don't you?"

"Um-hm." She nodded. "I think so."

"I so feared I'd give myself away, make a fool of myself, or frighten you into thinking I was some sort of lunatic, that I pushed you off rather rudely."

"Your documents from King John. Did you inherit those, too?"

"No, sweetling. I purposely brought them with me. I bloody well wasn't going to leave that bit of business to chance! It's why they're so bloody well-preserved," Andrew added, chuckling.

"But what happened after I left on Halloween? Come to think of it," Judy added, patting his tanned, bare knee, "why are you wearing shorts? What day is this?"

"July 15."

"What!"

He nodded. "July 15th, 2002."

"2002!" The shock jolted through her like a nearby explosion. "You mean I lost almost four years?"

"Yes. It would appear time travel's not very precise, and because you leave on a certain day doesn't mean you'll arrive on that same date in another year. You left here that first time on Samhain, in 1998. But you appeared in my world sometime in April, did you not?"

"Yeah." Judy tried to absorb the ramifications of this information. Grabbing his arm, she exclaimed, "Andrew! What about my parents and Carla? They think I'm dead, don't they? I've been away so long."

"Hush, sweetling." He tucked his cheek against Judy's, the cheek that didn't hurt with a toothache. "It's been hard for them, I admit. I felt almost as frantic as Carla when you first turned up missing. I knew where you'd gone—God's teeth, I knew I was with you in some twist of time! Yet I was also without you, and I'd no idea when you might return to your own time, if at all. I never lost all hope, but I must admit, in the last couple of years, I've grown more and more despondent. To see you here this morning...!"

He sighed and hugged her more tightly, as though he were afraid she might slip away from him again.

"When you first left," he said, "I contacted your parents, who flew here. The police were called in, of course. Everyone surmised you'd been abducted. But as time went on, and you never reappeared and your body was never recovered, the authorities concluded you'd gone off on your own accord, just turned your back on your life and started over with a new identity."

"Mom would never believe that."

"No, she didn't. She grieved for you, as did Tony and your brothers."

"Tony? You're on a first name basis with my parents?"

"I am, actually. We speak by telephone every few months. I believe your father first suspected I was the culprit behind your disappearance, but I think we've moved beyond that."

"I hope so," Judy concurred. "After all, you're his son-in-law."

Andrew laughed and looked at Judy with those heavy-lidded, syrupy eyes she so adored. "Methinks we're the longest wedded couple in history, don't you? Who could top almost 800 years?"

"I think we're going to have to start over, Andrew. A big, formal wedding in my parents' parish back in New York. You don't mind?"

"I'll marry you anywhere, every day for the rest of my life, if it pleases you." He kissed her before continuing, "I can't tell you how I felt when I spied you sitting up here near the old bailey walls! You understand, I couldn't be sure you'd return while I remained alive. I had hoped you'd reappear the morning after Samhain last year. When you didn't, I was as distraught as I'd been when you left me in 1215. I've come here every bloody morning since All Saints' Day of 1998."

"This is so strange," Judy admitted. "To me, we made love in our bed only last night. Yet to you, that happened years ago."

"Henceforth, there'll be no such gaps in our lovemaking." With a wink, Andrew stood, slapped his cap back onto his head, and reached down to Judy. When she gave him her hand, he pulled her to her feet. "We'll return to the inn now and make a few phone calls. There's my dentist, whom you'll wish to see promptly, and the police who must be notified. As well, you'll want to call your parents and Carla." He whipped a flip phone out of the leather pack belted to his waist and handed it to Judy with a grin. "If you don't wish to wait, you can ring up your mother while we're walking."

Judy laughed. "Your cell phone's nicer than mine, but electronics have advanced, no doubt, since I was here last. Andrew, did you understand at all when I first tried to explain how these things are used?"

"Nay. Nor did I imagine such things as airplanes and televisions, DVDs or automobiles! By the way, I have my own driver's license now," he confided as they strolled toward town. "I even own my own car."

"The library," Judy gasped. "All those books at Laycock Inn—they're really yours! You've read them."

"Indeed. I had almost a thousand years of history, science and invention to catch up on."

He stopped suddenly. "Wait, Judith. Before we go on and you place a call, I've been bringing something else with me on my hike to the ruins each morn." He pulled her old tape player from the leather pouch. "I played it every time I didn't find you here. I should like to play it now, since you've come back to me.

"You must remember this." He smiled as he pressed the "play" button, and the strains of "As Time Goes By" joined the other, more mundane sounds of the countryside.

Judy set down the phone, the water bottle, and her tote. She slipped one hand into Andrew's as she stepped very close to him and rested her other hand on his shoulder. When she put her cheek against his, they danced together in the warm, yellow dawn that had broken in this new millennium, just as once they had danced under the cool, twilight sky in another age.

Volume 1

An Erotic Collection

Alexa Nichols

Quickies Series

CUMPILATION, VOLUME 1
QUICKIES SERIES

For information contact **Alexa Nichols**

alexa.nichols.author@gmail.com
http://alexanichols.com

@AlexaNicholsAuthor
@AlexaNichols69
alexa.nichols.author
alexanicholsauthor
alexanichols69
alexanichols

ISBN: 9781519010780

First Print Edition: August 2016

10 9 8 7 6 5 4 3 2 1

Contents...

Acknowledgements

This has to be the hardest part of the book to write, because there are so many people that influence and encourage me... choosing which ones to thank here is truly more daunting than you might think.

So, in this, my first Quickies! *Cumpilation*, I want to thank them all.

You know who you are, and I don't want to embarrass anyone by name-dropping them in an erotic collection, so we'll just leave it at that.

I love you. All of you.

Siempre.

NO, Daddy! I'm NOt MOmmy!

Chapter 1

Amber lay on her stomach, on her bed, with her diary wide open in front of her as she stared at the blank page for today's entry lost in thought. She was trying to think of how to start. Ever since she was a little girl she had written in her diary nearly every day – in 20 years' time, she had only missed three days. Usually, an entry came out with next to little thought, but so much had happened today that she wasn't quite sure if she even *should* write some of it down.

Her first day home, the first day of her vacation from college, actually, had not gone *anywhere near* how she thought it would. Not that anything that had happened was necessarily *bad*...

She tapped her pen against her diary's open pages.

What to write…

Part of the problem was that her thoughts were all over the place. They usually were. See, Amber wasn't your normal, run-of-the-mill girl in any sense of the word.

Not only was she the dorm mother of the newest sorority on her campus, Phi Beta Pie, but she was also practically rich thanks to the numerous *fundraisers* she conned the girls into doing.

It was a fabulous hustle.

But it wasn't all good. Though her finances were terrific, her love life was anything but. Her long-time boyfriend, Jake, was constantly leeching funds off her idea and did practically

nothing to contribute to it. Same with Dean Whitman, who was in on the scam with her. **They** didn't have to live with the damn girls, didn't have to deal with the bickering and constant cat-fighting, and they especially didn't have to deal with *Penny*, the current queen of the dorm, whom Amber had come to at once hate and respect.

Amber wiggled her bottom until her panties shifted out of her butt crack, then stared down forlornly at her diary. She then smiled as she realized that she was holding her pen more like a knife than a writing instrument.

"Fuck it. I'm writing down everything," she said to herself as she positioned her pen properly and began to do just that.

If you're going to hell, she thought to herself, you might as well document why.

After all, sometimes the road to hell is paved with gold, right?

And semen...

Chapter 2

Dear Diary...

So it's my first day back from college, and if today is any indication of how the rest of the week is going to go, it's going to be one hell of an interesting vacation!

First thing: that asshole of a boyfriend of mine, Jake, is not returning any of my calls or texts. He's probably out fucking one of the girls in Pie. Knowing my luck, it's probably Penny. So fuck him.

Second: I had a bit of an interesting situation a few minutes ago. Me, my baby sister Amy, my mother's new (and retarded rich) husband Mark, and my mother were all sitting on the couch watching TV, some lame ass reality show about the ex-wife of a basketball player and her daughter. God, I hate that show.

I amused myself by messing with Amy's long light blonde hair (she was sitting on my lap) and playing on my phone, trying to keep from showing too much of my panties to Mark. I had thought he was asleep when I wandered into the front room, wearing only a flannel shirt and a pair of white cotton panties, but then he slipped in like a fucking ninja wearing his night robe and sat down next to me.

Amy arrived seconds later and plopped on my lap.

I had originally wanted to be there to spend time with my mother, whom I really missed, and watching TV together was always one of the ways that we bonded. Pathetic, I know.

Anyway, her new husband is really physically unremarkable: overweight, old, and generally just sloppy

looking. He had maybe two things going for him: he always *smelled good, and his longish black hair was absolutely beautiful. If my mom didn't marry him for the money, I was damn sure it was over that hair. I would mate with that hair if I could.*

Just saying.

Despite his sloppy appearance, he's actually a really good person. He practically oozes charisma when he wants to, and he seems to genuinely care for us.

My mother could definitely do worse. Has, actually. Several times.

Mark, who was sitting in-between me and my mother with his arm casually draped over my shoulder, offered me a drink of whatever foul-smelling alcoholic beverage he was guzzling down. It had a strong, pungent odor, and Amy made an over-exaggerated face at the smell of it. In her defense, it did smell really foul – like a sick elderly dog defecated and then threw up atop of it to cover its indiscretion.

I turned it down, mumbling something about being a cheerleader and having to keep myself in shape.

He seemed to have bought it; or, at least, didn't care enough to pursue the matter further.

Besides, last time I drank, I ended up running down the street naked and yelling at the top of my lungs over a dare. My friends thought it was hilarious. They uploaded the videos to YouTube, but it was taken down, being that I was a minor at the time and all. The lesson I learned from that: I had the alcohol tolerance of a mouse.

And to not get drunk around asshole friends with cameras on their phones.

Something Jake knew and tried to exploit often.

Did I mention my boyfriend was an asshole in this entry yet?

Anyway.

My curiosity started stabbing at me, however, and I really wanted to ask him what kind of animals he blended together to make a drink that smelled like that. My sister, who turned and looked at my face, must have read my mind because she answered my unspoken question by whispering in my ear.

"It's Jägermeister, sis. Trust me, you don't want any. Tastes foul."

Her comment made me start, and I looked at her with wide eyes. How the hell did she *know what kind of drink that was? Or how it tasted??*

We were going to have a talk later.

I returned my attention to my game and my sister returned hers to the television, and time began to pass quickly.

Mark was starting to get woozy, no doubt from the lateness of the day and the alcohol – excuse me, the Jägermeister *- and Amy was practically asleep on my lap, snoring in that ultra-girly way of hers. But I didn't mind; I liked having her in my lap. I knew it was just a matter of time before Mark tapped out and went to bed, and then it would just be me, my sister, and my mom. Which, in a way, I was not looking forward to, because I knew my mom and sister were going to grill me about* everything *having to do with my college experience.*

My mother surprised me, however, by telling us she was going to bed and kissing both me and Mark goodnight, then taking Amy from my lap and carrying her off.

Mark mumbled something that sounded like he would be there in a minute.

I looked over at him - he already looked 3/4 asleep.

I was about to find out, however, that just because the big head was sleepy didn't mean the little head wasn't wide awake...

Chapter 3

Amber looked down at her journal, wondering if she should *really* write down everything that had happened tonight. What if someone managed to get ahold of her diary? After all, Mark was the one putting her through college, and he was actually a really decent guy. Sure, he kind of creepily insisted that she call him *daddy*, but that was more a joke than a serious demand.

She jumped as her phone beeped beside her. A text message. She looked at her phone's lock-screen and grinned, thinking of creative ways to tell Jake to eat a dick.

But it wasn't from Jake, it was from Penny.

"hA girl! Enjoying yor tym home?"

Amber frowned at her phone. She hated shorthand text-messaging and definitely hated having to translate it in her head before she could respond.

[*Hey girl! Enjoying your time home?*]

She rolled her eyes and swiped the message away, ignoring it.

She wished it had been from Jake. She had a lot of steam to vent at that motherfucker. She refused to text him first, however - especially when he promised he would message her as soon as he got to his parent's place.

She looked down at her diary, tapping her pen against it like it was a drum.

"Screw it," she mumbled, continuing her entry.

After my mom left I put my phone down and grabbed the remote, flipping through all the channels in record time, trying to find something interesting to watch. Within minutes I heard loud snorting sounds coming from Mark; he was finally starting to fall asleep. Within minutes I knew I would be by myself. Now it was simply a waiting game.

That's what I thought, at least, until about 10 minutes later when I felt his body fall to the side and lean against mine, completely asleep.

I tried to gently shake him awake, but he refused. He was truly out cold.

Then I heard him starting to mumble.

"Shirley, I need release..."

Shirley was my mother, and all kinds of alarms went off in my head. He was thinking I was my mother.

"Mark. Wake up. Go to bed," I said, shaking my body gently, causing him to rattle.

Instead of waking up, however, his body turned slightly towards me. Moments later I felt his hand sloppily exploring my body.

Mark was a big man, and it was impossible to push him off without tossing him off the couch entirely, so I continued saying his name and shaking him.

It didn't work.

I tried to turn away from his overly explorative hand, but I couldn't - his body had mine locked into place.

I sighed heavily and gave up, figuring it would only be a matter of minutes before he completely passed out. Hopefully. I turned to the television, trying my best to ignore him.

"Shirley... I love... Ur breasts..."

His hand-

Ambers phone beeped. She stopped writing and looked at her lock screen.

It was Penny.

Again.

"Hey, girl, we hav a prob. d lSBN twins went missing. n one's cn dem since U L."

This one took a while to mentally decode. She even had to go to the internet to translate a few of the abbreviations, like ISBN, which she thought meant *International Standard Book Number*.

[*Hey, girl, we have a problem. The lesbian twins went missing. No one's seen them since you left.*]

Amber looked hard at her phone. She didn't *want* to answer, but she was the dorm mother...

Grumbling, she snatched her phone off the bed and tapped out her response. "Did they go home to visit their parents?"

Minutes passed before she received Penny's response.

"Oh, shit! Yeah, dey did! I'll caL off d srch thN. & d cops. Hey, whatcha doin ^ so late?"

Amber rolled her eyes. So childish.

[*Oh, shit! Yeah, they did! I'll call off the search then. And the cops. Hey, whatcha doin' up so late?*]

Amber gritted her teeth. "Grudge-fucking Jake," she responded, tossing her phone across the bed and looking back down at her journal. She continued drum-tapping her pen on it.

Minutes passed.

Penny didn't respond.

Her lack of a response bothered Amber for some reason.

She started to reach for her phone, then stopped herself. She was not about to text Penny asking her what she was doing. The fewer doors she opened with that girl the better. Besides, she knew that as soon as she continued writing in her journal Penny would interrupt her anyway.

Either that… or Penny was with Jake...

The tapping of her pen on her diary increased as she looked back and forth between it and her phone.

She exhaled a deep breath and continued her entry.

After all, she was just getting to the good part...

Chapter 4

His hand slid across my stomach, causing me to instinctively tighten my abdominal muscles. I had a really hard time ignoring him as his hand slid further up my shirt, to my breasts, cupping one and gently squeezing and kneading it. I looked at his face - he was definitely still asleep. So he was, what, instead of sleepwalking, sleep groping? He leaned more into me, pinning me against the couch completely while his mouth sloppily found my neck and began kiss-licking it like some kind of thirsty camel.

"Mark!" I hissed quietly, not wanting to awaken my mother, "I'm not Shirley! I'm Amber! Go to bed!"

He mumbled something completely unintelligible and jerkily slid his hand down my stomach and in between my legs.

I was so shocked that I didn't respond for several seconds, and by the time I closed my legs he was already at the crotch of my panties. It was no problem for him to slide his fingers underneath them, to touch and stroke me in my softest, most sensitive of places.

I hissed as his finger found my opening, mentally cursing myself and confused to find myself wet and hot down there. I was not attracted to this man at all, *but it had been so long since me and Jake had done anything that my body was going into automatic sex mode.*

His finger entered me.

Deeply.

I-

Amber dropped her pen and snatched her phone off the bed.

"Where the fuck are you, what the fuck are you doing, and why haven't you texted or called me all day?!" She texted to Jake, then stared at her phone hard willing his response to pop up on her screen.

It didn't.

She let out a small growl of frustration, then opened up her favorite radio streaming service and tossed her phone to the side, picking her pen back up.

She was going to kill Jake. Literally.

There was no doubt in her mind about this.

"-just now joining us, we're talking with Miel Lucrox and her husband Piotr about her new bestselling book, *The Secret Life of Miel*. So, Miel, I'm going to be honest, your book is kind of a mindfuck. I mean-"

Penny rolled her eyes and grabbed her phone, shutting her radio app down.

She continued her diary entry.

I tried to push him off, but I couldn't - he was too fat, and I too small.

His finger wiggling around inside me excited me more than I understood, and my traitorous body was becoming way more excited about this than I wanted.

"No, daddy! I'm not mommy!" I harshly whispered into his ear, hoping to snap him into consciousness with the daddy endearment. He grunted and his finger quit moving inside me. I felt him slowly pull his finger out, and my body calmed as I assumed that he was finally starting to wake up.

But he wasn't. In fact, his head slid slowly down to my stomach to my lap, and his nose ended up resting firmly against my panties, right on top of my clitoris. He stayed this way for a while, taking deep breaths.

Like he was breathing in my scent.

And then I felt his tongue-

Ambers phone beeped, causing her to jump.

It was from Penny. "k"

Amber stared at her phone, confused. OK? OK to what? She went to her text messages and found their conversation. Ah. She had told her she was grudge-fucking Jake. Why did it take her this long to respond?

"What are you doing?" She texted Penny.

Penny's response came seconds later. "Hanging out w Song n d queen's r%m. getin redE 2 go 2 slp. Jake jst L. Why?"

Amber painfully went through the annoying task of translating her text. When she finished, her eyes widened in alarm.

[*Hanging out with Song in the queen's room. Getting ready to go to sleep. Jake just left. Why?*]

Her hands were a blur on her phone's virtual keyboard.

"Why was that motherfucker in-"

She received another text from Penny before she could complete hers. "I mEnt Antonio. Antonio jst L. SBTA. Tired."

It took her a second to translate that one.

[*I meant Antonio. Antonio just left. Sorry. Tired.*]

Antonio? Who was Antonio? She erased what she had been writing and asked Penny who Antonio was.

"Tanya's bf. He's also 1 of my best fRnds. swEt guy. Goodnight."

[*Tanya's boyfriend. He's also one of my best friends. Sweet guy. Goodnight.*]

Amber fought with herself not to pursue the topic. She knew Penny was lying, and she was certain Jake really *did* just leave her room.

She let out a small exasperated yell.

All hell was going to break loose when she got ahold of that asshole. She reached back and adjusted her panties again, removing them from her crotch and butt crack. Pretty soon she was going to have to shower, but she wanted to finish this diary entry first.

She started to continue her entry.

There was a knock on her door.

Chapter 5

Ambers' heart started beating triple time. What if it was Mark? What if it was her mother, and she had somehow found out...

She pushed herself off the bed and shuffled over to her door.

It was her mother.

"Hey – wait, why are you looking at me like I'm a ghost? Is everything OK? I keep hearing strange sounds coming from here, like your yelling or grunting or something. Are you feeling OK?"

Amber smiled in relief. Her mother apparently didn't know. "I'm fine, mom. It's just Jake. He's being an asshole. Nothing new. We're having issues right now."

Amber's mom nodded, then yawned. "You want to talk about it, honey?"

She shook her head. "Nah, I'm OK. I'm just going to finish my diary entry and jump in the shower, then go to bed. I'll be OK."

Her mother smiled, then reached out and ruffled her hair. "I love you, Doodlebug. Remember that, K?"

Amber smiled. She had been *Doodlebug* since she was a little girl, and every time her mother called her that she melted a little inside. She absolutely loved the name.

"I know. I'll talk to you in the morning, OK? Tell you all about it."

Ambers mother smiled, then kissed her daughter on the cheek.

Amber waited until her mother was halfway down the hall before she closed the door and launched herself on her bed, grabbing her pen and rereading what she wrote so she could finish her entry. She continued...

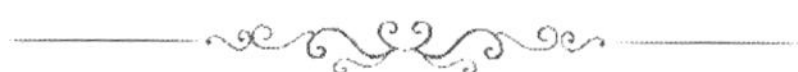

And then I felt his tongue licking the general area of my clitoris like a thirsty enthusiastic dog. Even though he was passed out, drunk, and ugly as all sin, it felt absolutely amazing. Before I knew it, I was running my hands all through his long beautiful hair.

I felt a jolt of naughtiness course through my body, and I responded to it by reaching down and moving my panties to the side, giving him unobstructed access to my most holy of parts.

And his tongue...

It was amazing...

In what seemed like seconds I felt jitters race through my body like electricity and I came – hard - all over his unshaven face. My orgasm was intense and sudden, causing me to shake and cry out, and I ground my crotch into his face as hard as I could as my inner fluids exploded out of me. It was something I could not control; the pleasure was just too intense.

And he didn't stop.

I managed to-

Her phone beeped. She ignored it, continuing her entry.

I managed to slide out from underneath him and prepared to race back into my room-

-but then I noticed his impressive erection bulging underneath his underwear. Apparently, that's all he was wearing underneath his night robe. And me and my little sister had been sitting next to him all night.

A hundred thoughts raced through my mind. Eventually, I quit thinking and carefully dropped down to my knees, watching him as I did so.

He was still out cold.

I leaned forward and put my mouth on his underwear directly on top of his bulbous penis tip, which was very (impressively) visible. I wanted to make him come - after all, he just made me have what had to have been the most powerful orgasm of my life.

I gently suckled him through his underwear, taking as much of it into my mouth as I could.

And then something came over me.

I decided to expedite the process by-

Ambers phone rang. She reached up and swiped to ignore the call, and continued her entry.

-expedite the process by carefully pulling his penis out of his underwear hole and taking it into my mouth.

Compared to Jakes, Mark's penis was enormous.

I looked up at him as I created a gentle yet strong suction with my mouth. He was still passed out.

If I kept doing this, I knew it would only be minutes – maybe even seconds - before he came.

I continued pleasuring him, but in the back of my mind, I was fiercely wondering what it would feel like to have a penis this engorged inside of me. I tried to swat the thought away, but it was persistent.

And powerful.

I stopped my sucking and carefully removed him from my mouth, then moved him so he was laying on his back and

-

Her phone rang again.

She dropped her pen and snatched up her phone, aggravated.

Then felt her heart squeezed painfully within her.

It was Jake…

Chapter 6

She answered the phone, but didn't give him a chance to speak. "Where the fuck are you, and why haven't you been texting or calling me all day?!"

"Hey babe," was his slurred response.

Hey, babe. That's it. *Hey, babe*.

Ambers door creaked open, and her little sister, Amy, groggily walked in and stepped up onto her bed, then plopped down atop her, laying across her back.

"I asked you a question, Jake," she said through gritted teeth as she pressed her head against Amy's.

"No. Asked-asked me two… questions. I think…"

Amber went silent, listening carefully to the sounds in the background. She could make out other guys... low music... some laughing...

Amy wrapped her arms around Ambers' neck and laid her head flat against hers. Full body hug. Amber loved it. She returned her attention to the asshole on the phone.

"You're drunk, aren't you Jake? You didn't even leave the campus, did you?"

"Yes'm."

Amber let out an aggravated grunt and hung up. She'll tear him a new asshole when he was sober - it wasn't any fun when he was drunk.

She turned her phone off.

“Who was that, sis?” Amy asked, a slight feminine yawn punctuating her sentence.

“Jake. Being an asshole. Nothing new. I think he’s drunk.”

“You’re still with him? I thought,” a yawn silenced her for several seconds, “that you left that slob already. All he wants is in your pants.”

Amber giggled. “Who taught you how to talk like that?!”

“You did,” Amy said as she squeezed her older sisters neck, “besides, I’m already 15. Just because I’m small for my age doesn’t mean I’m not a woman.”

Amber smiled. “A woman, huh? Does that mean you’ve finally had your- “

“Eww. No. Thank god. Mom says any minute I will, though. So not looking forward to it.”

Amber felt Amy’s head move and come to rest beside hers. “Whatcha’ writing?”

Ambers eyes widened as she snapped her journal entry shut. “Nothing! Well, my diary. Private stuff.”

Seconds later Amber was almost startled out of her skin by a gentle rapping on her window.

Amy grumbled. "It's probably Alicia. I'll get it."

Amber watched her little sister slide off the bed and shuffle over to the window, shoulders slumped. "Alicia? Isn't that supposed to be your best friend?"

"Something like that," Amy grumbled as she opened the curtains and lifted the window. Sure enough, it was Alicia - a girl they had known since she was literally a baby.

The years had changed her drastically, however.

Amber remembered Alicia as a curly haired, shy, slightly chunky girl - crawling through the window was a slender, gothic, shapely near-woman.

Alicia smoothed her tight-fitting leather outfit out as Amy closed the window behind her.

"Why didn't you return my texts?" She asked Amy over her shoulder, then, at Amber "Hey chicky. Looking good. College agrees with you."

And then a slight wink and smile.

What the fuck had happened to her?! Was this suddenly an alternate universe or something?

For a moment, Amber didn't know what to say.

Amy came to stand in front of Alicia, blocking her from Amber's view, saving her from the embarrassment of not responding. "Because my phone's in my room. Why are you even here? I told you I was spending time with my sister this week."

"Babe... look, don't be ignoring my texts. You know how I get. And… look, I'm sorry about earlier, I just get - you know how I get. Jealous. I heard rumors..."

"Yeah, well, unless you hear it from me, don't assume," Amy said sourly as she crossed her arms over her chest and looked away from her.

Amber cocked her head at her little sisters back. What exactly was she witnessing here?

The teens stood there for several moments quietly, just looking at each other. Amber almost said something but was beaten by Alicia, who broke the silence by moving some of Amy's long Blonde hair to the side, then moving her head until she was facing her.

And then by kissing her.

On the mouth.

Amber's mouth dropped open.

"Come on, let's go to your room. I brought my tarot cards. Promise I'll be out before your parents wake up this time," Alicia said to Amy as they pulled themselves apart from each other, keeping their arms locked around each other's waists.

"K. Night, Amber," was all Amy said as her and Alicia latched hands and made their way to the door.

Before Amber could say anything they had slipped out and closed the door behind them. Amber stared at the door unblinkingly for a while, then shook it off and continued her diary entry.

-moving him so he was laying on his back and carefully, slowly, straddling him. I watched his face as I did this, making sure he wasn't waking up.

He wasn't.

He wasn't sleeping, I don't think, but he was too drunk to care what was happening. I knew if I left him in his horny state that he would end up with a painful set of blue balls.

And I didn't dislike him enough to do that to him.

When I finished straddling him I reached down and moved my saturated panties to the side, using my other hand to direct his engorged meat to my wetness.

God, he was huge.

I lowered myself onto him slowly, and even though I was wetter than I had ever been, he didn't enter me as smoothly as I had anticipated. It had been too long since I last had sex, apparently, and I was nearly virgin-tight down there.

I gyrated slowly and pushed down, trying to fit him inside of me, feeling my labia slowly separate as I managed to squeeze in his enormous tip.

It was no easy feat.

I stifled a squeal.

It.

Hurt.

I stayed still for a moment, adjusting to the unexpected pain.

When it finally subsided, I lowered myself even more, taking his length deep into my insides. When I finally managed to take him all in, I swear I felt him hitting the entrance to my womb.

Just the thought of that made my body supernova.

I had never felt like this with Jake.

I started-

Amber reached over and turned her phone back on. She was starting to develop a nervous twitch wondering if she was missing calls, social media posts, and text messages. While her phone booted up she continued her diary entry.

I started to make small micro-movements, stroking him with my insides.

I looked down at his face, letting go of my panties and placing my hands beside his head. He was mumbling something, it sounded like my mother's name, and I honestly didn't give a damn. I bent down and placed my mouth on his, still keeping him firmly and completely lodged inside of me, completely losing all forms of common sense.

I kissed him. Deeply.

And he kissed me back.

I became lost in the moment, in our motions, in his mouth, and the world around me completely evaporated. My mother could have walked in right at that moment and I would not have stopped.

Not until we were finished.

I grunted into his mouth as I continued to stroke him with my movements, and to my surprise, he started to kiss me back. His kisses were sloppy, and the taste of alcohol in his mouth was revolting, but that didn't stop me from kissing him. Didn't even slow me down.

Suddenly his body tightened all at once and he-

Amber was so startled by her phone ringing that she drew a small line across the page she was writing on.

She looked at the screen in wide-eyed fury.

It was Penny.

She snatched the phone up and accepted the call. "What the f-what do you want, Penny? I thought you were sleeping."

"I can't sleep," Penny responded in a whiny little girl voice, "and I think someone's trying to break in."

Amber frowned. "Why do you think that?"

The line went dead…

Chapter 7

Alarmed, Amber immediately tried calling Penny back, but her call went straight to voicemail.

Three times.

She tried calling Jake.

The line rang, but no one picked up.

Options. What were her options…

She didn't have many. Especially when she was three states away.

She pushed off her bed and started pacing her room, thinking furiously about the things she could do. She couldn't call the cops because Phi Beta Pie was an illegal sorority, and any kind of digging would reveal this. There wasn't-

-then it occurred to her.

She could call Dean Whitman. He would take care of it. Even if it was late. The last thing he wanted was for his cash cow to get burglarized.

She dialed Dean Whitman's number, a smug smile on her face, and waited for him to answer. He did on the fourth ring.

She rapidly filled him in, and he assured her (groggily) that he would make sure everything was OK.

She hung up, pleased with herself, and belly-flopped back onto her bed, snatching up her pen and focusing once again on her diary.

Suddenly his body tightened and he made a strange grunting sound into my mouth as he began to pulsate, shake, and empty himself inside of me.

I froze, focusing on the warm splashing sensations. He was so far deep inside of me that I knew his sperm was going straight into my womb, and...

Amber blinked. Something had just occurred to her, something that she hadn't thought about during the heat of the moment. She wasn't on the pill, or the shot, or any kind of birth-control really. And he definitely wasn't using a condom.

She could be pregnant right now. With her stepfather's baby...

A burst of thunder startled her. The rain drops tapping on her window moments later, however, had a strangely soothing effect on her. What if she was pregnant? What would she do? Where would she go? After all, she just told the girls of her sorority that coming up pregnant was grounds for immediate expulsion.

She blinked and returned her attention to her diary.

...and I pressed my bottom firmly down on top of his geyser, taking all of his ejaculations inside of me, squeezing my insides around his hardness to encourage him to come more.

And he did.

Volumes.

When he finally finished (and it took a lot *longer than I anticipated) I slowly slid off of him, tightening my inside to keep his expelled semen inside of me.*

I started to rush back to my room but stopped before I got there. Guys leak *after they come, and if Mark wakes up to find any kind of sperm residue, he's going to know that something happened.*

So I had some decisions to make.

I inched my way back towards Mark, watching and listening for any signs of my mother or sister, or her apparent girlfriend. *Nothing.*

I finally reached him and dropped back to my knees, taking his flaccid member into my mouth and gently suckling it, draining it of any residue that might have been left behind.

His residual emissions tasted overly sour, and I was glad he didn't have much left.

I then rushed to my room, plopped on my bed, and started this journal entry that you're re-reading right now..

Amber looked up from her diary and stared the wall, not looking at anything in particular, just lost in thought. She gently closed her diary, setting the pen she had been writing with beside

it, and turned on her back, spreading her legs and placing her hands in-between them as she relaxed her internal muscles.

His cum was still pooled inside of her.

Sticky.

Hot.

Thick.

And probably making a baby at this very moment.

She scooped some of it with her fingers and brought it to her face, smelling it, sticking her tongue out and licking it. Her body began heating up all over again, and she wondered what the probability was that he was still out there on the couch.

And if maybe she could make him go another round.

Maybe even wake him up first…

She leaned to the side and slipped off the bed, bouncing to her feet and heading towards the shower. Her stomach and insides started twisting, almost as if they realized that soon there may be a baby growing inside of them.

Or maybe it was mom's lasagna.

But she doubted it.

This was going to be an interesting week...

Please Don't Get me Pregnant!

Chapter 1

Louis was jacking himself off so fast that Daedre knew it was only a matter of moments before he came. His hand was practically a blur, and his face was screwed up in the goofiest expression she had ever seen him make. She tried to spread her legs just a little bit wider as she played with herself, hiking her dress up with her free hand so he could see her sex without any kind of obstruction.

She had never done anything like this before.

She wanted to orgasm *with* him, so deduced that the best way to accomplish this was to synchronize her movements with his - but it was hard to focus on bringing yourself to orgasm when you had to keep an ear out for your mother at the same time.

True, her mother didn't have much of a reason to come into the barn - she was, after all, cleaning the house - and Daedre herself was supposed to be tending to the various animals across the farm.

Which, in a sense, she was…

She increased the rapidity of her finger movements on her clitoris as Louis increased his stroking and was surprised to feel her body jerk in a miniature orgasm. She was wetter than she had ever been down there, and this knowledge served to excite her even more as she continued to explore her innermost parts with the rest of her fingers. This was not the first time she had pleasured herself, of course, but it was definitely the first time she had done so in front of another person.

It was...

Invigorating.

She could smell the strong, sharp scent of her excited sex, and knew that Louis could too. Knowing this served to turn her on even more, just as it no doubt did to him.

"Are you gonna come yet?" she asked her crush, watching mesmerized as he rapidly stroked his meat, fascinated by it.

In response Louis used his free hand and gently pushed her backward, leaning over her as he continued to masturbate, looking down intently at Daedre's exposed nether regions.

She raised her hands to his chest to stop his advance. "Nuh uh. You can't put it in. I ain't tryin' to get pregnant!"

Louis didn't stop stroking himself - in fact, his masturbation seemed to quicken. "Can uh - ok - can I put it on top of your belly?"

Daedre considered this. She knew she couldn't get pregnant if he put it on top of her, as long as he didn't get any on top of her dress everything should be OK. So she nodded her head, feeling her entire body flush, and quickly pulled her dress even further up so it was just underneath her breast.

"I wanna see em!" Louis said huskily as he used one hand to prop himself up and the other to quicken his stroking.

Daedre pulled her dress up even further, struggling with the large gemmed necklace that her mother gave her when she was just a little girl. It felt uncharacteristically heavy and almost seemed to put up a fight as she pulled her dress over it and, next, her breasts. She even managed to somehow get her hands caught up in it.

She heard Louis cry out and felt his weight drop down on her body, and seconds later felt a sharp deep sting in-between

her legs. He had completely penetrated her, stealing her virginity, something she was trying to save for her marriage bed. Half a second after his brutal invasion she felt spurts of hot wetness being unleashed into her womb. He had pushed his entire length inside of her, and with each spurt, she could feel his overly swollen testicles throb and twitch as they emptied themselves of semen.

"Louis!"

She tried to push him off of her, but she couldn't; he had used both of his hands to brace himself, and was lodged deeply - completely - inside of her.

"So-sorry..." he mumbled, not sounding sorry in the least bit.

She knew he wasn't sorry. Even when he was done, he didn't pull out, he just went lax, keeping himself deeply lodged within her, still leaking his baby making juices.

"Daedre?"

Daedre's heart stopped. It was her mother.

In the barn...

Chapter 2

Fortunately for Daedre, she had a little bit of foresight before her and Louis started this little erotic foray. She had found the best hiding place in the barn: a large section of hay, somewhere her mother wouldn't immediately see them. But that could easily change if her mother came anywhere near where they were.

Louis slowly rolled off of her and tried to pull his pants back up, but Daedre stopped him - it would make far too much noise, and at the moment any kind of noise would likely get her mother's attention.

"Daedre? Are you in here?"

Daedre mentally swore to herself. She could hear her mother walking around the barn, could imagine her looking around, searching, investigating. Why would she think she was in here to begin with?!

Unless she had already checked the rest of the farm first.

Daedre mentally swore again. She hadn't thought about that. Truth be told, she thought her and Louis would be done long before her mother thought to look for her.

Her crush started squirming. She looked at him in confusion and put a single finger in front of her mouth, but the expression on his face told her he was extremely uncomfortable, and being quiet wasn't going to happen.

"I have to pee," he mouthed to her.

She widened her eyes and shook her head, then held her finger up to tell him to wait.

"I can't. I have to pee *now*," he mouthed.

Daedre could hear her mother coming closer. It wouldn't take much to get her attention.

Letting Louis pee was definitely out of the question.

Daedre did the only thing she could think of doing: she bent over and took Louis flaccid member all the way into her mouth.

Louis tried to push her head away, but she swatted at him. She could feel his stomach muscles contract, and could sense him trying hard - fighting - to hold his urine.

But he couldn't.

Seconds later his piss was being released into her mouth, and Daedre tried hard not to think about what was happening as she drank it down as quickly as she could.

It was disgustingly salty and strong and came out faster than she thought it would.

When he had finally finished he let out a small sigh of relief and went limp against the hay. Daedre kept him inside her mouth, waiting for the sounds of her mother leaving the barn.

Instead, she heard her mother doing… something. Organizing things? Cleaning?

After several minutes of waiting, she began to feel Louis' manhood growing erect once again.

She panicked.

Louis reached down and held her head in place as his erection continued to harden, filling her mouth and, eventually, part of her throat. She fought not to gag and was surprised to find

it was easier than she thought. Apparently, she didn't have much of a gag reflex, something she hadn't known before.

Of course, she wouldn't have had a way to know – Louis was her first.

She mentally tried to hurry her mother, because the penis in her mouth, while tolerable, was getting increasingly uncomfortable.

Not knowing what else to do, she started suckling it, something that caused Louis' eyes to roll in the back of his head.

For some reason this made her feel even naughtier than she previously had, and she grinned around the meaty appendage in her mouth.

The sounds of her mother moving about the barn receded into the background as she began focusing on messing with Louis, trying things she had never dreamed of doing before.

She pushed her face flush against his pelvis and slid her tongue out, running it underneath his hard-on, managing to get some of his testicles. She moved her hand up to his delicate man-orbs, moving them gently as she fellated him, and was both surprised and amused when his body responded to her ministrations by letting loose small little twitches. She became so caught up in her games that she squealed in muffled shock as Louis reached down and held her head tight as he shook and ejaculated violently into her mouth.

It was a weird sensation.

When he finally finished, he let her go, and she immediately pulled back and spat his thick milky white juices onto the ground beside her.

She could hear the sounds of her mother finally retreating towards the barns exit, and closed her eyes in relief.

Then she heard her mother's footsteps stop.

"When you're done, Daedre, please meet me in the kitchen. I need your help with the pie I'm making."

The barn door closed moments later...

Chapter 3

Daedre timidly sat in the kitchen chair as her mother went about getting the necessary ingredients for her famous blackberry pie.

She could feel Louis' semen, mixed with the blood of her virginity, oozing out of her birth canal, and tried to clench her internal muscles to keep it inside instead.

If she kept it inside her, did that mean she was more likely to get pregnant? The thought made her heart thump like a hummingbird's wings in her chest.

She didn't want to be pregnant. She did like Louis, a lot, but she wasn't sure she *loved* him. She highly doubted he would make a good father.

"So who was the boy? Was that Louis, the boy from the next farm over?"

Daedre hung her head. "Yeah. How-how did you know?"

"How did I know it was Louis, or that he was in there to begin with?"

Daedre looked up at her mother and tilted her head, interested in the lack of rage in her mother's voice. "Both."

Her mother smiled. "He's the only boy I know of around your age anywhere near us. And I knew he was in the barn because I saw him sneak in when I was cleaning the front room."

Daedre closed her eyes and shook her head. Stupid. She knew they were there all along. The hiding - and the drinking of his urine - was all pointless.

She snapped her eyes open. "Wait, why aren't you mad at me?"

For a long time, her mother said nothing.

"Come here. Beat, crack, and whip these eggs while I form the crust."

Daedre stood up, immediately regretting it; not only did Louis semen (and her virgin blood) begin slowly oozing out of her and down her leg, but her abdomen in general subjected her to a quick burst of pain.

"Was he your first?" her mother asked without looking at her.

She looked at her mother, squinting in pain. "Unintentionally."

Daedre's mother nodded and began to work on the crust.

For a while they said nothing, simply focusing on making the pie.

"Mom?"

"Hmmm?"

“Why aren’t you yelling at me right now?”

Her mother laughed lightly. “Do you want me to start yelling at you? Would that make you feel better? I can hardly yell at you when I myself have done far worse than that, sweetie. I am no hypocrite.”

Daedre nodded, focusing on her tasks.

“What kind of- “

“We are not having this conversation, Daedre. Not right now. Now hurry up, I’m almost done with the crust.”

Daedre sighed but did as she was told.

For a bit.

"How was your first time? Did it hurt? And was it with my father?" she blurted out, bracing herself for her mother's rage.

Her mother let out a deep breath and stopped prepping the pan, looking down at her hands with an unreadable expression on her face.

An expression she had never seen on her mother's face before.

"Well, you're not a child. I guess I can tell you."

Daedre blinked. Something told her that her mother's first time was going to be an interesting story.

"What I'm about to tell you I've never told another soul. I want this to stay between us. People might find it hard to see me as a respectable alchemist if they knew some of the things I have done."

Daedre nodded. This must be one hell of a story!

"It started when I was just a bit younger than you..."

Chapter 4

My father had died when I was just a little girl; I was so young that I barely remembered him at all. It had always been just my mother and I. Fortunately, we lived a good way away from the city proper - in a cabin out in the woods, in fact - surviving primarily by living off the land. Everything we ate and wore came from the land and animals around us. We never had a reason to venture out into town, and I had little desire to. From what my mother had told me, there was nothing there for a girl like me anyways.

We lived a peaceful little life in that cabin, just the two of us. It was perfect.

My mother had only one rule: do not enter the forest alone.

It was a rule I had a hard time understanding because the forest absolutely fascinated me. It wasn't that I was naive enough to think it devoid of any danger - I knew that it wasn’t. It was full of all manner of strange and fascinating creatures: The Espers, ghost-like fey creatures that were deceptively menacing; the beautiful yet wild wolf-riding Silvestri, and even the occasional bestial Tauron, who looked like a horrid mixture of bull and man. While I knew they were there, I also knew that they lived deeper in the forest than I would ever go and that they were not harmful to Humans by default.

If I was being honest with myself, however, I had to admit that I *wanted* to meet something non-human, something completely alien and different than me. As a little girl, my mother used to tell me story upon story of strange and fascinating creatures... now that I was a woman, I wanted to see

them for myself. And then there were the various animals, plants, and lakes.... so many beautiful, natural things for me to see. The desire to see them all burned away at my insides the same way a strong alcoholic beverage might, and I finally decided that the next time I got a chance, I would explore it to my heart's content.

So one day, when my mother said she needed some flowers and herbs for some medicine she was concocting, I jumped at the chance to get them.

She agreed, sending me off with the usual warning.

"Don't go too far in the forest. Come back as soon as you get what I need. Don't dawdle."

I agreed, grabbing my basket, and left.

Seconds later I was deep in the woods, farther than I had ever gone before, and quickly became lost. Of course, Aeriel, the god of the sky and travelers, would decide to pick that day to make the sky pregnant with rain.

But I didn't care. In a way, the rain was beneficial to me, for it ensured that I would be unmolested by some of the forests more dangerous creatures.

Or so I thought.

It seemed like I was wandering around for hours. I might have been. Eventually, however, I was found.

Not by monsters.

By bandits...

Chapter 5

Daedre gasped. "Mom! Are you trying to say-"?

"Are you going to listen, or are we going to bake?"

Daedre blinked. "Listen. I'm going to listen. Ma'am."

Daedre's mother nodded.

"As I was saying: I was found by a group of bandits. I didn't know they were bandits, of course, because I had never actually seen a bandit before - but then, except for my father and the occasional villager that came to my mother for various elixirs and potions, I had never seen a man up close before either. So I had no idea what to make of these men.

They had no problem figuring out what to make of me.

They captured me easily and took me to a cave; before I fully realized what they intended to do they had torn my shirt off, exposing my breasts, and I was pushed to the ground, with one holding my hands behind me while the other pushed my skirt up and lowered his pants, exposing his hardness. The other bandits were laughing and joking amongst themselves even as they disrobed, even as the man forcing my legs apart started stroking himself, lowering himself and placing the tip of his engorged manhood to my virginal entrance. I screamed, cried, struggled, but this only seemed to excite the men - especially the one in between my legs. I could feel him moving the tip of his hardness between my lower lips, seeking and finding my entrance and forcing himself inside it with one quick, brutal thrust.

I screamed. It hurt - badly - and my struggling only seemed to amuse the men.

I remembered everything they said. Especially the one who had stolen my virginity.

"Holy shit she's tight! Got ourselves a bona fide virgin here ya'll! Well, *was* a virgin!"

The men laughed as if this was the funniest thing they had heard all week.

It probably was.

I cried, begging him to take it out, telling him in gasps how much it hurt, but this only seemed to excite him even more.

He continued to violently piston himself inside me, squeezing my inner thighs hard with an iron-like grip, keeping my legs open wide so that I had no choice but to accept his thrusts.

It was a strange sensation, feeling a man's member moving in and out of me. I had never felt anything like it and had never heard anything about what to expect. I was completely unprepared.

The man humping me shuddered and cried out, and I cried out too as his fingers dug deeper into my legs. Moments later I felt an odd wetness splashing around inside me, and I could feel his engorged member rapidly pulsating, shooting his disgusting baby-making juices.

I was powerless. All I could do was wait until he was finished. He seemed to pour his seed into me for a very long time, as if he had been saving it up for years just for this occasion.

When he did finally finish he pulled his spent member out of me, and I could feel his emissions, mixed with my first blood, leaking out of my body.

My crying became sobbing.

It was finally finished.

Or so I thought. As it turns out, it was only just beginning..."

Chapter 6

Daedre was captivated by her mother's story. She wanted to say something comforting because she knew her mother's recollection was painful for her, but she couldn't bring herself to talk - or even move. Without thinking, she reached up and grabbed the necklace her mother had given her long ago, drawing comfort from it. It had always soothed her, and had done so since she was a little girl, and now wasn't any different.

Her mother looked out the nearest window and continued.

"The man that had been holding my arms flipped me over so that I was on my knees, my chest flush against the cave floor. I didn't even have time to wonder what was going to happen next - his hardness quickly pressed at my… anus, and before I could protest he grunted and forced himself inside.

I wasn't ready for pain on that kind of scale.

I screeched, and his hands painfully dug into my buttocks as he repeatedly and rapidly forced his way in and out of my stomach.

I was crying so hard that it blurred my vision. Even over my sounds of misery, I could still hear the men surrounding me: laughing, drinking, and having all manner of casual conversations as I was being raped. Like this was an everyday thing for them; like my worth as a person was negligible. I was simply a collection of holes to them, little more.

The man thrusting into my bowels did not last long - in a matter of minutes he grabbed my sides painfully and pressed

himself flush against my backside, and I felt his man-juices gushing into me.

He pulled out as soon as he was finished, and I immediately felt his emissions leaking out.

I was raped every day - for several days - after that. They put me in all manner of positions to satisfy their lust: standing with my hands against the wall as I was penetrated from behind, on my back as they rutted away in between my legs, and even using my mouth, forcing me to swallow their ejaculations over and over again.

Whenever I objected to one of their requests, something I did frequently as they found new and inventive ways to use my body, they beat me brutally.

However, although I was often beat, I was not beaten; I always kept my eye on the cave's exit and planned my escape in a myriad of ways.

It was only a matter of time, I knew, before they let their guard down. As soon as that happened, I would be gone. That was the only thing that kept me sane.

My hopes of escape were quickly and thoroughly shattered, however..."

Chapter 7

“A slave trader who was apparently on good terms with the bandits stopped by, and the men had little hesitation to sell me to him. Perhaps it was because the slaver was not an ordinary slaver, if such a thing exists, especially since slavery is supposed to be outlawed in our land. No, he was not ordinary; he was an Agari."

Daedre gasped, interrupting her mother’s story. "Mom! I thought they only lived in the Wildlands and-"

Her mother silenced her with a look. "Things don't always do what they are supposed to, honey, now do they?"

This caused Daedre to fall silent. She knew exactly what her mother was referring to: she was, after all, just in the barn with Louis doing very un-ladylike things...

Before she could utter an apology, however, her mother continued her story.

"Now as you have probably heard, Agari are very humanlike, save for their massive size, skin color, and mean temperamental dispositions. This Agari made the ones you hear about seem like servants of Angelica, the love goddess. The slavers were quick to agree with whatever terms he dictated.

It was like this that I was sold for a silver coin.

That was all I was worth to them. A single silver coin.

I realized then that I would never see my home - or my mother - again, and that knowledge hurt me worse than anything the bandits had ever done to me. Even as I was placed in a large wagon with several other girls the slaver had collected during his

travels, I could not stop crying… and the girls did nothing to comfort me. We were all naked, all alone, and all past the point of return.

We were no longer people, but objects.

And we knew it.

I remember very little of how long we were in that wagon, or of the stops that we took.

I did, however, remember the moons.

They were one of the only things that kept me lucid during our seemingly endless journey in that small, stinking wagon. The moons. Because of the holes in the wagons covering (which did nothing to keep the rain away from us), I was able to watch them every night before I fell asleep.

The moons...

I had never really noticed them before. I knew they were there, of course, but I had never really *looked* at them.

Nyla. Aylana. They were beautiful. I could see why so many people had written poems and stories about them. I watched them until I fell asleep most nights, their constant and sporadic twinkling barely visible but magical to me nonetheless.

Sometimes I felt as if the goddesses they were said to be were looking down upon me, soothing me, comforting me, telling me in their silent yet magical way that everything was not only going to be all right but also somehow better because of what I was going through.

As it turns out, they were right…

As beautiful and soothing as the dual moons were, however, the three suns were not. They beat down on us ferociously throughout the day, an unforgiving barrage of heat

that seemed to not only ignore the wagons flimsy covering but become magnified by it.

Because of the constant heat, of our sweating, of the proximity of our naked bodies, an undeniable pungent odor began to fill the wagon, lessened only by the sporadic rains. One of the girls ended up dying, and our Agarin slaver callously discarded her body as soon as he was made aware.

He cared nothing for us, for our lives. To him, we were simply wares.

We were truly alone.

Our final stop was a port city. We were quickly sold to a group of sailors about to embark on a long voyage.

I remember the *examination* process well: they had each of us line up on a long table, our legs spread, and examined our sex, looking for signs of damage or looseness. Several girls were turned away, but most were not.

I was one of the ones that were not.

I remember vividly being led onto the ship. It was my first time ever being on one, ever even seeing one, and I was both terrified and fascinated at the same time.

They spent a little time letting us get accustomed to our new home, however, grabbing whichever one of us they fancied using for our intended purposes. Hours after the ship departed from the port we were all placed in cubicles with small mattresses and told to stay there; as the days and nights passed so many different men came and had sex with us that they all kind of just blurred together.

They used us in any manner they wanted, and were all extremely rough – and, even worse, they cared so little for our

personal welfare that without fail they each spent themselves inside of us.

It was only a matter of time before we all became pregnant.

And they didn't care.

This thought terrified me. I begged each of them to not finish inside me, begging them to please not get me pregnant, but this impassioned plea only seemed to steel their resolve to do exactly that.

And they were all so violent... oftentimes I was brought to the point of fainting before they finally finished.

Yet, not all of them were like this.

Some of them were actually kind.

My favorite of which was a man that I had come to know as Aliest. He was not a sailor like the others, but a practitioner of the Arts, and he would often amuse me with esoteric tales, even show me magical fascinating tricks that most normal mortals would never see.

Of course, he would still occasionally use my body to placate his needs, but I welcomed this, and our joining was more than simply the moving together of bodies; it was a deep, intimate act between two people who genuinely cared for one another.

We were not fucking, in my mind; we were making love.

He was not simply a man to me. And he was more than my lover. He was my best friend, my only friend, and I cared for him far more than I had ever cared for anyone else before him.

And I remember our last time together well.

He came to me and told me that he was needed elsewhere, that he had to deal with a situation that was far more urgent than the petty concerns of sailors. He promised to one day see me again - as a type of collateral, he gave me his favorite necklace, a necklace he had been given by his mother. He said if I ever wanted to feel close to him, I would only have to hold the necklace, and there I would find his soul.

When he placed the necklace on me, I could immediately feel its magic.

"What does it truly do?" I asked him, the wonder very evident in my voice.

"What makes you think it does anything?" he responded, smirking playfully at me.

I immediately looked at the floor, embarrassed at my assumption. After all, I was little more than a whore, why would an Art user give me anything of true value?

I remember his response as if he had uttered it yesterday.

He lifted my chin up with his fingers and turned my face until our eyes locked.

"It allows me to always be able to find you, wherever you are. Most people would not be able to feel the subtle yet powerful magic resonating within it. I am very impressed."

I beamed at him, and I vowed then to never take the necklace off.

A vow I kept. Until the day I gave it to you."

Daedre's eyes slowly became huge. She looked down at the necklace that she had been unconsciously gripping as her mother told her of her past, a necklace that her mother had given her back when she was a little girl. It was beautifully crafted, no

doubt, but to have once been the property of an Art user… she carefully raised it to her eyes to examine it further.

"Yes," her mother said, turning to her and smiling, "that would be the necklace. You have been wearing the necklace of a powerful Art practitioner since you were a little girl."

Daedre was absolutely speechless.

“I remember well our last night together,” her mother continued, “after he had spent himself I grabbed him fiercely, willing every drop of his juices out of his body, praying to all the gods that I knew to let his seed take hold and make me with child. It was a long time before I unlatched my legs from his side and let him go, allowing him to lay down at my side, holding me as he often did.

I felt complete.

Whole.

At peace.

In love.

I knew then that I was in love for the first time in my life.

"I have to go now," he told me eventually, his voice practically dripping with regret. My heart – to be honest, I really can’t explain what I was feeling at that exact moment. Hurt is the closest I can come to it.

I am positive he knew this.

"I will find you. I promise," were his last words to me as he kissed me on the lips. He then dissolved into countless colorful, floating bubbles which themselves disintegrated into colorful particles of air, which quickly dissipated into the air around me, becoming invisible.

He was gone.

I held my stomach, closing my eyes and again praying fiercely that his life-giving seed bless me with child.

I believe the gods heard me.

A short time later I discovered I was pregnant...”

Chapter 8

"Mom!"

"Daedre, you are going to either let me finish my story or we will stop talking and I will never speak of this again."

Daedre was conflicted. There was so much she wanted to say, a hundred questions she wanted to ask. One important question in particular. After much internal warfare, she finally acquiesced and put her hand over her mouth, indicating to her mother that she wouldn't say anything else.

Her mother eyed for a long moment before she continued.

"Once my pregnancy became evident I was taken off the ship at one of the many port cities they stopped at and sold to a place I now know was a *brothel* – which is a place they keep women who have sex with men for money. I didn't know this at the time, of course, but it was something I quickly discovered.

They put me to work right away. The things I did for the men was not all that different than what I did day in and day out on the ship - except the food in the brothel was better, and the men that came in were quite a bit more creative.

Some were very creative.

It was there that I learned all about *fetishes*. One man, for example, liked to put his member deep into my throat while I sucked as hard as I could until I brought him to orgasm. He would simply stand there, unmoving, while I drank his disgustingly salty emissions, his testicles resting on my chin. It was a strange sensation, feeling a set of large hairy testicles

rapidly contracting against my chin as they produced the sperm that was being poured down my throat. I would just grab his legs, massaging them in the manner he had instructed me to, waiting for it to all be over with. There was little else I could do.

Others preferred me atop of them, laying back and watching me as I took them inside and rode them, my pregnant belly bouncing ever so slightly as I rode them to orgasm.

I quickly learned that it was far easier on me if these men came quickly, so I learned little tricks to make them do exactly that. Telling them they could come whenever they wanted, asking them if I was too heavy, asking them how my tightness felt to them, kissing them even as I rode them, even as I felt them filling my insides with their semen.

I would ask them if they came a lot, would even take their emissions into my hand as it drained out of me and drink it like it was the sweetest of nectars.

Being a part of a brothel was not all bad, however.

There were several distinct advantages: the food was much better, we were allotted more than enough time to rest, and we were allowed to bathe as often as we wanted.

The bathing was one of my favorite past times - they supplied us with all manner of sweet-smelling soaps and oils, and sometimes I would spend hours just soaking in the baths hot luxurious waters.

And our clothes were always clean and varying, which was definitely a switch from the ship.

All in all, if it were not for the constant sex on demand, it was much like one would picture a paradise to be.

Then something unexpected happened: the sex slaves rioted and took control of the brothel, disbanding it and killing the owner… and suddenly, I was a free woman.

Something I had not been in a very long time.

I was also a broke woman, however, and there was only one thing I knew how to do to earn money..."

Chapter 9

Daedre was practically dancing in her chair. She wanted to ask so many questions, but she knew if she did her mother would quit telling her story, and she absolutely *had* to know how they wound up here living the life that they did now.

Her mother noticed this, ignored it, and continued.

"Since I did not have money, I had to rely on the lusts of men to obtain it. Looking back, the price I was asking for was overly small, but in my defense, I knew nothing of the business end of such things - that was something I had never been privy to. So I found an old, dirty mattress in an empty alleyway and set up shop, letting men fuck me over and over again, sometimes multiple men at once. Satisfying men like this was not easy: trying to pleasure one with my mouth, another with my hands, all the while keeping my insides contracted while another pistoned himself in and out of me.

Oftentimes they would all come at the same time, and that was a very strange sensation: having a man spurt in my mouth, hand, and womanhood all at the same time.

Meanwhile, my belly got bigger, making it completely impossible to hide my pregnancy from anyone. Especially from the men that I pleasured.

It turns out that there are some men that find this a turn on, however. They loved to have me stand as they entered me from behind, some even grabbing my belly as they slammed into me, losing themselves completely over my fat, engorged body.

And then I started lactating and quickly discovered it to be something of a coin magnet. All manner of men loved to

drink my breast milk even as they fucked me, even as they came inside me, and it was a disturbing feeling to have a man drink from you and fill you both at the same time.

I would bring them to orgasm in all manner of ways, despite my enormous belly: on top of them, knelt over so they could drink of me; sitting on their lap, draining them even as they drained me.

Some even preferred to suckle on my nipple like a newborn babe as I masturbated them. Their cum was always voluminous, creamy as if they were far more excited and aroused than any of the other men had been.

Finally, however, my body had enough; after one of my customers had finished, giving me the requested copper, my belly started hurting in a manner I had never experienced before, and I cried out for help as I slid down the alleyways walls.

No one came to help me.

Even as I felt my previous customer's semen leaving my body, I felt my lower muscles contracting, and soon I began giving birth..."

Chapter 10

"I had a bit of a revelation after your birth, realizing that what I had been doing was wrong on many levels, and vowed to raise you in a proper way, not on the streets as a prostitute. So I made my way throughout the city, looking for proper employment, and eventually found the ear of an older woman who was acting as the cities herbalist. She taught me everything I knew, and eventually I took over her trade - and when she passed - her home..."

Daedre's mouth dropped. "You mean, this house-"

Her mother nodded. "Yes. This house, and the farm surrounding it were hers."

"So..." Daedre's mind reeled. She had never even suspected that her mother had been through all that. It was mind boggling. She slid off her chair and went to her mother, giving her an all-encompassing hug.

"Why are you hugging me?" her mother asked with a hint of amusement in her voice.

Daedre fought to speak through her tears. "I-I had no idea you went through all of that. I'm so sorry, mother."

Daedre's mother pulled back and smiled at her daughter. "Honey. What, wait, why does your breath smell so foul? What have you been eating?"

Daedre's eye's widened and her face went beet red.

Daedre and her mother both jumped as the door to their tiny home slammed open.

In the doorway, smiling, stood a large imposing man in an even more imposing robe.

Her mother gasped.

Daedre's amulet glowed...

Cramming sis!

Chapter 1

Alicia lay in her bed naked, hot, and extremely aroused, with nothing but a thin nearly transparent sheet covering her sinuous nakedness from the world.

Her body yearned for Amy. It wasn't just her companionship she craved, however. It was her mouth… her fingers… her hot, erotic softness...

But Amy was not here.

She slowly, gently, slid her finger just a little inside herself, feeling her internal virginal muscles instantly and tightly contract around it. With her other hand, she manipulated her tiny sensitive nub, feeling her breath catching powerfully at erratic intervals.

She could almost taste Amy then. Her unique saltiness, her sweet nectar-like honey-

"Can I come in?"

She froze. It was Amy's voice. Her eyes flew open, but it was too dark to see.

"Yes!" She exclaimed, sitting up, her pulse quickening through her veins.

Her room door opened.

It was not Amy…

Chapter 2

"Hey. You know where the soap is? Everyone's sleeping, and I just got off work and want to take a shower," the voice in the doorway said.

It was her step-brother Link. And she was sitting up in her bed, completely exposed.

"What are you doing in here?" Alicia snapped, pulling her bedsheet up to cover herself.

He looked at her with an unreadable expression. "You told me to come in. I knocked and asked if I could."

Alicia sighed. It was a dream. It was *his* voice, not Amy's. She reached up and moved her long black hair away from her eyes, hooking it around her ear. "We must be out. Of soap. Usually it's in the bathroom closet. Looks like you'll have to stink for a while. Now get the fuck out of my room."

Link frowned and his shoulders drooped. "Yeah. OK. Sorry for bothering you..."

Alicia studied him as he turned to leave.

He was, she had to admit, handsome in a unique kind of way. And he was especially well-tempered considering everything he had been through – like his longtime girlfriend pulling a straight up bitch move and leaving him right before he was released from prison about a month ago. Which was when Alicia met him.

She didn't know what she'd do if Amy ever went to prison. Given that her girlfriend was a drug dealer (small time, but still), that was definitely a possibility. She doubted prison

would change Amy the way it had Link, however. He was pretty much the definition of a whipped dog, spending all his time working some lame-ass construction job for minimum wage because they were the only ones in town that would hire a felon. According to his mother, her new step-mother, this new attitude was nothing like the way he used to be.

A strange, unfamiliar feeling of sympathy pinged her.

"Link, wait. I have some soap, but it's perfumed - Amy got it as a gift for me a few weeks ago. So... you can have it if you want."

Link turned. "I don't want to use something your - ah - girlfriend got you. Wouldn't that piss her off?"

Alicia half-smirked, a habit she had since she was a teenager. "You'd be doing me a favor. I don't use perfumed soap like that."

Linked ruffled his hair and softly laughed. "Yeah, OK, thanks. That would be great. Don't really care much about what I smell like. Just want to be clean. I feel like someone buried me or something."

Alicia got out of bed and went towards her dresser where the small basket of soap was.

"Here," she said as she spun around and held it out to him, "go ahead and keep it. Just give me the basket back so-"

The look on Link's face startled her. His eyes were huge, and he didn't seem to be breathing.

She closed her eyes and sighed the second she realized why.

She was stark-naked, and her nether regions were moist and swollen, completely exposed.

Link reached out and took the basket, then quickly left the room and closed the door behind him.

She was going to have a hell of a time getting back to sleep...

Chapter 3

The sound of screaming kids and the smell of bacon woke Alicia up the next morning.

She had, predictably, a hard time finally getting to sleep last night. When she did, however, it was a surprisingly restful one.

Link was the first thing that popped into her mind. He was the first man that had ever seen her naked, a fact she was definitely not sharing with Amy.

She stirred beneath her sheets, yawning and stretching as sunlight poured into her room. It took her a moment to remember that her house was full of visiting relatives from out of state - a memory triggered by small footsteps rumbling up the stairs toward her room.

She quickly slid out of bed and got dressed, putting on the first objects of clothing she could find: old black sweatpants and a tiny black shirt with the words *Satan Inside* inscribed on its front.

No sooner did she pull the shirt over her head than her bedroom door flew open and her two younger cousins bounced their way into her room. They excitedly raced toward her bed and jumped on it, using it as a makeshift trampoline.

"Alicia! Alicia!" they shouted gleefully as they bounced.

"Good morning, munchkins," Alicia said, yawning and rubbing her eyes.

"Uncle is taking us to the mall later," One of them blurted out.

The other fidgeted excitedly. "He said we could come wake you up."

Alicia half-smirked. "Oh did he? I'll make sure to thank him for that later. I can't remember the last time Daddy took me to the mall, you lucky ducks."

The two of them giggled and bounded off together, out of her room and back down the stairs.

Alicia walked over to her full-length mirror to look at just how presentable she was. She stretched, loving how her body looked. She was tone and fit from being on the track and swim teams all throughout high school, and now, even two years later, she had managed to maintain her physique.

Which was good, because she and Amy were about to head off to college, and she wanted to look good.

No one was about to take Amy away from her.

She flexed her stomach. She had the best abs of anyone she knew, and the reason for this was simple: she was one of those crazy people who actually loved running. She was so busy admiring the lines of definition in her stomach and the way her breasts were filling out that she failed to notice the reflection of someone in her mirror standing at her doorway.

"Hey you," came a deep voice.

Alicia spun around and yelped, hating herself instantly for it.

It was Link, holding the soap basket out to her.

"You scared me," Alicia practically hissed, snatching the basket out from his hand, instantly remembering standing stark-naked in front of him last night.

Allowing him to see what no one besides Amy had ever seen.

"You're missing breakfast," Link said, obviously trying to avert his eyes from her, but not entirely succeeding. Alicia felt a strange sense of pride - and mischievousness - about this.

It's a damn good thing that Amy wasn't there right at that moment.

"I'm coming," Alicia snapped as she started picking up clothes off her floor, setting the basket on top of her dresser where it had originally been.

She looked up. Link had still not moved.

"Look - I just wanted to say thanks. For the soap. You didn't have to, and-"

"You're welcome. Now leave me alone so I can clean."

Link frowned, nodded, and left.

Something was different in the air between them now, however. Alicia couldn't put her finger on exactly what it was.

Amy needed to hurry up and get back from her vacation...

Chapter 4

It was a hot day. On days like this, Alicia usually wore as little as she could get away with - partly because wearing clothes when it was hot was nearly unbearable to her, and partly because she loved the way Amy looked at her when she dressed skimpily. She even loved the attention of some of the guys, even though she would never admit it.

Amy was supposed to be back from her vacation today, which was the reason that Alicia was tearing through her room looking for the skimpiest running shorts she could find, along with Amy's favorite dark blue bikini top.

She didn't bother trying to find any panties. She hated wearing those too.

When she finally found the clothes she was looking for, she modeled herself in the mirror, fighting the urge to grab her phone for the hundredth time since she woke up to text her better half. It wasn't easy, but she knew from experience that constantly texting or calling Amy would drive both of them crazy.

Besides, she was spending the week with her starting tonight. She could wait a few more hours.

She wondered idly if this particular outfit was the smartest thing to wear with all her relatives around. Her shorts were dark black and a bit loose, so without panties underneath she would have to keep her legs closed or else someone might see her goods.

Her mind flashed to last night.

To Link.

Who saw absolutely everything.

She felt her body heat rise, and forced the memory out of her mind and hurried out the door towards the bathroom -

- and slammed straight into a naked, wet Link...

Chapter 5

Several things popped into Alicia's mind at once.

The first: Link had an impressive erection, which was now pressed against her exposed midriff.

The second: he was not actually naked, but wearing a pair of baggy faded swim trunks.

For several long moments they both simply stood there, motionless, neither knowing what to do.

Then, at the same time, they both took a step away from the other.

A million things swam through her mind.

He reached out and moved her long black hair away from her eyes.

"You know, it’s still hard to think of you as my *sister*. I mean, I've only known you a month, and if we'd met under different circumstances..." he shook his head and smiled. "Are you OK? They sent me up here to get you for breakfast again. I was swimming."

She felt her eyes travel on their own accord to his chest and arms. Prison and construction work were apparently a winning combination for him. He was in fantastic shape.

"Have to pee." Was all she could manage to say. She pushed her way past him and stormed into the bathroom, closing and locking the door behind her.

Why was she so flabbergasted?! So he saw her naked. She had never, ever felt like this around anyone before.

Flustered.

Uncomfortable.

Aroused.

When she finished peeing and went to wipe herself, she was alarmed at how moist she was. Did she have a wet dream she didn't remember last night? Or was it Link? Normally only Amy could get her body this riled up.

Alicia unconsciously squeezed her thighs together as her sex tingled.

She went quiet, listening to the sounds outside the door. No one was near the bathroom.

Good.

She carefully split her vaginal lips and dipped her index finger just slightly into herself. Her hole was hot, tight, and silky, and she contemplated making herself come right there, but since she had been summoned twice for breakfast already, she decided against it and quickly finished sanitizing herself and went downstairs.

Her body, however, screamed for release...

Chapter 6

Breakfast was always fun at Alicia's house. Alicia's step-mother was the perfect model housewife: a great cook, doting over her husband, and showed the precise amount of concern and love necessary. In fact, Alicia had to admit, the woman was more than just beautiful: she was elegant.

Her father, on the other hand, was gruff, stoic, and insultingly honest.

And Alicia adored him for that.

All throughout breakfast, her little cousins were going on and on about all the fun they were going to have while they were visiting for the week. So far it was just Alicia's aunt and uncle that were here, but more family were on their way. She knew that either she or Link were going to have to give up their beds, or maybe both.

For some reason, that made her feel strange inside.

But there was a huge light at the end of this tunnel: Amy. She should be back in town tonight, and she already got the OK from her father for her to stay the week.

Amy...

All of Alicia's first experiences with sexual feelings, kissing, and touching another person in an intimate way were all with Amy, and this vacation Amy was on practically killed her.

And then there was Link.

Alicia hurried with her breakfast and trotted upstairs to her room, wanting to shower and get ready for the day.

She quickly cleaned up her room, trying to be considerate considering someone else might be sleeping there this week, picking up undergarments and other pieces of clothing from the floor and stashing them quickly into her closet. For how disciplined she was with fitness and health, she was remarkably messy with her room.

She was still cleaning when someone cleared their throat behind her.

Link was standing in her doorway, for the second time this morning.

"What?" She snapped a little harsher than she intended, still cleaning up.

Link took a deep breath. "I just wanted to apologize for walking in on you last night," he said, leaning against the door frame.

Alicia half-smirked in his general direction. "It's fine. No big deal. It was bound to happen."

She could tell Link was fishing for something, so she kept cleaning while she waited.

"Do you... always walk around your room naked?" he finally asked.

Alicia laughed. "What, you don't?"

Link apparently missed the sarcasm. "Yeah, I do."

Alicia arched her eyebrow and turned to face him. "OK. Good to know. Now why are you asking me this?"

Alicia bent to pick up the last of the clothes then turned to face him, awaiting his response.

"I dunno," Link replied, blushing. "It's kinda sexy, is all."

Alicia's eyes widened. That was not the response she was expecting.

A strange emotion filled her, one she had never felt before. She stepped to within a few feet of him. "I figured I wasn't your type," she said, enjoying his nervous reaction.

"What do you mean?"

She shrugged, pretending to be casual. "You know, guys like women with big boobs and a big ass, right?"

Link laughed. "Yeah, I guess that is typical. But I go for the athletic type."

Alicia raised an eyebrow and cocked her head, feeling her long black hair cascade across her face. An intentional act of coyness. "Like me?"

Link nodded. "Yeah, I suppose."

Not really knowing what came over her, Alicia reached up and lifted her bikini top just enough to expose her breasts. "You don't think these are too small?" she asked.

Link's eyes were glued to her chest. He was caught off guard.

"Not at all," he said, a slight crack in his voice. There was some degree of guilt in the back of Alicia's mind - this was, technically, her step-brother, and he shouldn't be seeing this… but that guilt was practically trampled over by the unexpected intensity of his reaction.

"You're sweet," Alicia said, just about to pull her top back down, then changing her mind. "You know, I'm giving you a treat for that." She stepped closer to Link and waited, keeping

her top open. He finally looked up at her face, but he was utterly confused as to what she was doing.

"Go ahead," she said. "Touch them."

Link's eyes widened. "What?"

"Touch them."

Link was extremely hesitant – almost insultingly so.

"If you don't want to, I can always-"

Links hands were suddenly on her breasts.

Alicia laughed at his speed and accuracy. He gently and firmly squeezed them but otherwise remained mostly still. Her nipples reacted strongly to his touch, hardening and poking at his palms.

"They feel..." Link could barely find his words. "...great…"

He took a step towards her. Neither of them realized how excited this was making him, and to both of their surprise, his erection - now much larger and angrier than before - was pressing up against his shorts and resting against Alicia's stomach again.

Her eyes widened, and she had to fight to not look down at what was no doubt an impressive bulge. She didn't want to embarrass him, so she fought the urge.

He swallowed loudly. "I'm sorry," he said, releasing her chest from his grasp and trying in vain to adjust his shorts to hide his excitement.

"I'm glad you enjoyed them," Alicia said softly, lowering her bikini top to cover herself.

"I...um..." Link stood there, not wanting to turn and run like an idiot, but embarrassed about his erection. So he remained in place and allowed his step-sister to finally see his shorts tenting out obscenely. Alicia's eyes drifted slowly south, and her expression turned to one of shock. Her step-brother's shorts were tenting out farther than she had imagined.

Just as slowly as her eyes had drifted down, they drifted back up to meet his face.

"Wow," she said, not bothering to hide her surprise. "I've never seen you... excited."

Link took a step back, then turned and headed for the door.

"Wait, Link - is that really because of me? I mean, do you really feel that way?"

Link couldn't look her in the eyes; he could only nod silently.

"Wow..." Alicia had never known that he thought of her that way, and considering her own sudden attraction to him, this presented an interesting circumstance.

Incest.

Could they possibly do it? She didn't know how to feel now, aside from the initial shock and ensuing arousal.

"Don't tell anyone, ok?" he said, his voice sounding scared and weak.

Her usual sarcastic, bad-girl persona melted away.

"Link, I would never..." Alicia said as she approached him and touched his arm. "You have no idea how flattered I am. Seriously."

Link smiled at her, but he was still aching to leave and retreat to his own room.

"You're going to jerk off now, right?" Alicia asked, trying to keep him focused on her for as long as possible. Link's face turned deep red, but he couldn't lie. He was a lot of things, but a liar was not one of them. He nodded.

"Take some of me with you," she said as she reached her hand boldly down into her running shorts. Link watched in awe as she touched herself in front of him, dipping a finger into her womanhood and rubbing it around for a few seconds, her eyes locked onto his. She withdrew her hand from her shorts and held it out to him. Link could clearly see, and smell, the silky fluid that decorated her finger.

It smelled sweet and milky. He had been with a few girls by now, but none had smelled so sweet.

"Please," Alicia said when he didn't budge, "taste me."

Link hesitated, then sucked her finger into his mouth and licked her nectar off of it. Alicia groaned, finding the sensation more arousing than she thought it would be. Link's eyes were closed for a few moments as he savored her taste, and she had to force herself to keep from reaching down to grab his aching erection as it visibly throbbed in its confines.

“So how does a virgin taste?” Alicia asked as he suckled her finger.

Link's eyes snapped open. Without a word, just a quick glance up at her face, he turned and left her room. His saliva dripped from the end of her finger, and Alicia couldn't resist. She closed her door and hurried to her bed, where she pulled aside the leg of her loose running shorts and softly pressed her wet finger against her clitoris. Link's spit felt so sexy against her nearly bare pussy, which she religiously shaved and trimmed.

Her own fluids mixed with her step-brother's to form a wonderful sheen of lubrication.

Imagining Link stroking himself a few rooms down, Alicia rubbed herself to a wonderful orgasm that ended with a small stream of clear fluid squirting out onto her bed. She sank back onto her pillow, bathing in the afterglow of her climax. It was so powerful; she was surprised she had never thought of Link before when she masturbated. Lazily rubbing her mound, bringing small electric pulses of orgasmic pleasure to her wetness, Alicia wondered how far she would be willing to go with Link.

Did he really want to fool around with her? Was it just plain wrong for them to be doing even this much? The timing was horrible since the house would be full of people by tonight and they most likely wouldn't have a chance to be alone for at least a week.

And what about Amy? Would she tell her lover what had happened? The two of them shared everything...

Alicia's pussy throbbed again, eager for another release. She was already masturbating, she was surprised to realize. She had been lost in her own thoughts and her body had been acting almost on its own, her finger rubbing her clitoris from side to side in small, frantic movements. Within a minute, she was softly crying out as her hips thrust upward and her body convulsed. With another more powerful spurt of clear fluid, Alicia orgasmed. She couldn't believe how good it felt, but she was making a bit of a mess on her bed.

She had squirted on rare occasions before, but this time, it had been powerful and she could really feel the hot burst of pleasure it gave her body. Panting and sweating now, she needed a shower more than ever.

She tried to get to her feet, promptly fell to the floor, and laughed at herself.

If just masturbating to thoughts of him did this to her, she wondered what actually having sex with him would do…

Chapter 7

In his room, Link barely got his shorts down around his knees before sitting back on his bed and stroking his dick. The taste of Alicia's pussy on his tongue was more than he could handle, and barely thirty seconds into it he was coming.

Masturbating under normal circumstances, with porn or just a hot mental image, was usually just a short session of stroking, coming, and cleaning up. This time, as the sperm was rising in his shaft and his warm cum spurted out of him, it just wasn't enough. While he shot his load out onto his stomach, his hand kept jerking even through his bliss; something animalistic in him spurred him to keep going faster, harder.

With a sudden spark of intensity, he thrust his hips upwards and his hand clamped down on his shaft. His orgasm multiplied within itself, and his vision blurred as he had the real, final orgasm. His load had been minimal up to this point, but now he was firing streams of thick white sperm high into the air and all the way up to his neck. He groaned loudly, his teeth clenched together, still tasting his step-sister's pussy. He nearly strained his muscles as he came and came, finding hidden reserves somewhere to supply this endless need for cum that his body was demanding.

Finally, with a guttural grunt, Link finished his orgasm and he just lay there, panting. He had never before experienced something this wonderful. If just masturbating to the thought of her made him come like this, how hard would he come if he actually fucked her?

He couldn't keep his mind from racing, thinking of all the possibilities of the two of them together. Surely she had to

want it too, right? She had practically been here with him, after all. She knew what he was doing - had encouraged him to do it. The only thing left now was to actually have sex…

Chapter 8

That night, the rest of the family arrived: another aunt, an uncle, and two more cousins.

And Amy!

Alicia was thrilled to see her paramour; She looked better than ever!

Once all of the greetings were exchanged and everyone brought their luggage into the house, the rooms were arranged. One set of parents would be in Link's room, another in Alicia's.

To her surprise, everyone else was being put in the basement. That wasn't a huge deal, as it was a finished basement and there was a big screen TV down there with some couches and lots of room for sleeping bags. The only awkward part would be that Link was the only boy. Her two little cousins were going to stay in their parents' room on the floor.

After a huge dinner, everyone talked and laughed, and Alicia tried her best not to look at Link, instead attempting to focus her attention and affection on Amy.

It was more difficult than she thought.

Somewhere around midnight the parents finally retired for the evening. Alicia, Link, Amy, and her older cousin Aiya all changed into pajamas and took blankets and pillows downstairs. Alicia was hauling an armful of pillows when her father stopped her.

"Hey pumpkin," he whispered, "be a good girl to Link, ok? Don't you girls go teasing him too much."

Alicia half-smirked. "OK, dad." She then trotted off into the basement to meet up with the rest of her clique. It was very cozy down there, with carpeting and soft couches to relax on while watching TV. Link was already sprawled out on one of them, the remote in his hand as he channel-surfed. Amy and Aiya were spreading out their blankets and pillows.

Alicia admired Amy's body as she did so: long light blonde hair, amazing skin, and thin shapely body. She was perfect, and Alicia instantly felt her body grow hotter.

And then there was Aiya.

Aiya was perhaps the strangest person Alicia had ever met, and that was really saying something.

It wasn't that she was Asian, or that she had long naturally white hair.

It was her eyes. Though they were slanted like most normal Asians, there was something unnerving about them when she looked at you too long that just made you feel off balance.

And then there were her mannerisms. It wasn't just that she was deaf – she had gotten over the uniqueness of that a long time ago – it was the way she moved, her body language in general.

"Do you think your parents can hear us down here?" Amy asked, jerking Alicia's attention away from the Asian.

"No way," Alicia said, then louder, "I mean, no fucking way!"

Amy laughed. "Babe! Stop that! You'll get us all in trouble!"

"No one upstairs can hear us, trust me," Link said, not taking his eyes off the TV.

"That's good to know," Amy whispered to Alicia, “because I brought some treats!”

Amy began pulling various types of drugs out of her purse like she was Mary Poppins. Alicia smacked her hand and put them right back in. This wasn’t going to be that kind of party.

“Why would you even be carrying all that around, anyway? I know you’re not selling all that – are you taking now too?”

Amy narrowed her eyes. “What if I was? In the past couple of years my mother died of cancer, my father became a professional alcoholic, and my sister - my best friend - has apparently given birth to a baby and vanished off the face of the earth. If anyone had a reason to use, it’s me.”

Alicia’s eyes widened, but Amy held up a hand and silenced her with a quick kiss.

“Look, beautiful, I’m sorry. None of those things are your fault. I’ve just had a lot of my mind lately. These make it… easier.”

Alicia wasn’t sure what to say to that. “We’re talking about this later, in private.”

Amy nodded. “I know. Let’s just try and enjoy the week for now, OK?”

Alicia nodded, slipping her hand into Amy’s.

Eventually, all three of the girls found themselves camped out on the floor, while Link remained on the couch. They all watched TV with him for a few minutes, too tired from their trip to really do anything else.

Or so Alicia thought.

"We should play a game," Amy said suddenly, propping herself up on her elbow.

"Like what?" Alicia asked wearily.

Link just rolled his eyes, knowing he wouldn't want any part of whatever they had planned. Alicia remembered what her father had said to her earlier.

"We have to include Link if we're gonna play something," she said.

"Ok, fine," Amy replied, thinking it over. "I'm the only non-family member here, so I should get to choose."

"Come on, Link!" Alicia said to her step-brother. "Please play with us?"

Link sighed and turned the TV off, then rolled off the couch and sat on the floor with the girls. Even sitting directly across from her, Link didn't dare look Alicia in the eye. She wondered if he had regretted what happened between them. She hoped not, because she sure as hell didn't.

"What's the game, then?" Alicia asked.

Amy sat straight up, brushing her long blonde hair over her shoulder.

"How about..." Amy looked inquisitively at each of them, studying them to see what they would be up for. "...if we start off with truth or dare, but without the dare. Let's save that for later."

Link laughed. "That's a game 12-year-olds play. Are you serious?"

Amy looked mockingly offended. "I'll have you know that me and Alicia played it all through high school, thank you very much."

Aiya smiled one of her creepy, mysterious smiles, then rapidly signed to Amy, the only one among them that knew sign language.

"Aiya says she's heard about some of those games." Amy translated, then laughed and slapped her shoulder. "Shush! I told you that in confidence!"

Everyone laughed, but Amy was serious about playing.

"Just to show that I'm not going to wuss out," Amy said, "I will let you all ask me a question each."

"Wait, we all have to come up with a question?" Alicia asked. "I don't even know what I'd ask."

"Don't worry about it," Amy said as she crossed her legs in front of her, inadvertently hiking up the football jersey she was wearing as pajamas and showing her white panties to everyone.

Alicia could tell that Link noticed, but he was good about not staring.

Aiya raised her hand and made deft hand motions. "Aiya says she'll go first," Amy translated.

"Shoot, chickie," Amy said playfully, "I accept all questions, regardless of subject."

Aiya tapped her chin, then signed. Amy translated. "How many hours' total did you spend on your knees in high school?" Amy smacked Aiya hard on the arm, making everyone laugh out loud. Aiya rubbed her arm, but she was laughing too much to show any hurt.

She rapidly signed again. "Ok, just kidding. I already know it was a lot." She giggled and thought of a new question. "I got it! How old were you when you had your first orgasm?"

Link was blushing by now, and Alicia couldn't keep from covering her mouth in embarrassment. Amy was true to her word, though. "14 Years old."

Everyone's eyes widened. "Oh my god, really?" Alicia blurted.

"It was the first time I tried masturbation," Amy answered, not missing a beat. "I was damn well gonna figure out how to do it right the first time!"

Aiya was rolling on her back with laughter, her tiny body shaking. Link was a little too aroused by this, Alicia noticed. She also noticed how uncomfortable he was.

"I'll go next," she offered. "What's the most embarrassing thing you've ever done in front of someone?"

Amy thought carefully. "Hmm, well I've peed while someone watched me."

Alicia half-smirked. "That was a bullshit answer. You've done that several times in front of me, and you definitely weren't embarrassed."

Amy gave her a sly glance. "I didn't say in front of you."

Everyone was silent for a moment. Aiya signed fluidly. "You did that for a guy, you mean?"

Amy nodded.

Alicia noticed that Link shifted his sweat pants not two seconds later, as the mental image no doubt sank in.

Alicia wasn't quite sure how she felt about this revelation.

"Your turn, Link," Amy said.

Link coughed nervously. "I have no idea what to ask."

Amy smiled warmly at him, causing Alicia's adrenaline to begin spiking. "The subject is, apparently, sex. Think of something."

Link propped his knees up to hide his tent. "Ok, fine. What's the craziest thing you ever did?"

Aiya leaned forward on her elbows, excitedly listening. Alicia was equally as interested.

"Ok, fine. I'll tell you all what happened the night before graduation." Amy paused and eyed each one of them. "But you all have to do something for me first."

“I thought we weren't doing the dare part?" Alicia asked.

"This isn't a dare, it's a requirement for the truth game to keep going. You want me to reveal my secrets? Then you have to reveal yours to me."

None of them knew what she was referring to, but to their shock, Amy reached down to her waist and pulled her jersey up and over her head.

Their game was about to get interesting...

Chapter 9

Alicia's mouth hung open in shock as she stared at her lover's bare chest, whereupon sat a very cute pair of firm C cups.

She ignored Link's equally shocked, albeit aroused, expression and Aiya's strangely happy one.

Amy, annoyingly enough, enjoyed Link's reaction. "What, you've never seen a pair before?"

Link shook his head. "I mean, yeah of course. But I can't believe you're showing them to us."

"Come on, guys." Amy looked seriously at them all for the first time since the game started. "This is my last hurrah before me and Alicia go away to college. I want to have fun. Nothing but fun the whole week."

Aiya was hilariously trying, somehow in vain, to get her oversized t-shirt off. She had it caught around her neck, but eventually, her small tits came into view.

Alicia was surprised at how open these two were being. She was even more surprised that she wasn't feeling murderous at her lover's exhibitionism. She was normally a very jealous, possessive girl.

"I agree," Aiya signed, her hair a mess now.

"You want us all to be naked?" Link asked. "Is that what you mean?"

Amy shrugged, making her tits jiggle just slightly. "We don't have to do anything you don't want to do. But we could all have some real fun this week if we just agree to be totally open

with each other. No hiding anything, no lying, no secrets. It'll be our pact for the week."

Alicia felt her own t-shirt itching against her skin suddenly, the thought of being as open with all of them as she normally only was with Amy exciting her. She hooked her thumb under her shirt and hesitated.

"Are you serious?" Alicia asked her girlfriend.

Amy smiled lovingly at her. "Do I have to prove how serious I am? I'll take the panties off too."

Link rubbed his eyes. "I can't believe this is happening."

Amy leaned closer to him and nudged her shoulder against his. "See? It's not so bad having to hang around your step-sister's girlfriend, is it?"

"Come on, Link!" Aiya signed, fidgeting in just her blue panties.

Alicia's eyes widened. She had never seen Aiya this adventurous, this bold. Especially with someone she had only just met.

Sighing, Alicia whipped off her shirt, and was immediately rewarded with Amy's catcalls.

Link pulled his shirt off, too, but it wasn't quite the same as the girls doing it. Still, though, he received appreciative looks from them as they saw his muscular chest and arms.

"Wow, you're pretty hunky," Amy said appreciatively, "you're not a virgin, right?"

Link was caught off guard by the question but managed to shake his head.

Amy nodded. "Good. Then it's two against two."

"Hey!" Aiya signed indignantly.

"Oh, be quiet, Aiya," Amy said, winking, "it's not like your alone. Alicia's a virgin too. Before the night is over, both of you might finally grow up."

Warning signals went off in Alicia's mind. Was Amy planning for sexual activity between the four of them?

"Wait," Aiya signed. "Let's all get naked together, ok?"

Amy nodded, though Alicia noticed that she was eyeing Link mostly. "On the count of three then."

Each of them looked nervously at the other, and the girls would certainly all be looking at Link once his pants came off. Alicia bet that he was so horny at this point that he would do whatever they wanted him to do.

"One...two..." Amy led the count, each of them ready to strip their panties off and Link ready to drop his sweatpants.

"Three!" In a muddled burst of energy, panties flew up in the air and there were four thuds as their bare butts hit the floor. For a few seconds, the thrill of being naked in front of each other was clouding the reality of what they were doing. Once the thrill died down for a moment, silence followed as Alicia saw Aiya and Amy both staring at Link. She followed their eyes and gasped.

Link sat there naked, his erection proudly at full mast, and there was nothing he could do to hide it. He didn't even try - he just sank back onto his elbows and let the girls have a look at his body.

"Holy fucking shit, Link!" Amy exclaimed.

"My god," Aiya signed, looking at Amy, "how big is that thing?"

Alicia just stared, though eventually, her eyes met Links. There was still a strange connection between the two of them after last night, and a small part of her felt instantly regretful. Amy was right next to her and had no idea...

"Bigger than any I've had in me," Amy breathed, her arousal clear in her voice. "Well, I think so, anyway."

"Why don't you get closer and be sure?" Aiya signed teasingly.

Amy's eyes were locked on Links. "Come on, girls," Amy insisted, "do you want to lose your virginities or not?"

Aiya clapped her hands and squealed. No sign interpretation was necessary for that. Aiya was definitely game.

Link's dick twitched, the thought of fucking all these beauties a bit too much for him. "I... there's no way I can last that long. I'm about to come right now."

Amy smiled. "He's right, girls."

Aiya frowned, no doubt afraid that her fun would be spoiled.

Amy crawled forward and put her hands on Link's thighs. "If he's gonna last long enough to pop your cherries, he'd gonna need to let one go first."

Link groaned...

Chapter 10

Before her face even descended to his crotch, he knew Amy was going to take him inside her mouth.

He felt his testicles begin to tighten. "Oh god, I don't know if I can stand it," he sighed, trying to hold it in.

Amy's hot breath on his twitching erection wasn't helping either. "You want that, Link? Do you want to cum in my mouth?"

Link clenched his eyes shut, forcing his body to calm down. His legs were starting to quiver under Amy's hands. He wasn't a virgin, by any means. He had been truthful in telling her that. But this was a whole new experience, and he might as well have been one.

Amy's lips closed over his tip, and Link groaned loudly as he felt her tongue begin to slowly swirl along the underside of his shaft. Aiya was watching intently, her quiet, intense focus turning Link on even more.

Alicia watched as well, feeling conflicted.

Link's eyes finally popped open, and he looked right at Alicia.

His expression reflected her deep longing and her eyes were almost pleading with him. He returned the look, and then gave in to the intense wave of pleasure that Amy's skilled mouth was giving him.

She was very good at what she was doing.

"Oh my god!" he cried out and thrust his hips upwards into Amy's face.

Her hand snaked across the floor and she grasped Alicia's fingers.

Alicia watched as Amy smiled up at Link with her mouth full of his penis, and her eyes closed sensually and she groaned as his cock began spewing semen into her throat. She sucked hard on him, milking his cum from his balls.

There was no hesitation or reluctance on her part. She was completely giving her mouth to him. Link shivered as Amy held on for the ride, letting him shoot out everything he had, and then resuming her suck job. Without a word, they all watched as Amy sucked on him even more, enjoying the taste of his sperm. She reached a hand down to her crotch and began rubbing herself.

Alicia's eyes glazed over at the obscene show.

"How did that feel, Link?" Alicia asked her step-brother.

Link just sighed deeply, raggedly. "It was amazing. It still is."

Amy purred in his lap, impaling her throat on his dick until she felt his balls against her chin. Link grunted, and she swore she felt a weak stream of cum leave his cock. His penis tasted... sweet to her.

"Come on, girls," Amy said finally, strings of saliva and sperm trailing from her lips to Link's dick head, "do it with me."

Aiya looked at her friend for a long moment, then snaked her hand down to herself and began masturbating. She motioned for Alicia to do so as well, but she was very shy suddenly.

"Aiya, show Alicia what you like to do when you're feeling especially naughty," Amy encouraged.

Aiya smiled at her friend and got on her hands and knees. Propping herself with one hand, she reached the other back and gently began drifting the fingertip of her middle finger up and down her crack. She purred to herself as she enjoyed the naughty feelings that her ass gave her.

"You want to try it with her, love?" Amy asked Alicia.

Link was eagerly watching it all as Amy's mouth returned to his cock. He stroked Amy's hair softly, watching Alicia intensely. Alicia found herself wanting nothing more than to make her step-brother happy, and found a thrill at the thought of performing for him. Everyone else was doing it; she might as well join in.

"Fine." She kicked her feet out from under her and spread her legs wide. Link's mouth watered as he saw his step-sister's pussy for the first time. He could see why it had tasted so good earlier. She had the softest, smoothest pussy he had ever seen. She had a nice strip of short hair above her clit, but her pussy lips were nice and big for someone so petite.

Alicia smiled shyly at him while her fingers began to explore her pussy, then closed her eyes as she gave in to the wonderful feelings her body was giving her. Amy watched eagerly as well, finally pulling away from Link's cock after it had regained its stiffness. Link was shocked yet again when she climbed on top of him and sat herself down on his lap. Their faces were inches apart, and her breathing was really turning him on. She guided his cock to her steaming entrance, and gently slipped him inside of her.

"You're fucking?!" Alicia said, alarmed. "Amy!"

Amy closed her eyes, enjoying the feeling of him twitching inside of her pussy. "I couldn't help myself, he tasted too good."

Alicia's fingers froze as she watched her girlfriend start fucking her step-brother. Normally she would have turned murderous... but it was different with Link.

She wasn't jealous. She was envious.

She took a deep breath and began fondling herself again, watching the scene between Link and Amy unfold.

"Tell me something secret," Amy said to Link, rocking her pussy into him. "I want to hear you reveal something to us."

Link was pretty hazy by this point, having just cum and now already fucking this hot girl. But there was nothing to hide anymore. What they were doing was wrong enough; there wasn't anything left to feel guilty about now.

"I..." Amy's pussy gripped him tight as he tried to speak, and the breath was taken out of him for a moment. Her tits in his face didn't help things either.

"I tasted Alicia's pussy on her finger."

Alicia's fingers were a blur now, rubbing her clit furiously. Hearing Link reveal something so forbidden was too sensuous for her to handle, and instead of being embarrassed, the revelation made her intensely horny. She could feel her pussy contracting.

"Yes..." she hissed. "I fingered myself and let him taste, so he could jerk off thinking about me."

Aiya's gentle drifting fingers turned to focused probing, and she was openly spreading her cheeks and touching her

asshole. Amy kept her pace fucking Link, but her smile said that she enjoyed hearing his revelation.

"Good," she breathed. "Good boy! Secrets make this all the more enjoyable, don't they?"

Link just nodded his head, concentrating on the feel of her smooth pussy dragging along his shaft.

"It's my turn now," Amy said, still fucking Link but slowing down a bit.

"Aiya and I ate each other's pussies when we were younger."

Aiya grinned one of her mysterious grins. She was so close to coming...

"How young?" Alicia asked, actually interested in knowing but also incredibly aroused by the thought.

"Too young," Amy said, "before me and you."

Alicia felt better knowing that.

Alicia wanted to be completely open now, just as her best friend had been, and as Amy and Aiya were being.

"I've been dying to fuck Link since I first met him about a month ago," she blurted. Link's eyes shot over to her, though Amy was still riding him.

Amy smiled and stopped moving on him. "You should get to do that, right now," Amy said. She glanced down at Link. "That OK, stud?"

Link just nodded, the thought of fucking Alicia sending a new pulse of pleasure through his groin as Amy slid off of him. Alicia cautiously approached her step-brother, eyeing his big

dick. She wanted to feel it so bad inside of her, she didn't care how bad it hurt the first time.

"Do it, Alicia!" Aiya signed as she started to cum.

Amy sat next to Aiya and gently stroked her back while she climaxed.

When she finally finished her orgasm, she laid her head in Amy's lap and closed her eyes.

Link licked his lips as Alicia came over to him, her naked body looking delicious. Her pussy smelled sweet even from a few feet away.

Amy's cream was all over his dick, a fact that Aiya didn't want to miss out on. "Wait!" she signed to Amy. She crawled over to where Link and Alicia were. "I want to taste before this happens."

Aiya didn't wait for approval – she bent over and sucked Link's cock right into her mouth, savoring the taste of her best friend's pussy.

"Ok, Alicia," she signed, apparently satisfied.

"Fuck your bro good," Amy said to Alicia, causing her to smile.

Aiya unexpectedly leaned forward and kissed Alicia dead on the mouth, and they shared a deep, wet kiss that included the sharing of Amy's cream.

Alicia was definitely ready to fuck now...

Chapter 11

Alicia carefully sat on Link's lap, his huge cock sprouting up between their stomachs. It was as if the two of them were alone in the room now. Their eyes met, and Alicia's hand gently touched Link's penis. Fluid from the tip leaked out onto her belly where it was resting. She smiled at him, enjoying this closeness.

"Are you going to fuck me, big brother?" she asked as she looked deep into his eyes.

Link groaned, feeling her hand squeeze his cock.

"Please, let me." Alicia lifted herself just a bit, positioning his penis at the steaming hole of her pussy, and very carefully began to slide down his pole. He was stretching her little virgin slit immensely, making it hard to completely enjoy the moment. But Alicia's determination stuck, and she finally bottomed out on his pubic hair.

And they kissed. They didn't even hear the slurping sounds behind her, as Amy and Aiya 69'ed right next to them. They were totally focused on each other, on the thickness of Link's penis, and on the slick friction of Alicia's pussy as it slid up and down on him.

"Fuck me, Link," she whispered into his mouth.

"Oh god, Alicia..."

"I've wanted this for so long," she purred. "You have no idea. I've masturbated to this."

Link sped up his pace, spurred on by her words. "I've wanted you too. I've never cum so hard as when I've jerked off thinking about you."

"Cum in me." She whispered in his ear.

Link cried out as they both reached their crescendo, and Alicia's pussy exploded around Link's spewing cock. They both grunted and groaned together, sweat from their stomachs mingling and saliva trailing between their lips. Alicia's pussy eagerly accepted Link's generous load, throbbing and convulsing around his shaft to coax out everything he had. Link held onto Alicia's hips as he fired away inside of her.

After, when their focus expanded, Alicia turned to see Amy and Aiya still in the 69 position, but completely focused on the show. She blushed but held her big brother tightly in her vagina.

"Congratulations," Amy said proudly, "you are now a woman." Link sucked on Alicia's tits as he continued to twitch inside her tight pussy. Alicia mewed as her step-brother fed at her breasts.

She squeezed his cock tight inside her body, locking him there. Amy made her way over to them and gently lifted Alicia off of Link’s spent cock, laying her on the ground and siphoning Links sperm out of her birth canal.

“Can’t have you getting pregnant now. You’re not on birth control.” She murmured.

A thought that had not occurred to Alicia. But then, she had never imagined that she would lose her virginity to her step-brother, either.

She reached for Links' hand and held it as his sperm was drained from within her…

Chapter 12

"Hey you guys, check it out!" Amy whispered later on that night to Link and Alicia.

It didn't take long for them to notice what Amy was fascinated by.

Aiya was asleep, but her body was twitching, and her hips were softly thrusting into the air underneath her sleeping bag. Aiya carefully peeled it back, exposing her naked body underneath Link's hiked up t-shirt. She was moaning softly, little-muffled cries of pleasure escaping her mouth.

She was having an erotic dream.

"I've never seen someone be so into it," Amy said, her eyes locked onto Aiya's stomach as it quivered, and her tight little pussy as it contracted.

"Is she coming?" Alicia whispered.

"Wow, I think so," Link responded, his aching cock throbbing. Aiya cried out, still in her sleep, and her pussy oozed out thick fluid followed by a squirt of clear pussy juice.

She was squirting!

"Holy shit," Amy said, enthralled by what was happening, "she really comes when she has a wet dream!"

"She's still coming, look!" Alicia pointed at Aiya's tiny pussy, which as still contracting and squeezing at an invisible penis.

"Can you imagine fucking her?" Amy said to Link, a smile slowly spreading across her face.

Link gulped in response. Alicia didn't like where this was going.

Amy reached down and gently spread Aiya's labia, watching her vaginal muscles contract.

"Guys, she's still a virgin." Link said, his voice deep and husky.

"No shit. I told you that earlier, stud," Amy replied, bumping Link playfully, "maybe you can fix that for her really quick."

Alicia looked at her girlfriend, startled. "Say what?!"

Link looked just as incredulous. "I-I can't. She's sleeping. I can't take her virginity while she's sleeping," Link said, his mouth watering at the sight of Aiya's tiny moist pussy.

Amy didn't respond. Instead, she carefully spread the petite Asian's legs and reached down and firmly grabbed Link's shaft, then positioned its tip at the entrance to Aiya's sex.

Link looked at Alicia, who narrowed her eyes but slightly nodded. She was alarmed at how possessive she was beginning to feel towards him.

Amy pulled Link's cock, causing the tip of it to just barely enter Aiya. She let out a small whimper in her sleep, slightly moving her pelvis, causing her softness to lightly stroke the tip of Links hardness.

Link gasped at the intense pleasure. He was already close to orgasm.

"Link," Amy interrupted, "you're going to have to come *before* you put it in her. Otherwise, she won't get any pleasure out of it."

Link shook his head. He was confident that he could hold off long enough.

"Ok. Fine," Amy said, "then wake her up while your inside of her."

Link frowned. "I still don't know about this. She's a virgin. Maybe she's saving it..."

Amy rolled her eyes while Alicia moved behind him. "Just remember that it's her first time, babe. Don't be too rough," Alicia said softly in his ear.

He smiled as Alicia pressed against his back and took his member out of Amy's hand almost possessively. "I'll take care of this," She told her lover, then, to Link, "just focus on not coming."

Link nodded as she began to slowly stroke him, making sure to keep his tip inside of the small Asian while she pleasured him. It was all driving him crazy. He needed to come. Alicia pushed his back a bit, causing him to slip into the sleeping Asian another quarter of an inch.

"Do you want to come?" Alicia whispered in his ear.

He nodded the best he could.

"I'll make you come," She whispered again, "either in my hand or in Aiya. Just tell me what you want."

Link felt himself beginning to hyperventilate. It was simply too much bliss, too much eroticism, for him to handle. He was being overloaded with pleasure, and his sanity completely left him.

Alicia let go of his member as he pushed his way into Aiya's sleeping form.

She awoke immediately, squealing in pain and fear. She tried to push Link off of her, but couldn't. His mind was completely gone, lust replacing reason.

"Just relax, baby," Amy said to the diminutive Asian as she stroked her hair, "the hard part is done, now you just need to hold still."

Aiya's eyes widened as Link wedged himself even deeper inside of her, stroking in and out of her tightness as best as he could, using the pre-cum and her natural juices to get in just a bit deeper than he had previously. Aiya had the tiniest vagina he had ever seen, and his penis was massively stretching it.

Alicia massaged his back as his thrusts grew even more frantic.

Aiya struggled wildly, slapping and hitting anyone she could get her hands on, then alarmed Link by grabbing him and forcing him down to her, her mouth locking fiercely onto his as he continued to erase her virginity.

Link became lost in his lust, feeling his cock swell up inside her.

"Going... come..." He gasped as he finally managed to bottom out within her, trying to push himself even deeper into her small shapely body.

Aiya grabbed him by the hair and pulled their mouths apart, causing him to look her dead in the eyes, soundlessly giving her consent to let loose inside of her.

"Are... you on... pill...?" He gasped, quickly losing his ability to speak.

In response, Aiya wrapped her legs around his waist, making it impossible for him to pull out, and clamped down with her formerly virginal silk passage, causing him to place himself inside her as deeply as he could and floor her womb with his reproductive fluids.

Amy and Alicia watched on in amazement.

"Is she on birth control?" Alicia asked her girlfriend while Link emptied himself into the tiny Asian.

"Nope. Nothing at all. She was a virgin, remember?"

"Holy shit..."

Amy smiled. "Jealous?" She asked playfully.

Alicia was shocked when she realized that she was.

Amy leaned against her girlfriend. "Remember who you belong to, woman."

Alicia watched the pair in silence…

Chapter 13

The four of them finally drifted off to sleep, the girls staying naked even though at any time someone could come downstairs to wake them up or check on them.

Link awoke first.

Aiya stirred next, sleepily looking around as if she couldn't remember where she was. She saw Link and smiled.

Their eyes locked. Something clicked. Aiya began crawling over to him.

When she reached him, she took his manhood and started stroking it, causing him to involuntarily groan. She continued stroking him as she licked down his shaft and to his balls, where she tongued them delicately, even gently sucking on them at times.

He tilted his head back as her sweet, soft tongue danced around his testicles.

Her mouth left his sac and locked onto his dick, sucking the shaft as deep as she could take it in her tiny mouth seconds before he began spewing scalding hot cum down her throat. He thrust up into her face, holding her head with his hands as he fired away blissfully into her tiny eager mouth. Aiya swallowed everything, sucking what was left out of him.

Finally, he relaxed and just stroked her hair while she continued to blow him.

"God you're amazing," he finally said as Aiya withdrew from his dick.

Aiya smiled one of her beautiful, mysterious smiles. She then winked and climbed atop of him, wrapping her small frame around his body.

Link sighed contentedly. Aiya reached for his t-shirt and deftly donned it.

"I bet your boyfriend doesn't do things like this, does he?" he asked her as he placed his hands around her waist, keeping her body pressed against his.

Aiya tilted her head.

"She doesn't have a boyfriend," Amy said as she yawned and stood up, causing both Aiya and Link to jump, "most guys are too creeped out by the whole not being able to speak thing. She seems to like you a lot, though - more than I've ever seen with any other guy."

Aiya rested her head back on Link's shoulder and flipped Amy off in a casual, playful manner.

Link chuckled.

"Yeah, well, I like her too..."

Alicia woke up moments later, yawning ferociously and kicking Amy playfully on the butt as she walked by.

"Like what?" she asked.

"Each other," Amy replied. "I think Link and Aiya just became a couple."

Link laughed. "I never said -" but was stopped by Aiya's mouth pressing against his.

Alicia watched all of this with an unreadable expression on her face. Amy plopped next to her lover and kissed her. Hard.

"I know you're not developing feelings for him, right?" Amy asked Alicia quietly.

“Of course not,” Amy said dismissively, hoping her lover didn’t detect the deception in her voice.

Amy nodded. "Good. Because I’m fine with the whole weeklong experimentation thing, but anything beyond that…"

Alicia gave her a level look. "I told you I wasn’t. Now can we drop it?"

"We should plan something fun for today, besides crazy sex," Amy said abruptly as she got up and searched for the rest of her clothes.

Link agreed. "Yeah, let's go out and do something."

"First, breakfast," Alicia said, "I'm starving!"

As everyone expressed their agreeance, Amy noticed the expression on Alicia’s face: and her eyes as they lingered on Link and Aiya…

Chapter 14

The day was eventful for everyone - and, surprisingly, the sex had nothing to do with it.

Link found it hard to look at the girls - especially the beautiful, enigmatic Aiya - without picturing her wrapped around him, riding him, making him climax. But they all managed to hide their new relationship from everyone else.

Alicia and Amy were inseparable as usual, and Aiya tried to inconspicuously stay as close to Link as possible. After a nice long dinner, all the older adults were exhausted, so the foursome all made their way down to the basement to spend the rest of the evening together. Link was the last one down there; the others were practically racing.

He just barely closed the door to the basement when Aiya was flying through the air, wrapping her legs around his waist, attacking his mouth with hers.

He stumbled towards the couch, feeling Amy's hands gently directing him, another set of hands stealthily reaching for his crotch, manipulating his hardness underneath his pants.

Alicia’s hands.

By the time he collapsed onto the couch, he was hard as a rock.

Aiya practically melted into Link, and he into her.

Everything around them was simply background.

"You want him, don't you?" Amy whispered in Alicia’s ear.

Alicia thought fast. "Just the sex, not like as a boyfriend or anything."

"Fine. Let's make a deal. Get all the dick from him you can – but after we go to college, no one else's cock better be anywhere near you."

Alicia's eyes widened as her heartbeat quickened. "I promise."

Amy smirked - obviously trying to imitate Alicia's patented half-smirk. "Oh Link?" Amy called out in a sing-song voice.

Link and Aiya paused their intense make-out session long enough to look in her general direction.

"I want you to ravage my girlfriend's body."

Aiya's eyes widened, then narrowed.

Amy laughed. "Hey, he's all yours when we go off to college! We only have a few more days before we leave. Be a share-bear."

Aiya seemed to think about it, then smoothed her face. She carefully dismounted Link, and Amy watched as Links length slid out of the small Asians depths.

"You guys were already fucking?!" Amy asked, laughing.

Aiya shrugged, covering her bottom half while she leaned over and gave Link a quick, hard kiss.

Amy slinked over to him. "Do you wanna let one go first?"

Link looked at Alicia, who slightly shook her head. She wanted all of his cum inside her.

Link shook his head and reached for his step-sister.

Alicia rewarded him with her patented half-smirk and dropped to the floor on her hands and knees, looking back at him with pleading anticipation in her eyes.

"Fuck me."

Link was behind her and gripping her sides tightly before anyone really realized what was happening.

He relished the feel of his step-sister's tightness as he slid into her insides.

"Grab my hair. Pull it." Alicia whispered.

Link did exactly that.

Alicia bit her lip, loving the slight discomfort of his enormous penis. She felt like an animal in heat. She highly doubted she could simply *stop* doing this with him after she and Amy left for college, however.

Alicia's tight little hole accepted him and responded to him wonderfully. They fucked and fucked, changing positions and returning to doggie style so he could stick his finger in her butt while he pounded away at her tight little body.

The two of them were too caught up in their sex to really notice Aiya and Amy mere feet away, fingering their own pussies while they watched their performance.

Finally, after Alicia had come more times than she could count, Link felt the stirrings of his orgasm. They were doing it missionary style, and Alicia was passionately kissing his neck as he grinded away inside her.

"Do it," Alicia whispered in his ear, sensing his oncoming orgasm, "inside me. Come inside me."

She felt his cock throb and expand almost as if in response.

Link relentlessly thrusted himself inside her until he felt the explosion starting to build. In the back of his mind, he heard his newly crowned girlfriend cry out in orgasm, followed quickly by Amy.

He squeezed his eyes shut and let his cock spew endless bursts of cum into his step-sister.

The two of them groaned deeply, their bodies in perfect sync. Link had never had a better orgasm, except maybe in Alicia that first time. He helplessly twitched and ground his hips, pouring out load after load of his semen into her young, tight little womb.

"Oh god," Alicia murmured, massaging his back as he came, trying to coax more cum from his testicles. "My pussy is so sore, but I love it…"

Amy crawled over to her girlfriend and kissed her gently on the face. Aiya hugged her boyfriend from behind, squeezing her arms around his chest.

"That was so beautiful," Amy said as she gently separated the two, moving to place her face in between her girlfriend's legs to once again siphon out Links juices.

But Alicia closed her legs, preventing Amy from going in between them.

And she had no idea why…

Afterword

Hopefully, you liked this compilation (err, *Cumpilation*) because I plan on releasing one sometime after releasing 3 Quickies! stories. Most likely it will be a *while* after the third story because I have so many projects, but eventually, it will get released.

My novels have to come first. After all, these Quickies! stories are kind of just me taking a break from my novels, like snacking on junk food, in a way, where my novels are like the steak and potatoes of what I do.

My novels are my true loves.

My Quickies are basically a fling.

Anyways.

I hope you enjoyed reading this as much as I enjoyed compiling it.

And I love you all.

You haven't seen anything yet. ;-)

Coming Next

Quickies! Naughty Cheerleaders

Welcome back to the notorious sorority Phi Beta Pie! Now that Penny's in charge, her first act as house mother is to create a special "cheerleader’s division", comprised of the virgin freshmen sisters for an erotic cherry auction fundraiser!

Other Books By Alexa Nichols

Numbers indicate the chronological order that the stories were written in (for continuity purposes). Note that all of the stories stand on their own and can be read in any order you want - however, reading them in the numbered order will provide a much richer experience, as all of the stories contain characters and events that take place in the stories before it.

Various

3

Phi Beta Pie
($2.99 US)
ISBN: 9781310611698

4

The Secret Life of Miel
($3.99 US)
ISBN: 9781311289575

6

Cramming Sis!
($2.99 US)
ISBN: 9781311501158

7

Naughty Cheerleaders
($2.99 US)
ISBN: 9781310588471

Please Don't Get Me Pregnant!
($1.99 US)
ISBN: 9781310716812

Quickies

1

Knocked Up In Prison!
($.99 US)
ISBN: 9781311102898

2

When Daddy Was Away!
($2.99 US)
ISBN: 9781310333408

5

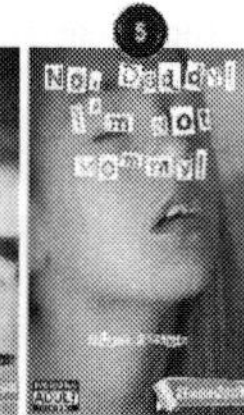

No, Daddy! I'm Not Mommy!
($1.99 US)
ISBN: 9781311200815

Cumpilation Volume 1
($3.99 US)
ISBN: 9781311245397

Cumpilation Volume 2
($3.99 US)
ISBN: 9781370527489

About The Author

Alexa Nichols is a full-time writer who refuses to stray away from erotica - the reading of it, the writing of it, and definitely the enjoying of it.

She's a lover of all things sexual and is a strong supporter of lesbian and gay rights. She herself is bisexual, though she does lean more towards the males than the females.

Currently, she is watching the Netflix series "Orange Is the New Black" and reading the “Beautiful Creatures” series of books.

She lives in Corpus Christi with her brother, J.C., and is currently (fantastically) single.

Lightning Source UK Ltd.
Milton Keynes UK
UKOW041941190313

207902UK00001B/74/A